PENGUIN 🐧 C

THE YELLOW WALL-PAPER, HERLAND, AND SELECTED WRITINGS

CHARLOTTE PERKINS GILMAN (1860–1935) was born in New England, a descendant of the prominent and influential Beecher family. Despite the affluence of her famous ancestors, she was born into poverty. Her father abandoned the family when she was a child, and she received just four years of formal education. At an early age she vowed never to marry, hoping instead to devote her life to public service. In 1882, however, at the age of twenty-one, she was introduced to Charles Walter Stetson (1858–1911), a handsome Providence, Rhode Island, artist, and the two were married in 1884. Charlotte Stetson became pregnant almost immediately after their marriage, gave birth to a daughter, and sank into a deep depression that lasted for several years. She eventually entered a sanitarium in Philadelphia to undergo the "rest cure," a controversial treatment for nervous prostration, which forbade any type of physical activity or intellectual stimulation. After a month, she returned to her husband and child and subsequently suffered a nervous breakdown. In 1888, she left Stetson and moved with her daughter to California, where her recovery was swift. In the early 1890s, she began a career in writing and lecturing, and in 1892, she published the now-famous story "The Yellow Wall-Paper." A volume of poems, *In This Our World*, followed a year later. In 1894, she relinquished custody of her young daughter to her ex-husband and endured public condemnation for her actions. In 1898, her most famous nonfiction book, *Women and Economics*, was published. With its publication, and its subsequent translation into seven languages, Gilman earned international acclaim. In 1900, she married her first cousin, George Houghton Gilman. Over the next thirty-five years, she wrote and published hundreds of stories and poems and more than a dozen books, including *Concerning Children* (1900), *The Home: Its Work and Influence* (1903), *Human Work* (1904), *The Man Made World; Or, Our Androcentric Culture* (1911), *Moving the Mountain* (1911), *Herland* (1915), *With Her in Ourland* (1916), *His Religion and Hers: A Study of the Faith of Our Fathers and the Work of Our Mothers* (1923), and *The Living of Charlotte*

Perkins Gilman: An Autobiography (1935). From 1909 to 1916 she singlehandedly wrote, edited, and published her own magazine, *The Forerunner*, in which the utopian romance *Herland* first appeared. In 1932, Gilman learned that she had inoperable breast cancer. Three years later, at the age of seventy-five, she committed suicide, intending her death to demonstrate her advocacy of euthanasia. In 1993, Gilman was named in a poll commissioned by the Siena Research Institute as the sixth most influential woman of the twentieth century. In 1994, she was inducted posthumously into the National Women's Hall of Fame in Seneca Falls, New York.

KATE BOLICK's first book, the bestselling *Spinster: Making a Life of One's Own*, was named a *New York Times* Notable Book of 2015. A contributing editor for *The Atlantic*, Bolick writes frequently for a variety of publications including *Bookforum*, the *New York Times*, and *Vogue* and hosts "Touchstones at The Mount," an annual interview series at Edith Wharton's country estate in Lenox, Massachusetts. Previously, she was executive editor of *Domino* and a columnist for the *Boston Globe*'s Ideas section. She teaches writing at New York University, in both the Cultural Reporting and Criticism MA program and the Gallatin School of Individualized Study, and lives in Brooklyn, New York. Bolick speaks frequently at colleges and conferences and has appeared on the *Today* show, *CBS Sunday Morning*, CNN, MSNBC, and numerous NPR programs across the country.

CHARLOTTE PERKINS GILMAN

The Yellow Wall-Paper, Herland, and Selected Writings

Introduction by
KATE BOLICK

PENGUIN BOOKS

PENGUIN BOOKS

An imprint of Penguin Random House LLC
penguinrandomhouse.com

The collection under the title *Herland, The Yellow Wall-Paper, and Selected Writings*
first published in Penguin Books 1999
This edition with an introduction by Kate Bolick published 2019

Introduction copyright © 2019 by Kate Bolick
Penguin supports copyright. Copyright fuels creativity, encourages diverse voices,
promotes free speech, and creates a vibrant culture. Thank you for buying an authorized
edition of this book and for complying with copyright laws by not reproducing, scanning, or
distributing any part of it in any form without permission. You are supporting writers and
allowing Penguin to continue to publish books for every reader.

Library of Congress Cataloging in Publication Control Number: 2018057219
ISBN 9780143105855 (paperback)

Printed in the United States of America
22nd Printing

Set in Sabon LT Std Roman

Contents

THE YELLOW WALL-PAPER, HERLAND, AND SELECTED WRITINGS

POETRY 337

Introduction

Like many people born in the 1970s, during the second wave of the women's movement, I was assigned to read Charlotte Perkins Gilman's famous short story "The Yellow Wall-Paper"—in high school or college, I can't remember which. Her symbolic fictionalization of her own postpartum depression shocked readers when it first appeared in 1892 and fascinated scholars some eighty years later, who promptly added the forgotten masterpiece to the then-nascent feminist canon. But the story didn't make much of an impression on my unworldly teenage self. Coming of age as I did in the early 1990s, at the dawn of today's so-called campus hookup culture, and blithely taking for granted the ready availability of birth control, the faraway prospects of marriage, childbirth, and its aftermath were as alien to my experience as Gilman and her posse of prim, corseted suffragists, or so I imagined.

Now I consider "The Yellow Wall-Paper" among American literature's most significant short stories and Gilman herself one of our most compelling feminist writers. She was the rare type of public intellectual who had *fun* with her work, conveying provocative views with wit, creativity, and a great ear for story. Though she was an active participant in feminism's long first wave, organized around the attainment of suffrage, her take on women's place in society far transcended her own moment; many of her ideas were so prescient and original that today they still feel brand new.

Not everything she advocated for has aged well, however. Particularly specious are her opinions about race, which didn't hold up under the scrutiny of detractors even in her own time.

Nearly a century after her death, Gilman's controversial legacy continues to be up for debate.

I would also come to learn that she never did wear a corset. But I'm getting ahead of myself.

Charlotte Anna Perkins was born squarely within the Victorian era, on July 3, 1860, in Hartford, Connecticut, twelve years after the first-ever women's rights convention, held in Seneca Falls, New York, and less than a year before the Civil War broke out. Her childhood and adolescence took place during an exceptionally dramatic swath of American history. One of her earliest memories was of the black-bordered newspaper announcing Lincoln's assassination. She grew into adolescence as Reconstruction was effectively sabotaged. Her young adulthood coincided with an unprecedented surge of educational and vocational opportunities for women, who entered universities, factories, and offices in staggering numbers, altering the workplace in ways that are still being negotiated to this day. By the time Gilman died, on August 17, 1935, age seventy-five, she'd seen her country go to war, women achieve the vote, and the early years of the Great Depression. She'd also glimpsed more than a few of the material advances that would come to reshape the lives of women and families, among them the legalization of condoms, the invention of the zipper, and the sale of frozen foods.

Gilman was never merely a witness to history's unfolding, however. From an early age, she yearned to actively mold society to her vision, an impulse she inherited from her paternal line, the prominent nineteenth-century Beecher clan. Her great-grandfather, Lyman Beecher, and great-uncle, Henry Ward Beecher, were influential ministers. Her great-aunts included Harriet Beecher Stowe, author of the bestselling 1852 abolitionist novel *Uncle Tom's Cabin*, Catharine Beecher, an author and educator who promoted women's higher education and founded her own school, and Isabella Beecher Hooker, a leader in the suffragist movement.

This lineage proved far more impressive than her father's fitness for parenthood; he vanished when Gilman and her fourteen-months-older brother were still infants, leaving his wife to raise the children alone. Over the next eighteen years, the threesome moved nineteen times, living in boardinghouses and the homes of various family members throughout New England. The familial generosity ceased in 1873, when Gilman's mother finally filed for divorce, an extremely rare decision at the time, of which the Beechers did not approve.

This unstable upbringing had an enormous effect on the eventual adult. Though by background and appearance a denizen of the white upper middle class, Gilman enjoyed very few of its attendant privileges, whether comforts like new clothing or the less tangible advantages of a formal education. (All told, she clocked four years among seven different elementary and secondary schools, ending when she was fifteen.) Someone less willful might have experienced these lacks as setbacks. For Gilman, they were welcome challenges to be surmounted with good cheer. By age five she was sewing for her mother and had taught herself to read and was already conceiving of herself as a "world-server," in other words, a Beecher. In her autobiography, she recalls waking one morning as a child "with a vast concept my inadequate vocabulary utterly failed to describe" and telling her family about a feeling of "'having the whole world on my toes' . . . an enormous sense of social responsibility with power to handle it." (They laughed in response.)

During early adolescence, she fashioned herself as a stoic, consciously cultivating personal deprivations and choosing the bracing rewards of intellectual study and physical exercise over all else. Also, the joys of imagination: "I could make a world to suit me," she recollected thinking in her autobiography. This creativity extended to the sartorial realm. She designed and sewed her own clothes, even her own special "species of brassière," and at a time when tight, constricting corsets were a staple of women's wardrobes, she refused to wear one. At seventeen she confided to her diary that she would never marry, because doing so would thwart her plans to better humanity.

It isn't difficult to see in this fiercely individualistic young woman the seeds of a radical. Possibly, the combination of her self-directed reading and lack of traditional schooling allowed for the habit of unconventional thinking that characterized her long career. (Though it also left her uneasy in the company of college graduates, who overwhelmingly helmed the social movements she was part of but never felt at home in.) Certainly, witnessing the travails of her visibly unhappy mother, forced to rely on the charity of extended family, impressed upon the girl the necessity of financial independence. In 1878, at age eighteen, she enrolled in classes at the Rhode Island School of Design and began earning money as a commercial artist.

In 1879, Gilman fell in love with a young woman her age, Martha Luther. It was her first significant romantic relationship, and she fervently hoped they would become life partners. Intense same-sex attachments were common among women during the nineteenth century, whether adolescent "romantic friendships," in which two girls exchanged passionate endearments, or adult "Boston marriages," in which two spinsters set up house without the economic support of a husband. But eventually Luther called off the relationship and announced her engagement to a man. Gilman was devastated. In her 1882 journal, she emphatically swore off "love and happiness" and doubled down on her commitment to public service, declaring "work" would be her emotional salvation.

You know what's said about best-laid plans: Ten days after writing that journal entry, Gilman met a charismatic young painter, Charles Walter Stetson. For two years she refused his repeated proposals, until finally breaking her antimarriage vow and saying yes. On May 2, 1884, she and Stetson were wed in a small ceremony in Providence, Rhode Island.

Subsequent events moved quickly. Less than a year after the wedding, Gilman gave birth to their daughter, Katharine, and promptly succumbed to what eventually became history's most famous postpartum depression, lasting nearly three years. In the spring of 1887, desperate for help, she traveled to Philadelphia to undergo the now-infamous "rest cure" with Dr. Silas Weir Mitchell, the era's venerated nerve specialist (Edith Wharton was his patient as well). His treatment: "Live as domestic a life as possible," and "never touch pen, brush, or pencil again as long as I lived," Gilman later wrote in an essay.

She tried to do as he said—and then she suffered a nervous breakdown.

Ironically, this series of personal, "domestic" misfortunes served as the chrysalis for Gilman's public self. Even while battling these demons, in 1888 she published her first book, *Art Gems for the Home and Fireside*, an annotated compendium of forty-nine works by famous artists. Women were publishing more than ever before, but usually under a pseudonym or their married name. Gilman chose the latter: Mrs. Charles Walter Stetson. She doesn't mention the book in her autobiography, perhaps because she considered it a compilation and not an original work, but it's worth noting that already this soon-to-be-famous social reformer was dreaming up ways to improve the home. (Incidentally, Edith Wharton's first book was also devoted to domestic aesthetics, the 1897 design manual *The Decoration of Houses*.)

It wasn't long before Gilman found the strength to reject her doctor's orders and make her own diagnosis. The emotional confines of marriage and motherhood were smothering her, she decided, and she would pursue her own course of treatment, what she cheekily called her "west cure." In the summer of 1888 she persuaded Stetson to agree to a separation, then moved with Katharine across the country to Pasadena, California, where, after a bumpy start, she finally embarked on her ambition to become a "world-server" and began writing and publishing in earnest.

In purely literary terms, Gilman was never a masterful writer. Unlike her near-exact contemporary Edith Wharton, who created some of America's greatest fictional heroines, Gilman wasn't interested in (or, more likely, capable of) puppeteering a wide cast of characters with complex inner lives, or perfecting a lyrical prose style. Even so, what she brought to the page remains unparalleled in American letters: a captivating mix of perspicacity, subversiveness, and humor, fueled by an admirable taste for experimentation (and an inexhaustible work ethic). All of this can be glimpsed in her early stories— relatively short, often satirical, almost-parables in which she stealthily embeds social commentary within the familiar tropes of popular genre fiction.

"The Unexpected" (1890), one of Gilman's first published works, pivots on a case of mistaken identity. Without spoiling the mystery's surprise twist, it can be said that in a brisk few pages she addresses gender, ambition, adultery, and that most modern of concepts—a man happily married to a woman more professionally successful than he is. "The Giant Wistaria" (1891) masquerades as a Gothic tale—a moldering mansion, a jocular house party, a mysterious corpse—while also commenting on domestic violence, female rebellion, and the tragic consequences of stigmatizing so-called illegitimate births. "An Extinct Angel" (1891), a spoof on a fairy tale, is a subtle attack on the Victorian cult of domesticity and its "angel in the house," the then-popular fantasy of a charming, passive, self-sacrificing wife-mother who lives only to serve others.

"The Yellow Wall-Paper" has been rightly celebrated as Gilman's best fictional work, a skillful merging of style and substance. Drawing on her own experience from several years prior, she wrote it in a two-day white heat during the summer of 1890, but it didn't appear in *The New England Magazine* until January 1892. (Her rejection letter from *The Atlantic* read, "Dear Madam, I could not forgive myself if I made others as miserable as I have made myself.") A chronicle of one woman's descent into madness, the story is most commonly interpreted as a feminist critique of Victorian America's patriarchal medical system. It is also, however, a stellar example of Gothic fiction, recalling the unreliable narrator of Edgar Allan Poe's "The Tell-Tale Heart," published a half century before, and anticipating Shirley Jackson's similarly themed psychological suspense stories to come a half century later.

The plot begins straightforwardly. A never-named narrator and her physician husband, John, have retired for the summer with their newborn to a long-abandoned country house, so she may rest. The narrator is suffering from what her husband patronizingly dismisses as a "temporary nervous depression—a slight hysterical tendency." Forbidden to work, she is confined to a nursery at the top of the house, a spacious room with windows on all sides and a "repellant" yellow wallpaper stripped off in giant patches. "I never saw a worse paper in my life. One of those sprawling flamboyant patterns committing every artistic sin," the narrator confides in the secret diary that comprises the story. More ominous: "There is a recurrent spot where the pattern lolls like a broken neck." Soon she detects the figure of a woman trapped inside the paper, "creeping" behind the pattern, with whom she eventually merges completely. The ambiguous ending is left deliciously unresolved: When John faints after discovering his wife crawling around the perimeter of the room, is the narrator triumphant? Or does the fact that she continues to "creep over" his body mean she's now trapped in a never-ending cycle?

In December 1892, Gilman's husband filed for divorce. The legal dissolution of marriage was much more common than it had been in her parents' time, but Gilman's status as a published author and frequent lecturer drew media attention to her personal affairs, and her name became "a football for all the papers on the coast," she complained in a letter to a friend. Two years later, when the divorce was finalized, Gilman relinquished full custody of her daughter to Stetson, garnering even more public approbation. Her story "The Unnatural Mother," drafted in 1893 and first published in *The Impress* in 1895, about a young mother who warns the townspeople of a coming flood instead of tending to the safety of her baby, plays on popular conceptions of maternal feeling; the mother saves the town, dying in the process, but is posthumously castigated anyhow for risking her child, who survives. (Intriguingly, the mother's name, Esther Greenwood, is also that of the heroine of Sylvia Plath's 1963 autobiographical novel *The Bell Jar*. Though it's possible that Plath read Gilman, scholars still haven't determined if the reference was intentional.)

The two other stories from this period collected here extend Gilman's exploration of women's relationship to the home, both literally and metaphorically. In "The Rocking-Chair" (1893), two newspapermen, lifelong close friends, spy through a boardinghouse window an enchantingly gilded-haired girl-woman in a rocking chair—that eminently domestic piece of furniture, suggestive of a mother nursing or a grandmother nodding over her needlepoint. They take a room, but each man's desire to possess the beauty—whether she's real or a ghost, nobody knows—quickly devolves into mutual suspicion, jealousy, and recrimination, until the rocking chair becomes an actual wedge between the friends. In "Through This" (1893), the female narrator, again unnamed, spends dawn until dusk cooking and cleaning for her family, her only time to herself spent waking up or falling asleep, contemplating the walls of her bedroom. Mild and uncomplaining, she could easily pass as a perfectly content "angel in the house." But the discerning reader sees in her selflessness the painful self-abnegation expected of women.

Once she'd found her stride, Gilman was unstoppable. In 1893 she published her debut poetry collection, *In This Our World*, to warm reviews. As with her fiction, in her poems she combined conventional forms with social critique, resulting in often didactic works that address through meter and rhyme the political and philosophical themes she held dear. Around this time, she decided her primary concern to be the "woman question," particularly suffrage and economic independence. She also became involved in the so-called Nationalist movement, a short-lived nineteenth-century network of socialist groups committed to nationalizing private property, hence the name (that is, no relation to our contemporary understanding of "nationalism"). Inspired by Edward Bellamy's 1888 blockbuster utopian science-fiction novel, *Looking Backward: 2000–1887*, the movement's core principles—most notably a devotion to optimism and progress, and an emphasis on the communal over the individual—made a profound impact on Gilman and permanently expanded her approach to the "woman question." She incorporated ideas about cooperative living into her feminism and spent the years between 1895 and 1900 traveling nonstop as a public speaker, a woman "at large," as she liked to put it when asked to give her address.

In 1898, she put forth her new worldview in her first important nonfiction book, *Women and Economics*, a deeply researched synthesis of sociology, history, and psychology arguing for the necessity of female economic independence to the improvement of marriage and the family. Foreseeing our current debate over "work-life balance," she advocated for professionalizing housework and for building communal living spaces with public kitchens so that women wouldn't be permanently stuck alone cooking and cleaning. The book revived arguments initially made in Mary Wollstonecraft's groundbreaking *A Vindication of the Rights of Woman* (1792) and was compared favorably to John Stuart Mill's *The Subjection of Women* (1869), catapulting Gilman into a yet higher sphere of influence and crowning her the leading intellectual of the women's movement.

The new century inaugurated a new chapter in Gilman's eventful life. In 1900, she married her first cousin, George Houghton Gilman, a Wall Street attorney, and settled down with him in New York City. Over the next several years she published three more nonfiction books: *Concerning Children* (1900), *The Home: Its Work and Influence* (1903), and *Human Work* (1904). Meanwhile, in keeping with her populist spirit, she frequently contributed articles to a wide range of mass-market magazines and newspapers, as well as academic journals, under titles as disparate as "Esthetic Dyspepsia" (*Saturday Evening Post*, 1900) and "Social Darwinism" (*American Journal of Sociology*, 1907).

In 1909 Gilman launched her most ambitious endeavor yet: her own monthly one-woman publication, *The Forerunner*. For seven-plus years, she wrote, edited, designed, typeset, and produced every last inch of eighty-six issues, each twenty-eight pages long and going out to 1,500 subscribers. (An annual subscription was one dollar, the equivalent of twenty-five dollars today.) Free to unleash her voice whenever and however she wanted, without having to constantly navigate the complicated strictures of the publishing marketplace, she let loose in an inspired torrent of "stories short and serial, article and essay; drama, verse, satire and sermon; dialogue, fable and fantasy, comment and review," as she described in her statement of purpose. The cover image, her own pen-and-ink illustration, beautifully captures her politics: a genderless infant stands atop a globe flanked by a couple—the woman supports the child with her left arm, the man supports the woman with his right arm, and with their free hands, they hold the globe between them, that is, the fate of the family and of the world at large. All told, she'd use *The Forerunner* to publish ten serialized book-length works of fiction and nonfiction, two short plays, thirty short stories (thirteen of which are collected in this volume, along with four of her many poems that appeared in the periodical). It was in these pages that she first published, over the course of 1915, what is widely considered to be her greatest work, the satirical, utopian science-fiction novel *Herland*.

While most science fiction takes place in the future, *Herland* is about an all-female society set in Gilman's present day. Two thousand years before the story takes place, a volcanic eruption blocked off the country's only point of egress, killing most of the men in the process; those who remained, murderous slaves attempting to violently seize power, were obliterated by an uprising of women. Eventually the survivors, all female, discovered that via parthenogenesis (asexual reproduction) they could get pregnant and give birth to five girls apiece, who were also parthenogenetic. In this way Herland had created and maintained a thriving population over the millennia. When they'd reached the risk of overpopulation, they instituted the practice of *choosing* biological motherhood; that is, a woman could decide for herself if she'd give birth to a child or instead channel her generative energies into designing a new building, for instance, or writing a novel.

The story begins when three American men on a scientific expedition—Terry, a male chauvinist playboy; Jeff, a sentimental doctor; and Vandyck, a sociologist and the feminist-minded narrator—stumble upon this mythical place they'd long heard about and never believed to be real. The book's comedy turns on the many ways in which their sexist presumptions—many of which, sadly, still hold true today—are toppled. Far from the "sublimated summer resort—just Girls and Girls and Girls" that Terry had imagined Herland to be, they discover instead an ideal society that is communal, co-operative, and peaceful. Herlanders maintain a simple vegetarian diet and exercise daily. Their clothes are simple, airy, and comfortable; there isn't a corset, or even a special brassiere, to be found in all the land. The means of production are entirely self-sustaining. Laws are revised every twenty years.

There is a snake in this garden, however—not in the plot, but in Gilman's conception of this utopia-in-her-time: a desire for racial purity. For all her open-mindedness, Gilman was seriously xenophobic, a regrettably common response to the waves of immigrants resettling in urban areas at the turn of the last century, but one that she doubled down on with her simultaneous embrace of eugenics.

Unpacking Gilman's relationship to this controversial belief system is complicated enough on its own, and it's made more so by the passage of time. In the early 1900s, eugenics was a respectable academic field, studied at Harvard and Princeton. Between her passion for science and sociology and her constitutional faith in the forward march of progress, Gilman was quick to see merit in the idea that some human populations are genetically superior to others, and that by playing to the strengths inherent to each race, poverty could be eradicated and society vastly improved. Moreover, at a time when sex education and effective birth control weren't widely available, she saw in eugenics an answer to the scourges of sexually transmitted diseases (a major public-health issue until penicillin was found to treat syphilis in 1943) and involuntary motherhood—that is, women giving birth to more children than they could care for because they didn't know how not to get pregnant. Feminists and activists in general were divided: Margaret Sanger, Emma Goldman, and Olive Schreiner all shared Gilman's views, while Jane Addams, Lillian Wald, and Florence Kelley fought against them.

Viewed one way, the practice in Herland of women consciously deciding whether or not to give birth is a refreshing rejoinder to the age-old expectation that all women must become mothers, and even puts a positive spin on a decision that some still interpret as "choosing nothing over something," as

I've heard it said. Viewed another way, it appears perilously similar to the then-widespread use of involuntary eugenic sterilization as a means for controlling "undesirable" populations. Now considered a gross abuse of human rights, in the twentieth century eugenic sterilization was practiced in thirty states, starting in 1907, when it was first passed into Indiana law, and lasting into the 1970s. Of course, sterilization does not appear in *Herland*, and there is no evidence that Gilman advocated for the practice in real life, but it cannot be overlooked that she did believe native-born white people to be genetically superior to all other groups.

Gilman's "race awareness," as she called it, did not win her many followers, and over the course of the 1920s she came to be regarded as far less relevant than she once had been. When she died in 1935, all her books were out of print, and early posthumous efforts to keep her reputation alive foundered on disinterest. Hence the rush of excitement that scholars in the 1970s felt upon rediscovering this forgotten writer—which was replaced, as her writings on race came to light, with a sense of confusion, anger, and betrayal. How could it be that this progressive feminist activist followed such an injurious line of thinking? Why didn't her nuanced understanding of gender inequality extend to race? Women of the third wave, who struggled to make people see that the standard forms of discrimination—sexism, racism, classism—aren't distinct categorizations, but in fact overlap and interconnect, couldn't find a place for her within this new movement of intersectional feminism.

And yet, so much of what Gilman fought for has reverberated over the decades. Her vision of a companionate marriage founded on economic equality between the sexes, and the need to free women from the burdens of housework, anticipated many of the issues later taken up by the movement's second wave, from America's fights in the 1960s for equal employment and pay to Italy's 1972 Wages for Housework campaign. Likewise, her conviction that gender identity is fluid and not fixed foretold the third wave's understanding of a gender continuum. *The Forerunner* can be seen as a precursor to the riot grrrl practice of self-publishing zines. Her ingenious schemes for striking a balance between work and family—such as communal living arrangements with public kitchens—are echoed in the contemporary trend of "microhousing" and live-work spaces. Select concerns of the fourth wave, including the continued sexual predation of women in the workplace, can be traced back to Gilman: Her hope that revolutionizing marriage would free wives from the conjugal obligation to serve their husbands' erotic needs—"sex slavery," as she called it—did happen, after a fashion, though as we've learned, male sexual entitlement remains pervasive across all industries, from the most ordinary roadside diner to the exclusive redoubts of Hollywood.

Even Gilman's manner of death presaged today's right-to-die movement. On August 17, 1935, three years after being diagnosed with incurable breast cancer, she "chose chloroform over cancer," as she wrote in her suicide note, and killed herself with an overdose. At the time against the law, today euthanasia is legal in only a handful of states. In death, as in life, Gilman chose to observe her own rules.

It isn't merely Gilman's prescience, however, that makes her a figure worthy of continued study. She also stands as an example of the perils of optimism—a cautionary tale for an era besotted with genetic testing and assisted reproductive technologies. If we don't constantly remind ourselves that there is no such thing as a quick fix, and continually push back against the impulse to form and abide by hierarchies—whether according to race, gender, class, beauty, biological fitness, or as yet unarticulated designations—we risk not only the hope of progress, but our own humanity. Those figures who are uncommonly brilliant but also flawed, as Gilman was, serve the rare function of not only inspiring our best selves, but also keeping us in contact with our own weaknesses, without which we wouldn't be human at all.

KATE BOLICK

Suggestions for Further Reading

Ahmad, Dohra. *Landscapes of Hope: Anti-Colonial Utopianism in America*. New York: Oxford University Press, 2009.

Awkward-Rich, Cameron. "The Fiction of Ethnography in Charlotte Perkins Gilman's *Herland*," *Science Fiction Studies* 43, 2016, 331–50.

Betjemann, Peter. "Eavesdropping with Charlotte Perkins Gilman: Fiction, Transcription, and the Ethics of Interior Design," *American Literary Realism* 46, 2014, 95–115.

Christensen, Andrew G. "Charlotte Perkins Gilman's *Herland* and the Tradition of the Scientific Utopia," *Utopian Studies* 28, 2017, 286–304.

Craig, Layne Parish. *When Sex Changed: Birth Control Politics and Literature between the World Wars*. New Brunswick, NJ: Rutgers University Press, 2013.

Davis, Cynthia J. *Charlotte Perkins Gilman: A Biography*. Stanford, CA: Stanford University Press, 2010.

Davis, Cynthia J. "Concerning Children: Charlotte Perkins Gilman, Mothering, and Biography," *Victorian Review* 27, 2001, 102–15.

Davis, Cynthia J., and Denise D. Knight, eds. *Charlotte Perkins Gilman and Her Contemporaries: Literary and Intellectual Contexts*. Tuscaloosa: University of Alabama Press, 2004.

Edelstein, Sari. *Between the Novel and the News: The Emergence of American Women's Writing*. Charlottesville: University of Virginia Press, 2014.

Egan, Kristen R. "Conservation and Cleanliness: Racial Environmental Purity in Ellen Richards and Charlotte Perkins Gilman," *Women's Studies Quarterly* 39, 2011, 77–92.

Hayden, Dolores. *The Grand Domestic Revolution: A History of Feminist Designs for American Homes, Neighborhoods, and Cities*. Cambridge: MIT Press, 1981.

Knight, Denise D. "'Only a Husband's Opinion': Walter Stetson's View of Gilman's 'The Yellow Wall-Paper'—An Inscription," *American Literary Realism* 36, 2003, 86–87.

Lombardo, Paul A., ed. *A Century of Eugenics in America: From the Indiana Experiment to the Human Genome Era.* Bloomington: Indiana University Press, 2011.

Magarey, Susan. "Dreams and Desires: Four 1970s Feminist Visions of Utopia," *Australian Feminist Studies* 22, 2007, 325–41.

Nadkarni, Asha. *Eugenic Feminism: Reproductive Nationalism in the United States and India.* Minneapolis: University of Minnesota Press, 2014.

Oliver, Lawrence J. "W. E. B. Du Bois, Charlotte Perkins Gilman, and 'A Suggestion on the Negro Problem,'" *American Literary Realism* 48, 2015, 25–39.

Sutton-Ramspeck, Beth. *Raising the Dust: The Literary Housekeeping of Mary Ward, Sarah Grand, and Charlotte Perkins Gilman.* Athens: Ohio University Press, 2004.

Trigg, Mary K. *Feminism as Life's Work: Four Modern American Women through Two World Wars.* New Brunswick, NJ: Rutgers University Press, 2014.

Van Wienen, Mark W. *American Socialist Triptych: The Literary-Political Work of Charlotte Perkins Gilman, Upton Sinclair, and W. E. B. Du Bois.* Ann Arbor: University of Michigan Press, 2012.

Works by Charlotte Perkins Gilman

Benigna Machiavelli. Serialized in *Forerunner* 5, 1914. Reprint, Santa Barbara, Calif.: Bandanna Books, 1993.

Charlotte Perkins Gilman Reader. Edited with an introduction by Ann J. Lane. New York: Pantheon, 1980.

Concerning Children. Boston: Small, Maynard & Co., 1900.

The Crux. Seralized in *Forerunner* 2, 1911. Reprinted, New York: Charlton, 1911.

The Diaries of Charlotte Perkins Gilman. 2 vols. Edited by Denise D. Knight. Charlottesville: University Press of Virginia, 1994.

Forerunner 1–7, 1909–1916. Reprinted, with an introduction by Madeleine B. Stern, New York: Greenwood, 1968.

His Religion and Hers: A Study of the Faith of Our Fathers and the Work of Our Mothers. New York: The Century Company, 1923.

The Home: Its Work and Influence. New York: McClure, Phillips & Co., 1903.

Human Work. New York: McClure, Phillips & Co., 1904.

In This Our World. Oakland, Calif.: McCombs & Vaughn, 1893. 3rd ed., Boston: Small, Maynard & Co., 1898. Reprint, New York: Arno, 1974.

The Later Poetry of Charlotte Perkins Gilman. Edited by Denise D. Knight. Newark: University of Delaware Press, 1996.

The Living of Charlotte Perkins Gilman: An Autobiography. Foreword by Zona Gale. New York: Appleton-Century, 1935. Reprinted, with an introduction by Ann J. Lane, Madison: University of Wisconsin Press, 1990.

Mag-Marjorie. Serialized in *Forerunner* 3, 1912.

The Man-Made World; Or, Our Androcentric Culture. *Forerunner* 1, 1909–1910. Reprint, New York: Charlton, 1911.

"Moving the Mountain." *Forerunner* 2, 1911. Reprint, New York: Charlton, 1911.

Our Brains and What Ails Them. Serialized in *Forerunner* 3, 1911.

Social Ethics. Serialized in *Forerunner* 4, 1914.

Unpunished. Catherine J. Golden and Denise D. Knight, eds. New York: Feminist Press, 1997.

"What Diantha Did." *Forerunner* 1, 1909–1910. Reprint, New York: Charlton, 1910.

With Her in Ourland: The Sequel to Herland. Serialized in *Forerunner* 7, 1916. Reprinted, with an introduction by Mary Jo Deegan and Michael R. Hill, eds., Westport, Conn.: Greenwood, 1997.

Women and Economics: A Study of the Economic Relation Between Men and Women as a Factor in Social Evolution. Boston: Small, Maynard & Co., 1898. Reprinted, with an introduction by Carl Degler, New York: Harper & Row, 1966.

Won Over. Serialized in *Forerunner* 4, 1913.

The Yellow Wall-Paper. Boston: Small, Maynard & Co., 1899. Reprint, with an afterword by Elaine Hedges. 2nd ed. New York: Feminist Press, 1996.

The Yellow Wall-Paper and Selected Stories of Charlotte Perkins Gilman. Edited with an introduction by Denise D. Knight. Newark: University of Delaware Press, 1994.

Secondary Sources

Allen, Polly Wynn. *Building Domestic Liberty: Charlotte Perkins Gilman's Architectural Feminism*. Amherst: University of Massachusetts Press, 1988.

Bauer, Dale M. *The Yellow Wallpaper.* Boston: Bedford Books, 1998.

Biamonte, Gloria A. "'there is a story, if we could only find it': Charlotte Perkins Gilman's 'The Giant Wistaria,'" *Legacy* 5, 1988, 33–43.

Cane, Aleta. "Charlotte Perkins Gilman's *Herland* as a Feminist Response to Male Quest Romance," *Jack London Journal* 2, 1995, 25–38.

Ceplair, Larry, ed. *Charlotte Perkins Gilman: A Nonfiction Reader.* New York: Columbia University Press, 1992.

Degler, Carl N. "Charlotte Perkins Gilman on the Theory and Practice of Feminism," *American Quarterly* 8, spring 1956, 21–39.

DeLamotte, Eugenia C. "Male and Female Mysteries in 'The Yellow Wallpaper,'" *Legacy* 5:1, spring 1988, 3–14.

Donaldson, Laura E. "The Eve of De-Struction: Charlotte Perkins Gilman and the Feminist Recreation of Paradise," *Women's Studies* 16, 1989, 373–87.

Fishkin, Shelley Fisher. "Making a Change: Strategies of Subversion in Gilman's Journalism and Short Fiction." In *Critical Essays on Charlotte Perkins Gilman.* Edited by Joanne Karpinski. New York: G. K. Hall, 1992, 234–48.

Fleenor, Julian E. "The Gothic Prism: Charlotte Perkins Gilman's Gothic Stories and Her Autobiography." In *The Female Gothic.* Edited by Julian E. Fleenor. Montreal: Eden, 1983, 227–41.

Gilbert, Sandra, and Susan Guber. *The Madwoman in the Attic: The Woman Writer and the Nineteenth Century Imagination.* New Haven: Yale University Press, 1979.

Golden, Catherine. *The Captive Imagination: A Casebook on "The Yellow Wall-Paper."* New York: The Feminist Press, 1992.

Hedges, Elaine. Afterword to "The Yellow Wall-Paper." 2nd ed. New York: Feminist Press, 1996.

Hill, Mary A. *Charlotte Perkins Gilman: The Making of a Radical Feminist, 1860–1896.* Philadelphia: Temple University Press, 1980.

———. *Endure: The Diaries of Charles Walter Stetson.* Philadelphia: Temple University Press, 1985.

———. *A Journey from Within: The Love Letters of Charlotte Perkins Gilman and Houghton Gilman, 1897–1900.* Lewisburg, Pa.: Bucknell University Press, 1995.

Howe, Harriet. "Charlotte Perkins Gilman—As I Knew Her," *Equal Rights: Independent Feminist Weekly* 5, September 1936, 211–16.

Hume, Beverly A. "Gilman's Interminable Grotesque: The Narrator of 'The Yellow Wallpaper,'" *Studies in Short Fiction* 28:4, fall 1991, 477–84.

Johnson, Greg. "Gilman's Gothic Allegory: Rage and Redemption in 'The Yellow Wallpaper,'" *Studies in Short Fiction* 26:4, fall 1989, 521–30.

Karpinski, Joanne B. *Critical Essays on Charlotte Perkins Gilman.* Boston: G. K. Hall, 1992.

Kasmer, Lisa. "'The Yellow Wallpaper': A Symptomatic Reading," *Literature and Psychology* 36:3, 1990, 1–15.

Kessler, Carol Farley. "Brittle Jars and Bitter Jangles: Light Verse by Charlotte Perkins Gilman," *Regionalism and the Female Imagination* 4, winter 1979. Reprinted in *Charlotte Perkins Gilman: The Woman and Her Work.* Edited by Sheryl L. Meyering. Ann Arbor, Mich.: UMI Research Press, 1989, 133–43.

——. *Charlotte Perkins Gilman: Her Progress Toward Utopia with Selected Writings.* Syracuse, N.Y.: Syracuse University Press, 1995. Knight, Denise D. *Charlotte Perkins Gilman: A Study of the Short Fiction.* New York: Twayne Publishers, 1997.

——. "'Such a hopeless task before her': Some observations on Hawthorne and Gilman." In *Scribbling Women: Engendering and Expanding the Hawthorne Tradition.* Edited by John Idol and Melinda M. Ponder. Amherst: University of Massachusetts Press, 1999.

——. "The Reincarnation of Jane: 'Through This'—Gilman's Companion to 'The Yellow Wall-Paper,'" *Women's Studies* 20, 1992, 287–302.

——. "'With the first grass-blade': Whitman's Influence on the Poetry of Charlotte Perkins Gilman," *Walt Whitman Quarterly Review*, summer 1993, 18–29.

Lane, Ann J. *To Herland and Beyond: The Life and Work of Charlotte Perkins Gilman.* New York: Pantheon, 1980.

Matossian, Lou Ann. "A Woman-Made Language: Charlotte Perkins Gilman and *Herland,*" *Women and Language* 10, 1987, 16–20.

Meyering, Sheryl L., ed. *Charlotte Perkins Gilman: The Woman and Her Work.* Foreword by Cathy N. Davidson. Ann Arbor, Mich.: UMI Research Press, 1989.

Peyser, Thomas G. "Reproducing Utopia: Charlotte Perkins Gilman and *Herland,*" *Studies in American Fiction* 20, 1992, 1–16.

Scharnhorst, Gary. *Charlotte Perkins Gilman.* Boston: Twayne, 1985.

———. *Charlotte Perkins Gilman: A Bibliography*. Metuchen, N.J.: Scarecrow, 1985.

———. "Reconstructing *Here Also*: On the Later Poetry of Charlotte Perkins Gilman." In *Critical Essays on Charlotte Perkins Gilman*. Edited by Joanne Karpinski. New York: G. K. Hall, 1992, 249–68.

Shumaker, Conrad. "'Too Terribly Good to Be Printed': Charlotte Perkins Gilman's 'The Yellow Wallpaper,'" *American Literature* 57, 1985, 588–99.

Stern, Madeleine B. Introduction to the reprint edition of *Forerunner*, vol. 1. New York: Greenwood, 1968.

Veeder, William. "Who Is Jane? The Intricate Feminism of Charlotte Perkins Gilman," *Arizona Quarterly* 44:3, 1988, 40–79.

Vertinsky, Patricia. *The Eternally Wounded Woman: Women, Doctors, and Exercise in the Late Nineteenth Century*. Manchester, England: Manchester University Press, 1990.

Wilson, Christopher P. "Charlotte Perkins Gilman's Steady Burghers: The Terrain of *Herland*," *Women's Studies* 12, 1986, 271–92.

A Note on the Texts

The text of *Herland* that follows is taken from the original 1915 edition serialized in *Forerunner*. Editions published after 1915 dropped sentences, substituted wording, altered syntax, and eliminated capitalization without documentation. This publication restores the text of *Herland* to its original appearance. Except for minor editorial emendations to enhance readability, Gilman's spelling, punctuation, capitalization, indentations, and italics have been retained. I have silently corrected obvious typographical errors.

The word "wallpaper" appears variously in the title of different editions of "The Yellow Wall-Paper" as one word (Wallpaper), two words (Wall Paper) and as a hyphenated word, both with a lowercase and uppercase "p" (Wall-paper; Wall-Paper). In quoting titles of critical articles, I have retained the spelling as it appears. In general discussion of the story, I have used "Wall-Paper," taken from the title of the first published edition of the story in *New England Magazine* in 1892.

The texts of the stories are taken from the following sources: "The Unexpected," from the May 21, 1890, issue of *Kate Field's Washington*; "The Giant Wistaria," from the June 1891 issue of *New England Magazine*; "An Extinct Angel," from the September 23, 1891, issue of *Kate Field's Washington*; "The Yellow Wall-Paper," from the January 1892 issue of *New England Magazine*; "The Rocking-Chair," from the May 1893 issue of *Worthington's Illustrated*; "Through This," from the September 13, 1893, issue of *Kate Field's Washington*; "The Boys and The Butter," from the October 1910 issue of *Forerunner*; "Mrs. Beazley's Deeds," from the March 27, 1911, issue of *Woman's*

World; "Turned," from the September 1911 issue of *Forerunner*; "Old Water" from the October 1911 issue of *Forerunner*; "Making a Change," from the December 1911 issue of *Forerunner*; "Mrs. Elder's Idea," from the February 1912 issue of *Forerunner*; "The Chair of English," from the March 1913 issue of *Forerunner*; "Bee Wise," from the July 1913 issue of *Forerunner*; "His Mother," from the July 1914 issue of *Forerunner*; "Dr. Clair's Place," from the June 1915 issue of *Forerunner*; "Joan's Defender," from the June 1916 issue of *Forerunner*; "The Vintage," from the October 1916 issue of *Forerunner*; "The Unnatural Mother," from the November 1916 issue of *Forerunner*.

The texts of the poems are taken from the following sources: "One Girl of Many," from the February 1, 1884, issue of *Alpha*; "Closed Doors," from the November 1898 issue of *Scribner's*; "The Purpose," from the March 12, 1904, issue of *Woman's Journal*; "Birth," "In Duty Bound," "Seeking," "Too Much," "On the Paw-tuxet," "A Moonrise," "Similar Cases," "A Conservative," "An Obstacle," "She Walketh Veiled and Sleeping," and "To the Young Wife," from the third edition of *In This Our World*, published in 1908 by Small, Maynard & Company in Boston; "Locked Inside," from the January 1910 issue of *Forerunner*; "The Artist," from the May 1911 issue of *Forerunner*; "More Females of the Species," from the December 1911 issue of *Forerunner*; "Matriatism," from the November 1914 issue of *Forerunner*.

The Yellow Wall-Paper,
Herland, and
Selected Writings

HERLAND

CHAPTER I

A NOT UNNATURAL
ENTERPRISE

This is written from memory, unfortunately. If I could have brought with me the material I so carefully prepared, this would be a very different story. Whole books full of notes, carefully copied records, first-hand descriptions, and the pictures—that's the worst loss. We had some bird's-eyes of the cities and parks; a lot of lovely views of streets, of buildings, outside and in, and some of those gorgeous gardens, and, most important of all, of the women themselves.

Nobody will ever believe how they looked. Descriptions aren't any good when it comes to women, and I never was good at descriptions anyhow. But it's got to be done somehow; the rest of the world needs to know about that country.

I haven't said where it was for fear some self-appointed missionaries, or traders, or land-greedy expansionists, will take it upon themselves to push in. They will not be wanted, I can tell them that, and will fare worse than we did if they do find it.

It began this way. There were three of us, classmates and friends—Terry O. Nicholson (we used to call him the Old Nick, with good reason), Jeff Margrave, and I, Vandyck Jennings.

We had known each other years and years, and in spite of our differences we had a good deal in common. All of us were interested in science.

Terry was rich enough to do as he pleased. His great aim was exploration. He used to make all kinds of a row because there was nothing left to explore now, only patchwork and filling in, he said. He filled in well enough—he had a lot of talents—great on mechanics and electricity. Had all kinds of boats and motor cars, and was one of the best of our airmen.

We never could have done the thing at all without Terry.

Jeff Margrave was born to be a poet, a botanist—or both—but his folks persuaded him to be a doctor instead. He was a good one, for his age, but his real interest was in what he loved to call "the wonders of science."

As for me, Sociology's my major. You have to back that up with a lot of other sciences, of course. I'm interested in them all.

Terry was strong on facts—geography and meteorology and those; Jeff could beat him any time on biology, and I didn't care what it was they talked about, so long as it connected with human life, somehow. There are few things that don't.

We three had a chance to join a big scientific expedition. They needed a doctor, and that gave Jeff an excuse for dropping his just opening practice; they needed Terry's experience, his machine, and his money; and as for me, I got in through Terry's influence.

The expedition was up among the thousand tributaries and enormous hinterland of a great river, up where the maps had to be made, savage dialects studied, and all manner of strange flora and fauna expected.

But this story is not about that expedition. That was only the merest starter for ours.

My interest was first roused by talk among our guides. I'm quick at languages, know a good many, and pick them up readily. What with that and a really good interpreter we took with us, I made out quite a few legends and folk-myths of these scattered tribes.

And as we got farther and farther upstream, in a dark tangle of rivers, lakes, morasses, and dense forests, with here and there an unexpected long spur running out from the big mountains beyond, I noticed that more and more of these savages had a story about a strange and terrible "Woman Land" in the high distance.

"Up yonder," "Over there," "Way up"—was all the direction they could offer, but their legends all agreed on the main point—that there was this strange country where no men lived—only women and girl children.

None of them had ever seen it. It was dangerous, deadly, they said, for any man to go there. But there were tales of long ago, when some brave investigator had seen it—a Big Country, Big Houses, Plenty People—All Women.

Had no one else gone? Yes—a good many—but they never came back. It was no place for men—that they seemed sure of.

I told the boys about these stories, and they laughed at them. Naturally I did myself. I knew the stuff that savage dreams are made of.

But when we had reached our farthest point, just the day before we all had to turn around and start for home again, as the best of expeditions must in time, we three made a discovery.

The main encampment was on a spit of land running out into the main stream, or what we thought was the main stream. It had the same muddy color we had been seeing for weeks past, the same taste.

I happened to speak of that river to our last guide, a rather superior fellow, with quick, bright eyes.

He told me that there was another river—"over there—short river, sweet water—red and blue."

I was interested in this and anxious to see if I had understood, so I showed him a red and blue pencil I carried, and asked again.

Yes, he pointed to the river, and then to the southwestward. "River—good water—red and blue."

Terry was close by and interested in the fellow's pointing.

"What does he say, Van?"

I told him.

Terry blazed up at once.

"Ask him how far it is."

The man indicated a short journey; I judged about two hours, maybe three.

"Let's go," urged Terry. "Just us three. Maybe we can really find something. May be cinnabar in it."

"May be indigo," Jeff suggested, with his lazy smile.

It was early yet; we had just breakfasted; and leaving word that we'd be back before night, we got away quietly, not wishing to be thought too gullible if we failed, and secretly hoping to have some nice little discovery all to ourselves.

It was a long two hours, nearer three. I fancy the savage could have done it alone much quicker. There was a desperate tangle of wood and water and a swampy patch we never should have found our way across alone. But there was one, and I could see Terry, with compass and notebook, marking directions and trying to place landmarks.

We came after a while to a sort of marshy lake, very big, so that the circling forest looked quite low and dim across it. Our guide told us that boats could go from there to our camp—but "long way—all day."

This water was somewhat clearer than we had left, but we could not judge well from the margin. We skirted it for another half hour or so, the ground growing firmer as we advanced, and presently turned the corner of a wooded promontory and saw a quite different country—a sudden view of mountains, steep and bare.

"One of those long easterly spurs," Terry said appraisingly. "May be hundreds of miles from the range. They crop out like that."

Suddenly we left the lake and struck directly toward the cliffs. We heard running water before we reached it, and the guide pointed proudly to his river.

It was short. We could see where it poured down a narrow vertical cataract from an opening in the face of the cliff. It was sweet water. The guide drank eagerly and so did we.

"That's snow water," Terry announced. "Must come from way back in the hills."

But as to being red and blue—it was greenish in tint. The guide seemed not at all surprised. He hunted about a little and showed us a quiet marginal pool where there were smears of red along the border; yes, and of blue.

Terry got out his magnifying glass and squatted down to investigate.

"Chemicals of some sort—I can't tell on the spot. Look to me like dye-stuffs. Let's get nearer," he urged, "up there by the fall."

We scrambled along the steep banks and got close to the pool that foamed and boiled beneath the falling water. Here we searched the border and found traces of color beyond dispute. More—Jeff suddenly held up an unlooked-for trophy.

It was only a rag, a long, ravelled fragment of cloth. But it was a well-woven fabric; with a pattern, and of a clear scarlet that the water had not faded. No savage tribe that we had heard of made such fabrics.

The guide stood serenely on the bank, well pleased with our excitement.

"One day blue—one day red—one day green," he told us, and pulled from his pouch another strip of bright-hued cloth.

"Come down," he said, pointing to the cataract. "Woman Country—up there."

Then we were interested. We had our rest and lunch right there and pumped the man for further information. He could tell us only what the others had—a land of women—no men— babies, but all girls. No place for men—dangerous. Some had gone to see—none had come back.

I could see Terry's jaw set at that. No place for men? Dangerous? He looked as if he might shin up the waterfall on the spot. But the guide would not hear of going up, even if there had been any possible method of scaling that sheer cliff, and we had to get back to our party before night.

"They might stay if we told them," I suggested.

But Terry stopped in his tracks. "Look here, fellows," he said. "This is our find. Let's not tell those cocky old professors. Let's go on home with 'em, and then come back—just us—have a little expedition of our own."

We looked at him, much impressed. There was something attractive to a bunch of unattached young men in finding an undiscovered country of a strictly Amazonian nature.

Of course we didn't believe the story—but yet!

"There is no such cloth made by any of these local tribes," I announced, examining those rags with great care.

"Somewhere up yonder they spin and weave and dye—as well as we do."

"That would mean a considerable civilization, Van. There couldn't be such a place—and not known about."

"Oh, well, I don't know; what's that old republic up in the Pyrenees somewhere—Andorra? Precious few people know anything about that, and it's been minding its own business for a thousand years. Then there's Montenegro—splendid little state—you could lose a dozen Montenegroes up and down these great ranges."

We discussed it hotly, all the way back to camp. We discussed it, with care and privacy, on the voyage home. We discussed it after that, still only among ourselves, while Terry was making his arrangements.

He was hot about it. Lucky he had so much money—we might have had to beg and advertise for years to start the thing, and then it would have been a matter of public amusement—just sport for the papers.

But T. O. Nicholson could fix up his big steam yacht, load his specially made big motor-boat aboard, and tuck in a "dissembled" biplane without any more notice than a snip in the society column.

We had provisions and preventives and all manner of supplies. His previous experience stood him in good stead there. It was a very complete little outfit.

We were to leave the yacht at the nearest safe port and go up that endless river in our motor, just the three of us and a pilot; then drop the pilot when we got to that last stopping place of the previous party, and hunt up that clear water stream ourselves.

The motorboat we were going to leave at anchor in that wide shallow lake. It had a special covering of fitted armor, thin but strong, shut up like a clamshell.

"Those natives can't get into it, or hurt it, or move it," Terry explained proudly. "We'll start our flier from the lake and leave the motor as a base to come back to."

"If we come back," I suggested cheerfully.

"'Fraid the ladies will eat you?" he scoffed.

"We're not so sure about those ladies, you know," drawled Jeff. "There may be a contingent of gentlemen with poisoned arrows or something."

"You don't need to go if you don't want to," Terry remarked drily.

"Go? You'll have to get an injunction to stop me!" Both Jeff and I were sure about that.

But we did have differences of opinion, all the long way.

An ocean voyage is an excellent time for discussion. Now we had no eavesdroppers, we could loll and loaf in our deck-chairs and talk and talk—there was nothing else to do. Our absolute lack of facts only made the field of discussion wider.

"We'll leave papers with our consul where the yacht stays," Terry planned. "If we don't come back in—say a month—they can send a relief party after us."

"A punitive expedition," I urged. "If the ladies do eat us we must make reprisals."

"They can locate that last stopping place easy enough, and I've made a sort of chart of that lake and cliff and waterfall."

"Yes, but how will they get up?" asked Jeff.

"Same way we do, of course. If three valuable American citizens are lost up there, they will follow somehow—to say nothing of the glittering attractions of that fair land—let's call it Feminisia,'" he broke off.

"You're right, Terry. Once the story gets out, the river will crawl with expeditions and the airships rise like a swarm of mosquitoes." I laughed as I thought of it. "We've made a great mistake not to let Mr. Yellow Press in on this. Save us! What headlines!"

"Not much!" said Terry grimly. "This is our party. We're going to find that place alone."

"What are you going to do with it when you do find it—if you do?" Jeff asked mildly.

Jeff was a tender soul. I think he thought that country—if there was one—was just blossoming with roses and babies and canaries and tidies—and all that sort of thing.

And Terry, in his secret heart, had visions of a sort of subli-mated summer resort—just Girls and Girls and Girls—and that he was going to be—well, Terry was popular among women even when there were other men around, and it's not to be wondered at that he had pleasant dreams of what might happen. I could see it in his eyes as he lay there, looking at the long blue rollers slipping by, and fingering that impressive mustache of his.

But I thought—then—that I could form a far clearer idea of what was before us than either of them.

"You're all off, boys," I insisted. "If there is such a place— and there does seem some foundation for believing it—you'll find it's built on a sort of matriarchal principle—that's all. The men have a separate cult of their own, less socially developed than the women, and make them an annual visit—a sort of wedding call. This is a condition known to have existed— here's just a survival. They've got some peculiarly isolated valley or tableland up there, and their primeval customs have survived. That's all there is to it."

"How about the boys?" Jeff asked.

"Oh, the men take them away as soon as they are five or six, you see."

"And how about this danger theory all our guides were so sure of?"

"Danger enough, Terry, and we'll have to be mighty careful. Women of that stage of culture are quite able to defend themselves and have no welcome for unseasonable visitors."

We talked and talked.

And with all my airs of sociological superiority I was no nearer than any of them.

It was funny though, in the light of what we did find, those extremely clear ideas of ours as to what a country of women would be like. It was no use to tell ourselves and one another that all this was idle speculation. We were idle and we did speculate, on the ocean voyage and the river voyage, too.

"Admitting the improbability," we'd begin solemnly, and then launch out again.

"They would fight among themselves," Terry insisted. "Women always do. We mustn't look to find any sort of order and organization."

"You're dead wrong," Jeff told him. "It will be like a nunnery under an Abbess—a peaceful, harmonious sisterhood."

I snorted derision at this idea.

"Nuns, indeed! Your peaceful sisterhoods were all celibate, Jeff, and under vows of obedience. These are just women, and mothers, and where there's motherhood you don't find sisterhood—not much."

"No, sir—they'll scrap," agreed Terry. "Also we mustn't look for inventions and progress; it'll be awfully primitive."

"How about that cloth mill?" Jeff suggested.

"Oh, cloth! Women have always been spinsters. But there they stop—you'll see."

We joked Terry about his modest impression that he would be warmly received, but he held his ground.

"You'll see," he insisted. "I'll get solid with them all—and play one bunch against another. I'll get myself elected King in no time—whew! Solomon will have to take a back seat!"

"Where do we come in on that deal?" I demanded. "Aren't we Viziers or anything?"

"Couldn't risk it," he asserted solemnly. "You might start a revolution—probably would. No, you'll have to be beheaded, or bowstrung—or whatever the popular method of execution is."

"You'd have to do it yourself, remember," grinned Jeff. "No husky black slaves and mamelukes! And there'd be two of us and only one of you—eh, Van?"

Jeff's ideas and Terry's were so far apart that sometimes it was all I could do to keep the peace between them. Jeff idealized women in the best Southern style. He was full of chivalry and sentiment, and all that. And he was a good boy; he lived up to his ideals.

You might say Terry did, too, if you can call his views about women anything so polite as ideals. I always liked Terry. He was a man's man, very much so, generous and brave and clever; but I don't think any of us in college days was quite pleased to have him with our sisters. We weren't very stringent, heavens no! But Terry was "the limit." Later on—why, of course a man's life is his own, we held, and asked no questions.

But barring a possible exception in favor of a not impossible wife, or of his mother, or, of course, the fair relatives of his friends, Terry's idea seemed to be that pretty women were just so much game and homely ones not worth considering.

It was really unpleasant sometimes to see the notions he had.

But I got out of patience with Jeff, too. He had such rose-colored haloes on his women folks. I held a middle ground, highly scientific, of course, and used to argue learnedly about the physiological limitations of the sex.

We were not in the least "advanced" on the woman question, any of us, then.

So we joked and disputed and speculated, and after an interminable journey, got to our old camping place at last.

It was not hard to find the river, just poking along that side till we came to it, and it was navigable as far as the lake.

When we reached that and slid out on its broad glistening bosom, with that high gray promontory running out toward us, and the straight white fall clearly visible, it began to be really exciting.

There was some talk, even then, of skirting the rock wall and seeking a possible foot-way up, but the marshy jungle made that method look not only difficult but dangerous.

Terry dismissed the plan sharply.

"Nonsense, fellows! We've decided that. It might take months—we haven't the provisions. No, sir—we've got to take our chances. If we get back safe—all right. If we don't, why, we're not the first explorers to get lost in the shuffle. There are plenty to come after us."

So we got the big biplane together and loaded it with our scientifically compressed baggage—the camera, of course; the glasses; a supply of concentrated food. Our pockets were magazines of small necessities, and we had our guns, of course—there was no knowing, what might happen.

Up and up and up we sailed, way up at first, to get "the lay of the land" and make note of it.

Out of that dark green sea of crowding forest this high-standing spur rose steeply. It ran back on either side, apparently, to the far-off white-crowned peaks in the distance, themselves probably inaccessible.

"Let's make the first trip geographical," I suggested. "Spy out the land, and drop back here for more gasoline. With your tremendous speed we can reach that range and back all right. Then we can leave a sort of map on board—for that relief expedition."

"There's sense in that," Terry agreed. "I'll put off being king of Ladyland for one more day."

So we made a long skirting voyage, turned the point of the cape which was close by, ran up one side of the triangle at our best speed, crossed over the base where it left the higher mountains, and so back to our lake by moonlight.

"That's not a bad little kingdom," we agreed when it was roughly drawn and measured. We could tell the size fairly by our speed. And from what we could see of the sides—and that icy ridge at the back end—"It's a pretty enterprising savage who would manage to get into it," Jeff said.

Of course we had looked at the land itself—eagerly, but we were too high and going too fast to see much. It appeared to be well forested about the edges, but in the interior there were wide plains, and everywhere parklike meadows and open places.

There were cities, too; that I insisted. It looked—well, it looked like any other country—a civilized one, I mean.

We had to sleep after that long sweep through the air, but we turned out early enough next day, and again we rose softly up the height till we could top the crowning trees and see the broad fair land at our pleasure.

"Semitropical. Looks like a first-rate climate. It's wonderful what a little height will do for temperature." Terry was studying the forest growth.

"Little height! Is that what you call little?" I asked. Our instruments measured it clearly. We had not realized the long gentle rise from the coast perhaps.

"Mighty lucky piece of land, I call it," Terry pursued. "Now for the folks—I've had enough scenery."

So we sailed low, crossing back and forth, quartering the country as we went, and studying it. We saw—I can't remember now how much of this we noted then and how much was supplemented by our later knowledge, but we could not help seeing this much, even on that excited day—a land in a state of perfect cultivation, where even the forests looked as if they were cared for; a land that looked like an enormous park, only it was even more evidently an enormous garden.

"I don't see any cattle," I suggested, but Terry was silent. We were approaching a village.

I confess that we paid small attention to the clean, well-built roads, to the attractive architecture, to the ordered beauty of the little town. We had our glasses out, even Terry, setting his machine for a spiral glide, clapped the binoculars to his eyes.

They heard our whirring screw. They ran out of the houses—they gathered in from the fields, swift-running light figures, crowds of them. We stared and stared until it was almost too late to catch the levers, sweep off and rise again; and then we held our peace for a long run upward.

"Gosh!" said Terry, after a while.

"Only women there—and children," Jeff urged excitedly.

"But they look—why, this is a *civilized* country!" I protested. "There must be men."

"Of course there are men," said Terry. "Come on, let's find 'em."

He refused to listen to Jeff's suggestion that we examine the country further before we risked leaving our machine.

"There's a fine landing place right there where we came over," he insisted, and it was an excellent one—a wide, flat-topped rock, overlooking the lake, and quite out of sight from the interior.

"They won't find this in a hurry," he asserted, as we scrambled with the utmost difficulty down to safer footing. "Come on, boys—there were some good lookers in that bunch."

Of course it was unwise of us.

It was quite easy to see afterward that our best plan was to have studied the country more fully before we left our swooping airship and trusted ourselves to mere foot service. But we were three young men. We had been talking about this country for over a year, hardly believing that there was such a place, and now—we were in it.

It looked safe and civilized enough, and among those up-turned, crowding faces, though some were terrified enough—there was great beauty—that we all agreed.

"Come on!" cried Terry, pushing forward. "Oh, come on! Here goes for Herland!"

CHAPTER II

RASH ADVANCES

Not more than ten or fifteen miles we judged it from our landing rock to that last village. For all our eagerness we thought it wise to keep to the woods and go carefully.

Even Terry's ardor was held in check by his firm conviction that there were men to be met, and we saw to it that each of us had a good stock of cartridges.

"They may be scarce, and they may be hidden away somewhere—some kind of a matriarchate, as Jeff tells us; for that matter, they may live up in the mountains yonder and keep the women in this part of the country—sort of a national harem! But there are men somewhere—didn't you see the babies?"

We had all seen babies, children big and little, everywhere that we had come near enough to distinguish the people. And though by dress we could not be sure of all the grown persons, still there had not been one man that we were certain of.

"I always liked that Arab saying, 'First tie your camel and then trust in the Lord,'" Jeff murmured; so we all had our weapons in hand, and stole cautiously through the forest. Terry studied it as we progressed.

"Talk of civilization," he cried softly in restrained enthusiasm. "I never saw a forest so petted, even in Germany. Look, there's not a dead bough—the vines are trained—actually! And see here"—he stopped and looked about him, calling Jeff's attention to the kinds of trees.

They left me for a landmark and made a limited excursion on either side.

"Food-bearing, practically all of them," they announced

returning. "The rest, splendid hard-wood. Call this a forest?
It's a truck farm!"

"Good thing to have a botanist on hand," I agreed. "Sure
there are no medicinal ones? Or any for pure ornament?"

As a matter of fact they were quite right. These towering
trees were under as careful cultivation as so many cabbages. In
other conditions we should have found those woods full of fair
foresters and fruit gatherers; but an airship is a conspicuous
object, and by no means quiet—and women are cautious.

All we found moving in those woods, as we started through
them, were birds, some gorgeous, some musical, all so tame
that it seemed almost to contradict our theory of cultivation—
at least until we came upon occasional little glades, where
carved stone seats and tables stood in the shade beside clear
fountains, with shallow bird baths always added.

"They don't kill birds, and apparently they do kill cats,"
Terry declared. "*Must* be men here. Hark!"

We had heard something: something not in the least like
a bird-song, and very much like a suppressed whisper of
laughter—a little happy sound, instantly smothered. We stood
like so many pointers, and then used our glasses, swiftly, carefully.

"It couldn't have been far off," said Terry excitedly. "How
about this big tree?"

There was a very large and beautiful tree in the glade we
had just entered, with thick wide-spreading branches that
sloped out in lapping fans like a beech, or pine. It was trimmed
underneath some twenty feet up, and stood there like a huge
umbrella, with circling seats beneath.

"Look," he pursued. "There are short stumps of branches
left to climb on. There's someone up that tree, I believe."

We stole near, cautiously.

"Look out for a poisoned arrow in your eye," I suggested,
but Terry pressed forward, sprang up on the seat-back, and
grasped the trunk. "In my heart, more likely," he answered.
"Gee!—Look, boys!"

We rushed close in and looked up. There among the boughs
overhead was something—more than one something—that

clung motionless, close to the great trunk at first, and then, as one and all we started up the tree, separated into three swift-moving figures and fled upwards. As we climbed we could catch glimpses of them scattering above us. By the time we had reached about as far as three men together dared push, they had left the main trunk and moved outwards, each one balanced on a long branch that dipped and swayed beneath the weight.

We paused uncertain. If we pursued further, the boughs would break under the double burden. We might shake them off, perhaps, but none of us was so inclined. In the soft dappled light of these high regions, breathless with our rapid climb, we rested awhile, eagerly studying our objects of pursuit; while they in turn, with no more terror than a set of frolicsome children in a game of tag, sat as lightly as so many big bright birds on their precarious perches and frankly, curiously, stared at us.

"Girls!" whispered Jeff, under his breath, as if they might fly if he spoke aloud.

"Peaches!" added Terry, scarcely louder. "Peacherinos—Apricot-nectarines! Whew!"

They were girls, of course, no boys could ever have shown that sparkling beauty, and yet none of us was certain at first.

We saw short hair, hatless, loose, and shining; a suit of some light firm stuff, the closest of tunics and kneebreeches, met by trim gaiters; as bright and smooth as parrots and as unaware of danger, they swung there before us, wholly at ease, staring as we stared, till first one, and then all of them burst into peals of delighted laughter.

Then there was a torrent of soft talk, tossed back and forth; no savage sing-song, but clear musical fluent speech.

We met their laughter cordially, and doffed our hats to them, at which they laughed again, delightedly.

Then Terry, wholly in his element, made a polite speech, with explanatory gestures, and proceeded to introduce us, with pointing finger. "Mr. Jeff Margrave," he said clearly; Jeff bowed as gracefully as a man could in the fork of a great limb. "Mr. Vandyck Jennings"—I also tried to make an effective salute and nearly lost my balance.

Then Terry laid his hand upon his chest—a fine chest he had, too, and introduced himself: he was braced carefully for the occasion and achieved an excellent obeisance.

Again they laughed delightedly, and the one nearest me followed his tactics.

"Celis," she said distinctly, pointing to the one in blue; "Alima"—the one in rose; then, with a vivid imitation of Terry's impressive manner, she laid a firm delicate hand on her gold-green jerkin—"Ellador." This was pleasant, but we got not nearer.

"We can't sit here and learn the language," Terry protested. He beckoned to them to come nearer, most winningly—but they gaily shook their heads. He suggested, by signs, that we all go down together; but again they shook their heads, still merrily. Then Ellador clearly indicated that we should go down, pointing to each and all of us, with unmistakable firmness; and further seeming to imply by the sweep of a lithe arm that we not only go downwards, but go away altogether—at which we shook our heads in turn.

"Have to use bait," grinned Terry. "I don't know about you fellows, but I came prepared." He produced from an inner pocket a little box of purple velvet, that opened with a snap—and out of it he drew a long sparkling thing, a necklace of big varicolored stones that would have been worth a million if real ones. He held it up, swung it, glittering in the sun, offered it first to one, then to another, holding it out as far as he could reach toward the girl nearest him. He stood braced in the fork, held firmly by one hand—the other, swinging his bright temptation, reached far out along the bough, but not quite to his full stretch.

She was visibly moved, I noted, hesitated, spoke to her companions. They chattered softly together, one evidently warning her, the other encouraging. Then, softly and slowly, she drew nearer. This was Alima, a tall long-limbed lass, well-knit and evidently both strong and agile. Her eyes were splendid, wide, fearless, as free from suspicion as a child's who has never been rebuked. Her interest was more that of an intent boy playing a fascinating game than of a girl lured by an ornament.

The others moved a bit farther out, holding firmly, watching. Terry's smile was irreproachable, but I did not like the look in his eyes—it was like a creature about to spring. I could already see it happen—the dropped necklace, the sudden clutching hand—the girl's sharp cry as he seized her and drew her in. But it didn't happen. She made a timid reach with her right hand for the gay swinging thing—he held it a little nearer—then, swift as light, she seized it from him with her left, and dropped on the instant to the bough below.

He made his snatch, quite vainly, almost losing his position as his hand clutched only air; and then, with inconceivable rapidity, the three bright creatures were gone. They dropped from the ends of the big boughs to those below, fairly pouring themselves off the tree, while we climbed downward as swiftly as we could. We heard their vanishing gay laughter, we saw them fleeting away in the wide open reaches of the forest, and gave chase, but we might as well have chased wild antelopes; so we stopped at length somewhat breathless.

"No use," gasped Terry. "They got away with it. My word! The men of this country must be good sprinters!"

"Inhabitants evidently arboreal," I grimly suggested. "Civilized and still arboreal—peculiar people."

"You shouldn't have tried that way," Jeff protested. "They were perfectly friendly; now we've scared them."

But it was no use grumbling, and Terry refused to admit any mistake. "Nonsense," he said. "They expected it. Women like to be run after. Come on, let's get to that town; maybe we'll find them there. Let's see, it was in this direction and not far from the woods, as I remember."

When we reached the edge of the open country we reconnoitered with our field glasses. There it was, about four miles off, the same town, we concluded, unless, as Jeff ventured, they all had pink houses. The broad green fields and closely cultivated gardens sloped away at our feet, a long easy slant, with good roads winding pleasantly here and there, and narrower paths besides.

"Look at that!" cried Jeff suddenly. "There they go!"

Sure enough, close to the town, across a wide meadow, three bright-hued figures were running swiftly.

"How could they have got that far in this time? It can't be the same ones," I urged. But through the glasses we could identify our pretty tree-climbers quite plainly, at least by costume.

Terry watched them, we all did for that matter, till they disappeared among the houses. Then he put down his glass and turned to us, drawing a long breath. "Mother of Mike, boys—what Gorgeous Girls! To climb like that! to run like that! and afraid of nothing. This country suits me all right. Let's get ahead."

"Nothing venture, nothing have," I suggested, but Terry preferred "'Faint heart ne'er won fair lady.'"

We set forth in the open, walking briskly. "If there are any men, we'd better keep an eye out," I suggested, but Jeff seemed lost in heavenly dreams, and Terry in highly practical plans.

"What a perfect road! What a heavenly country! See the flowers, will you."

This was Jeff, always an enthusiast; but we could agree with him fully.

The road was some sort of hard manufactured stuff, sloped slightly to shed rain, with every curve and grade and gutter as perfect as if it were Europe's best. "No men, eh?" sneered Terry. On either side a double row of trees shaded the footpaths; between the trees bushes or vines, all fruit-bearing, now and then seats and little wayside fountains; everywhere flowers.

"We'd better import some of these ladies and set 'em to parking the United States," I suggested. "Mighty nice place they've got here." We rested a few moments by one of the fountains, tested the fruit that looked ripe, and went on, impressed, for all our gay bravado by the sense of quiet potency which lay about us.

Here was evidently a people highly skilled, efficient, caring for their country as a florist cares for his costliest orchids. Under the soft brilliant blue of that clear sky, in the pleasant shade of those endless rows of trees, we walked unharmed, the placid silence broken only by the birds.

Presently there lay before us at the foot of a long hill the town or village we were aiming for. We stopped and studied it.

Jeff drew a long breath. "I wouldn't have believed a collection of houses could look so lovely," he said.

"They've got architects and landscape gardeners in plenty, that's sure," agreed Terry.

I was astonished myself. You see, I come from California, and there's no country lovelier, but when it comes to towns—! I have often groaned at home to see the offensive mess man made in the face of nature, even though I'm no art sharp, like Jeff. But this place—! It was built mostly of a sort of dull rose-colored stone, with here and there some clear white houses; and it lay abroad among the green groves and gardens like a broken rosary of pink coral.

"Those big white ones are public buildings evidently," Terry declared. "This is no savage country, my friend. But no men? Boys, it behooves us to go forward most politely."

The place had an odd look, more impressive as we approached. "It's like an exposition." "It's too pretty to be true—" "Plenty of palaces, but where are the homes?" "Oh there are little ones enough—but—." It certainly was different from any towns we had ever seen.

"There's no dirt," said Jeff suddenly. "There's no smoke," he added after a little.

"There's no noise," I offered; but Terry snubbed me—"That's because they are laying low for us; we'd better be careful how we go in there."

Nothing could induce him to stay out, however, so we walked on.

Everything was beauty, order, perfect cleanness, and the pleasantest sense of home over it all. As we neared the center of the town the houses stood thicker, ran together as it were, grew into rambling palaces grouped among parks and open squares, something as college buildings stand in their quiet greens.

And then, turning a corner, we came into a broad paved space and saw before us a band of women standing close together in even order, evidently waiting for us.

We stopped a moment and looked back. The street behind was closed by another band, marching steadily, shoulder to shoulder. We went on—there seemed no other way to go—and presently found ourselves quite surrounded by this close-massed multitude; women, all of them, but—

They were not young. They were not old. They were not, in the girl sense, beautiful, they were not in the least ferocious; and yet, as I looked from face to face, calm, grave, wise, wholly unafraid, evidently assured and determined, I had the funniest feeling—a very early feeling—a feeling that I traced back and back in memory until I caught up with it at last. It was that sense of being hopelessly in the wrong that I had so often felt in early youth when my short legs' utmost effort failed to overcome the fact that I was late to school.

Jeff felt it too; I could see he did. We felt like small boys, very small boys, caught doing mischief in some gracious lady's house. But Terry showed no such consciousness. I saw his quick eyes darting here and there, estimating numbers, measuring distances, judging chances of escape. He examined the close ranks about us, reaching back far on every side, and murmured softly to me, "Every one of 'em over forty as I'm a sinner."

Yet they were not old women. Each was in the full bloom of rosy health, erect, serene, standing sure-footed and light as any pugilist. They had no weapons, and we had, but we had no wish to shoot.

"I'd as soon shoot my aunts," muttered Terry again. "What do they want with us anyhow? They seem to mean business." But in spite of that business-like aspect, he determined to try his favorite tactics. Terry had come armed with a theory.

He stepped forward, with his brilliant ingratiating smile, and made low obeisance to the women before him. Then he produced another tribute, a broad soft scarf of filmy texture, rich in color and pattern, a lovely thing, even to my eye, and offered it with a deep bow to the tall unsmiling woman who seemed to head the ranks before him. She took it with a gracious nod of acknowledgment, and passed it on to those behind her. He tried again, this time bringing out a circlet of rhinestones, a glittering crown that should have pleased any woman on earth.

He made a brief address, including Jeff and me as partners in his enterprise, and with another bow presented this.

Again his gift was accepted and, as before, passed out of sight.

"If they were only younger," he muttered between his teeth. "What on earth is a fellow to say to a regiment of old Colonels like this?"

In all our discussions and speculations we had always unconsciously assumed that the women, whatever else they might be, would be young. Most men do think that way, I fancy.

"Woman" in the abstract is young, and, we assume, charming. As they get older they pass off the stage, somehow, into private ownership mostly, or out of it altogether. But these good ladies were very much on the stage, and yet any one of them might have been a grandmother.

We looked for nervousness—there was none.

For terror, perhaps—there was none.

For uneasiness, for curiosity, for excitement—and all we saw was what might have been a vigilance committee of women doctors, as cool as cucumbers, and evidently meaning to take us to task for being there.

Six of them stepped forward now, one on either side of each of us, and indicated that we were to go with them. We thought it best to accede, at first anyway, and marched along, one of these close at each elbow, and the others in close masses before, behind, on both sides.

A large building opened before us, a very heavy thick-walled impressive place, big, and old-looking; of grey stone, not like the rest of the town.

"This won't do!" said Terry to us, quickly. "We mustn't let them get us in this, boys. All together, now—"

We stopped in our tracks. We began to explain, to make signs pointing away toward the big forest—indicating that we would go back to it—at once.

It makes me laugh, knowing all I do now, to think of us three boys—nothing else; three audacious impertinent boys—butting into an unknown country without any sort of a guard or defense. We seemed to think that if there were men we could fight them, and if there were only women—why, they would be no obstacles at all.

Jeff, with his gentle romantic old-fashioned notions of women as clinging vines; Terry, with his clear decided practical theories that there were two kinds of women—those he wanted and those he didn't; Desirable and Undesirable was his demarcation. The last was a large class, but negligible—he had never thought about them at all.

And now here they were, in great numbers, evidently indifferent to what he might think, evidently determined on some purpose of their own regarding him, and apparently well able to enforce their purpose.

We all thought hard just then. It had not seemed wise to object to going with them, even if we could have; our one chance was friendliness—a civilized attitude on both sides.

But once inside that building, there was no knowing what these determined ladies might do to us. Even a peaceful detention was not to our minds, and when we named it imprisonment it looked even worse.

So we made a stand, trying to make clear that we preferred the open country. One of them came forward with a sketch of our flier, asking by signs if we were the aerial visitors they had seen.

This we admitted.

They pointed to it again, and to the outlying country, in different directions—but we pretended we did not know where it was—and in truth we were not quite sure and gave a rather wild indication of its whereabouts.

Again they motioned us to advance, standing so packed about the door that there remained but the one straight path open. All around us and behind they were massed solidly—there was simply nothing to do but go forward—or fight.

We held a consultation.

"I never fought with women in my life," said Terry, greatly perturbed, "but I'm not going in there. I'm not going to be—herded in—as if we were in a cattle chute."

"We can't fight them, of course," Jeff urged. "They're all women, in spite of their nondescript clothes; nice women, too; good strong sensible faces. I guess we'll have to go in."

"We may never get out, if we do," I told them. "Strong and sensible, yes; but I'm not so sure about the good. Look at those faces!"

They had stood at ease, waiting while we conferred together, but never relaxing their close attention.

Their attitude was not the rigid discipline of soldiers; there was no sense of compulsion about them. Terry's term of a "vigilance committee" was highly descriptive. They had just the aspect of sturdy burghers, gathered hastily to meet some common need or peril, all moved by precisely the same feelings, to the same end.

Never, anywhere before, had I seen women of precisely this quality. Fishwives and market women might show similar strength, but it was coarse and heavy. These were merely athletic, light, and powerful. College professors, teachers, writers—many women showed similar intelligence but often wore a strained nervous look while these were as calm as cows, for all their evident intellect.

We observed pretty closely just then, for all of us felt that it was a crucial moment.

The leader gave some word of command and beckoned us on, and the surrounding mass moved a step nearer.

"We've got to decide quick," said Terry. "I vote to go in," Jeff urged. But we were two to one against him and he loyally stood by us. We made one more effort to be let go, urgent, but not imploring. In vain.

"Now for a rush, boys!" Terry said. "And if we can't break 'em, I'll shoot in the air."

Then we found ourselves much in the position of the Suffragette trying to get to the Parliament buildings through a triple cordon of London police.

The solidity of those women was something amazing. Terry soon found that it was useless, tore himself loose for a moment, pulled his revolver, and fired upward. As they caught at it, he fired again—we heard a cry—.

Instantly each of us was seized by five women, each holding arm or leg or head; we were lifted like children, straddling helpless children, and borne onward, wriggling indeed, but most ineffectually.

We were borne inside, struggling manfully, but held secure most womanfully, in spite of our best endeavors.

So carried and so held, we came into a high inner hall, gray and bare, and were brought before a majestic grey-haired woman who seemed to hold a judicial position.

There was some talk, not much, among them, and then suddenly there fell upon each of us at once a firm hand holding a wetted cloth before mouth and nose—an odor of swimming sweetness—anesthesia.

CHAPTER III

A PECULIAR
IMPRISONMENT

From a slumber as deep as death, as refreshing as that of a healthy child, I slowly awakened.

It was like rising up, up, up through a deep warm ocean, nearer and nearer to full light and stirring air. Or like the return to consciousness after concussion of the brain. I was once thrown from a horse while on a visit to a wild mountainous country quite new to me, and I can clearly remember the mental experience of coming back to life, through lifting veils of dream. When I first dimly heard the voices of those about me, and saw the shining snowpeaks of that mighty range, I assumed that this too would pass, and I should presently find myself in my own home.

That was precisely the experience of this awakening: receding waves of half-caught swirling vision, memories of home, the steamer, the boat, the air-ship, the forest—at last all sinking away one after another, till my eyes were wide open, my brain clear, and I realized what had happened.

The most prominent sensation was of absolute physical comfort. I was lying in a perfect bed: long, broad, smooth; firmly soft and level; with the finest linen, some warm light quilt of blanket, and a counterpane that was a joy to the eye. The sheet turned down some fifteen inches, yet I could stretch my feet at the foot of the bed, free but warmly covered.

I felt as light and clean as a white feather. It took me some time to consciously locate my arms and legs, to feel the vivid sense of life radiate from the wakening center to the extremities.

A big room, high and wide, with many lofty windows whose closed blinds let through soft green-lit air; a beautiful room, in proportion, in color, in smooth simplicity; a scent of blossoming gardens outside.

I lay perfectly still, quite happy, quite conscious, and yet not actively realizing what had happened till I heard Terry.

"Gosh!" was what he said.

I turned my head. There were three beds in this chamber, and plenty of room for them.

Terry was sitting up, looking about him, alert as ever. His remarks, though not loud, roused Jeff also. We all sat up.

Terry swung his legs out of bed, stood up, stretched himself mightily. He was in a long night-robe, a sort of seamless garment, undoubtedly comfortable—we all found ourselves so covered. Shoes were beside each bed, also quite comfortable and good-looking though by no means like our own.

We looked for our clothes—they were not there, nor anything of all the varied contents of our pockets.

A door stood somewhat ajar; it opened into a most attractive bathroom, copiously provided with towels, soap, mirrors, and all such convenient comforts, with indeed our toothbrushes and combs, our notebooks, and thank goodness, our watches—but no clothes.

Then we made a search of the big room again and found a large airy closet, holding plenty of clothing, but not ours.

"A council of war!" demanded Terry. "Come on back to bed—the bed's all right anyhow. Now then, my scientific friend, let us consider our case dispassionately."

He meant me, but Jeff seemed most impressed.

"They haven't hurt us in the least!" he said. "They could have killed us—or—or anything—and I never felt better in my life."

"That argues that they *are* all women," I suggested, "and highly civilized. You know you hit one in the last scrimmage—I heard her sing out—and we kicked awfully."

Terry was grinning at us. "So you realize what these ladies have done to us?" he pleasantly inquired. "They have taken away *all* our possessions, *all* our clothes—every stitch. We have been stripped and washed and put to bed like so many yearling babies—by these highly civilized women."

Jeff actually blushed. He had a poetic imagination. Terry had imagination enough, of a different kind. So had I, also different. I always flattered myself I had the scientific imagination, which, incidentally, I considered the highest sort. One has a right to a certain amount of egotism if founded on fact—and kept to one's self—*I* think.

"No use kicking, boys," I said. "They've got us, and apparently they're perfectly harmless. It remains for us to cook up some plan of escape like any other bottled heroes. Meanwhile we've got to put on these clothes—Hobson's choice."

The garments were simple in the extreme, and absolutely comfortable, physically, though of course we all felt like supes in the theater. There was a one-piece cotton undergarment, thin and soft, that reached over the knees and shoulders, something like the one-piece pajamas some fellows wear, and a kind of half-hose, that came up to just under the knee and stayed there—had an elastic top of their own, and covered the edges of the first.

Then there was a thicker variety of union suit, a lot of them in the closet, of varying weights and somewhat sturdier material—evidently they would do at a pinch with nothing further. Then there were tunics, knee length, and some long robes. Needless to say, we took tunics.

We bathed and dressed quite cheerfully.

"Not half bad," said Terry, surveying himself in a long mirror. His hair was somewhat longer than when we left the last barber, and the hats provided were much like those seen on the prince in the fairy-tale, lacking the plume.

The costume was similar to that which we had seen on all the women, though some of them, those working in the fields, glimpsed by our glasses when we first flew over, wore only the first two.

I settled my shoulders and stretched my arms, remarking: "They have worked out a mighty sensible dress, I'll say that for them." With which we all agreed.

"Now then," Terry proclaimed, "we've had a fine long

sleep—we've had a good bath—we're clothed and in our right minds, though feeling like a lot of neuters. Do you think these highly civilized ladies are going to give us any breakfast?"

"Of course they will," Jeff asserted confidently. "If they had meant to kill us, they would have done it before. I believe we are going to be treated as guests."

"Hailed as deliverers, I think," said Terry.

"Studied as curiosities," I told them. "But anyhow, we want food. So now for a sortie!"

A sortie was not so easy.

The bathroom only opened into our chamber, and that had but one outlet, a big heavy door, which was fastened.

We listened.

"There's someone outside," Jeff suggested. "Let's knock."

So we knocked, whereupon the door opened.

Outside was another large room, furnished with a great table at one end, long benches or couches against the wall, some smaller tables and chairs. All these were solid, strong, simple in structure, and comfortable in use; also, incidentally, beautiful.

This room was occupied by a number of women, eighteen to be exact, some of whom we distinctly recalled.

Terry heaved a disappointed sigh. "The Colonels!" I heard him whisper to Jeff.

Jeff, however, advanced and bowed in his best manner; so did we all, and we were saluted civilly by the tall-standing women.

We had no need to make pathetic pantomime of hunger; the smaller tables were already laid with food, and we were gravely invited to be seated. The tables were set for two; each of us found ourselves placed vis-à-vis with one of our hosts, and each table had five other stalwarts nearby, unobtrusively watching. We had plenty of time to get tired of those women!

The breakfast was not profuse, but sufficient in amount and excellent in quality. We were all too good travelers to object to novelty, and this repast with its new but delicious fruit, its dish of large rich-flavored nuts, and its highly satisfactory little cakes was most agreeable. There was water to drink, and a hot beverage of a most pleasing quality, some preparation like cocoa.

And then and there, willy-nilly, before we had satisfied our appetites, our education began.

By each of our plates lay a little book, a real printed book, though different from ours both in paper and binding, as well, of course, as in type. We examined them curiously.

"Shades of Sauveur!" muttered Terry. "We're to learn the language!"

We were indeed to learn the language, and not only that, but to teach our own. There were blank books with parallel columns, neatly ruled, evidently prepared for the occasion, and in these, as fast as we learned and wrote down the name of anything, we were urged to write our own name for it by its side.

The book we had to study was evidently a school-book, one in which children learned to read, and we judged from this, and from their frequent consultation as to methods, that they had had no previous experience in the art of teaching foreigners their language, or of learning any other.

On the other hand, if they lacked in experience, they made up for in genius. Such subtle understanding, such instant recognition of our difficulties, and readiness to meet them, were a constant surprise to us.

Of course, we were willing to meet them half-way. It was wholly to our advantage to be able to understand and speak with them, and as to refusing to teach them—why should we? Later on we did try open rebellion, but only once.

That first meal was pleasant enough, each of us quietly studying his companion, Jeff with sincere admiration, Terry with that highly technical look of his, as of a past master—like a lion-tamer, a serpent charmer, or some such professional. I myself was intensely interested.

It was evident that those sets of five were there to check any outbreak on our part. We had no weapons, and if we did try to do any damage, with a chair, say, why five to one was too many for us, even if they were women; that we had found out to our sorrow. It was not pleasant, having them always around, but we soon got used to it.

"It's better than being physically restrained ourselves," Jeff philosophically suggested when we were alone. "They've given us a room—with no great possibility of escape—and personal liberty—heavily chaperoned. It's better than we'd have been likely to get in a man-country."

"Man-Country! Do you really believe there are no men here, you innocent? Don't you know there must be?" demanded Terry.

"Ye—es," Jeff agreed. "Of course—and yet—"

"And yet—what! Come, you obdurate sentimentalist—what are you thinking about?"

"They may have some peculiar division of labor we've never heard of," I suggested. "The men may live in separate towns, or they may have subdued them—somehow—and keep them shut up. But there must be some."

"That last suggestion of yours is a nice one, Van," Terry protested. "Same as they've got us subdued and shut up! You make me shiver."

"Well, figure it out for yourself, anyway you please. We saw plenty of kids, the first day, and we've seen those girls—"

"Real girls!" Terry agreed, in immense relief. "Glad you mentioned 'em. I declare, if I thought there was nothing in the country but those grenadiers I'd jump out the window."

"Speaking of windows," I suggested, "let's examine ours."

We looked out of all the windows. The blinds opened easily enough, and there were no bars, but the prospect was not reassuring.

This was not the pink-walled town we had so rashly entered the day before. Our chamber was high up, in a projecting wing of a sort of castle, built out on a steep spur of rock. Immediately below us were gardens, fruitful and fragrant, but their high walls followed the edge of the cliff which dropped sheer down, we could not see how far. The distant sound of water suggested a river at the foot.

We could look out east, west, and south. To the southeastward stretched the open country, lying bright and fair in the morning light, but on either side, and evidently behind, rose great mountains.

"This thing is a regular fortress—and no women built it, I can tell you that," said Terry. We nodded agreeingly. "It's right up among the hills—they must have brought us a long way."

"And pretty fast, too," I added.

"We saw some kind of swift-moving vehicles the first day," Jeff reminded us. "If they've got motors, they *are* civilized."

"Civilized or not, we've got our work cut out for us to get away from here. I don't propose to make a rope of bedclothes and try those walls till I'm sure there is no better way."

We all concurred on this point, and returned to our discussion as to the women.

Jeff continued thoughtful. "All the same, there's something funny about it," he urged. "It isn't just that we don't see any men—but we don't see any signs of them. The—the—reaction of these women is different from any that I've ever met."

"There is something in what you say, Jeff," I agreed. "There is a different—atmosphere."

"They don't seem to notice our being men," he went on. "They treat us—well—just as they do one another. It's as if our being men was a minor incident."

I nodded. I'd noticed it myself. But Terry broke in rudely.

"Fiddlesticks!" he said. "It's because of their advanced age. They're all grandmas, I tell you—or ought to be. Great aunts, anyhow. Those girls were girls all right, weren't they?"

"Yes—" Jeff agreed, still slowly. "But they weren't afraid—they flew up that tree and hid, like school-boys caught out of bounds—not like shy girls."

"And they ran like marathon winners—you'll admit that, Terry," [he] added.

Terry was moody as the days passed. He seemed to mind our confinement more than Jeff or I did; and he harped on Alima, and how near he'd come to catching her. "If I had—" he would say, rather savagely, "we'd have had a hostage and could have made terms."

But Jeff was getting on excellent terms with his tutor, and even his guards, and so was I. It interested me profoundly to note and study the subtle difference between these women and other women, and try to account for them. In the matter of personal appearance, there was a great difference. They all wore short hair, some few inches at most; some curly, some not; all light and clean and fresh-looking.

"If their hair was only long," Jeff would complain, "they would look so much more feminine."

I rather liked it myself, after I got used to it. Why we should so admire "a woman's crown of hair" and not admire a Chinaman's queue is hard to explain, except that we are so convinced that the long hair "belongs" to a woman. Whereas the "mane" in horses is on both, and in lions, buffalos, and such creatures only on the male. But I did miss it—at first.

Our time was quite pleasantly filled. We were free of the garden below our windows, quite long in its irregular rambling shape, bordering the cliff. The walls were perfectly smooth and high, ending in the masonry of the building; and as I studied the great stones I became convinced that the whole structure was extremely old. It was built like the pre-Incan architecture in Peru, of enormous monoliths, fitted as closely as mosaics.

"These folks have a history, that's sure," I told the others. "And *some* time they were fighters—else why a fortress?"

I said we were free of the garden, but not wholly alone in it. There was always a string of those uncomfortably strong women sitting about, always one of them watching us even if the others were reading, playing games, or busy at some kind of handiwork.

"When I see them knit," Terry said, "I can almost call them feminine."

"That doesn't prove anything," Jeff promptly replied. "Scotch shepherds knit—always knitting."

"When we get out—" Terry stretched himself and looked at the far peaks, "when we get out of this and get to where the real women are—the mothers, and the girls—"

"Well, what'll we do then?" I asked, rather gloomily. "How do you know we'll ever get out?"

This was an unpleasant idea, which we unanimously considered, returning with earnestness to our studies.

"If we are good boys and learn our lessons well," I suggested. "If we are quiet and respectful and polite and they are not afraid of us—then perhaps they will let us out. And anyway—when we do escape, it is of immense importance that we know the language."

Personally, I was tremendously interested in that language, and seeing they had books, was eager to get at them, to dig into their history, if they had one.

It was not hard to speak, smooth and pleasant to the ear, and so easy to read and write that I marvelled at it. They had an absolutely phonetic system, the whole thing was as scientific as Esperanto yet bore all the marks of an old and rich civilization.

We were free to study as much as we wished, and were not left merely to wander in the garden for recreation but introduced to a great gymnasium, partly on the roof and partly in the story below. Here we learned real respect for our tall guards. No change of costume was needed for this work, save to lay off outer clothing. The first one was as perfect a garment for exercise as need be devised, absolutely free to move in, and, I had to admit, much better looking than our usual one.

"Forty—over forty—some of 'em fifty, I bet—and look at 'em!" grumbled Terry in reluctant admiration.

There were no spectacular acrobatics, such as only the young can perform, but for all-around development they had a most excellent system. A good deal of music went with it, with posture dancing and, sometimes, gravely beautiful processional performances.

Jeff was much impressed by it. We did not know then how small a part of their physical culture methods this really was, but found it agreeable to watch, and to take part in.

Oh yes, we took part all right! It wasn't absolutely compulsory, but we thought it better to please.

Terry was the strongest of us, though I was wiry and had good staying power, and Jeff was a great sprinter and hurdler, but I can tell you those old ladies gave us cards and spades. They ran like deer, by which I mean that they ran not as if it was a performance, but as if it was their natural gait. We remembered those fleeting girls of our first bright adventure, and concluded that it was.

They leaped like deer, too, with a quick folding motion of the legs, drawn up and turned to one side with a sidelong twist of the body. I remembered the sprawling spread-eagle way in which some of the fellows used to come over the line—and tried to learn the trick. We did not easily catch up with these experts, however.

"Never thought I'd live to be bossed by a lot of elderly lady acrobats," Terry protested.

They had games, too, a good many of them, but we found them rather uninteresting at first. It was like two people playing solitaire to see who would get it first; more like a race or a—a competitive examination, than a real game with some fight in it.

I philosophized a bit over this and told Terry it argued against their having any men about. "There isn't a man-size game in the lot," I said.

"But they are interesting—I like them," Jeff objected, "and I'm sure they are educational."

"I'm sick and tired of being educated," Terry protested. "Fancy going to a dame school—at our age. I want to Get Out!"

But we could not get out, and we were being educated swiftly. Our special tutors rose rapidly in our esteem. They seemed of rather finer quality than the guards, though all were on terms of easy friendliness. Mine was named Somel, Jeff's Zava, and Terry's Moadine. We tried to generalize from the names, those of the guards, and of our three girls, but got nowhere.

"They sound well enough, and they're mostly short, but there's no similarity of termination—and no two alike. However, our acquaintance is limited as yet."

There were many things we meant to ask—as soon as we could talk well enough. Better teaching I never saw. From morning to night there was Somel, always on call except between two and four; always pleasant with a steady friendly kindness that I grew to enjoy very much. Jeff said Miss Zava—he would put on a title, though they apparently had none—was a darling; that she reminded him of his Aunt Esther at home; but Terry refused to be won, and rather jeered at his own companion, when we were alone.

"I'm sick of it!" he protested. "Sick of the whole thing. Here we are cooped up as helpless as a bunch of three-year-old orphans, and being taught what they think is necessary—whether we like it or not. Confound their old-maid impudence!"

Nevertheless we were taught. They brought in a raised map of their country, beautifully made, and increased our knowledge of geographical terms; but when we inquired for information as to the country outside, they smilingly shook their heads.

They brought pictures, not only the engravings in the books but colored studies of plants and trees and flowers and birds. They brought tools and various small objects—we had plenty of "material" in our school.

And, as we made progress, they brought more and more books.

If it had not been for Terry we would have been much more contented, but as the weeks ran into months he grew more and more irritable.

"Don't act like a bear with a sore head," I begged him. "We're getting on finely. Every day we can understand them better, and pretty soon we can make a reasonable plea to be let out—"

"*Let* out!" he stormed. "*Let* out—like children kept after school. I want to Get Out, and I'm going to. I want to find the men of this place and fight!—or the girls—"

"Guess it's the girls you're most interested in," Jeff commented. "What are you going to fight *with*—your fists?"

"Yes—or sticks and stones—I'd just like to!" And Terry squared off and tapped Jeff softly on the jaw. "Just for instance," he said.

"Anyhow," he went on, "we could get back to our machine and clear out."

"If it's there," I cautiously suggested.

"Oh, don't croak, Van! If it isn't there, we'll find our way down somehow—the boat's there, I guess—"

It was hard on Terry, so hard that he finally persuaded us to consider a plan of escape. It was difficult, it was highly dangerous, but he declared that he'd go alone if we wouldn't go with him, and of course we couldn't think of that.

It appeared he had made a pretty careful study of the environment. From our end window that faced the point of the promontory we could get a fair idea of the stretch of wall, and the drop below. Also from the roof we could make out more, and even, in one place, glimpse a sort of path below the wall.

"It's a question of three things," he said. "Ropes, agility, and not being seen."

"That's the hardest part," I urged, still hoping to dissuade him. "One or another pair of eyes is on us every minute except at night."

"Therefore we must do it at night," he answered. "That's easy."

"We've got to think that if they catch us we may not be so well treated afterward," said Jeff.

"That's the business risk we must take. I'm going—if I break my neck." There was no changing him.

The rope problem was not easy. Something strong enough to hold a man and long enough to let us down into the garden, and then down over the wall. There were plenty of strong ropes in the gymnasium—they seemed to love to swing and climb on them—but we were never there by ourselves.

We should have to piece it out from our bedding, rugs, and garments, and moreover, we should have to do it after we were shut in for the night, for every day the place was cleaned to perfection by two of our guardians.

We had no shears, no knives, but Terry was resourceful. "These Jennies have glass and china, you see. We'll break a glass from the bathroom and use that. 'Love will find out a way,'" he hummed. "When we're all out of the window, we'll stand three-man high and cut the rope as far up as we can reach, so as to have more for the wall. I know just where I saw that bit of path below, and there's a big tree there, too, or a vine or something—I saw the leaves."

It seemed a crazy risk to take, but this was, in a way, Terry's expedition, and we were all tired of our imprisonment.

So we waited for full moon, retired early, and spent an anxious hour or two in the unskilled manufacture of man-strong ropes.

To retire into the depths of the closet, muffle a glass in thick cloth, and break it without noise was not difficult, and broken glass will cut, though not as deftly as a pair of scissors.

The broad moonlight streamed in through four of our windows—we had not dared leave our lights on too long—and we worked hard and fast at our task of destruction.

Hangings, rugs, robes, towels, as well as bed-furniture—even the mattress covers—we left not one stitch upon another, as Jeff put it.

Then at an end window, as less liable to observation, we fastened one end of our cable, strongly, to the firm-set hinge of the inner blind, and dropped our coiled bundle of rope softly over.

"This part's easy enough—I'll come last, so as to cut the rope," said Terry.

So I slipped down first, and stood, well braced against the wall; then Jeff on my shoulders, then Terry, who shook us a little as he sawed through the cord above his head. Then I slowly dropped to the ground, Jeff following, and at last we all three stood safe in the garden, with most of our rope with us.

"Good-bye, Grandma!" whispered Terry, under his breath, and we crept softly toward the wall, taking advantage of the shadow of every bush and tree. He had been foresighted enough to mark the very spot, only a scratch of stone on stone, but we could see to read in that light. For anchorage there was a tough, fair-sized shrub close to the wall.

"Now I'll climb up on you two again and go over first," said Terry. "That'll hold the rope firm till you both get up on top. Then I'll go down to the end. If I can get off safely, you can see me and follow—or, say, I'll twitch it three times. If I find there's absolutely no footing—why I'll climb up again, that's all. I don't think they'll kill us."

From the top he reconnoitered carefully, waved his hand, and whispered, "o.k.," then slipped over. Jeff climbed up and I followed, and we rather shivered to see how far down that swaying, wavering figure dropped, hand under hand, till it disappeared in a mass of foliage far below.

Then there were three quick pulls, and Jeff and I, not without a joyous sense of recovered freedom, successfully followed our leader.

CHAPTER IV

OUR VENTURE

We were standing on a narrow, irregular, all too slanting little ledge, and should doubtless have ignominiously slipped off and broken our rash necks but for the vine. This was a thick-leaved, wide-spreading thing, a little like Amphelopsis.

"It's not *quite* vertical here, you see," said Terry, full of pride and enthusiasm. "This thing never would hold our direct weight, but I think if we sort of slide down on it, one at a time, sticking in with hands and feet, we'll reach that next ledge alive."

"As we do not wish to get up our rope again—and can't comfortably stay here—I approve," said Jeff solemnly.

Terry slid down first—said he'd show us how a Christian meets his death. Luck was with us. We had put on the thickest of those intermediate suits, leaving our tunics behind, and made this scramble quite successfully, though I got a pretty heavy fall just at the end, and was only kept on the second ledge by main force. The next stage was down a sort of "chimney"—a long irregular fissure; and so with scratches many and painful and bruises not a few, we finally reached the stream.

It was darker there, but we felt it highly necessary to put as much distance as possible behind us; so we waded, jumped, and clambered down that rocky river-bed, in the flickering black and white moonlight and leaf shadow, till growing daylight forced a halt.

We found a friendly nut-tree, those large, satisfying, soft-shelled nuts we already knew so well, and filled our pockets.

I see that I have not remarked that these women had pockets

in surprising number and variety. They were in all their garments, and the middle one in particular was shingled with them. So we stocked up with nuts till we bulged like Prussian privates in marching order, drank all we could hold, and retired for the day.

It was not a very comfortable place, not at all easy to get at, just a sort of crevice high up along the steep bank, but it was well veiled with foliage and dry. After our exhausting three- or four-hours scramble and the good breakfast food, we all lay down along the crack—heads and tails, as it were—and slept till the afternoon sun almost toasted our faces.

Terry poked a tentative foot against my head.

"How are you, Van? Alive yet?"

"Very much so," I told him. And Jeff was equally cheerful.

We had room to stretch, if not to turn around; but we could very carefully roll over, one at a time, behind the sheltering foliage.

It was no use to leave there by daylight. We could not see much of the country, but enough to know that we were now at the beginning of the cultivated area, and no doubt there would be an alarm sent out far and wide.

Terry chuckled softly to himself, lying there on that hot narrow little rim of rock. He dilated on the discomfiture of our guards and tutors, making many discourteous remarks.

I reminded him that we had still a long way to go before getting to the place where we'd left our machine, and no probability of finding it there; but he only kicked me, mildly, for a croaker.

"If you can't boost, don't knock," he protested. "I never said 'twould be a picnic. But I'd run away in the Antarctic ice fields rather than be a prisoner."

We soon dozed off again.

The long rest and penetrating dry heat were good for us, and that night we covered a considerable distance, keeping always in the rough forested belt of land which we knew bordered the whole country. Sometimes we were near the outer edge, and caught sudden glimpses of the tremendous depths beyond.

"This piece of geography stands up like a basalt column," Jeff said. "Nice time we'll have getting down if they have confiscated our machine!" For which suggestion he received summary chastisement.

What we could see inland was peaceable enough, but only moonlit glimpses; by daylight we lay very close. As Terry said, we did not wish to kill the old ladies—even if we could; and short of that they were perfectly competent to pick us up bodily and carry us back, if discovered. There was nothing for it but to lie low, and sneak out unseen if we could do it.

There wasn't much talking done. At night we had our Marathon-obstacle race; we "stayed not for brake and we stopped not for stone," and swam whatever water was too deep to wade and could not be got around; but that was only necessary twice. By day, sleep, sound and sweet. Mighty lucky it was that we could live off the country as we did. Even that margin of forest seemed rich in food-stuffs.

But Jeff thoughtfully suggested that that very thing showed how careful we should have to be, as we might run into some stalwart group of gardeners or foresters or nut-gatherers at any minute. Careful we were, feeling pretty sure that if we did not make good this time we were not likely to have another opportunity; and at last we reached a point from which we could see, far below, the broad stretch of that still lake from which we had made our ascent.

"That looks pretty good to me!" said Terry, gazing down at it. "Now, if we can't find the 'plane, we know where to aim if we have to drop over this wall some other way."

The wall at that point was singularly uninviting. It rose so straight that we had to put our heads over to see the base, and the country below seemed to be a far-off marshy tangle of rank vegetation. We did not have to risk our necks to that extent, however, for at last, stealing along among the rocks and trees like so many creeping savages, we came to that flat space where we had landed; and there, in unbelievable good fortune, we found our machine.

"Covered, too, by jingo! Would you think they had that much sense?" cried Terry.

"If they had that much, they're likely to have more," I warned him, softly. "Bet you the thing's watched."

We reconnoitered as widely as we could in the failing moonlight—moons are of a painfully unreliable nature; but the growing dawn showed us the familiar shape, shrouded in some heavy cloth like canvas and no slightest sign of any watchman near. We decided to make a quick dash as soon as the light was strong enough for accurate work.

"I don't care if the old thing'll go or not," Terry declared. "We can run her to the edge, get aboard, and just plane down—plop!—beside our boat there. Look there—see the boat!"

Sure enough—there was our motor, lying like a gray cocoon on the flat pale sheet of water.

Quietly but swiftly we rushed forward and began to tug at the fastenings of that cover.

"Confound the thing!" Terry cried in desperate impatience. "They've got it sewed up in a bag! And we've not a knife among us!"

Then, as we tugged and pulled at that tough cloth we heard a sound that made Terry lift his head like a war horse—the sound of an unmistakable giggle, yes—three giggles.

There they were—Celis, Alima, Ellador—looking just as they had when we first saw them, standing a little way off from us, as interested, as mischievous as three schoolboys.

"Hold on, Terry—hold on!" I warned. "That's too easy— look out for a trap."

"Let us appeal to their kind hearts," Jeff urged. "I think they will help us. Perhaps they've got knives."

"It's no use rushing them, anyhow." I was absolutely holding on to Terry. "We know they can out-run and out-climb us."

He reluctantly admitted this; and after a brief parley among ourselves, we all advanced slowly toward them, holding out our hands in token of friendliness.

They stood their ground till we had come fairly near, and then indicated that we should stop. To make sure, we advanced a step or two and they promptly and swiftly withdrew. So we stopped at the distance specified. Then we used their language, as far as we were able, to explain our plight, telling how we were imprisoned, how we had escaped—a good deal of pantomime here and vivid interest on their part—how we had traveled by night and hidden by day, living on nuts—and here Terry pretended great hunger.

I know he could not have been hungry; we had found plenty to eat and had not been sparing in helping ourselves. But they seemed somewhat impressed; and after a murmured consultation they produced from their pockets certain little packages, and with the utmost ease and accuracy tossed them into our hands.

Jeff was most appreciative of this; and Terry made extravagant gestures of admiration, which seemed to set them off, boy-fashion, to show their skill. While we ate the excellent biscuits they had thrown us, and while Ellador kept a watchful eye on our movements, Celis ran off to some distance, and set up a sort of "duck-on-a-rock" arrangement, a big yellow nut on top of three balanced sticks; Alima, meanwhile, gathering stones.

They urged us to throw at it, and we did, but the thing was a long way off, and it was only after a number of failures, at which those elvish damsels laughed delightedly, that Jeff succeeded in bringing the whole structure to the ground. It took me still longer, and Terry, to his intense annoyance, came third.

Then Celis set up the little tripod again, and looked back at us, knocking it down, pointing at it, and shaking her short curls severely. "No," she said. "Bad—wrong!" We were quite able to follow her.

Then she set it up once more, put the fat nut on top, and returned to the others; and there those aggravating girls sat and took turns throwing little stones at that thing, while one stayed by as a setter-up; and they just popped that nut off, two times out of three, without upsetting the sticks. Pleased as Punch they were, too, and we pretended to be, but weren't.

We got very friendly over this game, but I told Terry we'd be sorry if we didn't get off while we could, and then we begged for knives. It was easy to show what we wanted to do, and they each proudly produced a sort of strong clasp-knife from their pockets.

"Yes," we said eagerly, "that's it! Please—" We had learned quite a bit of their language, you see. And we just begged for those knives, but they would not give them to us. If we came a step too near they backed off, standing light and eager for flight.

"It's no sort of use," I said. "Come on—let's get a sharp stone or something—we must get this thing off."

So we hunted about and found what edged fragments we could, and hacked away, but it was like trying to cut sailcloth with a clamshell.

Terry hacked and dug, but said to us under his breath, "Boys—we're in pretty good condition—let's make a life and death dash and get hold of those girls—we've got to."

They had drawn rather nearer, to watch our efforts, and we did take them rather by surprise; also, as Terry said, our recent training had strengthened us in wind and limb, and for a few desperate moments those girls were scared and we almost triumphant.

But just as we stretched out our hands, the distance between us widened; they had got their pace apparently, and then, though we ran at our utmost speed, and much farther than I thought wise, they kept just out of reach all the time.

We stopped breathless, at last, at my repeated admonitions.

"This is stark foolishness," I urged. "They are doing it on purpose—come back or you'll be sorry."

We went back, much slower than we came, and in truth we were sorry.

As we reached our swaddled machine, and sought again to tear loose its covering, there rose up from all around the sturdy forms, the quiet determined faces we knew so well.

"Oh Lord!" groaned Terry. "The Colonels! It's all up— they're forty to one."

It was no use to fight. These women evidently relied on numbers, not so much as a drilled force but as a multitude actuated by a common impulse. They showed no sign of fear, and since we had no weapons whatever and there were at least a hundred of them, standing ten deep about us, we gave in as gracefully as we might.

Of course we looked for punishment—a closer imprisonment, solitary confinement maybe—but nothing of the kind happened. They treated us as truants only, and as if they quite understood our truancy.

Back we went; not under an anesthetic this time but skimming along in electric motors enough like ours to be quite recognizable, each of us in a separate vehicle with one able-bodied lady on either side and three facing him.

They were all pleasant enough, and talked to us as much as was possible with our limited powers. And though Terry was keenly mortified, and at first we all rather dreaded harsh treatment, I for one soon began to feel a sort of pleasant confidence and to enjoy the trip.

Here were my five familiar companions, all good-natured as could be, seeming to have no worse feeling than a mild triumph as of winning some simple game; and even that they politely suppressed.

This was a good opportunity to see the country, too, and the more I saw of it, the better I liked it. We went too swiftly for close observation, but I could appreciate perfect roads, as dustless as a swept floor; the shade of endless lines of trees; the ribbon of flowers that unrolled beneath them; and the rich comfortable country that stretched off and away, full of varied charm.

We rolled through many villages and towns, and I soon saw that the parklike beauty of our first-seen city was no exception. Our swift high-sweeping view from the plane had been most attractive, but lacked detail; and in that first day of struggle and capture, we noticed little; but now we were swept along at an easy rate of some thirty miles an hour and covered quite a good deal of ground.

We stopped for lunch in quite a sizeable town, and here, rolling slowly through the streets, we saw more of the population. They had come out to look at us everywhere we had passed, but here were more; and when we went in to eat, in a big garden place with little shaded tables among the trees and flowers, many eyes were upon us. And everywhere, open country, village, or city—only women. Old women and young women and a great majority who seemed neither young nor old, but just women; young girls, also, though these, and the children, seeming to be in groups by themselves generally, were less in evidence. We caught many glimpses of girls and children in what seemed to be schools or in playgrounds, and so far as we could judge there were no boys. We all looked, carefully. Everyone gazed at us politely, kindly, and with eager interest. No one was impertinent. We could catch quite a bit of the talk now, and all they said seemed pleasant enough.

Well—before nightfall we were all safely back in our big room. The damage we had done was quite ignored; the beds as smooth and comfortable as before, new clothing and towels supplied. The only thing those women did was to illuminate the gardens at night, and to set an extra watch. But they called us to account next day. Our three tutors, who had not joined in the recapturing expedition, had been quite busy in preparing for us, and now made explanation.

They knew well we would make for our machine, and also that there was no other way of getting down—alive. So our flight had troubled no one; all they did was to call the inhabitants to keep an eye on our movements all along the edge of the forest between the two points. It appeared that many of those nights we had been seen, by careful ladies sitting snugly in big trees by the riverbed, or up among the rocks.

Terry looked immensely disgusted, but it struck me as extremely funny. Here we had been risking our lives, hiding and prowling like outlaws, living on nuts and fruit, getting wet and cold at night, and dry and hot by day, and all the while these estimable women had just been waiting for us to come out.

Now they began to explain, carefully using such words as we could understand. It appeared that we were considered as guests of the country—sort of public wards. Our first violence had made it necessary to keep us safeguarded for a while, but as soon as we learned the language—and would agree to do no harm—they would show us all about the land.

Jeff was eager to reassure them. Of course he did not tell on Terry, but he made it clear that he was ashamed of himself, and that he would now conform. As to the language—we all fell upon it with redoubled energy. They brought us books, in greater numbers, and I began to study them seriously.

"Pretty punk literature," Terry burst forth one day, when we were in the privacy of our own room. "Of course one expects to begin on child-stories, but I would like something more interesting now."

"Can't expect stirring romance and wild adventure without men, can you?" I asked. Nothing irritated Terry more than to have us assume that there were no men; but there were no signs of them in the books they gave us, or the pictures.

"Shut up!" he growled. "What infernal nonsense you talk! I'm going to ask 'em outright—we know enough now."

In truth we had been using our best efforts to master the language, and were able to read fluently and to discuss what we read with considerable ease.

That afternoon we were all sitting together on the roof—we three and the tutors gathered about a table, no guards about. We had been made to understand some time earlier that if we would agree to do no violence they would withdraw their constant attendance, and we promised most willingly.

So there we sat, at ease; all in similar dress; our hair, by now, as long as theirs, only our beards to distinguish us. We did not want those beards, but had so far been unable to induce them to give us any cutting instruments.

"Ladies," Terry began, out of a clear sky, as it were, "are there no men in this country?"

"Men?" Somel answered. "Like you?"

"Yes, men," Terry indicated his beard, and threw back his broad shoulders. "Men, real men."

"No," she answered quietly. "There are no men in this country. There has not been a man among us for two thousand years."

Her look was clear and truthful and she did not advance this astonishing statement as if it was astonishing, but quite as a matter of fact.

"But—the people—the children," he protested, not believing her in the least, but not wishing to say so.

"Oh yes," she smiled. "I do not wonder you are puzzled. We are mothers—all of us—but there are no fathers. We thought you would ask about that long ago—why have you not?" Her look was as frankly kind as always, her tone quite simple.

Terry explained that we had not felt sufficiently used to the language, making rather a mess of it, I thought, but Jeff was franker.

"Will you excuse us all," he said, "if we admit that we find it hard to believe? There is no such—possibility—in the rest of the world."

"Have you no kind of life where it is possible?" asked Zava.

"Why, yes—some low forms, of course."

"How low—or how high, rather?"

"Well—there are some rather high forms of insect life in which it occurs. Parthenogenesis, we call it—that means virgin birth."

She could not follow him.

"*Birth*, we know, of course; but what is *virgin*?"

Terry looked uncomfortable, but Jeff met the question quite calmly. "Among mating animals, the term *virgin* is applied to the female who has not mated," he answered.

"Oh, I see. And does it apply to the male also? Or is there a different term for him?"

He passed this over rather hurriedly, saying that the same term would apply, but was seldom used.

"No?" she said. "But one cannot mate without the other surely. Is not each then—virgin—before mating? And, tell me, have you any forms of life in which there is birth from a father only?"

"I know of none," he answered, and I inquired seriously.

"You ask us to believe that for two thousand years there have been only women here, and only girl babies born?"

"Exactly," answered Somel, nodding gravely. "Of course we know that among other animals it is not so, that there are fathers as well as mothers; and we see that you are fathers, that you come from a people who are of both kinds. We have been waiting, you see, for you to be able to speak freely with us, and teach us about your country and the rest of the world. You know so much, you see, and we know only our own land."

In the course of our previous studies we had been at some pains to tell them about the big world outside, to draw sketches, maps, to make a globe, even, out of a spherical fruit, and show the size and relation of the countries, and to tell of the numbers of their people. All this had been scant and in outline, but they quite understood.

I find I succeed very poorly in conveying the impression I would like to of these women. So far from being ignorant, they were deeply wise—that we realized more and more; and for clear reasoning, for real brain scope and power they were A No. 1, but there were a lot of things they did not know.

They had the evenest tempers, the most perfect patience and good nature—one of the things most impressive about them all was the absence of irritability. So far we had only this group to study, but afterwards I found it a common trait.

We had gradually come to feel that we were in the hands of friends, and very capable ones at that—but we couldn't form any opinion yet of the general level of these women.

"We want you to teach us all you can," Somel went on, her firm shapely hands clasped on the table before her, her clear quiet eyes meeting ours frankly. "And we want to teach you what we have that is novel and useful. You can well imagine that it is a wonderful event to us, to have men among us— after two thousand years. And we want to know about your women."

What she said about our importance gave instant pleasure to Terry. I could see by the way he lifted his head that it pleased him. But when she spoke of our women—someway I had a queer little indescribable feeling, not like any feeling I ever had before when "women" were mentioned.

"Will you tell us how it came about?" Jeff pursued. "You said 'for two thousand years'—did you have men here before that?"

"Yes," answered Zava.

They were all quiet for a little.

"You should have our full history to read—do not be alarmed—it has been made clear and short. It took us a long time to learn how to write history. Oh, how I should love to read yours!"

She turned with flashing eager eyes, looking from one to the other of us.

"It would be so wonderful—would it not? To compare the history of two thousand years, to see what the differences are—between us, who are only mothers, and you, who are mothers and fathers, too. Of course we see, with our birds, that the father is as useful as the mother, almost; but among insects we find him of less importance, sometimes very little. Is it not so with you?"

"Oh, yes, birds and bugs," Terry said, "but not among animals—have you *no* animals?"

"We have cats," she said. "The father is not very useful."

"Have you no cattle—sheep—horses?" I drew some rough outlines of these beasts and showed them to her.

"We had, in the very old days, these," said Somel, and sketched with swift sure touches a sort of sheep or llama, "and these"—dogs, of two or three kinds, "and that"—pointing to my absurd but recognizable horse.

"What became of them?" asked Jeff.

"We do not want them anymore. They took up too much room—we need all our land to feed our people. It is such a little country, you know."

"Whatever do you do without milk?" Terry demanded incredulously.

"*Milk?* We have milk in abundance—our own."

"But—but—I mean for cooking—for grown people," Terry blundered, while they looked amazed and a shade displeased.

Jeff came to the rescue. "We keep cattle for their milk, as well as for their meat," he explained. "Cow's milk is a staple article of diet—there is a great milk industry—to collect and distribute it."

Still they looked puzzled. I pointed to my outline of a cow. "The farmer milks the cow," I said, and sketched a milk pail, the stool, and in pantomime showed the man milking. "Then it is carried to the city and distributed by milkmen—everybody has it at the door in the morning."

"Has the cow no child?" asked Somel earnestly.

"Oh, yes, of course, a calf, that is."

"Is there milk for the calf and you, too?"

It took some time to make clear to those three sweet-faced women the process which robs the cow of her calf, and the calf of its true food; and the talk led us into a further discussion of the meat business. They heard it out, looking very white, and presently begged to be excused.

CHAPTER V

A UNIQUE HISTORY

It is no use for me to try to piece out this account with adventures. If the people who read it are not interested in these amazing women and their history, they will not be interested at all.

As for us—three young men to a whole landful of women— what could we do? We did get away, as described, and were peacefully brought back again without, as Terry complained, even the satisfaction of hitting anybody.

There were no adventures because there was nothing to fight. There were no wild beasts in the country and very few tame ones. Of these I might as well stop to describe the one common pet of the country. Cats, of course. But such cats!

What do you suppose these lady Burbanks had done with their cats? By the most prolonged and careful selection and exclusion they had developed a race of cats that did not sing! That's a fact. The most those poor dumb brutes could do was to make a kind of squeak when they were hungry or wanted the door open, and, of course, to purr, and make the various mother-noises to their kittens.

Moreover, they had ceased to kill birds. They were rigorously bred to destroy mice and moles and all such enemies of the food supply; but the birds were numerous and safe.

While we were discussing birds, Terry asked them if they used feathers for their hats, and they seemed amused at the idea. He made a few sketches of our women's hats, with plumes and quills and those various tickling things that stick out so far; and they were eagerly interested, as at everything about our women.

As for them, they said they only wore hats for shade when

working in the sun; and those were big light straw hats, something like those used in China and Japan. In cold weather they wore caps or hoods.

"But for decorative purposes—don't you think they would be becoming?" pursued Terry, making as pretty a picture as he could of a lady with a plumed hat.

They by no means agreed to that, asking quite simply if the men wore the same kind. We hastened to assure her that they did not—and drew for them our kind of headgear.

"And do no men wear feathers in their hats?"

"Only Indians," Jeff explained, "savages, you know." And he sketched a war-bonnet to show them.

"And soldiers," I added, drawing a military hat with plumes.

They never expressed horror or disapproval, nor indeed much surprise—just a keen interest. And the notes they made!—miles of them!

But to return to our pussycats. We were a good deal impressed by this achievement in breeding, and when they questioned us— I can tell you we were well pumped for information—we told of what had been done for dogs and horses and cattle, but that there was no effort applied to cats, except for show purposes.

I wish I could represent the kind, quiet, steady, ingenious way they questioned us. It was not just curiosity—they weren't a bit more curious about us than we were about them, if as much. But they were bent on understanding our kind of civilization, and their lines of interrogation would gradually surround us and drive us in till we found ourselves up against some admissions we did not want to make.

"Are all these breeds of dogs you have made useful?" they asked.

"Oh—useful! Why, the hunting dogs and watch-dogs and sheepdogs are useful—and sled-dogs of course!—and ratters, I suppose, but we don't keep dogs for their *usefulness*. The dog is 'the friend of man,' we say—we love them."

That they understood. "We love our cats that way. They surely are our friends, and helpers, too. You can see how intelligent and affectionate they are."

It was a fact. I'd never seen such cats, except in a few rare instances. Big, handsome silky things, friendly with everyone and devotedly attached to their special owners.

"You must have a heartbreaking time drowning kittens," we suggested. But they said, "Oh, no! You see we care for them as you do for your valuable cattle. The fathers are few compared to the mothers, just a few very fine ones in each town; they live quite happily in walled gardens and the houses of their friends. But they only have a mating season once a year."

"Rather hard on Thomas, isn't it?" suggested Terry.

"Oh, no—truly! You see, it is many centuries that we have been breeding the kind of cats we wanted. They are healthy and happy and friendly, as you see. How do you manage with your dogs? Do you keep them in pairs, or segregate the fathers, or what?"

Then we explained that—well, that it wasn't a question of fathers exactly; that nobody wanted a—a mother dog; that, well, that practically all our dogs were males—there was only a very small percentage of females allowed to live.

Then Zava, observing Terry with her grave sweet smile, quoted back at him: "Rather hard on Thomas, isn't it? Do they enjoy it—living without mates? Are your dogs as uniformly healthy and sweet-tempered as our cats?"

Jeff laughed, eyeing Terry mischievously. As a matter of fact we began to feel Jeff something of a traitor—he so often flopped over and took their side of things; also his medical knowledge gave him a different point of view somehow.

"I'm sorry to admit," he told them, "that the dog, with us, is the most diseased of any animal—next to man. And as to temper—there are always some dogs who bite people—especially children."

That was pure malice. You see, children were the—the *raison d'être* in this country. All our interlocutors sat up straight at once. They were still gentle, still restrained, but there was a note of deep amazement in their voices.

"Do we understand that you keep an animal—an unmated male animal—that bites children? About how many are there of them, please?"

"Thousands—in a large city," said Jeff, "and nearly every family has one in the country."

Terry broke in at this. "You must not imagine they are all dangerous—it's not one in a hundred that ever bites anybody. Why, they are the best friends of the children—a boy doesn't have half a chance that hasn't a dog to play with!"

"And the girls?" asked Somel.

"Oh—girls—why they like them too," he said, but his voice flatted a little. They always noticed little things like that, we found later.

Little by little they wrung from us the fact that the friend of man, in the city, was a prisoner; was taken out for his meager exercise on a leash; was liable not only to many diseases, but to the one destroying horror of rabies, and, in many cases, for the safety of the citizens, had to go muzzled. Jeff maliciously added vivid instances he had known or read of injury and death from mad dogs.

They did not scold or fuss about it. Calm as judges, those women were. But they made notes; Moadine read them to us.

"Please tell me if I have the facts correct," she said. "In your country—and in others too?"

"Yes," we admitted, "in most civilized countries."

"In most civilized countries a kind of animal is kept which is no longer useful—"

"They are a protection," Terry insisted. "They bark if burglars try to get in."

Then she made notes of "burglars" and went on: "because of the love which people bear to this animal."

Zava interrupted here. "Is it the men or the women who love this animal so much?"

"Both!" insisted Terry.

"Equally?" she inquired.

And Jeff said, "Nonsense, Terry—you know men like dogs better than women do—as a whole."

"Because they love it so much—especially men. This animal is kept shut up, or chained."

"Why?" suddenly asked Somel. "We keep our father cats shut up because we do not want too much fathering; but they are not chained—they have large grounds to run in."

"A valuable dog would be stolen if he was let loose," I said. "We put collars on them, with the owner's name, in case they do stray. Besides, they get into fights—a valuable dog might easily be killed by a bigger one."

"I see," she said. "They fight when they meet—is that common?" We admitted that it was.

"They are kept shut up, or chained." She paused again, and asked, "Is not a dog fond of running? Are they not built for speed?" That we admitted, too, and Jeff, still malicious, enlightened them further.

"I've always thought it was a pathetic sight, both ways—to see a man or a woman taking a dog to walk—at the end of a string."

"Have you bred them to be as neat in their habits as cats are?" was the next question. And when Jeff told them of the effect of dogs on sidewalk merchandise and the streets generally, they found it hard to believe.

You see, their country was as neat as a Dutch kitchen, and as to sanitation—but I might as well start in now with as much as I can remember of the history of this amazing country before further description.

And I'll summarize here a bit as to our opportunities for learning it. I will not try to repeat the careful, detailed account I lost; I'll just say that we were kept in that fortress a good six months all told, and after that, three in a pleasant enough city where—to Terry's infinite disgust—there were only "Colonels" and little children—no young women whatever. Then we were under surveillance for three more—always with a tutor or a guard or both. But those months were pleasant because we were really getting acquainted with the girls. That was a chapter!—or will be—I will try to do justice to it.

We learned their language pretty thoroughly—had to; and they learned ours much more quickly and used it to hasten our own studies.

Jeff, who was never without reading matter of some sort, had two little books with him, a novel and a little anthology of verse; and I had one of those pocket encyclopedias—a fat little thing, bursting with facts. These were used in our education—and theirs. Then as soon as we were up to it, they furnished us with plenty of their own books, and I went in for the history part—I wanted to understand the genesis of this miracle of theirs.

And this is what happened, according to their records:

As to geography—at about the time of the Christian era this land had a free passage to the sea. I'm not saying where, for good reasons. But there was a fairly easy pass through that wall of mountains behind us, and there is no doubt in my mind that these people were of Aryan stock, and were once in contact with the best civilization of the old world. They were "white," but somewhat darker than our northern races because of their constant exposure to sun and air.

The country was far larger then, including much land beyond the pass, and a strip of coast. They had ships, commerce, an army, a king—for at that time they were what they so calmly called us—a bi-sexual race.

What happened to them first was merely a succession of historic misfortunes such as have befallen other nations often enough. They were decimated by war, driven up from their coastline till finally the reduced population, with many of the men killed in battle, occupied this hinterland, and defended it for years, in the mountain passes. Where it was open to any possible attack from below they strengthened the natural defenses so that it became unscalably secure, as we found it.

They were a polygamous people, and a slave-holding people, like all of their time; and during the generation or two of this struggle to defend their mountain home they built the fortresses, such as the one we were held in, and other of their oldest buildings, some still in use. Nothing but earthquakes could destroy such architecture—huge solid blocks, holding by their own weight. They must have had efficient workmen and enough of them in those days.

They made a brave fight for their existence, but no nation can stand up against what the steamship companies call "an act of God." While the whole fighting force was doing its best to defend their mountain pathway, there occurred a volcanic outburst, with some local tremors, and the result was the complete filling up of the pass—their only outlet. Instead of a passage, a new ridge, sheer and high, stood between them and the sea; they were walled in, and beneath that wall lay their whole little army. Very few men were left alive, save the slaves; and these now seized their opportunity, rose in revolt, killed their remaining masters even to the youngest boy, killed the old women too, and the mothers, intending to take possession of the country with the remaining young women and girls.

But this succession of misfortunes was too much for those infuriated virgins. There were many of them, and but few of these would-be masters, so the young women, instead of submitting, rose in sheer desperation and slew their brutal conquerors.

This sounds like Titus Andronicus, I know, but that is their account. I suppose they were about crazy—can you blame them?

There was literally no one left on this beautiful high garden land but a bunch of hysterical girls and some older slave women.

That was about two thousand years ago.

At first there was a period of sheer despair. The mountains towered between them and their old enemies, but also between them and escape. There was no way up or down or out—they simply had to stay there. Some were for suicide, but not the majority. They must have been a plucky lot, as a whole, and they decided to live—as long as they did live. Of course they had hope, as youth must, that something would happen to change their fate.

So they set to work, to bury the dead, to plow and sow, to care for one another.

Speaking of burying the dead, I will set down while I think of it, that they had adopted cremation in about the thirteenth century, for the same reason that they had left off raising cattle—they could not spare the room. They were much surprised to learn that we were still burying—asked our reasons for it, and were much dissatisfied with what we gave. We told them of the belief in the resurrection of the body, and they asked if our God was not as well able to resurrect from ashes as from long corruption. We told them of how people thought it repugnant to have their loved ones burn, and they asked if it was less repugnant to have them decay. They were inconveniently reasonable, those women.

Well—that original bunch of girls set to work to clean up the place and make their living as best they could. Some of the remaining slave women rendered invaluable service, teaching such trades as they knew. They had such records as were then kept, all the tools and implements of the time, and a most fertile land to work in.

There were a handful of the younger matrons who had escaped slaughter, and a few babies were born after the cataclysm—but only two boys, and they both died.

For five or ten years they worked together, growing stronger and wiser and more and more mutually attached, and then the miracle happened—one of these young women bore a child. Of course they all thought there must be a man somewhere, but none was found. Then they decided it must be a direct gift from the gods, and placed the proud mother in the Temple of Maaia—their Goddess of Motherhood—under strict watch. And there, as years passed, this wonder-woman bore child after child, five of them—all girls.

I did my best, keenly interested as I have always been in sociology and social psychology, to reconstruct in my mind the real position of these ancient women. There were some five or six hundred of them, and they were harem-bred; yet for the few preceding generations they had been reared in the atmosphere of such heroic struggle that the stock must have been toughened somewhat. Left alone in that terrific orphanhood, they had clung together, supporting one another and their little sisters, and developing unknown powers in the stress of new necessity. To this pain-hardened and work-strengthened group, who had lost not only the love and care of parents, but the hope of ever having children of their own, there now dawned the new hope.

Here at last was Motherhood, and though it was not for all of them personally, it might—if the power was inherited—found here a new race.

It may be imagined how those five Daughters of Maaia, Children of the Temple, Mothers of the Future—they had all the titles that love and hope and reverence could give—were reared. The whole little nation of women surrounded them with loving service, and waited, between a boundless hope and an as boundless despair, to see if they, too, would be Mothers.

And they were! As fast as they reached the age of twenty-five they began bearing. Each of them, like her mother, bore five daughters. Presently there were twenty-five New Women, Mothers in their own right, and the whole spirit of the country changed from mourning and mere courageous resignation to proud joy. The older women, those who remembered men, died off; the youngest of all the first lot of course died too, after a while, and by that time there were left one hundred and fifty-five parthenogenetic women, founding a new race.

They inherited all that the devoted care of that declining band of original ones could leave them. Their little country was quite safe. Their farms and gardens were all in full production. Such industries as they had were in careful order. The records of their past were all preserved, and for years the older women had spent their time in the best teaching they were capable of, that they might leave to the little group of sisters and mothers all they possessed of skill and knowledge.

There you have the start of Herland! One family, all descended from one mother! She lived to a hundred years old; lived to see her hundred and twenty-five great-granddaughters born; lived as Queen-Priestess-Mother of them all; and died with a nobler pride and a fuller joy than perhaps any human soul has ever known—she alone had founded a new race!

The first five daughters had grown up in an atmosphere of holy calm, of awed watchful waiting, of breathless prayer. To them the longed-for motherhood was not only a personal joy, but a nation's hope. Their twenty-five daughters in turn, with a stronger hope, a richer, wider outlook, with the devoted love and care of all the surviving population, grew up as a holy sisterhood, their whole ardent youth looking forward to their great office. And at last they were left alone; the white-haired First Mother was gone, and this one family, five sisters, twenty-five first cousins, and a hundred and twenty-five second cousins, began a new race.

Here you have human beings, unquestionably, but what we

were slow in understanding was how these ultra-women, inheriting only from women, had eliminated not only certain masculine characteristics, which of course we did not look for, but so much of what we had always thought essentially feminine.

The tradition of men as guardians and protectors had quite died out. These stalwart virgins had no men to fear and therefore no need of protection. As to wild beasts—there were none in their sheltered land.

The power of mother-love, that maternal instinct we so highly laud, was theirs of course, raised to its highest power; and a sister-love which, even while recognizing the actual relationship, we found it hard to credit.

Terry, incredulous, even contemptuous, when we were alone, refused to believe the story. "A lot of traditions as old as Herodotus—and about as trustworthy!" he said. "It's likely women—just a pack of women—would have hung together like that! We all know women can't organize—that they scrap like anything—are frightfully jealous."

"But these New Ladies didn't have anyone to be jealous of, remember," drawled Jeff.

"That's a likely story," Terry sneered.

"Why don't you invent a likelier one?" I asked him. "Here *are* the women—nothing but women, and you yourself admit there's no trace of a man in the country." This was after we had been about a good deal.

"I'll admit that," he growled. "And it's a big miss, too. There's not only no fun without 'em—no real sport—no competition; but these women aren't *womanly*. You know they aren't."

That kind of talk always set Jeff going; and I gradually grew to side with him. "Then you don't call a breed of women whose one concern is motherhood—womanly?" he asked.

"Indeed I don't," snapped Terry. "What does a man care for motherhood—when he hasn't a ghost of a chance at fatherhood? And besides—what's the good of talking sentiment when we are just men together? What a man wants of women is a good deal more than all this 'motherhood'!"

We were as patient as possible with Terry. He had lived about nine months among the "Colonels" when he made that outburst; and with no chance at any more strenuous excitement than our gymnastics gave us—save for our escape fiasco. I don't suppose Terry had ever lived so long with neither Love, Combat, nor Danger to employ his superabundant energies, and he was irritable. Neither Jeff nor I found it so wearing. I was so much interested intellectually that our confinement did not wear on me; and as for Jeff, bless his heart!—he enjoyed the society of that tutor of his almost as much as if she had been a girl—I don't know but more.

As to Terry's criticism, it was true. These women, whose essential distinction of motherhood was the dominant note of their whole culture, were strikingly deficient in what we call "femininity." This led me very promptly to the conviction that those "feminine charms" we are so fond of are not feminine at all, but mere reflected masculinity—developed to please us because they had to please us, and in no way essential to the real fulfillment of their great process. But Terry came to no such conclusion.

"Just you wait till I get out!" he muttered.

Then we both cautioned him. "Look here, Terry, my boy! You be careful! They've been mighty good to us—but do you remember the anesthesia? If you do any mischief in this virgin land, beware of the vengeance of the Maiden Aunts! Come, be a man! It won't be forever."

To return to the history:

They began at once to plan and build for their children, all the strength and intelligence of the whole of them devoted to that one thing. Each girl, of course, was reared in full knowledge of her Crowning Office, and they had, even then, very high ideas of the moulding powers of the mother, as well as those of education.

Such high ideals as they had! Beauty, Health, Strength, Intellect, Goodness—for these they prayed and worked.

They had no enemies; they themselves were all sisters and friends. The land was fair before them, and a great Future began to form itself in their minds.

The religion they had to begin with was much like that of old Greece—a number of gods and goddesses; but they lost all interest in deities of war and plunder, and gradually centered on their Mother Goddess altogether. Then, as they grew more intelligent, this had turned into a sort of Maternal Pantheism.

Here was Mother Earth, bearing fruit. All that they ate was fruit of motherhood, from seed or egg or their product. By motherhood they were born and by motherhood they lived— life was, to them, just the long cycle of motherhood.

But very early they recognized the need of improvement as well as of mere repetition, and devoted their combined intelligence to that problem—how to make the best kind of people. First this was merely the hope of bearing better ones, and then they recognized that however the children differed at birth, the real growth lay later—through education.

Then things began to hum.

As I learned more and more to appreciate what these women had accomplished, the less proud I was of what we, with all our manhood, had done.

You see, they had had no wars. They had had no kings, and no priests, and no aristocracies. They were sisters, and as they grew, they grew together—not by competition, but by united action.

We tried to put in a good word for competition, and they were keenly interested. Indeed, we soon found from their earnest questions of us that they were prepared to believe our world must be better than theirs. They were not sure; they wanted to know; but there was no such arrogance about them as might have been expected.

We rather spread ourselves, telling of the advantages of competition: how it developed fine qualities; that without it there would be "no stimulus to industry." Terry was very strong on that point.

"No stimulus to industry," they repeated, with that puzzled look we had learned to know so well. "*Stimulus? To Industry?* But don't you *like* to work?"

"No man would work unless he had to," Terry declared.

"Oh, no *man!* You mean that is one of your sex distinctions?"

"No, indeed!" he said hastily. "No one, I mean, man or woman, would work without incentive. Competition is the— the motor power, you see."

"It is not with us," they explained gently, "so it is hard for us to understand. Do you mean, for instance, that with you no mother would work for her children without the stimulus of competition?"

No, he admitted that he did not mean that. Mothers, he supposed, would of course work for their children in the home; but the world's work was different—that had to be done by men, and required the competitive element.

All our teachers were eagerly interested.

"We want so much to know—you have the whole world to tell us of, and we have only our little land! And there are two of you—the two sexes—to love and help one another. It must be a rich and wonderful world. Tell us—what is the work of the world, that men do—which we have not here?"

"Oh, everything," Terry said grandly. "The men do everything, with us." He squared his broad shoulders and lifted his chest. "We do not allow our women to work. Women are loved—idolized—honored—kept in the home to care for the children."

"What is 'the home'?" asked Somel a little wistfully.

But Zava begged: "Tell me first, do *no* women work, really?"

"Why, yes," Terry admitted. "Some have to, of the poorer sort."

"About how many—in your country?"

"About seven or eight million," said Jeff, as mischievous as ever.

CHAPTER VI

COMPARISONS ARE ODIOUS

I had always been proud of my country, of course. Everyone is. Compared with the other lands and other races I knew, the United States of America had always seemed to me, speaking modestly, as good as the best of them.

But just as a clear-eyed, intelligent, perfectly honest, and well-meaning child will frequently jar one's self-esteem by innocent questions, so did these women, without the slightest appearance of malice or satire, continually bring up points of discussion which we spent our best efforts in evading.

Now that we were fairly proficient in their language, had read a lot about their history, and had given them the general outlines of ours, they were able to press their questions closer.

So when Jeff admitted the number of "women wage earners" we had, they instantly asked for the total population, for the proportion of adult women, and found that there were but twenty million or so at the outside.

"Then at least a third of your women are—what is it you call them—wage earners? And they are all *poor*. What is *poor*, exactly?"

"Ours is the best country in the world as to poverty," Terry told them. "We do not have the wretched paupers and beggars of the older countries, I assure you. Why, European visitors tell us we don't know what poverty is."

"Neither do we," answered Zava. "Won't you tell us?"

Terry put it up to me, saying I was the sociologist, and I explained that the laws of nature require a struggle for existence, and that in the struggle the fittest survive, and the unfit perish. In our economic struggle, I continued, there was always plenty of opportunity for the fittest to reach the top, which they did, in great numbers, particularly in our country; that where there was severe economic pressure the lowest classes of course felt it the worst, and that among the poorest of all, the women were driven into the labor market by necessity.

They listened closely, with the usual note-taking.

"About one-third, then, belong to the poorest class," observed Moadine gravely. "And two-thirds are the ones who are—how was it you so beautifully put it?—'loved, honored, kept in the home to care for the children.' This inferior one-third have no children, I suppose?"

Jeff—he was getting as bad as they were—solemnly replied that, on the contrary, the poorer they were, the more children they had. That too, he explained, was a law of nature: "Reproduction is in inverse proportion to individuation."

"These 'laws of nature,'" Zava gently asked, "are they all the laws you have?"

"I should say not!" protested Terry. "We have systems of law that go back thousands and thousands of years—just as you do, no doubt," he finished politely.

"Oh no," Moadine told him. "We have no laws over a hundred years old, and most of them are under twenty. In a few weeks more," she continued, "we are going to have the pleasure of showing you over our little land and explaining everything you care to know about. We want you to see our people."

"And I assure you," Somel added, "that our people want to see you."

Terry brightened up immensely at this news, and reconciled himself to the renewed demands upon our capacity as teachers. It was lucky that we knew so little, really, and had no books to refer to, else, I fancy we might all be there yet, teaching those eager-minded women about the rest of the world.

As to geography, they had the tradition of the Great Sea, beyond the mountains; and they could see for themselves the endless thick-forested plains below them—that was all. But from the few records of their ancient condition—not "before the flood" with them, but before that mighty quake which had cut them off so completely—they were aware that there were other peoples and other countries.

In geology they were quite ignorant.

As to anthropology, they had those same remnants of information about other peoples, and the knowledge of the savagery of the occupants of those dim forests below. Nevertheless, they had inferred (marvelously keen on inference and deduction their minds were!) the existence and development of civilization in other places, much as we infer it on other planets.

When our biplane came whirring over their heads in that first scouting flight of ours, they had instantly accepted it as proof of the high development of Some Where Else, and had prepared to receive us as cautiously and eagerly as we might prepare to welcome visitors who came "by meteor" from Mars.

Of history—outside their own—they knew nothing, of course, save for their ancient traditions.

Of astronomy they had a fair working knowledge—that is a very old science; and with it, a surprising range and facility in mathematics.

Physiology they were quite familiar with. Indeed, when it came to the simpler and more concrete sciences, wherein the subject matter was at hand and they had but to exercise their minds upon it, the results were surprising. They had worked out a chemistry, a botany, a physics, with all the blends where a science touches an art, or merges into an industry, to such fullness of knowledge as made us feel like schoolchildren.

Also we found this out—as soon as we were free of the country, and by further study and question—that what one knew, all knew, to a very considerable extent.

I talked later with little mountain girls from the fir-dark valleys away up at their highest part, and with sunburned plainswomen and agile foresters, all over the country, as well as those in the towns, and everywhere there was the same high level of intelligence. Some knew far more than others about one thing—they were specialized, of course; but all of them knew more about everything—that is, about everything the country was acquainted with—than is the case with us.

We boast a good deal of our "high level of general intelligence" and our "compulsory public education," but in proportion to their opportunities they were far better educated than our people.

With what we told them, from what sketches and models we were able to prepare, they constructed a sort of working outline to fill in as they learned more.

A big globe was made, and our uncertain maps, helped out by those in that precious year-book thing I had, were tentatively indicated upon it.

They sat in eager groups, masses of them who came for the purpose, and listened while Jeff roughly ran over the geologic history of the earth, and showed them their own land in relation to the others. Out of that same pocket reference book of mine came facts and figures which were seized upon and placed in right relation with unerring acumen.

Even Terry grew interested in this work. "If we can keep this up, they'll be having us lecture to all the girls' schools and colleges—how about that?" he suggested to us. "Don't know as I'd object to being an Authority to such audiences."

They did, in fact, urge us to give public lectures later, but not to the hearers or with the purpose we expected.

What they were doing with us was like—like—well, say like Napoleon extracting military information from a few illiterate peasants. They knew just what to ask, and just what use to make of it; they had mechanical appliances for disseminating information almost equal to ours at home; and by the time we were led forth to lecture, our audiences had thoroughly mastered a well-arranged digest of all we had previously given to our teachers, and were prepared with such notes and questions as might have intimidated a university professor.

They were not audiences of girls, either. It was some time before we were allowed to meet the young women.

"Do you mind telling what you intend to do with us?" Terry burst forth one day, facing the calm and friendly Moadine with that funny half-blustering air of his. At first he used to storm and flourish quite a good deal, but nothing seemed to amuse them more; they would gather around and watch him as if it was an exhibition, politely, but with evident interest. So he learned to check himself, and was almost reasonable in his bearing—but not quite.

She announced smoothly and evenly: "Not in the least. I thought it was quite plain. We are trying to learn of you all we can, and to teach you what you are willing to learn of our country."

"Is that all?" he insisted.

She smiled a quiet enigmatic smile. "That depends."

"Depends on what?"

"Mainly on yourselves," she replied.

"Why do you keep us shut up so closely?"

"Because we do not feel quite safe in allowing you at large where there are so many young women."

Terry was really pleased at that. He had thought as much, inwardly; but he pushed the question. "Why should you be afraid? We are gentlemen."

She smiled that little smile again, and asked: "Are 'gentlemen' always safe?"

"You surely do not think that any of us," he said it with a good deal of emphasis on the "us," "would hurt your young girls?"

"Oh no," she said quickly, in real surprise. "The danger is quite the other way. They might hurt you. If, by any accident, you did harm any one of us, you would have to face a million mothers."

He looked so amazed and outraged that Jeff and I laughed outright, but she went on gently.

"I do not think you quite understand yet. You are but men, three men, in a country where the whole population are mothers—or are going to be. Motherhood means to us something which I cannot yet discover in any of the countries of which you tell us. You have spoken"—she turned to Jeff, "of Human Brotherhood as a great idea among you, but even that I judge is far from a practical expression?"

Jeff nodded rather sadly. "Very far—" he said.

"Here we have Human Motherhood—in full working use,"

she went on. "Nothing else except the literal sisterhood of our origin, and the far higher and deeper union of our social growth.

"The children in this country are the one center and focus of all our thoughts. Every step of our advance is always considered in its effect on them—on the race. You see, we are *Mothers*," she repeated, as if in that she had said it all.

"I don't see how that fact—which is shared by all women—constitutes any risk to us," Terry persisted. "You mean they would defend their children from attack. Of course. Any mothers would. But we are not Savages, my dear Lady; we are not going to hurt any mother's child."

They looked at one another and shook their heads a little, but Zava turned to Jeff and urged him to make us see—said he seemed to understand more fully than we did. And he tried.

I can see it now, or at least much more of it, but it has taken me a long time, and a good deal of honest intellectual effort.

What they call Motherhood was like this:

They began with a really high degree of social development, something like that of Ancient Egypt or Greece. Then they suffered the loss of everything masculine, and supposed at first that all human power and safety had gone too. Then they developed this virgin birth capacity. Then, since the prosperity of their children depended on it, the fullest and subtlest coordination began to be practiced.

I remember how long Terry balked at the evident unanimity of these women—the most conspicuous feature of their whole culture. "It's impossible!" he would insist. "Women cannot cooperate—it's against nature."

When we urged the obvious facts he would say: "Fiddle-sticks!" or "Hang your facts—I tell you it can't be done!" And we never succeeded in shutting him up till Jeff dragged in the hymenoptera.

"'Go to the ant, thou sluggard'—and learn something," he said triumphantly. "Don't they cooperate pretty well? You can't beat it. This place is just like an enormous anthill—you know an anthill is nothing but a nursery. And how about bees? Don't they manage to cooperate and love one another?

> 'As the birds do love the Spring
> Or the bees their careful king,'

as that precious Constable had it. Just show me a combination of male creatures, bird, bug, or beast, that works as well, will you? Or one of our masculine countries where the people work together as well as they do here! I tell you, women are the natural cooperators, not men!"

Terry had to learn a good many things he did not want to.

To go back to my little analysis of what happened:

They developed all this close inter-service in the interests of their children. To do the best work they had to specialize, of course; the children needed spinners and weavers, farmers and gardeners, carpenters and masons, as well as mothers.

Then came the filling up of the place. When a population multiplies by five every thirty years it soon reaches the limits of a country, especially a small one like this. They very soon eliminated all the grazing cattle—sheep were the last to go, I believe. Also, they worked out a system of intensive agriculture surpassing anything I ever heard of, with the very forests all reset with fruit- or nut-bearing trees.

Do what they would, however, there soon came a time when they were confronted with the problem of "the pressure of population" in an acute form. There was really crowding, and with it, unavoidably, a decline in standards.

And how did those women meet it?

Not by a "struggle for existence" which would result in an everlasting writhing mass of underbred people trying to get ahead of one another—some few on top, temporarily, many constantly crushed out underneath, a hopeless substratum of paupers and degenerates, and no serenity or peace for anyone—no possibility for really noble qualities among the people at large.

Neither did they start off on predatory excursions to get more land from somebody else, or to get more food from somebody else, to maintain their struggling mass.

Not at all. They sat down in council together and thought it out. Very clear, strong thinkers they were. They said: "With our best endeavors this country will support about so many people, with the standard of peace, comfort, health, beauty, and progress we demand. Very well. That is all the people we will make."

There you have it. You see, they were Mothers, not in our sense of helpless involuntary fecundity, forced to fill and over-fill the land, every land, and then see their children suffer, sin, and die, fighting horribly with one another; but in the sense of Conscious Makers of People. Mother-love with them was not a brute passion, a mere "instinct," a wholly personal feeling; it was—A Religion.

It included that limitless feeling of sisterhood, that wide unity in service which was so difficult for us to grasp. And it was National, Racial, Human—oh, I don't know how to say it.

We are used to seeing what we call "a mother" completely wrapped up in her own pink bundle of fascinating babyhood, and taking but the faintest theoretic interest in anybody else's bundle, to say nothing of the common needs of *all* the bundles. But these women were working all together at the grandest of tasks—they were Making People—and they made them well.

There followed a period of "negative Eugenics" which must have been an appalling sacrifice. We are commonly willing to "lay down our lives" for our country, but they had to forego motherhood for their country—and it was precisely the hardest thing for them to do.

When I got this far in my reading I went to Somel for more light. We were as friendly by that time as I had ever been in my life with any woman. A mighty comfortable soul she was, giving one the nice smooth mother-feeling a man likes in a woman, and yet giving also the clear intelligence and dependableness I used to assume to be masculine qualities. We had talked volumes already.

"See here," said I. "Here was this dreadful period when they got far too thick, and decided to limit the population. We have a lot of talk about that among us, but your position is so different that I'd like to know a little more about it.

"I understand that you make Motherhood the highest Social

Service—a Sacrament, really; that it is only undertaken once, by the majority of the population; that those held unfit are not allowed even that; and that to be encouraged to bear more than one child is the very highest reward and honor in the power of the State."

(She interpolated here that the nearest approach to an aristocracy they had was to come of a line of "Over Mothers"—those who had been so honored.)

"But what I do not understand, naturally, is how you prevent it. I gathered that each woman had five. You have no tyrannical husbands to hold in check—and you surely do not destroy the unborn—"

The look of ghastly horror she gave me I shall never forget. She started from her chair, pale, her eyes blazing.

"Destroy the unborn—!" she said in a hard whisper. "Do men do that in your country?"

"Men!" I began to answer, rather hotly, and then saw the gulf before me. None of us wanted these women to think that *our* women, of whom we boasted so proudly, were in any way inferior to them. I am ashamed to say that I equivocated. I told her about Malthus and his fears. I told her of certain criminal types of women—perverts, or crazy, who had been known to commit infanticide. I told her, truly enough, that there was much in our land which was open to criticism, but that I hated to dwell on our defects until they understood us and our conditions better.

And, making a wide detour, I scrambled back to my question of how they limited the population.

As for Somel, she seemed sorry, a little ashamed even, of her too clearly expressed amazement. As I look back now, knowing them better, I am more and more and more amazed as I appreciate the exquisite courtesy with which they had received over and over again statements and admissions on our part which must have revolted them to the soul.

She explained to me, with sweet seriousness, that as I had supposed, at first each woman bore five children; and that, in their eager desire to build up a nation, they had gone on in that way for a few centuries, till they were confronted with the absolute need of a limit. This fact was equally plain to all—all were equally interested.

They were now as anxious to check their wonderful power as they had been to develop it; and for some generations gave the matter their most earnest thought and study.

"We were living on rations before we worked it out," she said. "But we did work it out. You see, before a child comes to one of us there is a period of utter exaltation—the whole being is uplifted and filled with a concentrated desire for that child. We learned to look forward to that period with the greatest caution. Often our young women, those to whom motherhood had not yet come, would voluntarily defer it. When that deep inner demand for a child began to be felt she would deliberately engage in the most active work, physical and mental; and even more important, would solace her longing by the direct care and service of the babies we already had."

She paused. Her wise sweet face grew deeply, reverently tender.

"We soon grew to see that mother-love has more than one channel of expression. I think the reason our children are so—so fully loved, by all of us, is that we never—any of us—have enough of our own."

This seemed to me infinitely pathetic, and I said so. "We have much that is bitter and hard in our life at home," I told her, "but this seems to me piteous beyond words—a whole nation of starving mothers!"

But she smiled her deep contented smile, and said I quite misunderstood.

"We each go without a certain range of personal joy," she said, "but remember—we each have a million children to love and serve—*our* children."

It was beyond me. To hear a lot of women talk about "our children"! But I suppose that is the way the ants and bees would talk—do talk, maybe.

That was what they did, anyhow.

When a woman chose to be a mother, she allowed the child-longing to grow within her till it worked its natural miracle. When she did not so choose she put the whole thing out of her mind, and fed her heart with the other babies.

Let me see—with us, children—minors, that is—constitute about three-fifths of the population; with them only about one-third, or less. And precious—! No sole heir to an empire's throne, no solitary millionaire baby, no only child of middle-aged parents, could compare as an idol with these Herland Children.

But before I start on that subject I must finish up that little analysis I was trying to make.

They did effectually and permanently limit the population in numbers, so that the country furnished plenty for the fullest, richest life for all of them: plenty of everything, including room, air, solitude even.

And then they set to work to improve that population in quality—since they were restricted in quantity. This they had been at work on, uninterruptedly, for some fifteen hundred years. Do you wonder they were nice people?

Physiology, hygiene, sanitation, physical culture—all that line of work had been perfected long since. Sickness was almost wholly unknown among them, so much so that a previously high development in what we call the "science of medicine" had become practically a lost art. They were a clean-bred, vigorous lot, having the best of care, the most perfect living conditions always.

When it came to psychology—there was no one thing which left us so dumbfounded, so really awed, as the everyday working knowledge—and practice—they had in this line. As we learned more and more of it, we learned to appreciate the exquisite mastery with which we ourselves, strangers of alien race, of unknown opposite sex, had been understood and provided for from the first.

With this wide, deep, thorough knowledge, they had met and solved the problems of education in ways some of which I hope to make clear later. Those nation-loved children of theirs compared with the average in our country as the most perfectly cultivated, richly developed roses compare with—tumbleweeds. Yet they did not *seem* "cultivated" at all—it had all become a natural condition.

And this people, steadily developing in mental capacity, in

will power, in social devotion, had been playing with the arts and sciences—as far as they knew them—for a good many centuries now with inevitable success.

Into this quiet lovely land, among these wise, sweet, strong women, we, in our easy assumption of superiority, had suddenly arrived; and now, tamed and trained to a degree they considered safe, we were at last brought out to see the country, to know the people.

CHAPTER VII

OUR GROWING MODESTY

Being at last considered sufficiently tamed and trained to be trusted with scissors, we barbered ourselves as best we could. A close-trimmed beard is certainly more comfortable than a full one. Razors, naturally, they could not supply.

"With so many old women you'd think there'd be some razors," sneered Terry. Whereat Jeff pointed out that he never before had seen such complete absence of facial hair on women.

"Looks to me as if the absence of men made them more feminine in that regard, anyhow," he suggested.

"Well, it's the only one then," Terry reluctantly agreed. "A less feminine lot I never saw. A child apiece doesn't seem to be enough to develop what I call motherliness."

Terry's idea of motherliness was the usual one, involving a baby in arms, or "a little flock about her knees," and the complete absorption of the mother in said baby or flock. A motherliness which dominated society, which influenced every art and industry, which absolutely protected all childhood, and gave to it the most perfect care and training, did not seem motherly—to Terry.

We had become well used to the clothes. They were quite as comfortable as our own—in some ways more so—and undeniably better looking. As to pockets, they left nothing to be desired. That second garment was fairly quilted with pockets. They were most ingeniously arranged, so as to be convenient to the hand and not inconvenient to the body, and were so placed as at once to strengthen the garment and add decorative lines of stitching.

In this, as in so many other points we had now to observe,

there was shown the action of a practical intelligence, coupled with fine artistic feeling, and, apparently, untrammeled by any injurious influences.

Our first step of comparative freedom was a personally conducted tour of the country. No pentagonal bodyguard now! Only our special tutors, and we got on famously with them. Jeff said he loved Zava like an aunt—"only jollier than any aunt I ever saw"; Somel and I were as chummy as could be—the best of friends; but it was funny to watch Terry and Moadine. She was patient with him, and courteous, but it was like the patience and courtesy of some great man, say a skilled, experienced diplomat, with a schoolgirl. Her grave acquiescence with his most preposterous expression of feeling; her genial laughter, not only with, but, I often felt, at him—though impeccably polite; her innocent questions, which almost invariably led him to say more than he intended—Jeff and I found it all amusing to watch.

He never seemed to recognize that quiet background of superiority. When she dropped an argument he always thought he had silenced her; when she laughed he thought it tribute to his wit.

I hated to admit to myself how much Terry had sunk in my esteem. Jeff felt it too, I am sure; but neither of us admitted it to the other. At home we had measured him with other men, and, though we knew his failings, he was by no means an unusual type. We knew his virtues too, and they had always seemed more prominent than the faults. Measured among women—our women at home, I mean—he had always stood high. He was visibly popular. Even where his habits were known, there was no discrimination against him; in some cases his reputation for what was felicitously termed "gaiety" seemed a special charm.

But here, against the calm wisdom and quiet restrained humor of these women, with only that blessed Jeff and my inconspicuous self to compare with, Terry did stand out rather strong.

As "a man among men," he didn't; as a man among—I shall have to say, "females," he didn't; his intense masculinity seemed only fit complement to their intense femininity. But here he was all out of drawing.

Moadine was a big woman, with a balanced strength that seldom showed. Her eye was as quietly watchful as a fencer's. She maintained a pleasant relation with her charge, but I doubt if many, even in that country, could have done as well.

He called her "Maud," amongst ourselves, and said she was "a good old soul, but a little slow"; wherein he was quite wrong. Needless to say, he called Jeff's teacher "Java," and sometimes "Mocha," or plain "Coffee"; when specially mischievous, "Chicory," and even "Postum." But Somel rather escaped this form of humor, save for a rather forced "Some 'ell."

"Don't you people have but one name?" he asked one day, after we had been introduced to a whole group of them, all with pleasant, few-syllabled strange names, like the ones we knew.

"Oh yes," Moadine told him. "A good many of us have another, as we get on in life—a descriptive one. That is the name we earn. Sometimes even that is changed, or added to, in an unusually rich life. Such as our present Land-Mother—what you call president or king, I believe. She was called Mera, even as a child; that means 'thinker.' Later there was added Du—Du-mera—the wise thinker, and now we all know her as O-du-mera—great and wise thinker. You shall meet her."

"No surnames at all then?" pursued Terry, with his somewhat patronizing air. "No family name?"

"Why no," she said. "Why should we? We are all descended from a common source—all one 'family' in reality. You see, our comparatively brief and limited history gives us that advantage at least."

"But does not each mother want her own child to bear her name?" I asked.

"No—why should she? The child has its own."

"Why for—for identification—so people will know whose child she is."

"We keep the most careful records," said Somel. "Each one of us has our exact line of descent all the way back to our dear First Mother. There are many reasons for doing that. But as to everyone knowing which child belongs to which mother—why should she?"

Here, as in so many other instances, we were led to feel the difference between the purely maternal and the paternal attitude of mind. The element of personal pride seemed strangely lacking.

"How about your other works?" asked Jeff. "Don't you sign your names to them—books and statues and so on?"

"Yes, surely, we are all glad and proud to. Not only books and statues, but all kinds of work. You will find little names on the houses, on the furniture, on the dishes sometimes. Because otherwise one is likely to forget, and we want to know to whom to be grateful."

"You speak as if it were done for the convenience of the consumer—not the pride of the producer," I suggested.

"It's both," said Somel. "We have pride enough in our work."

"Then why not in your children?" urged Jeff.

"But we have! We're magnificently proud of them," she insisted.

"Then why not sign 'em?" said Terry triumphantly.

Moadine turned to him with her slightly quizzical smile. "Because the finished product is not a private one. When they are babies, we do speak of them, at times, as 'Essa's Lato,' or 'Novine's Amel'; but that is merely descriptive and conversational. In the records, of course, the child stands in her own line of mothers; but in dealing with it personally it is Lato, or Amel, without dragging in its ancestors."

"But have you names enough to give a new one to each child?"

"Assuredly we have, for each living generation."

Then they asked about our methods, and found first that "we" did so and so, and then that other nations did differently. Upon which they wanted to know which method has been proved best—and we had to admit that so far as we knew there had been no attempt at comparison, each people pursuing its own custom in the fond conviction of superiority, and either despising or quite ignoring the others.

With these women the most salient quality in all their institutions was reasonableness. When I dug into the records to follow out any line of development, that was the most astonishing thing—the conscious effort to make it better.

They had early observed the value of certain improvements, had easily inferred that there was room for more, and took the greatest pains to develop two kinds of minds—the critic and inventor. Those who showed an early tendency to observe, to discriminate, to suggest, were given special training for that function; and some of their highest officials spent their time in the most careful study of one or another branch of work, with a view to its further improvement.

In each generation there was sure to arrive some new mind to detect faults and show need of alterations; and the whole corps of inventors was at hand to apply their special faculty at the point criticized, and offer suggestions.

We had learned by this time not to open a discussion on any of their characteristics without first priming ourselves to answer questions about our own methods; so I kept rather quiet on this matter of conscious improvement. We were not prepared to show our way was better.

There was growing in our minds, at least in Jeff's and mine, a keen appreciation of the advantages of this strange country and its management. Terry remained critical. We laid most of it to his nerves. He certainly was irritable.

The most conspicuous feature of the whole land was the perfection of its food supply. We had begun to notice from that very first walk in the forest, the first partial view from our 'plane. Now we were taken to see this mighty garden, and shown its methods of culture.

The country was about the size of Holland, some ten or twelve thousand square miles. One could lose a good many Hollands along the forest-smothered flanks of those mighty mountains. They had a population of about three million—not a large one, but quality is something. Three million is quite enough to allow for considerable variation, and these people varied more widely than we could at first account for.

Terry had insisted that if they were parthenogenetic they'd be as alike as so many ants or aphids; he urged their visible differences as proof that there must be men—somewhere.

But when we asked them, in our later, more intimate conversations, how they accounted for so much divergence without cross-fertilization, they attributed it partly to the careful education, which followed each slight tendency to differ, and partly to the law of mutation. This they had found in their work with plants, and fully proven in their own case.

Physically they were more alike than we, as they lacked all morbid or excessive types. They were tall, strong, healthy, and beautiful as a race, but differed individually in a wide range of feature, coloring, and expression.

"But surely the most important growth is in mind—and in the things we make," urged Somel. "Do you find your physical variation accompanied by a proportionate variation in ideas, feelings, and products? Or, among people who look more alike, do you find their internal life and their work as similar?"

We were rather doubtful on this point, and inclined to hold that there was more chance of improvement in greater physical variation.

"It certainly should be," Zava admitted. "We have always thought it a grave initial misfortune to have lost half our little world. Perhaps that is one reason why we have so striven for conscious improvement."

"But acquired traits are not transmissible," Terry declared. "Weissman has proved that."

They never disputed our absolute statements, only made notes of them.

"If that is so, then our improvement must be due either to mutation, or solely to education," she gravely pursued. "We certainly have improved. It may be that all these higher qualities were latent in the original mother, that careful education is bringing them out, and that our personal differences depend on slight variations in prenatal condition."

"I think it is more in your accumulated culture," Jeff suggested. "And in the amazing psychic growth you have made. We know very little about methods of real soul culture—and you seem to know a great deal."

Be that as it might, they certainly presented a higher level of active intelligence, and of behavior, than we had so far really grasped. Having known in our lives several people who showed the same delicate courtesy and were equally pleasant to live with, at least when they wore their "company manners," we had assumed that our companions were a carefully chosen few. Later we were more and more impressed that all this gentle breeding was breeding; that they were born to it, reared in it, that it was as natural and universal with them as the gentleness of doves or the alleged wisdom of serpents.

As for the intelligence, I confess that this was the most impressive and, to me, most mortifying, of any single feature of Herland. We soon ceased to comment on this or other matters which to them were such obvious commonplaces as to call forth embarrassing questions about our own conditions.

This was nowhere better shown than in that matter of food supply, which I will now attempt to describe.

Having improved their agriculture to the highest point, and carefully estimated the number of persons who could comfortably live on their square miles; having then limited their population to that number, one would think that was all there was to be done. But they had not thought so. To them the country was a unit—it was Theirs. They themselves were a unit, a conscious group; they thought in terms of the community. As such, their time-sense was not limited to the hopes and ambitions of an individual life. Therefore, they habitually considered and carried out plans for improvement which might cover centuries.

I had never seen, had scarcely imagined, human beings undertaking such a work as the deliberate replanting of an entire forest area with different kinds of trees. Yet this seemed to them the simplest common sense, like a man's plowing up an inferior lawn and reseeding it. Now every tree bore fruit—edible fruit, that is. In the case of one tree, in which they took especial pride, it had originally no fruit at all—that is, none humanly edible—yet was so beautiful that they wished to keep it. For nine hundred years they had experimented, and now showed us this particularly lovely graceful tree, with a profuse crop of nutritious seeds.

That trees were the best food plants, they had early decided, requiring far less labor in tilling the soil, and bearing a larger amount of food for the same ground space; also doing much to preserve and enrich the soil.

Due regard had been paid to seasonable crops, and their fruit and nuts, grains and berries, kept on almost the year through.

On the higher part of the country, near the backing wall of mountains, they had a real winter with snow. Toward the southeastern point, where there was a large valley with a lake whose outlet was subterranean, the climate was like that of California, and citrus fruits, figs, and olives grew abundantly.

What impressed me particularly was their scheme of fertilization. Here was this little shut-in piece of land where one would have thought an ordinary people would have been starved out long ago or reduced to an annual struggle for life. These careful culturists had worked out a perfect scheme of refeeding the soil with all that came out of it. All the scraps and leavings of their food, plant waste from lumber work or textile industry, all the solid matter from the sewage, properly treated and combined—everything which came from the earth went back to it.

The practical result was like that in any healthy forest; an increasingly valuable soil was being built, instead of the progressive impoverishment so often seen in the rest of the world.

When this first burst upon us we made such approving comments that they were surprised that such obvious common sense should be praised; asked what our methods were; and we had some difficulty in—well, in diverting them, by referring to the extent of our own land, and the—admitted—carelessness with which we had skimmed the cream of it.

At least we thought we had diverted them. Later I found that besides keeping a careful and accurate account of all we told them, they had a sort of skeleton chart, on which the things we said and the things we palpably avoided saying were all set down and studied. It really was child's play for those profound educators to work out a painfully accurate estimate of our conditions—in some lines. When a given line of observation seemed to lead to some very dreadful inference, they always gave us the benefit of the doubt, leaving it open to further knowledge. Some of the things we had grown to accept as perfectly natural, or as belonging to our human limitations, they literally could not have believed; and, as I have said, we had all of us joined in a tacit endeavor to conceal much of the social status at home.

"Confound their grandmotherly minds!" Terry said. "Of course they can't understand a Man's World! They aren't human—they're just a pack of Fe-Fe-Females!" This was after he had to admit their parthenogenesis.

"I wish our grandfatherly minds had managed as well," said Jeff. "Do you really think it's to our credit that we have muddled along with all our poverty and disease and the like? They have peace and plenty, wealth and beauty, goodness and intellect. Pretty good people, I think!"

"You'll find they have their faults too," Terry insisted; and partly in self-defense, we all three began to look for those faults of theirs. We had been very strong on this subject before we got there—in those baseless speculations of ours.

"Suppose there are," Jeff would put it, over and over. "What'll they be like?"

And we had been cocksure as to the inevitable limitations, the faults and vices, of a lot of women. We had expected them to be given over to what we called "feminine vanity"—"frills and furbelows," and we found they had evolved a costume more perfect than the Chinese dress, richly beautiful when so desired, always useful, of unfailing dignity and good taste.

We had expected a dull submissive monotony, and found a daring social inventiveness far beyond our own, and a mechanical and scientific development fully equal to ours.

We had expected pettiness, and found a social consciousness besides which our nations looked like quarreling children—feebleminded ones at that.

We had expected jealousy, and found a broad sisterly affection, a fair-minded intelligence, to which we could produce no parallel.

We had expected hysteria, and found a standard of health and vigor, a calmness of temper, to which the habit of profanity, for instance, was impossible to explain—we tried it.

All these things even Terry had to admit, but he still insisted that we should find out the other side pretty soon.

"It stands to reason, doesn't it?" he argued. "The whole thing's deuced unnatural—I'd say impossible if we weren't in it. And an unnatural condition's sure to have unnatural results. You'll find some awful characteristics—see if you don't! For instance—we don't know yet what they do with their criminals—their defectives—their aged. You notice we haven't seen any! There's got to be something!"

I was inclined to believe that there had to be something, so I took the bull by the horns—the cow, I should say!—and asked Somel.

"I want to find some flaw in all this perfection," I told her flatly. "It simply isn't possible that three million people have no faults. We are trying our best to understand and learn—would you mind helping us by saying what, to your minds, are the worst qualities of this unique civilization of yours?"

We were sitting together in a shaded arbor, in one of those eating-gardens of theirs. The delicious food had been eaten, a plate of fruit still before us. We could look out on one side over a stretch of open country, quietly rich and lovely; on the other, the garden, with tables here and there, far apart enough for privacy. Let me say right here that with all their careful "balance of population" there was no crowding in this country. There was room, space, a sunny breezy freedom everywhere.

Somel set her chin upon her hand, her elbow on the low wall beside her, and looked off over the fair land.

"Of course we have faults—all of us," she said. "In one way you might say that we have more than we used to—that is, our standard of perfection seems to get farther and farther away. But we are not discouraged, because our records do show gain—considerable gain.

"When we began—even with the start of one particularly noble mother—we inherited the characteristics of a long race-record behind her. And they cropped out from time to time—alarmingly. But it is—yes, quite six hundred years since we have had what you call a 'criminal.'

"We have, of course, made it our first business to train out, to breed out, when possible, the lowest types."

"Breed out?" I asked. "How could you—with parthenogenesis?"

"If the girl showing the bad qualities had still the power to appreciate social duty, we appealed to her, by that, to renounce motherhood. Some of the few worst types were, fortunately, unable to reproduce. But if the fault was in a disproportionate egotism—then the girl was sure she had the right to have children, even that hers would be better than others."

"I can see that," I said. "And then she would be likely to rear them in the same spirit."

"That we never allowed," answered Somel quietly.

"Allowed?" I queried. "Allowed a mother to rear her own children?"

"Certainly not," said Somel, "unless she was fit for that supreme task."

This was rather a blow to my previous convictions.

"But I thought motherhood was for each of you—"

"Motherhood—yes, that is, maternity, to bear a child. But education is our highest art, only allowed to our highest artists."

"Education?" I was puzzled again. "I don't mean education. I mean by motherhood not only child-bearing, but the care of babies."

"The care of babies involves education and is entrusted only to the most fit," she repeated.

"Then you separate mother and child!" I cried in cold horror, something of Terry's feeling creeping over me, that there must be something wrong among these many virtues.

"Not usually," she patiently explained. "You see, almost every woman values her maternity above everything else. Each girl holds it close and dear, an exquisite joy, a crowning honor, the most intimate, most personal, most precious thing. That is, the child-rearing has come to be with us a culture so profoundly studied, practiced with such subtlety and skill, that the more we love our children the less we are willing to trust that process to unskilled hands—even our own."

"But a mother's love—" I ventured.

She studied my face, trying to work out a means of clear explanation.

"You told us about your dentists," she said, at length, "those quaintly specialized persons who spend their lives filling little holes in other persons' teeth—even in children's teeth sometimes."

"Yes?" I said, not getting her drift.

"Does mother-love urge mothers—with you—to fill their own children's teeth? Or to wish to?"

"Why no—of course not," I protested. "But that is a highly specialized craft. Surely the care of babies is open to any woman—any mother!"

"We do not think so," she gently replied. "Those of us who are the most highly competent fulfill that office; and a majority of our girls eagerly try for it—I assure you we have the very best."

"But the poor mother—bereaved of her baby—"

"Oh no!" she earnestly assured me. "Not in the least bereaved. It is her baby still—it is with her—she has not lost it. But she is not the only one to care for it. There are others whom she knows to be wiser. She knows it because she has studied as they did, practiced as they did, and honors their real superiority. For the child's sake, she is glad to have for it this highest care."

I was unconvinced. Besides, this was only hearsay; I had yet to see the motherhood of Herland.

CHAPTER VIII

THE GIRLS OF HERLAND

At last Terry's ambition was realized. We were invited, always courteously and with free choice on our part, to address general audiences and classes of girls.

I remember the first time—and how careful we were about our clothes, and our amateur barbering. Terry, in particular, was fussy to a degree about the cut of his beard, and so critical of our combined efforts, that we handed him the shears and told him to please himself. We began to rather prize those beards of ours; they were almost our sole distinction among those tall and sturdy women, with their cropped hair and sexless costume. Being offered a wide selection of garments, we had chosen according to our personal taste, and were surprised to find, on meeting large audiences, that we were the most highly decorated, especially Terry.

He was a very impressive figure, his strong features softened by the somewhat longer hair—though he made me trim it as closely as I knew how; and he wore his richly embroidered tunic with its broad, loose girdle with quite a Henry V air. Jeff looked more like—well, like a Huguenot Lover; and I don't know what I looked like, only that I felt very comfortable. When I got back to our own padded armor and its starched borders I realized with acute regret how comfortable were those Herland clothes.

We scanned that audience, looking for the three bright faces we knew; but they were not to be seen. Just a multitude of girls: quiet, eager, watchful, all eyes and ears to listen and learn.

We had been urged to give, as fully as we cared to, a sort of synopsis of world history, in brief, and to answer questions.

"We are so utterly ignorant, you see," Moadine had explained to us. "We know nothing but such science as we have worked out for ourselves, just the brain work of one small half-country; and you, we gather, have helped one another all over the globe, sharing your discoveries, pooling your progress. How wonderful, how supremely beautiful your civilization must be!"

Somel gave a further suggestion.

"You do not have to begin all over again, as you did with us. We have made a sort of digest of what we have learned from you, and it has been eagerly absorbed, all over the country. Perhaps you would like to see our outline?"

We were eager to see it, and deeply impressed. To us, at first, these women, unavoidably ignorant of what to us was the basic commonplace of knowledge, had seemed on the plane of children, or of savages. What we had been forced to admit, with growing acquaintance, was that they were ignorant as Plato and Aristotle were, but with a highly developed mentality quite comparable to that of Ancient Greece.

Far be it from me to lumber these pages with an account of what we so imperfectly strove to teach them. The memorable fact is what they taught us, or some faint glimpse of it. And at present, our major interest was not at all in the subject matter of our talk, but in the audience.

Girls—hundreds of them—eager, bright-eyed, attentive young faces; crowding questions, and, I regret to say, an increasing inability on our part to answer them effectively.

Our special guides, who were on the platform with us, and sometimes aided in clarifying a question or, oftener, an answer, noticed this effect, and closed the formal lecture part of the evening rather shortly.

"Our young women will be glad to meet you," Somel suggested, "to talk with you more personally, if you are willing?"

Willing! We were impatient and said as much, at which I saw a flickering little smile cross Moadine's face. Even then, with all those eager young things waiting to talk to us, a sudden question crossed my mind: "What was their point of view? What did they think of us?" We learned that later.

Terry plunged in among those young creatures with a sort of rapture, somewhat as a glad swimmer takes to the sea. Jeff, with a rapt look on his high-bred face, approached as to a sacrament. But I was a little chilled by that last thought of mine, and kept my eyes open. I found time to watch Jeff, even while I was surrounded by an eager group of questioners—as we all were—and saw how his worshipping eyes, his grave courtesy, pleased and drew some of them; while others, rather stronger spirits they looked to be, drew away from his group to Terry's or mine.

I watched Terry with special interest, knowing how he had longed for this time, and how irresistible he had always been at home. And I could see, just in snatches, of course, how his suave and masterful approach seemed to irritate them; his too-intimate glances were vaguely resented, his compliments puzzled and annoyed. Sometimes a girl would flush, not with drooped eyelids and inviting timidity, but with anger and a quick lift of the head. Girl after girl turned on her heel and left him, till he had but a small ring of questioners, and they, visibly, were the least "girlish" of the lot.

I saw him looking pleased at first, as if he thought he was making a strong impression; but, finally, casting a look at Jeff, or me, he seemed less pleased—and less.

As for me, I was most agreeably surprised. At home I never was "popular." I had my girl friends, good ones, but they were friends—nothing else. Also they were of somewhat the same clan, not popular in the sense of swarming admirers. But here, to my astonishment, I found my crowd was the largest.

I have to generalize, of course, rather telescoping many impressions; but the first evening was a good sample of the impression we made. Jeff had a following, if I may call it that, of the more sentimental—though that's not the word I want. The less practical, perhaps; the girls who were artists of some sort, ethicists, teachers—that kind.

Terry was reduced to a rather combative group: keen, logical, inquiring minds, not over sensitive, the very kind he liked least; while, as for me—I became quite cocky over my general popularity.

Terry was furious about it. We could hardly blame him.

"Girls!" he burst forth, when that evening was over and we were by ourselves once more. "Call those *girls!*"

"Most delightful girls, I call them," said Jeff, his blue eyes dreamily contented.

"What do *you* call them?" I mildly inquired.

"Boys! Nothing but boys, most of 'em. A standoffish, disagreeable lot at that. Critical, impertinent youngsters. No girls at all."

He was angry and severe, not a little jealous, too, I think. Afterward, when he found out just what it was they did not like, he changed his manner somewhat and got on better. He had to. For, in spite of his criticism, they were girls, and, furthermore, all the girls there were! Always excepting our three!—with whom we presently renewed our acquaintance.

When it came to courtship, which it soon did, I can of course best describe my own—and am least inclined to. But of Jeff I heard somewhat; he was inclined to dwell reverently and admiringly, at some length, on the exalted sentiment and measureless perfection of his Celis; and Terry—Terry made so many false starts and met so many rebuffs, that by the time he really settled down to win Alima, he was considerably wiser. At that, it was not smooth sailing. They broke and quarreled, over and over; he would rush off to console himself with some other fair one—the other fair one would have none of him—and he would drift back to Alima, becoming more and more devoted each time.

She never gave an inch. A big, handsome creature, rather exceptionally strong even in that race of strong women, with a proud head and sweeping level brows that lined across above her dark eager eyes like the wide wings of a soaring hawk.

I was good friends with all three of them but best of all with Ellador, long before that feeling changed, for both of us.

From her, and from Somel, who talked very freely with me, I learned at last something of the viewpoint of Herland toward its visitors.

Here they were, isolated, happy, contented, when the booming buzz of our biplane tore the air above them.

Everybody heard it—saw it—for miles and miles, word flashed all over the country, and a council was held in every town and village.

And this was their rapid determination:

"From another country. Probably men. Evidently highly civilized. Doubtless possessed of much valuable knowledge. May be dangerous. Catch them if possible; tame and train them if necessary. This may be a chance to re-establish a bi-sexual state for our people."

They were not afraid of us—three million highly intelligent women—or two million, counting only grown-ups—were not likely to be afraid of three young men. We thought of them as "Women," and therefore timid; but it was two thousand years since they had had anything to be afraid of, and certainly more than one thousand since they had outgrown the feeling.

We thought—at least Terry did—that we could have our pick of them. They thought—very cautiously and farsightedly—of picking us, if it seemed wise.

All that time we were in training they studied us, analyzed us, prepared reports about us, and this information was widely disseminated all about the land.

Not a girl in that country had not been learning for months as much as could be gathered about our country, our culture, our personal characters. No wonder their questions were hard to answer. But I am sorry to say, when we were at last brought out and—exhibited (I hate to call it that, but that's what it was), there was no rush of takers. Here was poor old Terry fondly imagining that at last he was free to stray in "a rosebud garden of girls"—and behold! the rosebuds were all with keen appraising eye, studying us.

They were interested, profoundly interested, but it was not the kind of interest we were looking for.

To get an idea of their attitude you have to hold in mind their extremely high sense of solidarity. They were not each choosing a lover; they hadn't the faintest idea of love—sex-love, that is. These girls—to each of whom motherhood was a lodestar, and that motherhood exalted above a mere personal function, looked forward to as the highest social service, as the sacrament of a lifetime—were now confronted with an opportunity to make the great step of changing their whole status, of reverting to their earlier bi-sexual order of nature.

Beside this underlying consideration there was the limitless interest and curiosity in our civilization, purely impersonal, and held by an order of mind beside which we were like—schoolboys.

It was small wonder that our lectures were not a success; and none at all that our, or at least Terry's, advances were so ill received. The reason for my own comparative success was at first far from pleasing to my pride.

"We like you the best," Somel told me, "because you seem more like us."

"More like a lot of women!" I thought to myself disgustedly, and then remembered how little like "women," in our derogatory sense, they were. She was smiling at me, reading my thought.

"We can quite see that we do not seem like—women—to you. Of course, in a bi-sexual race the distinctive feature of each sex must be intensified. But surely there are characteristics enough which belong to People, aren't there? That's what I mean about you being more like us—more like People. We feel at ease with you."

Jeff's difficulty was his exalted gallantry. He idealized women, and was always looking for a chance to "protect" or to "serve" them. These needed neither protection nor service. They were living in peace and power and plenty; we were their guests, their prisoners, absolutely dependent.

Of course we could promise whatsoever we might of advantages, if they would come to our country; but the more we knew of theirs, the less we boasted.

Terry's jewels and trinkets they prized as curious; handed them about, asking questions as to workmanship, not in the least as to value; and discussed not ownership, but which museum to put them in.

When a man has nothing to give a woman, is dependent wholly on his personal attraction, his courtship is under limitations.

They were considering these two things: the advisability of

making the Great Change; and the degree of personal adaptability which would best serve that end.

Here we had the advantage of our small personal experience with those three fleet forest girls; and that served to draw us together.

As for Ellador: Suppose you come to a strange land and find it pleasant enough—just a little more than ordinarily pleasant—and then you find rich farmland, and then gardens, gorgeous gardens, and then palaces full of rare and curious treasures—incalculable, inexhaustible, and then—mountains— like the Himalayas, and then the sea.

I liked her that day she balanced on the branch before me and named the trio. I thought of her most. Afterward I turned to her like a friend when we met for the third time, and continued the acquaintance. While Jeff's ultra-devotion rather puzzled Celis, really put off their day of happiness, while Terry and Alima quarreled and parted, re-met and re-parted, Ellador and I grew to be close friends.

We talked and talked. We took long walks together. She showed me things, explained them, interpreted much that I had not understood. Through her sympathetic intelligence I became more and more comprehending of the spirit of the people of Herland, more and more appreciative of its marvelous inner growth as well as outer perfection.

I ceased to feel a stranger, a prisoner. There was a sense of understanding, of identity, of purpose. We discussed— everything. And, as I traveled farther and farther, exploring the rich, sweet soul of her, my sense of pleasant friendship became but a broad foundation for such height, such breadth, such interlocked combination of feeling as left me fairly blinded with the wonder of it.

As I've said, I had never cared very much for women, nor they for me—not Terry-fashion. But this one—

At first I never even thought of her "in that way," as the girls have it. I had not come to the country with any Turkish-harem intentions, and I was no woman-worshipper like Jeff. I just liked that girl "as a friend," as we say. That friendship grew like a tree. She was *such* a good sport! We did all kinds of things together. She taught me games and I taught her games, and we raced and rowed and had all manner of fun, as well as higher comradeship.

Then, as I got on farther, the palace and treasures and snowy mountain ranges opened up. I had never known there could be such a human being. So—great. I don't mean talented. She was a forester—one of the best—but it was not that gift I mean. When I say *great*, I mean great—big, all through. If I had known more of those women, as intimately, I should not have found her so unique; but even among them she was noble. Her mother was an Over Mother—and her grandmother, too, I heard later.

So she told me more and more of her beautiful land; and I told her as much, yes, more than I wanted to, about mine; and we became inseparable. Then this deeper recognition came and grew. I felt my own soul rise and lift its wings, as it were. Life got bigger. It seemed as if I understood—as I never had before—as if I could Do things—as if I too could grow—if she would help me. And then It came—to both of us, all at once.

A still day—on the edge of the world, their world. The two of us, gazing out over the far dim forestland below, talking of heaven and earth and human life, and of my land and other lands and what they needed and what I hoped to do for them—

"If you will help me," I said.

She turned to me, with that high, sweet look of hers, and then, as her eyes rested in mine and her hands too—then suddenly there blazed out between us a farther glory, instant, overwhelming—quite beyond any words of mine to tell.

Celis was a blue-and-gold-and-rose person; Alima, black-and-white-and-red, a blazing beauty. Ellador was brown: hair dark and soft, like a seal coat; clear brown skin with a healthy red in it; brown eyes—all the way from topaz to black velvet they seemed to range—splendid girls, all of them.

They had seen us first of all, far down in the lake below, and flashed the tidings across the land even before our first exploring flight. They had watched our landing, flitted through the forest with us, hidden in that tree and—I shrewdly suspect—giggled on purpose.

They had kept watch over our hooded machine, taking turns at it; and when our escape was announced, had followed alongside for a day or two, and been there at the last, as described. They felt a special claim on us—called us "their men"—and when we were at liberty to study the land and people, and be studied by them, their claim was recognized by the wise leaders.

But I felt, we all did, that we should have chosen them among millions, unerringly.

And yet, "the path of true love never did run smooth"; this period of courtship was full of the most unsuspected pitfalls.

Writing this as late as I do, after manifold experiences both in Herland and, later, in my own land, I can now understand and philosophize about what was then a continual astonishment and often a temporary tragedy.

The "long suit" in most courtships is sex attraction, of course. Then gradually develops such comradeship as the two temperaments allow. Then, after marriage, there is either the establishment of a slow-growing, widely based friendship, the deepest, tenderest, sweetest of relations, all lit and warmed by the recurrent flame of love; or else that process is reversed, love cools and fades, no friendship grows, the whole relation turns from beauty to ashes.

Here everything was different. There was no sex-feeling to appeal to, or practically none. Two thousand years' disuse had left very little of the instinct; also we must remember that those who had at times manifested it as atavistic exceptions were often, by that very fact, denied motherhood.

Yet while the mother process remains, the inherent ground for sex-distinction remains also; and who shall say what long-forgotten feeling, vague and nameless, was stirred in some of these mother hearts by our arrival?

What left us even more at sea in our approach was the lack of any sex-tradition. There was no accepted standard of what was "manly" and what was "womanly."

When Jeff said, taking the fruit basket from his adored one, "A woman should not carry anything," Celis said, "Why?" with the frankest amazement. He could not look that fleet-footed, deep-chested young forester in the face and say, "Because she is weaker." She wasn't. One does not call a race horse weak because it is visibly not a cart horse.

He said, rather lamely, that women were not built for heavy work.

She looked out across the fields to where some women were working, building a new bit of wall out of large stones; looked back at the nearest town with its woman-built houses; down at the smooth, hard road we were walking on; and then at the little basket he had taken from her.

"I don't understand," she said quite sweetly. "Are the women in your country so weak that they could not carry such a thing as that?"

"It is a convention," he said. "We assume that motherhood is a sufficient burden—that men should carry all the others."

"What a beautiful feeling!" she said, her blue eyes shining.

"Does it work?" asked Alima, in her keen, swift way. "Do all men in all countries carry everything? Or is it only in yours?"

"Don't be so literal," Terry begged lazily. "Why aren't you willing to be worshipped and waited on? We like to do it."

"You don't like to have us do it to you," she answered.

"That's different," he said, annoyed; and when she said, "Why is it?" he quite sulked, referring her to me, saying, "Van's the philosopher."

Ellador and I talked it all out together, so that we had an easier experience of it when the real miracle time came. Also, between us, we made things clearer to Jeff and Celis. But Terry would not listen to reason.

He was madly in love with Alima. He wanted to take her by storm, and nearly lost her forever.

You see, if a man loves a girl who is in the first place young and inexperienced; who in the second place is educated with a background of caveman tradition, a middle-ground of poetry and romance, and a foreground of unspoken hope and interest all centering upon the one Event; and who has, furthermore, absolutely no other hope or interest worthy of the name—why, it is a comparatively easy matter to sweep her off her feet with a dashing attack. Terry was a past master in this process. He tried it here, and Alima was so affronted, so repelled, that it was weeks before he got near enough to try again.

The more coldly she denied him, the hotter his determination; he was not used to real refusal. The approach of flattery she dismissed with laughter, gifts and such "attentions" we could not bring to bear, pathos and complaint of cruelty stirred only a reasoning inquiry. It took Terry a long time.

I doubt if she ever accepted her strange lover as fully as did Celis and Ellador theirs. He had hurt and offended her too often; there were reservations.

But I think Alima retained some faint vestige of long-descended feeling which made Terry more possible to her than to others; and that she had made up her mind to the experiment and hated to renounce it.

However it came about, we all three at length achieved full understanding, and solemnly faced what was to them a step of measureless importance, a grave question as well as a great happiness; to us a strange, new joy.

Of marriage as a ceremony they knew nothing. Jeff was for bringing them to our country for the religious and the civil ceremony, but neither Celis nor the others would consent.

"We can't expect them to want to go with us—yet," said Terry sagely. "Wait a bit, boys. We've got to take 'em on their own terms—if at all." This, in rueful reminiscence of his repeated failures.

"But our time's coming," he added cheerfully. "These women have never been mastered, you see—" This, as one who had made a discovery.

"You'd better not try to do any mastering if you value your chances," I told him seriously; but he only laughed, and said, "Every man to his trade!"

We couldn't do anything with him. He had to take his own medicine.

If the lack of tradition of courtship left us much at sea in our wooing, we found ourselves still more bewildered by lack of tradition of matrimony.

And here again, I have to draw on later experience, and as

deep an acquaintance with their culture as I could achieve, to explain the gulfs of difference between us.

Two thousand years of one continuous culture with no men. Back of that, only traditions of the harem. They had no exact analogue for our word "home," any more than they had for our Roman-based "family."

They loved one another with a practically universal affection, rising to exquisite and unbroken friendships, and broadening to a devotion to their country and people for which our word "patriotism" is no definition at all.

Patriotism, red hot, is compatible with the existence of a neglect of national interests, a dishonesty, a cold indifference to the suffering of millions. Patriotism is largely pride, and very largely combativeness. Patriotism generally has a chip on its shoulder.

This country had no other country to measure itself by—save the few poor savages far below, with whom they had no contact.

They loved their country because it was their nursery, playground, and workshop—theirs and their children's. They were proud of it as a workshop, proud of their record of ever-increasing efficiency; they had made a pleasant garden of it, a very practical little heaven; but most of all they valued it—and here it is hard for us to understand them—as a cultural environment for their children.

That, of course, is the keynote of the whole distinction—their children.

From those first breathlessly guarded, half-adored race mothers, all up the ascending line, they had this dominant thought of building up a great race through the children.

All the surrendering devotion our women have put into their private families, these women put into their country and race. All the loyalty and service men expect of wives, they gave, not singly to men, but collectively to one another.

And the mother instinct, with us so painfully intense, so thwarted by conditions, so concentrated in personal devotion to a few, so bitterly hurt by death, disease, or barrenness, and even by the mere growth of the children, leaving the mother alone in her empty nest—all this feeling with them flowed out in a strong, wide current, unbroken through the generations, deepening and widening through the years, including every child in all the land.

With their united power and wisdom, they had studied and overcome the "diseases of childhood"—their children had none.

They had faced the problems of education and so solved them that their children grew up as naturally as young trees; learning through every sense; taught continuously but unconsciously—never knowing they were being educated.

In fact, they did not use the word as we do. Their idea of education was the special training they took, when half grown up, under experts. Then the eager young minds fairly flung themselves on their chosen subjects, and acquired with an ease, a breadth, a grasp, at which I never ceased to wonder.

But the babies and little children never felt the pressure of that "forcible feeding" of the mind that we call "education." Of this, more later.

CHAPTER IX

OUR RELATIONS
AND THEIRS

What I'm trying to show here is that with these women the whole relationship of life counted in a glad, eager growing-up to join the ranks of workers in the line best loved; a deep, tender reverence for one's own mother—too deep for them to speak of freely—and beyond that, the whole, free, wide range of sister-hood, the splendid service of the country, and friendships.

To these women we came, filled with the ideas, convictions, traditions, of our culture, and undertook to rouse in them the emotions which—to us—seemed proper.

However much, or little, of true sex-feeling there was be-tween us, it phrased itself in their minds in terms of friendship, the one purely personal love they knew, and of ultimate parentage. Visibly we were not mothers, nor children, nor compatriots; so, if they loved us, we must be friends.

That we should pair off together in our courting days was natural to them; that we three should remain much together, as they did themselves, was also natural. We had as yet no work, so we hung about them in their forest tasks; that was natural, too.

But when we began to talk about each couple having "homes" of our own, they could not understand it.

"Our work takes us all around the country," explained Celis. "We cannot live in one place all the time."

"We are together now," urged Alima, looking proudly at Terry's stalwart nearness. (This was one of the times when they were "on," though presently "off" again.)

"It's not the same thing at all," he insisted. "A man wants a home of his own, with his wife and family in it."

"Staying in it? All the time?" asked Ellador. "Not imprisoned, surely!"

"Of course not! Living there—naturally," he answered.

"What does she do there—all the time?" Alima demanded. "What is her work?"

Then Terry patiently explained again that our women did not work—with reservations.

"But what do they do—if they have no work?" she persisted.

"They take care of the home—and the children."

"At the same time?" asked Ellador.

"Why yes. The children play about, and the mother has charge of it all. There are servants, of course."

It seemed so obvious, so natural to Terry, that he always grew impatient; but the girls were honestly anxious to understand.

"How many children do your women have?" Alima had her notebook out now, and a rather firm set of lip. Terry began to dodge.

"There is no set number, my dear," he explained. "Some have more, some have less."

"Some have none at all," I put in mischievously.

They pounced on this admission and soon wrung from us the general fact that those women who had the most children had the least servants, and those who had the most servants had the least children.

"There!" triumphed Alima. "One or two or no children, and three or four servants. Now what do those women *do?*"

We explained as best we might. We talked of "social duties," disingenuously banking on their not interpreting the words as we did; we talked of hospitality, entertainment, and various "interests." All the time we knew that to these large-minded women whose whole mental outlook was so collective, the limitations of a wholly personal life were inconceivable.

"We cannot really understand it," Ellador concluded. "We are only half a people. We have our woman-ways and they have their man-ways and their both-ways. We have worked out a system of living which is, of course, limited. They must have a broader, richer, better one. I should like to see it."

"You shall, dearest," I whispered.

"There's nothing to smoke," complained Terry. He was in the midst of a prolonged quarrel with Alima, and needed a sedative. "There's nothing to drink. These blessed women have no pleasant vices. I wish we could get out of here!"

This wish was vain. We were always under a certain degree of watchfulness. When Terry burst forth to tramp the streets at night he always found a "Colonel" here or there; and when, on an occasion of fierce though temporary despair, he had plunged to the cliff edge with some vague view to escape, he found several of them close by. We were free—but there was a string to it.

"They've no unpleasant ones, either," Jeff reminded him.

"Wish they had!" Terry persisted. "They've neither the vices of men, nor the virtues of women—they're neuters!"

"You know better than that. Don't talk nonsense," said I, severely.

I was thinking of Ellador's eyes when they gave me a certain look, a look she did not at all realize.

Jeff was equally incensed. "I don't know what 'virtues of women' you miss. Seems to me they have all of them."

"They've no modesty," snapped Terry. "No patience, no submissiveness, none of that natural yielding which is woman's greatest charm."

I shook my head pityingly. "Go and apologize and make friends again, Terry. You've got a grouch, that's all. These women have the virtue of humanity, with less of its faults than any folks I ever saw. As for patience—they'd have pitched us over the cliffs the first day we lit among 'em, if they hadn't that."

"There are no—distractions," he grumbled. "Nowhere a man can go and cut loose a bit. It's an everlasting parlor and nursery."

"And workshop," I added. "And school, and office, and laboratory, and studio, and theater, and—home."

"*Home!*" he sneered. "There isn't a home in the whole piti-ful place."

"There isn't anything else, and you know it," Jeff retorted hotly. "I never saw, I never dreamed of, such universal peace and good will and mutual affection."

"Oh, well, of course, if you like a perpetual Sunday school, it's all very well. But I like Something Doing. Here it's all done."

There was something to this criticism. The years of pioneer-ing lay far behind them. Theirs was a civilization in which the initial difficulties had long since been overcome. The untrou-bled peace, the unmeasured plenty, the steady health, the large good will and smooth management which ordered everything, left nothing to overcome. It was like a pleasant family in an old established, perfectly run country place.

I liked it because of my eager and continued interest in the sociological achievements involved. Jeff liked it as he would have liked such a family and such a place anywhere.

Terry did not like it because he found nothing to oppose, to struggle with, to conquer.

"Life is a struggle, has to be," he insisted. "If there is no struggle, there is no life—that's all."

"You're talking nonsense—masculine nonsense," the peace-ful Jeff replied. He was certainly a warm defender of Herland. "Ants don't raise their myriads by a struggle, do they? Or the bees?"

"Oh, if you go back to insects—and want to live in an anthill—! I tell you the higher grades of life are reached only through struggle—combat. There's no Drama here. Look at their plays! They make me sick."

He rather had us there. The drama of the country was—to our taste—rather flat. You see, they lacked the sex motive and, with it, jealousy. They had no interplay of warring nations, no aristocracy and its ambitions, no wealth and poverty oppo-sition.

I see I have said little about the economics of the place; it should have come before, but I'll go on about the drama now.

They had their own kind. There was a most impressive array

of pageantry, of processions, a sort of grand ritual, with their arts and their religion broadly blended. The very babies joined in it. To see one of their great annual festivals, with the massed and marching stateliness of those great mothers; the young women brave and noble, beautiful and strong; and then the children, taking part as naturally as ours would frolic round a Christmas tree—it was overpowering in the impression of joyous, triumphant life.

They had begun at a period when the drama, the dance, music, religion, and education were all very close together; and instead of developing them in detached lines, they had kept the connection. Let me try again to give, if I can, a faint sense of the difference in the life view—the background and basis on which their culture rested.

Ellador told me a lot about it. She took me to see the children, the growing girls, the special teachers. She picked out books for me to read. She always seemed to understand just what I wanted to know, and how to give it to me.

While Terry and Alima struck sparks and parted—he always madly drawn to her and she to him—she must have been, or she'd never have stood the way he behaved—Ellador and I had already a deep, restful feeling, as if we'd always had one another. Jeff and Celis were happy; there was no question of that; but it didn't seem to me as if they had the good times we did.

Well, here is the Herland child facing life—as Ellador tried to show it to me. From the first memory, they knew Peace, Beauty, Order, Safety, Love, Wisdom, Justice, Patience, and Plenty. By "plenty" I mean that the babies grew up in an environment which met their needs, just as young fawns might grow up in dewy forest glades and brook-fed meadows. And they enjoyed it as frankly and utterly as the fawns would.

They found themselves in a big bright lovely world, full of the most interesting and enchanting things to learn about and to do. The people everywhere were friendly and polite. No Herland child ever met the overbearing rudeness we so commonly show to children. They were People, too, from the first; the most precious part of the nation.

In each step of the rich experience of living, they found the instance they were studying widen out into contact with an endless range of common interests. The things they learned were *related,* from the first; related to one another, and to the national prosperity.

"It was a butterfly that made me a forester," said Ellador. "I was about eleven years old, and I found a big purple-and-green butterfly on a low flower. I caught it, very carefully, by the closed wings, as I had been told to do, and carried it to the nearest insect teacher"—I made a note there to ask her what on earth an insect teacher was—"to ask her its name. She took it from me with a little cry of delight. 'Oh, you blessed child,' she said. 'Do you like obernuts?' Of course I liked obernuts, and said so. It is our best food-nut, you know. 'This is a female of the obernut moth,' she told me. 'They are almost gone. We have been trying to exterminate them for centuries. If you had not caught this one, it might have laid eggs enough to raise worms enough to destroy thousands of our nut trees—thousands of bushels of nuts—and make years and years of trouble for us.'

"Everybody congratulated me. The children all over the country were told to watch for that moth, if there were any more. I was shown the history of the creature, and an account of the damage it used to do and of how long and hard our foremothers had worked to save that tree for us. I grew a foot, it seemed to me, and determined then and there to be a forester."

This is but an instance; she showed me many. The big difference was that whereas our children grow up in private homes and families, with every effort made to protect and seclude them from a dangerous world, here they grew up in a wide, friendly world, and knew it for theirs, from the first.

Their child literature was a wonderful thing. I could have spent years following the delicate subtleties, the smooth simplicities with which they had bent that great art to the service of the child mind.

We have two life cycles: the man's and the woman's. To the man there is growth, struggle, conquest, the establishment of his family, and as much further success in gain or ambition as he can achieve.

To the woman, growth, the securing of a husband, the sub-
ordinate activities of family life, and afterward such "social"
or charitable interests as her position allows.

Here was but one cycle, and that a large one.

The child entered upon a broad open field of life, in which
motherhood was the one great personal contribution to the
national life, and all the rest the individual share in their common activities. Every girl I talked to, at any age above babyhood, had her cheerful determination as to what she was going
to be when she grew up.

What Terry meant by saying they had no "modesty" was
that this great life-view had no shady places; they had a high
sense of personal decorum, but no shame—no knowledge of
anything to be ashamed of.

Even their shortcomings and misdeeds in childhood never
were presented to them as sins; merely as errors and misplays—
as in a game. Some of them, who were palpably less agreeable
than others or who had a real weakness or fault, were treated
with cheerful allowance, as a friendly group at whist would
treat a poor player.

Their religion, you see, was maternal; and their ethics, based
on the full perception of evolution, showed the principle of
growth and the beauty of wise culture. They had no theory of
the essential opposition of good and evil; life to them was
Growth; their pleasure was in growing, and their duty also.

With this background, with their sublimated mother-love,
expressed in terms of widest social activity, every phase of
their work was modified by its effect on the national growth.
The language itself they had deliberately clarified, simplified,
made easy and beautiful, for the sake of the children.

This seemed to us a wholly incredible thing: first, that any nation should have the foresight, the strength, and the persistence
to plan and fulfill such a task; and second, that women should
have had so much initiative. We have assumed, as a matter of
course, that women had none; that only the man, with his natural
energy and impatience of restriction, would ever invent anything.

Here we found that the pressure of life upon the environment develops in the human mind its inventive reactions,

regardless of sex; and further, that a fully awakened motherhood plans and works without limit, for the good of the child.

That the children might be most nobly born, and reared in an environment calculated to allow the richest, freest growth, they had deliberately remodeled and improved the whole state.

I do not mean in the least that they stopped at that, any more than a child stops at childhood. The most impressive part of their whole culture beyond this perfect system of child-rearing was the range of interests and associations open to them all, for life. But in the field of literature I was most struck, at first, by the child motive.

They had the same gradation of simple repetitive verse and story that we are familiar with, and the most exquisite, imaginative tales; but where, with us, these are the dribbled remnants of ancient folk myths and primitive lullabies, theirs were the exquisite work of great artists; not only simple and unfailing in appeal to the child-mind, but *true*, true to the living world about them.

To sit in one of their nurseries for a day was to change one's views forever as to babyhood. The youngest ones, rosy fatlings in their mothers' arms, or sleeping lightly in the flower-sweet air, seemed natural enough, save that they never cried. I never heard a child cry in Herland, save once or twice at a bad fall; and then people ran to help, as we would at a scream of agony from a grown person.

Each mother had her year of Glory; the time to love and learn, living closely with her child, nursing it proudly, often for two years or more. This perhaps was one reason for their wonderful vigor.

But after the baby-year the mother was not so constantly in attendance, unless, indeed, her work was among the little ones. She was never far off, however, and her attitude toward the co-mothers, whose proud child-service was direct and continuous, was lovely to see.

As for the babies—a group of those naked darlings playing on short velvet grass, clean-swept; or rugs as soft; or in shallow pools of bright water; tumbling over with bubbling joyous baby laughter—it was a view of infant happiness such as I had never dreamed.

The babies were reared in the warmer part of the country, and gradually acclimated to the cooler heights as they grew older.

Sturdy children of ten and twelve played in the snow as joyfully as ours do; there were continuous excursions of them, from one part of the land to another, so that to each child the whole country might be home.

It was all theirs, waiting for them to learn, to love, to use, to serve; as our own little boys plan to be "a big soldier," or "a cowboy," or whatever pleases their fancy; and our little girls plan for the kind of home they mean to have, or how many children; these planned, freely and gaily with much happy chattering, of what they would do for the country when they were grown.

It was the eager happiness of the children and young people which first made me see the folly of that common notion of ours—that if life was smooth and happy, people would not enjoy it. As I studied these youngsters, vigorous, joyous, eager little creatures, and their voracious appetite for life, it shook my previous ideas so thoroughly that they have never been re-established. The steady level of good health gave them all that natural stimulus we used to call "animal spirits"—an odd contradiction in terms. They found themselves in an immediate environment which was agreeable and interesting, and before them stretched the years of learning and discovery, the fascinating, endless process of education.

As I looked into these methods and compared them with our own, my strange uncomfortable sense of race-humility grew apace.

Ellador could not understand my astonishment. She explained things kindly and sweetly, but with some amazement that they needed explaining, and with sudden questions as to how we did it that left me meeker than ever.

I betook myself to Somel one day, carefully not taking Ellador. I did not mind seeming foolish to Somel—she was used to it.

"I want a chapter of explanation," I told her. "You know my stupidities by heart, and I do not want to show them to Ellador—she thinks me so wise!"

She smiled delightedly. "It is beautiful to see," she told me, "this new wonderful love between you. The whole country is interested, you know—how can we help it!"

I had not thought of that. We say: "All the world loves a lover," but to have a couple of million people watching one's courtship—and that a difficult one—was rather embarrassing.

"Tell me about your theory of education," I said. "Make it short and easy. And, to show you what puzzles me, I'll tell you that in our theory great stress is laid on the forced exertion of the child's mind; we think it is good for him to overcome obstacles."

"Of course it is," she unexpectedly agreed. "All our children do that—they love to."

That puzzled me again. If they loved to do it, how could it be educational?

"Our theory is this," she went on carefully. "Here is a young human being. The mind is as natural a thing as the body, a thing that grows, a thing to use and to enjoy. We seek to nourish, to stimulate, to exercise the mind of a child as we do the body. There are the two main divisions in education—you have those of course?—the things it is necessary to know, and things it is necessary to do."

"To do? Mental exercises, you mean?"

"Yes. Our general plan is this: in the matter of feeding the mind, of furnishing information, we use our best powers to meet the natural appetite of a healthy young brain; not to overfeed it, to provide such amount and variety of impressions as seem most welcome to each child. That is the easiest part. The other division is in arranging a properly graduated series of exercises which will best develop each mind; the common faculties we all have, and most carefully, the especial faculties some of us have. You do this also, do you not?"

"In a way," I said rather lamely. "We have not so subtle and highly developed a system as you, not approaching it; but tell me more. As to the information—how do you manage? It appears that all of you know pretty much everything—is that right?"

This she laughingly disclaimed. "By no means. We are, as you soon found out, extremely limited in knowledge. I wish you could realize what a ferment the country is in over the new things you have told us; the passionate eagerness among thousands of us to go to your country and learn—learn—learn! But what we do know is readily divisible into common knowledge and special knowledge. The common knowledge we have long since learned to feed into the minds of our little ones with no waste of time or strength; the special knowledge is open to all, as they desire it. Some of us specialize in one line only. But most take up several—some for their regular work, some to grow with."

"To grow with?"

"Yes. When one settles too close in one kind of work there is a tendency to atrophy in the disused portions of the brain. We like to keep on learning, always."

"What do you study?"

"As much as we know of the different sciences. We have, within our limits, a good deal of knowledge of anatomy, physiology, nutrition—all that pertains to a full and beautiful personal life. We have our botany and chemistry, and so on—very rudimentary, but interesting; our own history, with its accumulating psychology."

"You put psychology with history—not with personal life?"

"Of course. It is ours; it is among and between us, and it changes with the succeeding and improving generations. We are at work, slowly and carefully, developing our whole people along these lines. It is glorious work—splendid! To see the thousands of babies improving, showing stronger clearer minds, sweeter dispositions, higher capacities—don't you find it so in your country?"

This I evaded flatly. I remembered the cheerless claim that the human mind was no better than in its earliest period of savagery, only better informed—a statement I had never believed.

"We try most earnestly for two powers," Somel continued.

"The two that seem to us basically necessary for all noble life: a clear, far-reaching judgment, and a strong well-used will. We spend our best efforts, all through childhood and youth, in developing these faculties, individual judgment and will."

"As part of your system of education, you mean?"

"Exactly. As the most valuable part. With the babies, as you may have noticed, we first provide an environment which feeds the mind without tiring it; all manner of simple and interesting things to do, as soon as they are old enough to do them; physical properties, of course, come first. But as early as possible, going very carefully, not to tax the mind, we provide choices, simple choices, with very obvious causes and consequences. You've noticed the games?"

I had. The children seemed always playing something; or else, sometimes, engaged in peaceful researches of their own. I had wondered at first when they went to school, but soon found that they never did—to their knowledge. It was all education but no schooling.

"We have been working for some sixteen hundred years, devising better and better games for children," continued Somel.

I sat aghast. "Devising games?" I protested. "Making up new ones, you mean?"

"Exactly," she answered. "Don't you?"

Then I remembered the kindergarten, and the "material" devised by Signora Montessori, and guardedly replied: "To some extent." But most of our games, I told her, were very old—came down from child to child, along the ages, from the remote past.

"And what is their effect?" she asked. "Do they develop the faculties you wish to encourage?"

Again I remembered the claims made by the advocates of "sports," and again replied guardedly that that was, in part, the theory.

"But do the children *like* it?" I asked. "Having things made up and set before them that way? Don't they want the old games?"

"You can see the children," she answered. "Are yours more contented—more interested—happier?"

Then I thought, as in truth I never had thought before, of the dull, bored children I had seen, whining: "What can I do now?"; of the little groups and gangs hanging about; of the value of some one strong spirit who possessed initiative and would "start something"; of the children's parties and the onerous duties of the older people set to "amuse the children"; also of that troubled ocean of misdirected activity we call "mischief," the foolish, destructive, sometimes evil things done by unoccupied children.

"No," said I grimly. "I don't think they are."

The Herland child was born not only into a world carefully prepared, full of the most fascinating materials and opportunities to learn, but into the society of plentiful numbers of teachers, teachers born and trained, whose business it was to accompany the children along that, to us, impossible thing—the royal road to learning.

There was no mystery in their methods. Being adapted to children it was at least comprehensible to adults. I spent many days with the little ones, sometimes with Ellador, sometimes without, and began to feel a crushing pity for my own childhood, and for all others that I had known.

The houses and gardens planned for babies had in them nothing to hurt—no stairs, no corners, no small loose objects to swallow, no fire—just a babies' paradise. They were taught, as rapidly as feasible, to use and control their own bodies, and never did I see such sure-footed, steady-handed, clear-headed little things. It was a joy to watch a row of toddlers learning to walk, not only on a level floor, but, a little later, on a sort of rubber rail raised an inch or two above the soft turf or heavy rugs, and falling off with shrieks of infant joy, to rush back to the end of the line and try again. Surely we have noticed how children love to get up on something and walk along it! But we have never thought to provide that simple and inexhaustible form of amusement and physical education for the young.

Water they had, of course, and could swim even before they walked. If I feared at first the effects of a too intensive system of culture, that fear was dissipated by seeing the long sunny days of pure physical merriment and natural sleep in which these heavenly babies passed their first years. They never knew they were being educated. They did not dream that in this association of hilarious experiment and achievement they were laying the foundation for that close beautiful group feeling into which they grew so firmly with the years. This was education for citizenship.

CHAPTER X

THEIR RELIGIONS AND OUR MARRIAGES

It took me a long time, as a man, a foreigner, and a species of Christian—I was that as much as anything—to get any clear understanding of the religion of Herland.

Its deification of motherhood was obvious enough; but there was far more to it than that; or, at least, than my first interpretation of that.

I think it was only as I grew to love Ellador more than I believed anyone could love anybody, as I grew faintly to appreciate her inner attitude and state of mind, that I began to get some glimpses of this faith of theirs.

When I asked her about it, she tried at first to tell me, and then, seeing me flounder, asked for more information about ours. She soon found that we had many, that they varied widely, but had some points in common. A clear methodical luminous mind had my Ellador, not only reasonable, but swiftly perceptive.

She made a sort of chart, superimposing the different religions as I described them, with a pin run through them all, as it were; their common basis being a Dominant Power or Powers, and some Special Behavior, mostly taboos, to please or placate. There were some common features in certain groups of religions, but the one always present was this Power, and the things which must be done or not done because of it. It was not hard to trace our human imagery of the Divine Force up through successive stages of bloodthirsty, sensual, proud, and cruel gods of early times to the conception of a Common Father with its corollary of a Common Brotherhood.

This pleased her very much, and when I expatiated on the Omniscience, Omnipotence, Omnipresence, and so on, of our God, and of the loving kindness taught by his Son, she was much impressed.

The story of the Virgin birth naturally did not astonish her, but she was greatly puzzled by the Sacrifice, and still more by the Devil, and the theory of Damnation.

When in an inadvertent moment I said that certain sects had believed in infant damnation—and explained it—she sat very still indeed.

"They believed that God was Love—and Wisdom—and Power?"

"Yes—all of that."

Her eyes grew large, her face ghastly pale.

"And yet that such a God could put little new babies to burn—for eternity?" She fell into a sudden shuddering and left me, running swiftly to the nearest Temple.

Every smallest village had its Temple, and in those gracious retreats sat wise and noble women, quietly busy at some work of their own until they were wanted, always ready to give comfort, light, or help, to any applicant.

Ellador told me afterward how easily this grief of hers was assuaged and seemed ashamed of not having helped herself out of it.

"You see, we are not accustomed to horrible ideas," she said, coming back to me rather apologetically. "We haven't any. And when we get a thing like that into our minds, it's like—oh, like red pepper in your eyes. So I just ran to her, blinded and almost screaming, and she took it out so quickly—so easily!"

"How?" I asked, very curious.

"'Why, you blessed child,' she said, 'you've got the wrong idea altogether. You do not have to think that there ever was such a God—for there wasn't. Or such a happening—for there wasn't. Nor even that this hideous false idea was believed by anybody. But only this—that people who are utterly ignorant will believe anything—which you certainly knew before.'"

"Anyhow," pursued Ellador, "she turned pale for a minute when I first said it."

This was a lesson to me. No wonder this whole nation of

women was peaceful and sweet in expression—they had no horrible ideas.

"Surely you had some when you began," I suggested.

"Oh, yes, no doubt. But as soon as our religion grew to any height at all we left them out of course."

From this, as from many other things, I grew to see what I finally put in words.

"Have you no respect for the past? For what was thought and believed by your foremothers?"

"Why, no," she said. "Why should we? They are all gone. They knew less than we do. If we are not beyond them, we are unworthy of them—and unworthy of the children who must go beyond us."

This set me thinking in good earnest. I had always imagined—simply from hearing it said, I suppose—that women were by nature conservative. Yet these women, quite unassisted by any masculine spirit of enterprise, had ignored their past and built daringly for the future.

Ellador watched me think. She seemed to know pretty much what was going on in my mind.

"It's because we began in a new way, I suppose. All our folks were swept away at once, and then, after that time of despair, came those wonder children—the first. And then the whole breathless hope of us was for *their* children—if they should have them. And they did! Then there was the period of pride and triumph till we grew too numerous; and after that, when it all came down to one child apiece, we began to really work—to make better ones."

"But how does this account for such a radical difference in your religion?" I persisted.

She said she couldn't talk about the difference very intelligently, not being familiar with other religions, but that theirs seemed simple enough. Their great Mother Spirit was to them what their own motherhood was—only magnified beyond human limits. That meant that they felt beneath and behind them an upholding, unfailing, serviceable love—perhaps it was really the accumulated mother-love of the race they felt—but it was a Power.

"Just what is your theory of worship?" I asked her.

"Worship? What is that?"

I found it singularly difficult to explain. This Divine Love which they felt so strongly did not seem to ask anything of them—"any more than our mothers do," she said.

"But surely your mothers expect honor, reverence, obedience, from you. You have to do things for your mothers, surely?"

"Oh, no," she insisted, smiling, shaking her soft brown hair. "We do things *from* our mothers—not *for* them. We don't have to do things *for* them—they don't need it, you know. But we have to live on—splendidly—because of them; and that's the way we feel about God."

I meditated again. I thought of that "God of Battles" of ours, that Jealous God, that "Vengeance-is-mine God." I thought of our world-nightmare—Hell.

"You have no theory of eternal punishment then, I take it?"

Ellador laughed. Her eyes were as bright as stars, and there were tears in them, too. She was so sorry for me.

"How could we?" she asked, fairly enough. "We have no punishments in life, you see, so we don't imagine them after death."

"Have you *no* punishments? Neither for children nor criminals—such mild criminals as you have?" I urged.

"Do you punish a person for a broken leg or a fever? We have preventive measures, and cures; sometimes we have to 'send the patient to bed,' as it were; but that's not a punishment—it's only part of the treatment," she explained.

Then studying my point of view more closely, she added: "You see, we recognize, in our human motherhood, a great tender limitless uplifting force—patience and wisdom and all subtlety of delicate method. We credit God—our idea of God—with all that and more. Our mothers are not angry with us—why should God be?"

"Does God mean a person to you?"

This she thought over a little. "Why—in trying to get close to it in our minds we personify the idea, naturally; but we certainly do not assume a Big Woman somewhere, who is God. What we call God is a Pervading Power, you know, an Indwelling Spirit, something inside of us that we want more of. Is your God a Big Man?" she asked innocently.

"Why—yes, to most of us, I think. Of course we call it an Indwelling Spirit just as you do, but we insist that it is Him, a Person, and a Man—with whiskers."

"Whiskers? Oh yes—because you have them! Or do you wear them because He does?"

"On the contrary, we shave them off—because it seems cleaner and more comfortable."

"Does He wear clothes—in your idea, I mean?"

I was thinking over the pictures of God I had seen—rash advances of the devout mind of man, representing his Omnipotent Deity as an old man in a flowing robe, flowing hair, flowing beard, and in the light of her perfectly frank and innocent questions this concept seemed rather unsatisfying.

I explained that the God of the Christian world was really the ancient Hebrew God, and that we had simply taken over the patriarchal idea—that ancient one which quite inevitably clothed its thought of God with the attributes of the patriarchal ruler, the Grandfather.

"I see," she said eagerly, after I had explained the genesis and development of our religious ideals. "They lived in separate groups, with a male head, and he was probably a little—domineering?"

"No doubt of that," I agreed.

"And we live together without any 'head,' in that sense—just our chosen leaders—that *does* make a difference."

"Your difference is deeper than that," I assured her. "It is in your common motherhood. Your children grow up in a world where everybody loves them. They find life made rich and happy for them by the diffused love and wisdom of all mothers. So it is easy for you to think of God in the terms of a similar diffused and competent love. I think you are far nearer right than we are."

"What I cannot understand," she pursued carefully, "is your preservation of such a very ancient state of mind. This patriarchal idea you tell me is thousands of years old?"

"Oh yes—four, five, six thousand—ever so many."

"And you have made wonderful progress in those years—in other things?"

"We certainly have. But religion is different. You see, our religions come from behind us, and are initiated by some great teacher who is dead. He is supposed to have known the whole thing and taught it, finally. All we have to do is Believe—and Obey."

"Who was the great Hebrew teacher?"

"Oh—there it was different. The Hebrew religion is an accumulation of extremely ancient traditions, some far older than their people, and grew by accretion down the ages. We consider it inspired—'the Word of God.'"

"How do you know it is?"

"Because it says so?"

"Does it say so in as many words? Who wrote that in?"

I began to try to recall some text that did say so, and could not bring it to mind.

"Apart from that," she pursued, "what I cannot understand is why you keep these early religious ideas so long. You have changed all your others, haven't you?"

"Pretty generally," I agreed. "But this we call 'revealed religion,' and think it is final. But tell me more about these little Temples of yours," I urged. "And these Temple Mothers you run to."

Then she gave me an extended lesson in applied religion, which I will endeavor to concentrate.

They developed their central theory of a Loving Power, and assumed that its relation to them was motherly—that it desired their welfare and especially their development. Their relation to it, similarly, was filial, a loving appreciation and a glad fulfillment of its high purposes. Then, being nothing if not practical, they set their keen and active minds to discover the kind of conduct expected of them. This worked out in a most admirable system of ethics. The principle of Love was universally recognized—and used.

Patience, gentleness, courtesy, all that we call "good breeding," was part of their code of conduct. But where they went far beyond us was in the special application of religious feeling to every field of life. They had no ritual, no little set of performances called "divine service," save those glorious pageants I have spoken of, and those were as much educational as religious, and as much social as either. But they had a clear established connection between everything they did—and God. Their cleanliness, their health, their exquisite order, the rich peaceful beauty of the whole land, the happiness of the children, and above all the constant progress they made—all this was their religion.

They applied their minds to the thought of God, and worked out the theory that such an inner power demanded outward expression. They lived as if God was real and at work within them.

As for those little temples everywhere—some of the women were more skilled, more temperamentally inclined, in this direction, than others. These, whatever their work might be, gave certain hours to the Temple Service, which meant being there with all their love and wisdom and trained thought, to smooth out rough places for anyone who needed it. Sometimes it was a real grief, very rarely a quarrel, most often a perplexity; even in Herland the human soul had its hours of darkness. But all through the country their best and wisest were ready to give help.

If the difficulty was unusually profound, the applicant was directed to someone more specially experienced in that line of thought.

Here was a religion which gave to the searching mind a rational basis in life, the concept of an immense Loving Power working steadily out through them, toward good. It gave to the "soul" that sense of contact with the inmost force, of perception of the uttermost purpose, which we always crave. It gave to the "heart" the blessed feeling of being loved, loved and *understood*. It gave clear, simple, rational directions as to how we should live—and why. And for ritual it gave first those triumphant group demonstrations, when with a union of all the arts, the revivifying combination of great multitudes moved rhythmically with march and dance, song and music, among their own noblest products and the open beauty of their groves and hills. Second, it gave these numerous little centers of wisdom where the least wise could go to the most wise and be helped.

"It is beautiful!" I cried enthusiastically. "It is the most practical, comforting, progressive religion I ever heard of. You *do* love one another—you *do* bear one another's burdens—you *do* realize that a little child is a type of the kingdom of heaven. You are more Christian than any people I ever saw. But—how about Death? And the Life Everlasting? What does your religion teach about Eternity?"

"Nothing," said Ellador. "What is Eternity?"

What indeed? I tried, for the first time in my life, to get a real hold on the idea.

"It is—never stopping."

"Never stopping?" She looked puzzled.

"Yes, life, going on forever."

"Oh—we see that, of course. Life does go on forever, all about us."

"But eternal life goes on *without dying.*"

"The same person?"

"Yes, the same person, unending, immortal." I was pleased to think that I had something to teach from our religion, which theirs had never promulgated.

"Here?" asked Ellador. "Never to die—here?" I could see her practical mind heaping up the people, and hurriedly reassured her.

"Oh no, indeed, not here—hereafter. We must die here, of course, but then we 'enter into eternal life.' The soul lives forever."

"How do you know?" she inquired.

"I won't attempt to prove it to you," I hastily continued. "Let us assume it to be so. How does this idea strike you?"

Again she smiled at me, that adorable, dimpling, tender, mischievous, motherly smile of hers. "Shall I be quite, quite honest?"

"You couldn't be anything else," I said, half gladly and half a little sorry. The transparent honesty of these women was a never-ending astonishment to me.

"It seems to me a singularly foolish idea," she said calmly. "And if true, most disagreeable."

Now I had always accepted the doctrine of personal immortality as a thing established. The efforts of inquiring Spiritualists, always seeking to woo their beloved ghosts back again, never seemed to me necessary. I don't say I had ever seriously and courageously discussed the subject with myself even; I had simply assumed it to be a fact. And here was the girl I loved, this creature whose character constantly revealed new heights and ranges far beyond my own, this superwoman of a superland, saying she thought immortality foolish! She meant it, too.

"What do you *want* it for?" she asked.

"How can you *not* want it!" I protested. "Do you want to go out like a candle? Don't you want to go on and on—growing and—and—being happy, forever?"

"Why, no," she said. "I don't in the least. I want my child—and my child's child—to go on—and they will. Why should *I* want to?"

"But it means Heaven!" I insisted. "Peace and Beauty and Comfort and Love—with God." I had never been so eloquent on the subject of religion. She could be horrified at Damnation, and question the justice of Salvation, but Immortality—that was surely a noble faith.

"Why, Van," she said, holding out her hands to me. "Why Van—darling! How splendid of you to feel it so keenly. That's what we all want, of course—Peace and Beauty, and Comfort and Love—with God! And Progress too, remember; Growth, always and always. That is what our religion teaches us to want and to work for, and we do!"

"But that is *here*," I said, "only for this life on earth."

"Well? And do not you in your country, with your beautiful religion of love and service have it here, too—for this life—on earth?"

None of us were willing to tell the women of Herland about the evils of our own beloved land. It was all very well for us to assume them to be necessary and essential, and to criticize—strictly among ourselves—their all-too-perfect civilization, but when it came to telling them about the failures and wastes of our own, we never could bring ourselves to do it.

Moreover, we sought to avoid too much discussion, and to press the subject of our approaching marriages.

Jeff was the determined one on this score.

"Of course they haven't any marriage ceremony or service, but we can make it a sort of Quaker wedding, and have it in the Temple—it is the least we can do for them."

It was. There was so little, after all, that we could do for them. Here we were, penniless guests and strangers, with no chance even to use our strength and courage—nothing to defend them from or protect them against.

"We can at least give them our names," Jeff insisted.

They were very sweet about it, quite willing to do whatever we asked, to please us. As to the names, Alima, frank soul that she was, asked what good it would do.

Terry, always irritating her, said it was a sign of possession. "You are going to be Mrs. Nicholson," he said, "Mrs. T. O. Nicholson. That shows everyone that you are my wife."

"What is a 'wife' exactly?" she demanded, a dangerous gleam in her eye.

"A wife is the woman who belongs to a man," he began.

But Jeff took it up eagerly: "And a husband is the man who belongs to a woman. It is because we are monogamous, you know. And marriage is the ceremony, civil and religious, that joins the two together—'until death do us part,'" he finished, looking at Celis with unutterable devotion.

"What makes us all feel foolish," I told the girls, "is that here we have nothing to give you—except, of course, our names."

"Do your women have no names before they are married?" Celis suddenly demanded.

"Why, yes," Jeff explained. "They have their maiden names—their father's names, that is."

"And what becomes of them?" asked Alima.

"They change them for their husbands', my dear," Terry answered her.

"Change them? Do the husbands then take the wives' 'maiden names'?"

"Oh, no," he laughed. "The man keeps his own and gives it to her, too."

"Then she just loses hers and takes a new one—how unpleasant! We won't do that!" Alima said decidedly.

Terry was good-humored about it. "I don't care what you do or don't do so long as we have that wedding pretty soon," he said, reaching a strong brown hand after Alima's, quite as brown and nearly as strong.

"As to giving us things—of course we can see that you'd like to, but we are glad you can't," Celis continued. "You see, we love you just for yourselves—we wouldn't want you to—to pay anything. Isn't it enough to know that you are loved personally—and just as men?"

Enough or not, that was the way we were married. We had a great triple wedding in the biggest Temple of all, and it looked as if most of the nation were present. It was very solemn and very beautiful. Someone had written a new song for the occasion, nobly beautiful, about the New Hope for their people—the New Tie with other lands—Brotherhood as well as Sisterhood, and, with evident awe, Fatherhood.

Terry was always restive under their talk of fatherhood. "Anybody'd think we were High Priests of—of Philoprogenitiveness!" he protested. "These women think of *nothing* but children, seems to me! We'll teach 'em!"

He was so certain of what he was going to teach, and Alima so uncertain in her moods of reception, that Jeff and I feared the worst. We tried to caution him—much good that did. The big handsome fellow drew himself up to his full height, lifted that great chest of his, and laughed.

"There are three separate marriages," he said. "I won't interfere with yours—nor you with mine."

So the great day came, and the countless crowds of women, and we three bridegrooms without any supporting "best men," or any other men to back us up, felt strangely small as we came forward.

Somel and Zava and Moadine were on hand; we were thankful to have them, too—they seemed almost like relatives.

There was a splendid procession, wreathing dances, the new Anthem I spoke of, and the whole great place pulsed with feeling—the deep awe, the sweet hope, the wondering expectation of a new miracle.

"There has been nothing like this in the country since our Motherhood began!" Somel said softly to me, while we watched the symbolic marches. "You see, it is the dawn of a new era. You don't know how much you mean to us. It is not only Fatherhood—that marvelous dual parentage to which we are strangers—the miracle of union in life-giving—but it is Brotherhood. You are the rest of the world. You join us to our kind—to all the strange lands and peoples we have never seen. We hope to know them—to love and help them—and to learn of them. Ah! You cannot know!"

Thousands of voices rose in the soaring climax of that great Hymn of The Coming Life. By the great Altar of Motherhood, with its crown of fruit and flowers, stood a new one, crowned as well. Before the Great Over Mother of the Land and her ring of High Temple Counsellors, before that vast multitude of calm-faced mothers and holy-eyed maidens, came forward our own three chosen ones, and we, three men alone in all that land, joined hands with them and made our marriage vows.

CHAPTER XI

OUR DIFFICULTIES

We say, "marriage is a lottery"; also "Marriages are made in Heaven"—but this is not so widely accepted as the other.

We have a well-founded theory that it is best to marry "in one's class," and certain well-grounded suspicions of international marriages, which seem to persist in the interests of social progress, rather than in those of the contracting parties.

But no combination of alien races, of color, caste, or creed, was ever so basically difficult to establish as that between us, three modern American men, and these three women of Herland.

It is all very well to say that we should have been frank about it beforehand. We had been frank. We had discussed—at least Ellador and I had—the conditions of The Great Adventure, and thought the path was clear before us. But there are some things one takes for granted, supposes are mutually understood, and to which both parties may repeatedly refer without ever meaning the same thing.

The differences in the education of the average man and woman are great enough, but the trouble they make is not mostly for the man; he generally carries out his own views of the case. The woman may have imagined the conditions of married life to be different; but what she imagined, was ignorant of, or might have preferred, did not seriously matter.

I can see clearly and speak calmly about this now, writing after a lapse of years, years full of growth and education, but at the time it was rather hard sledding for all of us—especially for Terry. Poor Terry! You see, in any other imaginable marriage among the peoples of the earth, whether the woman were black, red, yellow, brown, or white; whether she were ignorant or educated, submissive or rebellious, she would have behind her the marriage tradition of our general history. This tradition relates the woman to the man. He goes on with his business, and she adapts herself to him and to it. Even in citizenship, by some strange hocus-pocus, that fact of birth and geography was waved aside, and the woman automatically acquired the nationality of her husband.

Well—here were we, three aliens in this land of women. It was small in area, and the external differences were not so great as to astound us. We did not yet appreciate the differences between the race-mind of this people and ours.

In the first place, they were a "pure stock" of two thousand uninterrupted years. Where we have some long connected lines of thought and feeling, together with a wide range of differences, often irreconcilable, these people were smoothly and firmly agreed on most of the basic principles of their life; and not only agreed in principle, but accustomed for these sixty-odd generations to act on those principles.

This is one thing which we did not understand—had made no allowance for. When in our pre-marital discussions one of those dear girls had said: "We understand it thus and thus," or "We hold such and such to be true," we men, in our own deep-seated convictions of the power of love, and our easy views about beliefs and principles, fondly imagined that we could convince them otherwise. What we imagined, before marriage, did not matter any more than what an average innocent young girl imagines. We found the facts to be different.

It was not that they did not love us; they did, deeply and warmly. But there you are again—what they meant by "love" and what we meant by "love" were so different.

Perhaps it seems rather cold-blooded to say "we" and "they," as if we were not separate couples, with our separate joys and sorrows, but our positions as aliens drove us together constantly. The whole strange experience had made our friendship more close and intimate than it would ever have become in a free and easy lifetime among our own people. Also, as men, with our masculine tradition of far more than two thousand years, we were a unit, small but firm, against this far larger unit of feminine tradition.

I think I can make clear the points of difference without a too painful explicitness. The more external disagreement was in the matter of "the home," and the housekeeping duties and pleasures we, by instinct and long education, supposed to be inherently appropriate to women.

I will give two illustrations, one away up, and the other away down, to show how completely disappointed we were in this regard.

For the lower one, try to imagine a male ant, coming from some state of existence where ants live in pairs, endeavoring to set up housekeeping with a female ant from a highly developed ant-hill. This female ant might regard him with intense personal affection, but her ideas of parentage and economic management would be on a very different scale from his. Now, of course, if she was a stray female in a country of pairing ants, he might have had his way with her; but if he was a stray male in an ant-hill—!

For the higher one, try to imagine a devoted and impassioned man trying to set up housekeeping with a lady Angel, a real wings-and-harp-and-halo Angel, accustomed to fulfilling Divine missions all over interstellar space. This Angel might love the man with an affection quite beyond his power of return or even of appreciation, but her ideas of service and duty would be on a very different scale from his. Of course, if she was a stray Angel in a country of men, he might have had his way with her; but if he was a stray man among Angels—!

Terry, at his worst, in a black fury for which, as a man, I must have some sympathy, preferred the ant simile. More of Terry and his special troubles later. It was hard on Terry.

Jeff—well, Jeff always had a streak that was too good for this world! He's the kind that would have made a saintly priest in earlier times. He accepted the Angel theory, swallowed it whole, tried to force it on us—with varying effect. He so worshipped Celis, and not only Celis, but what she represented; he had become so deeply convinced of the almost supernatural advantages of this country and people, that he took his medicine like a—I cannot say "like a man," but more as if he wasn't one.

Don't misunderstand me for a moment. Dear old Jeff was no milksop or molly-coddle either. He was a strong, brave, efficient man, and an excellent fighter when fighting was necessary. But there was always this angel streak in him. It was rather a wonder, Terry being so different, that he really loved Jeff as he did; but it happens so sometimes, in spite of the difference—perhaps because of it.

As for me, I stood between. I was no such gay Lothario as Terry, and no such Galahad as Jeff. But for all my limitations I think I had the habit of using my brains in regard to behavior rather more frequently than either of them. I had to use brainpower now, I can tell you.

The big point at issue between us and our wives was, as may easily be imagined, in the very nature of the relation.

"Wives! Don't talk to me about wives!" stormed Terry. "They don't know what the word means."

Which is exactly the fact—they didn't. How could they? Back in their prehistoric records of polygamy and slavery there were no ideals of wifehood as we know it, and since then no possibility of forming such.

"The only thing they can think of about a man is *Fatherhood!*" said Terry in high scorn. "*Fatherhood!* As if a man was always wanting to be a *father!*"

This also was correct. They had their long, wide, deep, rich experience of Motherhood, and their only perception of the value of a male creature as such was for Fatherhood.

Aside from that, of course, was the whole range of personal love, love which as Jeff earnestly phrased it "passeth the love of women!" It did, too. I can give no idea—either now, after long and happy experience of it, or as it seemed then, in the first measureless wonder—of the beauty and power of the love they gave us.

Even Alima—who had a more stormy temperament than either of the others, and who, heaven knows, had far more provocation—even Alima was patience and tenderness and wisdom personified to the man she loved, until he—but I haven't got to that yet.

These, as Terry put it, "alleged or so-called wives" of ours, went right on with their profession as foresters. We, having no special leanings, had long since qualified as assistants. We had to do something, if only to pass the time, and it had to be work—we couldn't be playing forever.

This kept us out of doors with those dear girls, and more or less together—too much together sometimes.

These people had, it now became clear to us, the highest, keenest, most delicate sense of personal privacy, but not the faintest idea of that "*solitude à deux*" we are so fond of. They had, every one of them, the "two rooms and a bath" theory realized. From earliest childhood each had a separate bedroom with toilet conveniences, and one of the marks of coming of age was the addition of an outer room in which to receive friends.

Long since we had been given our own two rooms apiece, and as being of a different sex and race, these were in a separate house. It seemed to be recognized that we should breathe easier if able to free our minds in real seclusion.

For food we either went to any convenient eating-house, ordered a meal brought in, or took it with us to the woods, always and equally good. All this we had become used to and enjoyed—in our courting days.

After marriage there arose in us a somewhat unexpected urge of feeling that called for a separate house; but this feeling found no response in the hearts of those fair ladies.

"We *are* alone, dear," Ellador explained to me with gentle patience. "We are alone in these great forests; we may go and eat in any little summer-house—just we two, or have a separate table anywhere—or even have a separate meal in our own rooms. How could we be aloner?"

This was all very true. We had our pleasant mutual solitude about our work, and our pleasant evening talks in their apartments or ours; we had, as it were, all the pleasures of courtship carried right on; but we had no sense of—perhaps it may be called possession.

"Might as well not be married at all," growled Terry. "They only got up that ceremony to please us—please Jeff, mostly. They've no real idea of being married."

I tried my best to get Ellador's point of view, and naturally I tried to give her mine. Of course, what we, as men, wanted to make them see was that there were other, and as we proudly said "higher," uses in this relation than what Terry called "mere parentage." In the highest terms I knew I tried to explain this to Ellador.

"Anything higher than for mutual love to hope to give life, as we did?" she said. "How is it higher?"

"It develops love," I explained. "All the power of beautiful permanent mated love comes through this higher development."

"Are you sure?" she asked gently. "How do you know that it was so developed? There are some birds who love each other so that they mope and pine if separated, and never pair again if one dies, but they never mate except in the mating season. Among your people do you find high and lasting affection appearing in proportion to this indulgence?"

It is a very awkward thing, sometimes, to have a logical mind.

Of course I knew about those monogamous birds and beasts too, that mate for life and show every sign of mutual affection, without ever having stretched the sex relationship beyond its original range. But what of it?

"Those are lower forms of life!" I protested. "They have no capacity for faithful and affectionate, and apparently happy— but oh, my dear! my dear!—what can they know of such a love as draws us together? Why, to touch you—to be near you—to come closer and closer—to lose myself in you—surely you feel it too, do you not?"

I came nearer. I seized her hands.

Her eyes were on mine, tender, radiant, but steady and strong. There was something so powerful, so large and changeless, in those eyes that I could not sweep her off her feet by my own emotion as I had unconsciously assumed would be the case.

It made me feel as, one might imagine, a man might feel who loved a goddess—not a Venus, though! She did not resent my attitude, did not repel it, did not in the least fear it, evidently. There was not a shade of that timid withdrawal or pretty resistance which are so—provocative.

"You see, dearest," she said, "you have to be patient with us.

We are not like the women of your country. We are Mothers, and we are People, but we have not specialized in this line."

"We" and "we" and "we"—it was so hard to get her to be personal. And, as I thought that, I suddenly remembered how we were always criticizing *our* women for *being* so personal.

Then I did my earnest best to picture to her the sweet intense joy of married lovers, and the result in higher stimulus to all creative work.

"Do you mean," she asked quite calmly, as if I was not holding her cool firm hands in my hot and rather quivering ones, "that with you, when people marry, they go right on doing this in season and out of season, with no thought of children at all?"

"They do," I said, with some bitterness. "They are not mere parents. They are men and women, and they love each other."

"How long?" asked Ellador, rather unexpectedly.

"How long?" I repeated, a little dashed. "Why as long as they live."

"There is something very beautiful in the idea," she admitted, still as if she were discussing life on Mars. "This climactic expression, which, in all the other life-forms, has but the one purpose, has with you become specialized to higher, purer, nobler uses. It has—I judge from what you tell me—the most ennobling effect on character. People marry, not only for parentage, but for this exquisite interchange—and, as a result, you have a world full of continuous lovers, ardent, happy, mutually devoted, always living on that high tide of supreme emotion which we had supposed to belong only to one season and one use. And you say it has other results, stimulating all high creative work. That must mean floods, oceans of such work, blossoming from this intense happiness of every married pair! It is a beautiful idea!"

She was silent, thinking.

So was I.

She slipped one hand free, and was stroking my hair with it in a gentle motherly way. I bowed my hot head on her shoulder and felt a dim sense of peace, a restfulness which was very pleasant.

"You must take me there someday, darling," she was saying. "It is not only that I love you so much, I want to see your country—your people—your mother—" she paused reverently. "Oh, how I shall love your mother!"

I had not been in love many times—my experience did not compare with Terry's. But such as I had was so different from this that I was perplexed, and full of mixed feelings: partly a growing sense of common ground between us, a pleasant rested calm feeling, which I had imagined could only be attained in one way; and partly a bewildered resentment because what I found was not what I had looked for.

It was their confounded psychology! Here they were with this profound highly developed system of education so bred into them that even if they were not teachers by profession they all had a general proficiency in it—it was second nature to them.

And no child, stormily demanding a cookie "between meals," was ever more subtly diverted into an interest in housebuilding than was I when I found an apparently imperative demand had disappeared without my noticing it.

And all the time those tender mother eyes, those keen scientific eyes, noting every condition and circumstance, and learning how to "take time by the forelock" and avoid discussion before occasion arose.

I was amazed at the results. I found that much, very much, of what I had honestly supposed to be a physiological necessity was a psychological necessity—or so believed. I found, after my ideas of what was essential had changed, that my feelings changed also. And more than all, I found this—a factor of enormous weight—these women were not provocative. That made an immense difference.

The thing that Terry had so complained of when we first came—that they weren't "feminine," they lacked "charm," now became a great comfort. Their vigorous beauty was an aesthetic pleasure, not an irritant. Their dress and ornaments had not a touch of the "come-and-find-me" element.

Even with my own Ellador, my wife, who had for a time unveiled a woman's heart and faced the strange new hope and joy of dual parentage, she afterward withdrew again into the same good comrade she had been at first. They were women, *plus*, and so much plus that when they did not choose to let the womanness appear, you could not find it anywhere.

I don't say it was easy for me; it wasn't. But when I made appeal to her sympathies I came up against another immovable wall. She was sorry, honestly sorry, for my distresses, and made all manner of thoughtful suggestions, often quite useful, as well as the wise foresight I have mentioned above, which often saved all difficulty before it arose; but her sympathy did not alter her convictions.

"If I thought it was really right and necessary, I could perhaps bring myself to it, for your sake, dear; but I do not want to—not at all. You would not have a mere submission, would you? That is not the kind of high romantic love you spoke of, surely? It is a pity, of course, that you should have to adjust your highly specialized faculties to our unspecialized ones."

Confound it! I hadn't married the nation, and I told her so. But she only smiled at her own limitations and explained that she had to "think in we's."

Confound it again! Here I'd have all my energies focused on one wish, and before I knew it she'd have them dissipated in one direction or another, some subject of discussion that began just at the point I was talking about and ended miles away.

It must not be imagined that I was just repelled, ignored, left to cherish a grievance. Not at all. My happiness was in the hands of a larger, sweeter womanhood than I had ever imagined. Before our marriage my own ardor had perhaps blinded me to much of this. I was madly in love with not so much what was there as with what I supposed to be there. Now I found an endlessly beautiful undiscovered country to explore, and in it the sweetest wisdom and understanding. It was as if I had come to some new place and people, with a desire to eat at all hours, and no other interests in particular; and as if my hosts, instead of merely saying, "You shall not eat," had presently aroused in me a lively desire for music, for pictures, for games, for exercise, for playing in the water, for running some ingenious machine; and, in the multitude of my satisfactions, I forgot the one point which was not satisfied, and got along very well until mealtime.

One of the cleverest and most ingenious of these tricks was only clear to me many years after, when we were so wholly at one on this subject that I could laugh at my own predicament then. It was this: You see, with us, women are kept as different as possible and as feminine as possible. We men have our own world, with only men in it; we get tired of our ultra-maleness and turn gladly to the ultra-femaleness. Also, in keeping our women as feminine as possible, we see to it that when we turn to them we find the thing we want always in evidence. Well, the atmosphere of this place was anything but seductive. The very numbers of these human women, always in human relation, made them anything but alluring. When, in spite of this, my hereditary instincts and race-traditions made me long for the feminine response in Ellador, instead of withdrawing so that I should want her more, she deliberately gave me a little too much of her society—always de-feminized, as it were. It was awfully funny, really.

Here was I, with an Ideal in mind, for which I hotly longed, and here was she, deliberately obtruding in the foreground of my consciousness a Fact—a fact which I coolly enjoyed, but which actually interfered with what I wanted. I see now clearly enough why a certain kind of man, like Sir Almroth Wright, resents the professional development of women. It gets in the way of the sex ideal; it temporarily covers and excludes femininity.

Of course, in this case, I was so fond of Ellador my friend, of Ellador my professional companion, that I necessarily enjoyed her society on any terms. Only—when I had had her with me in her de-feminine capacity for a sixteen-hour day, I could go to my own room and sleep without dreaming about her.

The witch! If ever anybody worked to woo and win and hold a human soul, she did, great Superwoman that she was. I couldn't then half comprehend the skill of it, the wonder. But this I soon began to find: that under all our cultivated attitude of mind toward women, there is an older, deeper, more "natural" feeling, the restful reverence which looks up to the Mother Sex.

So we grew together in friendship and happiness, Ellador and I, and so did Jeff and Celis.

When it comes to Terry's part of it, and Alima's, I'm sorry—and I'm ashamed. Of course I blame her somewhat. She wasn't as fine a psychologist as Ellador, and what's more, I think she had a far-descended atavistic trace of more marked femaleness, never apparent till Terry called it out. But when all that is said, it doesn't excuse him. I hadn't realized to the full Terry's character—I couldn't, being a man.

The position was the same as with us, of course, only with these distinctions: Alima, a shade more alluring, and several shades less able as a practical psychologist; Terry, a hundredfold more demanding—and proportionately less reasonable.

Things grew strained very soon between them. I fancy at first, when they were together, in her great hope of parentage and his keen joy of conquest—that Terry was inconsiderate. In fact, I know it, from things he said.

"You needn't talk to me," he snapped at Jeff one day, just before our weddings. "There never was a woman yet that did not enjoy being *mastered*. All your pretty talk doesn't amount to a hill o'beans—I *know*." And Terry would hum:

> "I've taken my fun where I found it.
>   I've rogued and I've ranged in my time, and
>   The things that I learned from the yellow and black,
>   They 'ave helped me a 'eap with the white."

Jeff turned sharply and left him at the time. I was a bit disquieted myself.

Poor old Terry! The things he'd learned didn't help him a heap in Herland. His idea was To Take—he thought that was the way. He thought, he honestly believed, that women like it. Not the women of Herland! Not Alima!

I can see her now—one day in the very first week of their marriage, setting forth to her day's work with long determined strides and hard-set mouth, and sticking close to Ellador. She didn't wish to be alone with Terry—you could see that.

But the more she kept away from him, the more he wanted her—naturally.

He made a tremendous row about their separate establishments, tried to keep her in his rooms, tried to stay in hers. But there she drew the line sharply.

He came away one night, and stamped up and down the moonlit road, swearing under his breath. I was taking a walk that night too, but I wasn't in his state of mind. To hear him rage you'd not have believed that he loved Alima at all—you'd have thought that she was some quarry he was pursuing, something to catch and conquer.

I think that, owing to all those differences I spoke of, they soon lost the common ground they had at first, and were unable to meet sanely and dispassionately. I fancy too—this is pure conjecture—that he had succeeded in driving Alima beyond her best judgment, her real conscience, and that after that her own sense of shame, the reaction of the thing, made her bitter perhaps.

They quarreled, really quarreled, and after making it up once or twice, they seemed to come to a real break—she would not be alone with him at all. And perhaps she was a bit nervous, I don't know, but she got Moadine to come and stay next door to her. Also, she had a sturdy assistant detailed to accompany her in her work.

Terry had his own ideas, as I've tried to show. I daresay he thought he had a right to do as he did. Perhaps he even convinced himself that it would be better for her. Anyhow, he hid himself in her bedroom one night . . .

The women of Herland have no fear of men. Why should they have? They are not timid in any sense. They are not weak; and they all have strong trained athletic bodies. Othello could not have extinguished Alima with a pillow, as if she were a mouse.

Terry put in practice his pet conviction that a woman loves to be mastered, and by sheer brute force, in all the pride and passion of his intense masculinity, he tried to master this woman.

It did not work. I got a pretty clear account of it later from Ellador, but what we heard at the time was the noise of a tremendous struggle, and Alima calling to Moadine. Moadine was close by and came at once; one or two more strong grave women followed.

Terry dashed about like a madman; he would cheerfully have killed them—he told me that, himself—but he couldn't. When he swung a chair over his head one sprang in the air and caught it, two threw themselves bodily upon him and forced him to the floor; it was only the work of a few moments to have him tied hand and foot, and then, in sheer pity for his futile rage, to anesthetize him.

Alima was in a cold fury. She wanted him killed—actually.

There was a trial before the local Over Mother, and this woman, who did not enjoy being mastered, stated her case.

In a court in our country he would have been held quite "within his rights," of course. But this was not our country; it was theirs. They seemed to measure the enormity of the offense by its effect upon a possible fatherhood, and he scorned even to reply to this way of putting it.

He did let himself go once, and explained in definite terms that they were incapable of understanding a man's needs, a man's desires, a man's point of view. He called them neuters, epicenes, bloodless, sexless creatures. He said they could of course kill him—as so many insects could—but that he despised them nonetheless.

And all those stern grave mothers did not seem to mind his despising them, not in the least.

It was a long trial, and many interesting points were brought out as to their views of our habits, and after a while Terry had his sentence. He waited, grim and defiant. The sentence was: "You must go home!"

CHAPTER XII

EXPELLED

We had all meant to go home again. Indeed we had *not* meant—not by any means—to stay as long as we had. But when it came to being turned out, dismissed, sent away for bad conduct, we none of us really liked it.

Terry said he did. He professed great scorn of the penalty and the trial, as well as all the other characteristics of "this miserable half-country." But he knew, and we knew, that in any "whole" country we should never have been as forgivingly treated as we had been here.

"If the people had come after us according to the directions we left, there'd have been quite a different story!" said Terry. We found out later why no reserve party had arrived. All our careful directions had been destroyed in a fire. We might have all died there and no one at home have ever known our where-abouts.

Terry was under guard now, all the time, known as unsafe, convicted of what was to them an unpardonable sin.

He laughed at their chill horror. "Parcel of old maids!" he called them. "They're all old maids—children or not. They don't know the first thing about Sex."

When Terry said *Sex*, sex with a very large *S,* he meant the male sex, naturally; its special values, its profound conviction of being "the life force," its cheerful ignoring of the true life process, and its interpretation of the other sex solely from its own point of view.

I had learned to see these things very differently since living with Ellador; and as for Jeff, he was so thoroughly Herland-ized that he wasn't fair to Terry, who fretted sharply in his new restraint.

Moadine, grave and strong, as sadly patient as a mother with a degenerate child, kept steady watch on him, with enough other women close at hand to prevent an outbreak. He had no weapons, and well knew that all his strength was of small avail against those grim, quiet women.

We were allowed to visit him freely, but he had only his room, and a small high-walled garden to walk in, while the preparations for our departure were under way.

Three of us were to go: Terry, because he must; I, because two were safer for our flyer, and the long boat trip to the coast; Ellador, because she would not let me go without her.

If Jeff had elected to return, Celis would have gone too—they were the most absorbed of lovers; but Jeff had no desire that way.

"Why should I want to go back to all our noise and dirt, our vice and crime, our disease and degeneracy?" he demanded of me privately. We never spoke like that before the women. "I wouldn't take Celis there for anything on earth!" he protested. "She'd die! She'd die of horror and shame to see our slums and hospitals. How can you risk it with Ellador? You'd better break it to her gently before she really makes up her mind."

Jeff was right. I ought to have told her more fully than I did, of all the things we had to be ashamed of. But it is very hard to bridge the gulf of as deep a difference as existed between our life and theirs. I tried to.

"Look here, my dear," I said to her. "If you are really going to my country with me, you've got to be prepared for a good many shocks. It's not as beautiful as this—the cities, I mean, the civilized parts—of course the wild country is."

"I shall enjoy it all," she said, her eyes starry with hope. "I understand it's not like ours. I can see how monotonous our quiet life must seem to you, how much more stirring yours must be. It must be like the biological change you told me about when the second sex was introduced—a far greater movement, constant change, with new possibilities of growth."

I had told her of the later biological theories of sex, and she was deeply convinced of the superior advantages of having two, the superiority of a world with men in it.

"We have done what we could alone; perhaps we have some

things better in a quiet way, but you have the whole world—all the people of the different nations—all the long rich history behind you—all the wonderful new knowledge. Oh, I just can't wait to see it."

What could I do? I told her in so many words that we had our unsolved problems, that we had dishonesty and corruption, vice and crime, disease and insanity, prisons and hospitals; and it made no more impression on her than it would to tell a South Sea Islander about the temperature of the Arctic Circle. She could intellectually see that it was bad to have those things; but she could not *feel* it.

We had quite easily come to accept the Herland life as normal, because it was normal—none of us make any outcry over mere health and peace and happy industry. And the abnormal, to which we are all so sadly well acclimated, she had never seen.

The two things she cared most to hear about, and wanted most to see, were these: the beautiful relation of marriage and the lovely women who were mothers and nothing else; beyond these her keen, active mind hungered eagerly for the world life.

"I'm almost as anxious to go as you are yourself," she insisted, "and you must be desperately homesick."

I assured her that no one could be homesick in such a paradise as theirs, but she would have none of it.

"Oh, yes—I know. It's like those little tropical islands you've told me about, shining like jewels in the big blue sea—I can't wait to see the sea! The little island may be as perfect as a garden, but you always want to get back to your own big country, don't you? Even if it is bad in some ways?"

Ellador was more than willing. But the nearer it came to our really going, and to my having to take her back to our "civilization," after the clean peace and beauty of theirs, the more I began to dread it, and the more I tried to explain.

Of course I had been homesick at first, while we were prisoners, before I had Ellador. And of course I had, at first, rather idealized my country and its ways, in describing it. Also, I had always accepted certain evils as integral parts of our civilization and never dwelt on them at all. Even when I tried to tell her the worst, I never remembered some things—which, when she came to see them, impressed her at once, as they had never impressed me. Now, in my efforts at explanation, I began to see both ways more keenly than I had before; to see the painful defects of my own land, the marvelous gains of this.

In missing men we three visitors had naturally missed the larger part of life, and had unconsciously assumed that they must miss it too. It took me a long time to realize—Terry never did realize—how little it meant to them. When we say *men*, *man*, *manly*, *manhood,* and all the other masculine derivatives, we have in the background of our minds a huge vague crowded picture of the world and all its activities. To grow up and "be a man," to "act like a man"—the meaning and connotation is wide indeed. That vast background is full of marching columns of men, of changing lines of men, of long processions of men; of men steering their ships into new seas, exploring unknown mountains, breaking horses, herding cattle, ploughing and sowing and reaping, toiling at the forge and furnace, digging in the mine, building roads and bridges and high cathedrals, managing great businesses, teaching in all the colleges, preaching in all the churches; of men everywhere, doing everything—"the world."

And when we say *Women*, we think *Female*—the sex.

But to these women, in the unbroken sweep of this two-thousand-year-old feminine civilization, the word *woman* called up all that big background, so far as they had gone in social development; and the word *man* meant to them only *male*—the sex.

Of course we could *tell* them that in our world men did everything; but that did not alter the background of their minds. That man, "the male," did all these things was to them a statement, making no more change in the point of view than was made in ours when we first faced the astounding fact—to us—that in Herland women were "the world."

We had been living there more than a year. We had learned their limited history, with its straight, smooth, upreaching lines, reaching higher and going faster up to the smooth comfort of their present life. We had learned a little of their psychology, a much wider field than the history, but here we could not follow so readily. We were now well used to seeing women not as females but as people; people of all sorts, doing every kind of work.

This outbreak of Terry's, and the strong reaction against it, gave us a new light on their genuine femininity. This was given me with great clearness by both Ellador and Somel. The feeling was the same—sick revulsion and horror, such as would be felt at some climactic blasphemy.

They had no faintest approach to such a thing in their minds, knowing nothing of the custom of marital indulgence among us. To them the one high purpose of Motherhood had been for so long the governing law of life, and the contribution of the father, though known to them, so distinctly another method to the same end, that they could not, with all their effort, get the point of view of the male creature whose desires quite ignore parentage and seek only for what we euphoniously term "the joys of love."

When I tried to tell Ellador that women too felt so, with us, she drew away from me, and tried hard to grasp intellectually what she could in no way sympathize with.

"You mean—that with you—love between man and woman expresses itself in that way—without regard to motherhood? To parentage, I mean," she added carefully.

"Yes, surely. It is love we think of—the deep sweet love between two. Of course we want children, and children come—but that is not what we think about."

"But—but—it seems so against nature!" she said. "None of the creatures we know do that. Do other animals—in your country?"

"We are not animals!" I replied with some sharpness. "At least we are something more—something higher. This is a far nobler and more beautiful relation, as I have explained before. Your view seems to us rather—shall I say, practical? Prosaic? Merely a means to an end! With us—oh, my dear girl—cannot you see? Cannot you feel? It is the last, sweetest, highest consummation of mutual love."

She was impressed visibly. She trembled in my arms, as I held her close, kissing her hungrily. But there rose in her eyes that look I knew so well, that remote clear look as if she had gone far away even though I held her beautiful body so close, and was now on some snowy mountain regarding me from a distance.

"I feel it quite clearly," she said to me. "It gives me a deep sympathy with what you feel, no doubt more strongly still. But what I feel, even what you feel, dearest, does not convince me that it is right. Until I am sure of that, of course I cannot do as you wish."

Ellador, at times like this, always reminded me of Epictetus. "I will put you in prison!" said his master. "My body, you mean," replied Epictetus calmly. "I will cut your head off," said his master. "Have I said that my head could not be cut off?" A difficult person, Epictetus.

What is this miracle by which a woman, even in your arms, may withdraw herself, utterly disappear till what you hold is as inaccessible as the face of a cliff?

"Be patient with me, dear," she urged sweetly. "I know it is hard for you. And I begin to see—a little—how Terry was so driven to crime."

"Oh, come, that's a pretty hard word for it. After all, Alima was his wife, you know," I urged, feeling at the moment a sudden burst of sympathy for poor Terry. For a man of his temperament—and habits—it must have been an unbearable situation.

But Ellador, for all her wide intellectual grasp, and the broad sympathy in which their religion trained them, could not make allowance for such—to her—sacrilegious brutality.

It was the more difficult to explain to her, because we three, in our constant talks and lectures about the rest of the world, had naturally avoided the seamy side; not so much from a desire to deceive, but from wishing to put the best foot foremost for our civilization, in the face of the beauty and comfort of theirs. Also, we really thought some things were right, or at least unavoidable, which we could readily see would be repugnant to them, and therefore did not discuss. Again there was much of our world's life which we, being used to it, had not noticed as anything worth describing. And still further, there was about these women a colossal innocence upon which many of the things we did say had made no impression whatever.

I am thus explicit about it because it shows how unexpectedly strong was the impression made upon Ellador when she at last entered our civilization.

She urged me to be patient, and I was patient. You see, I loved her so much that even the restrictions she so firmly established left me much happiness. We were lovers, and there is surely delight enough in that.

Do not imagine that these young women utterly refused "the Great New Hope," as they called it, that of dual parentage. For that they had agreed to marry us, though the marrying part of it was a concession to our prejudices rather than theirs. To them the process was the holy thing—and they meant to keep it holy.

But so far only Celis, her blue eyes swimming in happy tears, her heart lifted with that tide of race-motherhood which was their supreme passion, could with ineffable joy and pride announce that she was to be a mother. "The New Motherhood" they called it, and the whole country knew. There was no pleasure, no service, no honor in all the land that Celis might not have had. Almost like the breathless reverence with which, two thousand years ago, that dwindling band of women had watched the miracle of virgin birth, was the deep awe and warm expectancy with which they greeted this new miracle of union.

All mothers in that land were holy. To them, for long ages, the approach to motherhood has been by the most intense and exquisite love and longing, by the Supreme Desire, the overmastering demand for a child. Every thought they held in connection with the processes of maternity was open to the day, simple yet sacred. Every woman of them placed motherhood not only higher than other duties, but so far higher that there were no other duties, one might almost say. All their wide mutual love, all the subtle interplay of mutual friendship and service, the urge of progressive thought and invention, the deepest religious emotion, every feeling and every act was related to this great central Power, to the River of Life pouring through them, which made them the bearers of the very Spirit of God.

Of all this I learned more and more—from their books, from talk, especially from Ellador. She was at first, for a brief moment, envious of her friend—a thought she put away from her at once and forever.

"It is better," she said to me. "It is much better that it has not come to me yet—to us, that is. For if I am to go with you to your country, we may have 'adventures by sea and land,' as you say (and as in truth we did), and it might not be at all safe for a baby. So we won't try again, dear, till it is safe—will we?"

This was a hard saying for a very loving husband.

"Unless," she went on, "if one is coming, you will leave me behind. You can come back, you know—and I shall have the child."

Then that deep ancient chill of male jealousy of even his own progeny touched my heart.

"I'd rather have you, Ellador, than all the children in the world. I'd rather have you with me—on your own terms—than not to have you."

This was a very stupid saying. Of course I would! For if she wasn't there I should want all of her and have none of her. But if she went along as a sort of sublimated sister—only much closer and warmer than that, really—why I should have all of her but that one thing. And I was beginning to find that Ellador's friendship, Ellador's comradeship, Ellador's sisterly affection, Ellador's perfectly sincere love—none the less deep that she held it back on a definite line of reserve—were enough to live on very happily.

I find it quite beyond me to describe what this woman was to me. We talk fine things about women, but in our hearts we know that they are very limited beings—most of them. We honor them for their functional powers, even while we dishonor them by our use of it; we honor them for their carefully enforced virtue, even while we show by our own conduct how little we think of that virtue; we value them, sincerely, for the perverted maternal activities which make our wives the most comfortable of servants, bound to us for life with the wages wholly at our own decision, their whole business, outside of the temporary duties of such motherhood as they may achieve, to meet our needs in every way. Oh, we value them, all right, "in their place," which place is the home, where they perform that mixture of duties so ably described by Mrs. Josephine Dodge Daskam Bacon, in which the services of "a mistress" are carefully specified. She is a very clear writer, Mrs. J. D. D. Bacon, and understands her subject—from her own point of view. But—that combination of industries, while convenient, and in a way economical, does not arouse the kind of emotion commanded by the women of Herland. These were women one had to love "up," very high up, instead of down. They were not pets. They were not servants. They were not timid, inexperienced, weak.

After I got over the jar to my pride (which Jeff, I truly think, never felt—he was a born worshipper, and which Terry never got over—he was quite clear in his ideas of "the position of women"), I found that loving "up" was a very good sensation after all. It gave me a queer feeling, way down deep, as of the stirring of some ancient dim prehistoric consciousness, a feeling that they were right somehow—that this was the way to feel. It was like—coming home to mother. I don't mean the underflannels-and-doughnuts mother, the fussy person that waits on you and spoils you and doesn't really know you. I mean the feeling that a very little child would have, who had been lost—for ever so long. It was a sense of getting home; of being clean and rested; of safety and yet freedom; of love that was always there, warm like sunshine in May, not hot like a stove or a featherbed—a love that didn't irritate and didn't smother.

I looked at Ellador as if I hadn't seen her before. "If you won't go," I said, "I'll get Terry to the coast and come back alone. You can let me down a rope. And if you will go—why you blessed wonder-woman—I would rather live with you all my life—like this—than to have any other woman I ever saw, or any number of them, to do as I like with. Will you come?"

She was keen for coming. So the plans went on. She'd have liked to wait for that Marvel of Celis's, but Terry had no such desire. He was crazy to be out of it all. It made him sick, he said, *sick;* this everlasting mother-mother-mothering. I don't think Terry had what the phrenologists call "the lump of philoprogenitiveness" at all well developed.

"Morbid one-sided cripples," he called them, even when from his window he could see their splendid vigor and beauty; even while Moadine, as patient and friendly as if she had never helped Alima to hold and bind him, sat there in the room, the picture of wisdom and serene strength. "Sexless, epicene, undeveloped neuters!" he went on bitterly. He sounded like Sir Almroth Wright.

Well—it was hard. He was madly in love with Alima, really; more so than he had ever been before, and their tempestuous courtship, quarrels, and reconciliations had fanned the flame. And then when he sought by that supreme conquest which seems so natural a thing to that type of man, to force her to love him as her master—to have the sturdy athletic furious woman rise up and master him—she and her friends—it was no wonder he raged.

Come to think of it, I do not recall a similar case in all history or fiction. Women have killed themselves rather than submit to outrage; they have killed the outrager; they have escaped; or they have submitted—sometimes seeming to get on very well with the victor afterward. There was that adventure of "false Sextus," for instance, who "found Lucrese combing the fleece, under the midnight lamp." He threatened, as I remember, that if she did not submit he would slay her, slay a slave and place him beside her and say he found him there. A poor device, it always seemed to me. If Mr. Lucretius had asked him how he came to be in his wife's bedroom overlooking her morals, what could he have said? But the point is Lucrese submitted, and Alima didn't.

"She kicked me," confided the embittered prisoner—he had to talk to someone. "I was doubled up with the pain, of course, and she jumped on me and yelled for this old harpy (Moadine couldn't hear him) and they had me trussed up in no time. I believe Alima could have done it alone," he added with reluctant admiration. "She's as strong as a horse. And of course a man's helpless when you hit him like that. No woman with a shade of decency—"

I had to grin at that, and even Terry did, sourly. He wasn't given to reasoning, but it did strike him that an assault like his rather waived considerations of decency.

"I'd give a year of my life to have her alone again," he said slowly, his hands clenched till the knuckles were white.

But he never did. She left our end of the country entirely, went up into the fir-forest on the highest slopes, and stayed there. Before we left he quite desperately longed to see her, but she would not come and he could not go. They watched him like lynxes. (Do lynxes watch any better than mousing cats, I wonder!)

Well—we had to get the flyer in order, and be sure there was enough fuel left, though Terry said we could glide all right, down to that lake, once we got started. We'd have gone gladly in a week's time, of course, but there was a great to-do all over the country about Ellador's leaving them. She had interviews with some of the leading ethicists—wise women with still eyes, and with the best of the teachers. There was a stir, a thrill, a deep excitement everywhere.

Our teaching about the rest of the world has given them all a sense of isolation, of remoteness, of being a little outlying sample of a country, overlooked and forgotten among the family of nations. We had called it "the family of nations," and they liked the phrase immensely.

They were deeply aroused on the subject of evolution; indeed, the whole field of natural science drew them irresistibly. Any number of them would have risked everything to go to the strange unknown lands and study; but we could take only one, and it had to be Ellador, naturally.

We planned greatly about coming back, about establishing a connecting route by water; about penetrating those vast forests and civilizing—or exterminating—the dangerous savages. That is, we men talked of that last—not with the women. They had a definite aversion to killing things.

But meanwhile there was high council being held among the wisest of them all. The students and thinkers who had been gathering facts from us all this time, collating and relating them, and making inferences, laid the result of their labors before the council.

Little had we thought that our careful efforts at concealment had been so easily seen through, with never a word to show us that they saw. They had followed up words of ours on the science of optics, asked innocent questions about glasses and the like, and were aware of the defective eyesight so common among us.

With the lightest touch, different women asking different questions at different times, and putting all our answers together like a picture puzzle, they had figured out a sort of skeleton chart as to the prevalence of disease among us. Even more subtly with no show of horror or condemnation, they had gathered something—far from the truth, but something pretty clear—about poverty, vice, and crime. They even had a goodly number of our dangers all itemized, from asking us about insurance and innocent things like that.

They were well posted as to the different races, beginning with their poison-arrow natives down below and widening out to the broad racial divisions we had told them about. Never a shocked expression of the face or exclamation of revolt had warned us; they had been extracting the evidence without our knowing it all this time, and now were studying with the most devout earnestness the matter they had prepared.

The result was rather distressing to us. They first explained the matter fully to Ellador, as she was the one who purposed visiting the Rest of the World. To Celis they said nothing. She must not be in any way distressed, while the whole nation waited on her Great Work.

Finally Jeff and I were called in. Somel and Zava were there, and Ellador, with many others that we knew.

They had a great globe, quite fairly mapped out from the small section maps in that compendium of ours. They had the different peoples of the earth roughly outlined, and their status in civilization indicated. They had charts and figures and estimates, based on the facts in that traitorous little book and what they had learned from us.

Somel explained: "We find that in all your historic period, so much longer than ours, that with all the interplay of services, the exchange of inventions and discoveries, and the wonderful progress we so admire, that in this widespread Other World of yours, there is still much disease, often contagious."

We admitted this at once.

"Also there is still, in varying degree, ignorance, with prejudice and unbridled emotion."

This too was admitted.

"We find also that in spite of the advance of democracy and the increase of wealth, that there is still unrest and sometimes combat."

Yes, yes, we admitted it all. We were used to these things and saw no reason for so much seriousness.

"All things considered," they said, and they did not say a hundredth part of the things they were considering, "we are unwilling to expose our country to free communication with the rest of the world—as yet. If Ellador comes back, and we approve her report, it may be done later—but not yet.

"So we have this to ask of you gentlemen (they knew that word was held a title of honor with us), that you promise not in any way to betray the location of this country until permission—after Ellador's return."

Jeff was perfectly satisfied. He thought they were quite right. He always did. I never saw an alien become naturalized more quickly than that man in Herland.

I studied it awhile, thinking of the time they'd have if some of our contagions got loose there, and concluded they were right. So I agreed.

Terry was the obstacle. "Indeed I won't!" he protested. "The first thing I'll do is to get an expedition fixed up to force an entrance into Ma-land."

"Then," they said quite calmly, "he must remain an absolute prisoner, always."

"Anesthesia would be kinder," urged Moadine.

"And safer," added Zava.

"He will promise, I think," said Ellador.

And he did. With which agreement we at last left Herland.

SHORT FICTION

THE UNEXPECTED

I

"It is the unexpected which happens," says the French proverb. I like the proverb, because it is true—and because it is French.

Edouard Charpentier is my name.

I am American by birth, but that is all. From infancy, when I had a French nurse; in childhood, when I had a French governess; through youth, passed in a French school; to manhood, devoted to French art, I have been French by sympathy and education.

France—modern France—and French art—modern French art—I adore!

My school is the very newest, and my master, could I but find him, is M. Duchesne. M. Duchesne has had pictures in the Salon for three years, and pictures elsewhere, eagerly bought, and yet Paris knows not M. Duchesne. We know his house, his horse, his carriage, his servants and his garden-wall, but he sees no one, speaks to no one; indeed, he has left Paris for a time, and we worship afar off.

I have a sketch by this master which I treasure jealously—a pencil sketch of a great picture yet to come. I await it.

M. Duchesne paints from the model, and I paint from the model, exclusively. It is the only way to be firm, accurate, true. Without the model we may have German fantasy or English domesticity, but no modern French art.

It is hard, too, to get models continually when one is but a student after five years' work, and one's pictures bring francs indeed, but not dollars.

Still, there is Georgette!

There, also, were Emilie and Pauline. But now it is Georgette, and she is adorable!

'Tis true, she has not much soul; but, then, she has a charming body, and 'tis that I copy.

Georgette and I get on together to admiration. How much better is this than matrimony for an artist! How wise is M. Daudet!

Antoine is my dearest friend. I paint with him, and we are happy. Georgette is my dearest model. I paint from her, and we are happy.

Into this peaceful scene comes a letter from America, bringing much emotion.

It appears I had a great-uncle there, in some northeastern corner of New England. Maine? No; Vermont.

And it appears, strangely enough, that this northeastern great-uncle was seized in his old age with a passion for French art; at least I know not how else to account for his hunting me up through a lawyer and leaving me some quarter of a million when he died.

An admirable great-uncle!

But I must go home and settle the property; that is imperative. I must leave Paris, I must leave Antoine, I must leave Georgette!

Could anything be further from Paris than a town in Vermont? No, not the Andaman Islands.

And could anything be further from Antoine and Georgette than the family of great-cousins I find myself among?

But one of them—ah, Heaven! some forty-seventh cousin who is so beautiful that I forget she is an American, I forget Paris, I forget Antoine—yes, and even Georgette! Poor Georgette! But this is fate.

This cousin is not like the other cousins. I pursue, I inquire, I ascertain.

Her name is Mary D. Greenleaf. I shall call her Marie.

And she comes from Boston.

But beyond the name, how can I describe her? I have seen beauty, yes, much beauty, in maid, matron and model, but I never saw anything to equal this country girl. What a figure!

No, not a "figure"—the word shames her. She has a body, the body of a young Diana, and a body and a figure are two very different things. I am an artist, and I have lived in Paris, and I know the difference.

The lawyers in Boston can settle that property, I find.

The air is delightful in northern Vermont in March. There are mountains, clouds, trees. I will paint here a while. Ah, yes; and I will assist this shy young soul!

"Cousin Marie," say I, "come, let me teach you to paint!"

"It would be too difficult for you, Mr. Carpenter—it would take too long!"

"Call me Edouard!" I cry. "Are we not cousins? Cousin Edouard, I beg of you! And nothing is difficult when you are with me, Marie—nothing can be too long at your side!"

"Thanks, cousin Edward, but I think I will not impose on your good nature. Besides, I shall not stay here. I go back to Boston, to my aunt."

I find the air of Boston is good in March, and there are places of interest there, rising American artists who deserve encouragement. I will stay in Boston a while to assist the lawyers in settling my property; it is necessary.

I visit Marie continually. Am I not a cousin?

I talk to her of life, of art, of Paris, of M. Duchesne. I show her my precious sketch.

"But," says she, "I am not wholly a wood nymph, as you seem fondly to imagine. I have been to Paris myself—with my uncle—years since."

"Fairest cousin," say I, "if you had not been even in Boston, I should still love you! Come and see Paris again—with me!" And then she would laugh at me and send me away. Ah, yes! I had come even to marriage, you see!

I soon found she had the usual woman's faith in those conventions. I gave her "Artists' Wives." She said she had read it. She laughed at Daudet and me!

I talked to her of ruined geniuses I had known myself, but she said a ruined genius was no worse than a ruined woman! One cannot reason with young girls!

Do not believe I succumbed without a struggle. I even tore myself away and went to New York. It was not far enough, I fear. I soon came back.

She lived with an aunt—my adorable little precisian!—with a horrible strong-minded aunt, and such a life as I led between them for a whole month!

I call continually. I bury her in flowers. I take her to the theatre, aunt and all. And at this the aunt seemed greatly surprised, but I disapprove of American familiarities. No; my wife—and wife she must be—shall be treated with punctilious respect.

Never was I so laughed at and argued with in my life as I was laughed at by that dreadful beauty, and argued with by that dreadful aunt.

The only rest was in pictures. Marie would look at pictures always, and seemed to have a real appreciation of them, almost an understanding, of a sort. So that I began to hope—dimly and faintly to hope—that she might grow to care for mine. To have a wife who would care for one's art, who would come to one's studio—but, then, the models! I paint from the model almost entirely, as I said, and *I* know what women are about models, without Daudet to tell me!

And this prudish New England girl! Well, she might come to the studio on stated days, and perhaps in time I might lead her gently to understand.

That I should ever live to commit matrimony!

But Fate rules all men.

I think that girl refused me nine times. She always put me off with absurd excuses and reasons: said I didn't know her yet; said we should never agree; said I was French and she was American; said I cared more for art than I did for her! At that I earnestly assured her that I would become an organ-grinder or a bank-clerk rather than lose her—and then she seemed downright angry, and sent me away again.

Women are strangely inconsistent!

She always sent me away, but I always came back.

After about a month of this torture, I chanced to find her, one soft May twilight, without the aunt, sitting by a window in the fragrant dusk.

She had flowers in her hand—flowers I had sent her—and sat looking down at them, her strong, pure profile clear against the saffron sky.

I came in quietly, and stood watching, in a rapture of hope and admiration. And while I watched I saw a great pearl tear roll down among my violets.

That was enough.

I sprang forward, I knelt beside her, I caught her hands in mine, I drew her to me, I cried, exultantly: "You love me! And I—ah, God! how I love you!"

Even then she would have put me from her. She insisted that I did not know her yet, that she ought to tell me—but I held her close and kissed away her words, and said: "You love me, perfect one, and I love you. The rest will be right."

Then she laid her white hands on my shoulders, and looked deep into my eyes.

"I believe that is true," said she; "and I will marry you, Edward."

She dropped her face on my shoulder then—that face of fire and roses—and we were still.

II

It is but two months' time from then; I have been married a fortnight. The first week was heaven—and the second was hell! O my God! my wife! That young Diana to be but—! I have borne it a week. I have feared and despised myself. I have suspected and hated myself. I have discovered and cursed myself. Aye, and cursed her, and *him*, whom this day I shall kill!

It is now three o'clock. I cannot kill him until four, for he comes not till then.

I am very comfortable here in this room opposite—very comfortable; and I can wait and think and remember.

Let me think.

First, to kill him. That is simple and easily settled.

Shall I kill her?

If she lived, could I ever see her again? Ever touch that hand—those lips—that, within two weeks of marriage—? No, she shall die!

And, if she lived, what would be before her but more shame, and more, till she felt it herself?

Far better that she die!

And I?

Could I live to forget her? To carry always in my heart a black stone across that door? To rise and rise, and do great work—*alone?*

Never! I cannot forget her!

Better die with her, even now.

Hark! Is that a step on the stair? Not yet.

My money is well bestowed. Antoine is a better artist than I, a better man, and the money will widen and lighten a noble life in his hands.

And little Georgette is provided for. How long ago, how faint and weak, that seems! But Georgette loved me, I believe, at least for a time—longer than a week.

To wait—until four o'clock!

To think—I have thought; it is all arranged!

These pistols, that she admired but day before yesterday, that we practised with together, both loaded full. What a shot she is! I believe she can do everything!

To wait—to think—to remember.

Let me remember.

I knew her a week, wooed her a month, have been married a fortnight.

She always said I didn't know her. She was always on the point of telling me something, and I would not let her. She seemed half repentant, half in jest—I preferred to trust her. Those clear, brown eyes—clear and bright, like brook water with the sun through it! And she would smile so! 'Tis not that I must remember.

Am I sure? Sure! I laugh at myself.

What would you call it, you—any man? A young woman steals from her house, alone, every day, and comes privately, cloaked and veiled, to this place, this den of Bohemians, this building of New York studios! Painters? I know them—I am a painter myself.

She goes to this room, day after day, and tells me nothing.

I say to her gently: "What do you do with your days, my love?"

"Oh, many things," she answers; "I am studying art—to please you!"

That was ingenious. She knew that she might be watched.

I say, "Cannot I teach you?" and she says, "I have a teacher I used to study with. I must finish. I want to surprise you!" So she would soothe me—to appearance.

But I watch and follow, I take this little room. I wait, and I see.

Lessons? Oh, perjured one! There is no tenant of that room but yourself, and to it *he* comes each day.

Is that a step? Not yet. I watch and wait. This is America, I say, not France. This is my wife. I will trust her. But the man comes every day. He is young. He is handsome—handsome as a fiend.

I cannot bear it. I go to the door. I knock. There is no response. I try the door. It is locked. I stoop and look through the key-hole. What do I see? Ah, God! The hat and cloak of that man upon a chair, and then only a tall screen. Behind that screen, low voices!

I did not go home last night. I am here to-day—with these!

That is a step. Yes! Softly, now. He has gone in. I heard her speak. She said: "You are late, Guillaume!"

Let me give them a little time.

Now—softly—I come, friends. *I* am not late!

III

Across the narrow passage I steal, noiselessly. The door is unlocked this time. I burst in.

There stands my young wife, pale, trembling, startled, unable to speak.

There is the handsome Guillaume—behind the screen. My fingers press the triggers. There is a sharp double report. Guillaume tumbles over, howling, and Marie flings herself between us.

"Edward! One moment! Give me a moment for my life! The pistols are harmless, dear—blank cartridges. I fixed them myself. I saw you suspected. But you've spoiled my surprise. I shall have to tell you now. This is my studio, love. Here is the picture you have the sketch of. *I* am 'M. Duchesne'—Mary Duchesne Greenleaf Carpenter—and this is my model!"

IV

We are very happy in Paris, with our double studio. We sometimes share our models. We laugh at M. Daudet.

THE GIANT WISTARIA

"Meddle not with my new vine, child! See! Thou hast already broken the tender shoot! Never needle or distaff for thee, and yet thou wilt not be quiet!"

The nervous fingers wavered, clutched at a small carnelian cross that hung from her neck, then fell despairingly.

"Give me my child, mother, and then I will be quiet!"

"Hush! hush! thou fool—some one might be near! See—there is thy father coming, even now! Get in quickly!"

She raised her eyes to her mother's face, weary eyes that yet had a flickering, uncertain blaze in their shaded depths.

"Art thou a mother and hast no pity on me, a mother? Give me my child!"

Her voice rose in a strange, low cry, broken by her father's hand upon her mouth.

"Shameless!" said he, with set teeth. "Get to thy chamber, and be not seen again to-night, or I will have thee bound!"

She went at that, and a hard-faced serving woman followed, and presently returned, bringing a key to her mistress.

"Is all well with her,—and the child also?"

"She is quiet, Mistress Dwining, well for the night, be sure. The child fretteth endlessly, but save for that it thriveth with me."

The parents were left alone together on the high square porch with its great pillars, and the rising moon began to make faint shadows of the young vine leaves that shot up luxuriantly around them; moving shadows, like little stretching fingers, on the broad and heavy planks of the oaken floor.

"It groweth well, this vine thou broughtest me in the ship, my husband."

"Aye," he broke in bitterly, "and so doth the shame I brought thee! Had I known of it I would sooner have had the ship founder beneath us, and have seen our child cleanly drowned, than live to this end!"

"Thou art very hard, Samuel, art thou not afeard for her life? She grieveth sore for the child, aye, and for the green fields to walk in!"

"Nay," said he grimly, "I fear not. She hath lost already what is more than life; and she shall have air enough soon. To-morrow the ship is ready, and we return to England. None knoweth of our stain here, not one, and if the town hath a child unaccounted for to rear in decent ways—why, it is not the first, even here. It will be well enough cared for! And truly we have matter for thankfulness, that her cousin is yet willing to marry her."

"Hast thou told him?"

"Aye! Thinkest thou I would cast shame into another man's house, unknowing it? He hath always desired her, but she would none of him, the stubborn! She hath small choice now!"

"Will he be kind, Samuel? can he—"

"Kind? What call'st thou it to take such as she to wife? Kind! How many men would take her, an' she had double the fortune? and being of the family already, he is glad to hide the blot forever."

"An' if she would not? He is but a coarse fellow, and she ever shunned him."

"Art thou mad, woman? She weddeth him ere we sail to-morrow, or she stayeth ever in that chamber. The girl is not so sheer a fool! He maketh an honest woman of her, and saveth our house from open shame. What other hope for her than a new life to cover the old? Let her have an honest child, an' she so longeth for one!"

He strode heavily across the porch, till the loose planks creaked again, strode back and forth, with his arms folded and his brows fiercely knit above his iron mouth.

Overhead the shadows flickered mockingly across a white face among the leaves, with eyes of wasted fire.

* * * * *

"O, George, what a house! what a lovely house! I am sure it's haunted! Let us get that house to live in this summer! We will have Kate and Jack and Susy and Jim of course, and a splendid time of it!"

Young husbands are indulgent, but still they have to recognize facts.

"My dear, the house may not be to rent; and it may also not be habitable."

"There is surely somebody in it. I am going to inquire!"

The great central gate was rusted off its hinges, and the long drive had trees in it, but a little foothpath showed signs of steady usage, and up that Mrs. Jenny went, followed by her obedient George. The front windows of the old mansion were blank, but in a wing at the back they found white curtains and open doors. Outside, in the clear May sunshine, a woman was washing. She was polite and friendly, and evidently glad of visitors in that lonely place. She "guessed it could be rented— didn't know." The heirs were in Europe, but "there was a lawyer in New York had the lettin' of it." There had been folks there years ago, but not in her time. She and her husband had the rent of their part for taking care of the place. "Not that they took much care on't either, but keepin' robbers out." It was furnished throughout, old-fashioned enough, but good; and "if they took it she could do the work for 'em herself, she guessed—if *he* was willin'!"

Never was a crazy scheme more easily arranged. George knew that lawyer in New York; the rent was not alarming; and the nearness to a rising sea-shore resort made it a still pleasanter place to spend the summer.

Kate and Jack and Susy and Jim cheerfully accepted, and the June moon found them all sitting on the high front porch.

They had explored the house from top to bottom, from the great room in the garret, with nothing in it but a rickety cradle, to the well in the cellar without a curb and with a rusty chain going down to unknown blackness below. They had explored the grounds, once beautiful with rare trees and shrubs, but now a gloomy wilderness of tangled shade.

The old lilacs and laburnums, the spirea and syringa, nodded against the second-story windows. What garden plants survived were great ragged bushes or great shapeless beds. A huge wistaria vine covered the whole front of the house. The trunk, it was too large to call a stem, rose at the corner of the porch by the high steps, and had once climbed its pillars; but now the pillars were wrenched from their places and held rigid and helpless by the tightly wound and knotted arms.

It fenced in all the upper story of the porch with a knitted wall of stem and leaf; it ran along the eaves, holding up the gutter that had once supported it; it shaded every window with heavy green; and the drooping, fragrant blossoms made a waving sheet of purple from roof to ground.

"Did you ever see such a wistaria!" cried ecstatic Mrs. Jenny. "It is worth the rent just to sit under such a vine,—a fig tree beside it would be sheer superfluity and wicked extravagance!"

"Jenny makes much of her wistaria," said George, "because she's so disappointed about the ghosts. She made up her mind at first sight to have ghosts in the house, and she can't find even a ghost story!"

"No," Jenny assented mournfully; "I pumped poor Mrs. Pepperill for three days, but could get nothing out of her. But I'm convinced there is a story, if we could only find it. You need not tell me that a house like this, with a garden like this, and a cellar like this, isn't haunted!"

"I agree with you," said Jack. Jack was a reporter on a New York daily, and engaged to Mrs. Jenny's pretty sister. "And if we don't find a real ghost, you may be very sure I shall make one. It's too good an opportunity to lose!"

The pretty sister, who sat next him, resented. "You shan't do anything of the sort, Jack! This is a *real* ghostly place, and I won't have you make fun of it! Look at that group of trees out there in the long grass—it looks for all the world like a crouching, hunted figure!"

"It looks to me like a woman picking huckleberries," said Jim, who was married to George's pretty sister.

"Be still, Jim!" said that fair young woman. "I believe in Jenny's ghost as much as she does. Such a place! Just look at this great wistaria trunk crawling up by the steps here! It looks for all the world like a writhing body—cringing—beseeching!"

"Yes," answered the subdued Jim, "it does, Susy. See its

waist,—about two yards of it, and twisted at that! A waste of good material!"

"Don't be so horrid, boys! Go off and smoke somewhere if you can't be congenial!"

"We can! We will! We'll be as ghostly as you please." And forthwith they began to see bloodstains and crouching figures so plentifully that the most delightful shivers multiplied, and the fair enthusiasts started for bed, declaring they should never sleep a wink.

"We shall all surely dream," cried Mrs. Jenny, "and we must all tell our dreams in the morning!"

"There's another thing certain," said George, catching Susy as she tripped over a loose plank; "and that is that you frisky creatures must use the side door till I get this Eiffel tower of a portico fixed, or we shall have some fresh ghosts on our hands! We found a plank here that yawns like a trap-door—big enough to swallow you,—and I believe the bottom of the thing is in China!"

The next morning found them all alive, and eating a substantial New England breakfast, to the accompaniment of saws and hammers on the porch, where carpenters of quite miraculous promptness were tearing things to pieces generally.

"It's got to come down mostly," they had said. "These timbers are clean rotted through, what ain't pulled out o' line by this great creeper. That's about all that holds the thing up."

There was clear reason in what they said, and with a caution from anxious Mrs. Jenny not to hurt the wistaria, they were left to demolish and repair at leisure.

"How about ghosts?" asked Jack after a fourth griddle cake. "I had one, and it's taken away my appetite!"

Mrs. Jenny gave a little shriek and dropped her knife and fork.

"Oh, so had I! I had the most awful—well, not dream exactly, but feeling. I had forgotten all about it!"

"Must have been awful," said Jack, taking another cake. "Do tell us about the feeling. My ghost will wait."

"It makes me creep to think of it even now," she said. "I woke up, all at once, with that dreadful feeling as if something were going to happen, you know! I was wide awake, and hearing every little sound for miles around, it seemed to me. There are so many strange little noises in the country for all it is so still. Millions of crickets and things outside, and all kinds of rustles in the trees! There wasn't much wind, and the moonlight came through in my three great windows in three white squares on the black old floor, and those fingery wistaria leaves we were talking of last night just seemed to crawl all over them. And—O, girls, you know that dreadful well in the cellar?"

A most gratifying impression was made by this, and Jenny proceeded cheerfully:

"Well, while it was so horridly still, and I lay there trying not to wake George, I heard as plainly as if it were right in the room, that old chain down there rattle and creak over the stones!"

"Bravo!" cried Jack. "That's fine! I'll put it in the Sunday edition!"

"Be still!" said Kate. "What was it, Jenny? Did you really see anything?"

"No, I didn't, I'm sorry to say. But just then I didn't want to. I woke George, and made such a fuss that he gave me bromide, and said he'd go and look, and that's the last I thought of it till Jack reminded me,—the bromide worked so well."

"Now, Jack, give us yours," said Jim. "Maybe, it will dovetail in somehow. Thirsty ghost, I imagine; maybe they had prohibition here even then!"

Jack folded his napkin, and leaned back in his most impressive manner.

"It was striking twelve by the great hall clock—" he began.

"There isn't any hall clock!"

"O hush, Jim, you spoil the current! It was just one o'clock then, by my old-fashioned repeater."

"Waterbury! Never mind what time it was!"

"Well, honestly, I woke up sharp, like our beloved hostess, and tried to go to sleep again, but couldn't. I experienced all those moonlight and grasshopper sensations, just like Jenny, and was wondering what could have been the matter with the supper, when in came my ghost, and I knew it was all a dream! It was a female ghost, and I imagine she was young and handsome, but all those crouching, hunted figures of last evening ran riot in my brain, and this poor creature looked just like them. She was all wrapped up in a shawl, and had a big bundle under her arm,—dear me, I am spoiling the story! With the air and gait of one in frantic haste and terror, the muffled figure glided to a dark old bureau, and seemed taking things from the drawers. As she turned, the moonlight shone full on a little red cross that hung from her neck by a thin gold chain—I saw it glitter as she crept noiselessly from the room! That's all."

"O Jack, don't be so horrid! Did you really? Is that all! What do you think it was?"

"I am not horrid by nature, only professionally. I really did. That was all. And I am fully convinced it was the genuine, legitimate ghost of an eloping chambermaid with kleptomania!"

"You are too bad, Jack!" cried Jenny. "You take all the horror out of it. There isn't a 'creep' left among us."

"It's no time for creeps at nine-thirty A.M., with sunlight and carpenters outside! However, if you can't wait till twilight for your creeps, I think I can furnish one or two," said George. "I went down cellar after Jenny's ghost!"

There was a delighted chorus of female voices, and Jenny cast upon her lord a glance of genuine gratitude.

"It's all very well to lie in bed and see ghosts, or hear them," he went on. "But the young householder suspecteth burglars, even though as a medical man he knoweth nerves, and after Jenny dropped off I started on a voyage of discovery. I never will again, I promise you!"

"Why, what *was* it?"

"Oh, George!"

"I got a candle—"

"Good mark for the burglars," murmured Jack.

"And went all over the house, gradually working down to the cellar and the well."

"Well?" said Jack.

"Now you can laugh; but that cellar is no joke by daylight, and a candle there at night is about as inspiring as a lightning-bug in the Mammoth Cave, I went along with the light, trying not to fall into the well prematurely; got to it all at once; held the light down and *then* I saw, right under my feet—(I nearly fell over her, or walked through her, perhaps),—a woman, hunched up under a shawl! She had hold of the chain, and the candle shone on her hands—white, thin hands,—on a little red cross that hung from her neck—*vide* Jack! I'm no believer in ghosts, and I firmly object to unknown parties in the house at night; so I spoke to her rather fiercely. She didn't seem to notice that, and I reached down to take hold of her,—then I came upstairs!"

"What for?"

"What happened?"

"What was the matter?"

"Well, nothing happened. Only she wasn't there! May have been indigestion, of course, but as a physician I don't advise any one to court indigestion alone at midnight in a cellar!"

"This is the most interesting and peripatetic and evasive ghost I ever heard of!" said Jack. "It's my belief she has no end of silver tankards, and jewels galore, at the bottom of that well, and I move we go and see!"

"To the bottom of the well, Jack?"

"To the bottom of the mystery. Come on!"

There was unanimous assent, and the fresh cambrics and pretty boots were gallantly escorted below by gentlemen whose jokes were so frequent that many of them were a little forced.

The deep old cellar was so dark that they had to bring lights, and the well so gloomy in its blackness that the ladies recoiled.

"That well is enough to scare even a ghost. It's my opinion you'd better let well enough alone?" quoth Jim.

"Truth lies hid in a well, and we must get her out," said George. "Bear a hand with the chain?"

Jim pulled away on the chain, George turned the creaking windlass, and Jack was chorus.

"A wet sheet for this ghost, if not a flowing sea," said he. "Seems to be hard work raising spirits! I suppose he kicked the bucket when he went down!"

As the chain lightened and shortened there grew a strained

silence among them; and when at length the bucket appeared, rising slowly through the dark water, there was an eager, half reluctant peering, and a natural drawing back. They poked the gloomy contents. "Only water."

"Nothing but mud."

"Something—"

They emptied the bucket up on the dark earth, and then the girls all went out into the air, into the bright warm sunshine in front of the house, where was the sound of saw and hammer, and the smell of new wood. There was nothing said until the men joined them, and then Jenny timidly asked:

"How old should you think it was, George?"

"All of a century," he answered. "That water is a preservative,—lime in it. Oh!—you mean?—Not more than a month; a very little baby!"

There was another silence at this, broken by a cry from the workmen. They had removed the floor and the side walls of the old porch, so that the sunshine poured down to the dark stones of the cellar bottom. And there, in the strangling grasp of the roots of the great wistaria, lay the bones of a woman, from whose neck still hung a tiny scarlet cross on a thin chain of gold.

AN EXTINCT ANGEL

There was once a species of angel inhabiting this planet, acting as "a universal solvent" to all the jarring, irreconcilable elements of human life.

It was quite numerous; almost every family had one; and, although differing in degree of seraphic virtue, all were, by common consent, angels.

The advantages of possessing such a creature were untold. In the first place, the chances of the mere human being in the way of getting to heaven were greatly increased by these semi-heavenly belongings; they gave one a sort of lien on the next world, a practical claim most comforting to the owner.

For the angels of course possessed virtues above mere humanity; and because the angels were so well-behaved, therefore the owners were given credit.

Beside this direct advantage of complimentary tickets up above were innumerable indirect advantages below. The possession of one of these angels smoothed every feature of life, and gave peace and joy to an otherwise hard lot.

It was the business of the angel to assuage, to soothe, to comfort, to delight. No matter how unruly were the passions of the owner, sometimes even to the extent of legally beating his angel with "a stick no thicker than his thumb," the angel was to have no passion whatever—unless self-sacrifice may be called a passion, and indeed it often amounted to one with her.

The human creature went out to his daily toil and comforted himself as he saw fit. He was apt to come home tired and cross, and in this exigency it was the business of the angel to wear a smile for his benefit—a soft, perennial, heavenly smile.

By an unfortunate limitation of humanity the angel was required, in addition to such celestial duties as smiling and soothing, to do kitchen service, cleaning, sewing, nursing, and other mundane tasks. But these things must be accomplished without the slightest diminution of the angelic virtues.

The angelic virtues, by the way, were of a curiously paradoxical nature.

They were inherent. A human being did not pretend to name them, could not be expected to have them, acknowledged them as far beyond his gross earthly nature; and yet, for all this, he kept constant watch over the virtues of the angel, wrote whole books of advice for angels on how they should behave, and openly held that angels would lose their virtues altogether should they once cease to obey the will and defer to the judgment of human kind.

This looks strange to us to-day as we consider these past conditions, but then it seemed fair enough; and the angels—bless their submissive, patient hearts!—never thought of questioning it.

It was perhaps only to be expected that when an angel fell the human creature should punish the celestial creature with unrelenting fury. It was so much easier to be an angel than to be human, that there was no excuse for an angel's falling, even by means of her own angelic pity and tender affection.

It seems perhaps hard that the very human creature the angel fell on, or fell with, or fell to—however you choose to put it—was as harsh as anyone in condemnation of the fall. He never assisted the angel to rise, but got out from under and resumed his way, leaving her in the mud. She was a great convenience to walk on, and, as was stoutly maintained by the human creature, helped keep the other angels clean.

This is exceedingly mysterious, and had better not be inquired into too closely.

The amount of physical labor of a severe and degrading sort required of one of these bright spirits, was amazing. Certain kinds of work—always and essentially dirty—were relegated wholly to her. Yet one of her first and most rigid duties was the keeping of her angelic robes spotlessly clean.

The human creature took great delight in contemplating the flowing robes of the angels. Their changeful motion suggested to him all manner of sweet and lovely thoughts and memories; also, the angelic virtues above mentioned were supposed largely to inhere in the flowing robes. Therefore flow they must, and the ample garments waved unchecked over the weary limbs of the wearer, the contiguous furniture and the stairs. For the angels unfortunately had no wings, and their work was such as required a good deal of going up and down stairs.

It is quite a peculiar thing, in contemplating this work, to see how largely it consisted in dealing with dirt. Yes, it does seem strange to this enlightened age; but the fact was that the angels waited on the human creatures in every form of menial service, doing things as their natural duty which the human creature loathed and scorned.

It does seem irreconcilable, but they reconciled it. The angel was an angel and the work was the angel's work and what more do you want?

There is one thing about the subject which looks a bit suspicious: The angels—I say it under breath—were not very bright!

The human creatures did not like intelligent angels—intelligence seemed to dim their shine, somehow, and pale their virtues. It was harder to reconcile things where the angels had any sense. Therefore every possible care was taken to prevent the angels from learning anything of our gross human wisdom.

But little by little, owing to the unthought-of consequences of repeated intermarriage between the angel and the human being, the angel longed for, found and ate the fruit of the forbidden tree of knowledge.

And in that day she surely died.

The species is now extinct. It is rumored that here and there in remote regions you can still find a solitary specimen—in places where no access is to be had to the deadly fruit; but the race as a race is extinct.

Poor dodo!

THE YELLOW WALL-PAPER

It is very seldom that mere ordinary people like John and myself secure ancestral halls for the summer.

A colonial mansion, a hereditary estate, I would say a haunted house, and reach the height of romantic felicity—but that would be asking too much of fate!

Still I will proudly declare that there is something queer about it.

Else, why should it be let so cheaply? And why have stood so long untenanted?

John laughs at me, of course, but one expects that in marriage.

John is practical in the extreme. He has no patience with faith, an intense horror of superstition, and he scoffs openly at any talk of things not to be felt and seen and put down in figures.

John is a physician, and *perhaps*—(I would not say it to a living soul, of course, but this is dead paper and a great relief to my mind—) *perhaps* that is one reason I do not get well faster.

You see he does not believe I am sick!

And what can one do?

If a physician of high standing, and one's own husband, assures friends and relatives that there is really nothing the matter with one but temporary nervous depression—a slight hysterical tendency—what is one to do?

My brother is also a physician, and also of high standing, and he says the same thing.

So I take phosphates or phosphites—whichever it is, and tonics, and journeys, and air, and exercise, and am absolutely forbidden to "work" until I am well again.

Personally, I disagree with their ideas.

Personally, I believe that congenial work, with excitement and change, would do me good.

But what is one to do?

I did write for a while in spite of them; but it *does* exhaust me a good deal—having to be so sly about it, or else meet with heavy opposition.

I sometimes fancy that in my condition if I had less opposition and more society and stimulus—but John says the very worst thing I can do is to think about my condition, and I confess it always makes me feel bad.

So I will let it alone and talk about the house.

The most beautiful place! It is quite alone, standing well back from the road, quite three miles from the village. It makes me think of English places that you read about, for there are hedges and walls and gates that lock, and lots of separate little houses for the gardeners and people.

There is a *delicious* garden! I never saw such a garden—large and shady, full of box-bordered paths, and lined with long grape-covered arbors with seats under them.

There were greenhouses, too, but they are all broken now.

There was some legal trouble, I believe, something about the heirs and co-heirs; anyhow, the place has been empty for years.

That spoils my ghostliness, I am afraid, but I don't care—there is something strange about the house—I can feel it.

I even said so to John one moonlight evening, but he said what I felt was a *draught*, and shut the window.

I get unreasonably angry with John sometimes. I'm sure I never used to be so sensitive. I think it is due to this nervous condition.

But John says if I feel so, I shall neglect proper self-control; so I take pains to control myself—before him, at least, and that makes me very tired.

I don't like our room a bit. I wanted one downstairs that opened on the piazza and had roses all over the window, and such pretty old-fashioned chintz hangings! but John would not hear of it.

He said there was only one window and not room for two beds, and no near room for him if he took another.

He is very careful and loving, and hardly lets me stir without special direction.

I have a schedule prescription for each hour in the day; he takes all care from me, and so I feel basely ungrateful not to value it more.

He said we came here solely on my account, that I was to have perfect rest and all the air I could get. "Your exercise depends on your strength, my dear," said he, "and your food somewhat on your appetite; but air you can absorb all the time." So we took the nursery at the top of the house.

It is a big, airy room, the whole floor nearly, with windows that look all ways, and air and sunshine galore. It was nursery first and then playroom and gymnasium, I should judge; for the windows are barred for little children, and there are rings and things in the walls.

The paint and paper look as if a boys' school had used it. It is stripped off—the paper—in great patches all around the head of my bed, about as far as I can reach, and in a great place on the other side of the room low down. I never saw a worse paper in my life.

One of those sprawling flamboyant patterns committing every artistic sin.

It is dull enough to confuse the eye in following, pronounced enough to constantly irritate and provoke study, and when you follow the lame uncertain curves for a little distance they suddenly commit suicide—plunge off at outrageous angles, destroy themselves in unheard of contradictions.

The color is repellant, almost revolting; a smouldering unclean yellow, strangely faded by the slow-turning sunlight.

It is a dull yet lurid orange in some places, a sickly sulphur tint in others.

No wonder the children hated it! I should hate it myself if I had to live in this room long.

There comes John, and I must put this away,—he hates to have me write a word.

* * * * *

We have been here two weeks, and I haven't felt like writing before, since that first day.

I am sitting by the window now, up in this atrocious nursery, and there is nothing to hinder my writing as much as I please, save lack of strength.

John is away all day, and even some nights when his cases are serious.

I am glad my case is not serious!

But these nervous troubles are dreadfully depressing.

John does not know how much I really suffer. He knows there is no *reason* to suffer, and that satisfies him.

Of course it is only nervousness. It does weigh on me so not to do my duty in any way!

I meant to be such a help to John, such a real rest and comfort, and here I am a comparative burden already!

Nobody would believe what an effort it is to do what little I am able,—to dress and entertain, and order things.

It is fortunate Mary is so good with the baby. Such a dear baby!

And yet I *cannot* be with him, it makes me so nervous.

I suppose John never was nervous in his life. He laughs at me so about this wall-paper!

At first he meant to repaper the room, but afterwards he said that I was letting it get the better of me, and that nothing was worse for a nervous patient than to give way to such fancies.

He said that after the wall-paper was changed it would be the heavy bedstead, and then the barred windows, and then that gate at the head of the stairs, and so on.

"You know the place is doing you good," he said, "and really, dear, I don't care to renovate the house just for a three months' rental."

"Then do let us go downstairs," I said, "there are such pretty rooms there."

Then he took me in his arms and called me a blessed little goose, and said he would go down cellar, if I wished, and have it whitewashed into the bargain.

But he is right enough about the beds and windows and things.

It is an airy and comfortable room as any one need wish, and, of course, I would not be so silly as to make him uncomfortable just for a whim.

I'm really getting quite fond of the big room, all but that horrid paper.

Out of one window I can see the garden, those mysterious deep-shaded arbors, the riotous old-fashioned flowers, and bushes and gnarly trees.

Out of another I get a lovely view of the bay and a little private wharf belonging to the estate. There is a beautiful shaded lane that runs down there from the house. I always fancy I see people walking in these numerous paths and arbors, but John has cautioned me not to give way to fancy in the least. He says that with my imaginative power and habit of story-making, a nervous weakness like mine is sure to lead to all manner of excited fancies, and that I ought to use my will and good sense to check the tendency. So I try.

I think sometimes that if I were only well enough to write a little it would relieve the press of ideas and rest me.

But I find I get pretty tired when I try.

It is so discouraging not to have any advice and companionship about my work. When I get really well, John says we will ask Cousin Henry and Julia down for a long visit; but he says he would as soon put fireworks in my pillow-case as to let me have those stimulating people about now.

I wish I could get well faster.

But I must not think about that. This paper looks to me as if it *knew* what a vicious influence it had!

There is a recurrent spot where the pattern lolls like a broken neck and two bulbous eyes stare at you upside down.

I get positively angry with the impertinence of it and the everlastingness. Up and down and sideways they crawl, and those absurd, unblinking eyes are everywhere. There is one place where two breadths didn't match, and the eyes go all up and down the line, one a little higher than the other.

I never saw so much expression in an inanimate thing before, and we all know how much expression they have! I used to lie awake as a child and get more entertainment and terror out of blank walls and plain furniture than most children could find in a toy-store.

I remember what a kindly wink the knobs of our big, old

bureau used to have, and there was one chair that always seemed like a strong friend.

I used to feel that if any of the other things looked too fierce I could always hop into that chair and be safe.

The furniture in this room is no worse than inharmonious, however, for we had to bring it all from downstairs. I suppose when this was used as a playroom they had to take the nursery things out, and no wonder! I never saw such ravages as the children have made here.

The wall-paper, as I said before, is torn off in spots, and it sticketh closer than a brother—they must have had persever-ance as well as hatred.

Then the floor is scratched and gouged and splintered, the plaster itself is dug out here and there, and this great heavy bed which is all we found in the room, looks as if it had been through the wars.

But I don't mind it a bit—only the paper.

There comes John's sister. Such a dear girl as she is, and so careful of me! I must not let her find me writing.

She is a perfect and enthusiastic housekeeper, and hopes for no better profession. I verily believe she thinks it is the writing which made me sick!

But I can write when she is out, and see her a long way off from these windows.

There is one that commands the road, a lovely shaded wind-ing road, and one that just looks off over the country. A lovely country, too, full of great elms and velvet meadows.

This wall-paper has a kind of subpattern in a different shade, a particularly irritating one, for you can only see it in certain lights, and not clearly then.

But in the places where it isn't faded and where the sun is just so—I can see a strange, provoking, formless sort of figure, that seems to skulk about behind that silly and conspicuous front design.

There's sister on the stairs!

* * * * *

Well, the Fourth of July is over! The people are all gone and I am tired out. John thought it might do me good to see a little company, so we just had mother and Nellie and the children down for a week.

Of course I didn't do a thing. Jennie sees to everything now. But it tired me all the same.

John says if I don't pick up faster he shall send me to Weir Mitchell in the fall.

But I don't want to go there at all. I had a friend who was in his hands once, and she says he is just like John and my brother, only more so!

Besides, it is such an undertaking to go so far.

I don't feel as if it was worth while to turn my hand over for anything, and I'm getting dreadfully fretful and querulous.

I cry at nothing, and cry most of the time.

Of course I don't when John is here, or anybody else, but when I am alone.

And I am alone a good deal just now. John is kept in town very often by serious cases, and Jennie is good and lets me alone when I want her to.

So I walk a little in the garden or down that lovely lane, sit on the porch under the roses, and lie down up here a good deal.

I'm getting really fond of the room in spite of the wall-paper. Perhaps *because* of the wall-paper.

It dwells in my mind so!

I lie here on this great immovable bed—it is nailed down, I believe—and follow that pattern about by the hour. It is as good as gymnastics, I assure you. I start, we'll say, at the bottom, down in the corner over there where it has not been touched, and I determine for the thousandth time that I *will* follow that pointless pattern to some sort of a conclusion.

I know a little of the principle of design, and I know this thing was not arranged on any laws of radiation, or alternation, or repetition, or symmetry, or anything else that I ever heard of.

It is repeated, of course, by the breadths, but not otherwise.

Looked at in one way each breadth stands alone, the bloated curves and flourishes—a kind of "debased Romanesque" with *delirium tremens*—go waddling up and down in isolated columns of fatuity.

But, on the other hand, they connect diagonally, and the

sprawling outlines run off in great slanting waves of optic horror, like a lot of wallowing seaweeds in full chase.

The whole thing goes horizontally, too, at least it seems so,
and I exhaust myself in trying to distinguish the order of its
going in that direction.

They have used a horizontal breadth for a frieze, and that
adds wonderfully to the confusion.

There is one end of the room where it is almost intact, and
there, when the crosslights fade and the low sun shines directly upon it, I can almost fancy radiation after all,—the interminable grotesques seem to form around a common centre
and rush off in headlong plunges of equal distraction.

It makes me tired to follow it. I will take a nap I guess.

* * * * *

I don't know why I should write this.

I don't want to.

I don't feel able.

And I know John would think it absurd. But I *must* say
what I feel and think in some way—it is such a relief!

But the effort is getting to be greater than the relief.

Half the time now I am awfully lazy, and lie down ever so
much.

John says I mustn't lose my strength, and has me take cod
liver oil and lots of tonics and things, to say nothing of ale and
wine and rare meat.

Dear John! He loves me very dearly, and hates to have me
sick. I tried to have a real earnest reasonable talk with him the
other day, and tell him how I wish he would let me go and
make a visit to Cousin Henry and Julia.

But he said I wasn't able to go, nor able to stand it after I got
there; and I did not make out a very good case for myself, for I
was crying before I had finished.

It is getting to be a great effort for me to think straight. Just
this nervous weakness I suppose.

And dear John gathered me up in his arms, and just carried
me upstairs and laid me on the bed, and sat by me and read to
me till it tired my head.

He said I was his darling and his comfort and all he had, and that I must take care of myself for his sake, and keep well.

He says no one but myself can help me out of it, that I must use my will and self-control and not let any silly fancies run away with me.

There's one comfort, the baby is well and happy, and does not have to occupy this nursery with the horrid wall-paper.

If we had not used it, that blessed child would have! What a fortunate escape! Why, I wouldn't have a child of mine, an impressionable little thing, live in such a room for worlds.

I never thought of it before, but it is lucky that John kept me here after all, I can stand it so much easier than a baby, you see.

Of course I never mention it to them any more—I am too wise,—but I keep watch of it all the same.

There are things in that paper that nobody knows but me, or ever will.

Behind that outside pattern the dim shapes get clearer every day.

It is always the same shape, only very numerous.

And it is like a woman stooping down and creeping about behind that pattern. I don't like it a bit. I wonder—I begin to think—I wish John would take me away from here!

* * * * *

It is so hard to talk with John about my case, because he is so wise, and because he loves me so.

But I tried it last night.

It was moonlight. The moon shines in all around just as the sun does.

I hate to see it sometimes, it creeps so slowly, and always comes in by one window or another.

John was asleep and I hated to waken him, so I kept still and watched the moonlight on that undulating wall-paper till I felt creepy.

The faint figure behind seemed to shake the pattern, just as if she wanted to get out.

I got up softly and went to feel and see if the paper *did* move, and when I came back John was awake.

"What is it, little girl?" he said. "Don't go walking about like that—you'll get cold."

I thought it was a good time to talk, so I told him that I really was not gaining here, and that I wished he would take me away.

"Why, darling!" said he, "our lease will be up in three weeks, and I can't see how to leave before.

"The repairs are not done at home, and I cannot possibly leave town just now. Of course if you were in any danger, I could and would, but you really are better, dear, whether you can see it or not. I am a doctor, dear, and I know. You are gaining flesh and color, your appetite is better, I feel really much easier about you."

"I don't weigh a bit more," said I, "nor as much; and my appetite may be better in the evening when you are here, but it is worse in the morning when you are away!"

"Bless her little heart!" said he with a big hug, "she shall be as sick as she pleases! But now let's improve the shining hours by going to sleep, and talk about it in the morning!"

"And you won't go away?" I asked gloomily.

"Why, how can I, dear? It is only three weeks more and then we will take a nice little trip of a few days while Jennie is getting the house ready. Really dear you are better!"

"Better in body perhaps—" I began, and stopped short, for he sat up straight and looked at me with such a stern, reproachful look that I could not say another word.

"My darling," said he, "I beg of you, for my sake and for our child's sake, as well as for your own, that you will never for one instant let that idea enter your mind! There is nothing so dangerous, so fascinating, to a temperament like yours. It is a false and foolish fancy. Can you not trust me as a physician when I tell you so?"

So of course I said no more on that score, and we went to sleep before long. He thought I was asleep first, but I wasn't, and lay there for hours trying to decide whether that front pattern and the back pattern really did move together or separately.

* * * * *

On a pattern like this, by daylight, there is a lack of sequence, a defiance of law, that is a constant irritant to a normal mind.

The color is hideous enough, and unreliable enough, and infuriating enough, but the pattern is torturing.

You think you have mastered it, but just as you get well underway in following, it turns a back-somersault and there you are. It slaps you in the face, knocks you down, and tramples upon you. It is like a bad dream.

The outside pattern is a florid arabesque, reminding one of a fungus. If you can imagine a toadstool in joints, an interminable string of toadstools, budding and sprouting in endless convolutions—why, that is something like it.

That is, sometimes!

There is one marked peculiarity about this paper, a thing nobody seems to notice but myself, and that is that it changes as the light changes.

When the sun shoots in through the east window—I always watch for that first long, straight ray—it changes so quickly that I never can quite believe it.

That is why I watch it always.

By moonlight—the moon shines in all night when there is a moon—I wouldn't know it was the same paper.

At night in any kind of light, in twilight, candlelight, lamplight, and worst of all by moonlight, it becomes bars! The outside pattern I mean, and the woman behind it is as plain as can be.

I didn't realize for a long time what the thing was that showed behind, that dim sub-pattern, but now I am quite sure it is a woman.

By daylight she is subdued, quiet. I fancy it is the pattern that keeps her so still. It is so puzzling. It keeps me quiet by the hour.

I lie down ever so much now. John says it is good for me, and to sleep all I can.

Indeed he started the habit by making me lie down for an hour after each meal.

It is a very bad habit I am convinced, for you see I don't sleep.

And that cultivates deceit, for I don't tell them I'm awake—O no!

The fact is I am getting a little afraid of John.

He seems very queer sometimes, and even Jennie has an inexplicable look.

It strikes me occasionally, just as a scientific hypothesis,—that perhaps it is the paper!

I have watched John when he did not know I was looking, and come into the room suddenly on the most innocent excuses, and I've caught him several times *looking at the paper!* And Jennie too. I caught Jennie with her hand on it once.

She didn't know I was in the room, and when I asked her in a quiet, a very quiet voice, with the most restrained manner possible, what she was doing with the paper—she turned around as if she had been caught stealing, and looked quite angry—asked me why I should frighten her so!

Then she said that the paper stained everything it touched, that she had found yellow smooches on all my clothes and John's, and she wished we would be more careful!

Did not that sound innocent? But I know she was studying that pattern, and I am determined that nobody shall find it out but myself!

* * * * *

Life is very much more exciting now than it used to be. You see I have something more to expect, to look forward to, to watch. I really do eat better, and am more quiet than I was.

John is so pleased to see me improve! He laughed a little the other day, and said I seemed to be flourishing in spite of my wall-paper.

I turned it off with a laugh. I had no intention of telling him it was *because* of the wall-paper—he would make fun of me. He might even want to take me away.

I don't want to leave now until I have found it out. There is a week more, and I think that will be enough.

* * * * *

I'm feeling ever so much better! I don't sleep much at night, for it is so interesting to watch developments; but I sleep a good deal in the daytime.

In the daytime it is tiresome and perplexing.

There are always new shoots on the fungus, and new shades

of yellow all over it. I cannot keep count of them, though I have tried conscientiously.

It is the strangest yellow, that wall-paper! It makes me think of all the yellow things I ever saw—not beautiful ones like buttercups, but old foul, bad yellow things.

But there is something else about that paper—the smell! I noticed it the moment we came into the room, but with so much air and sun it was not bad. Now we have had a week of fog and rain, and whether the windows are open or not, the smell is here.

It creeps all over the house.

I find it hovering in the dining-room, skulking in the parlor, hiding in the hall, lying in wait for me on the stairs.

It gets into my hair.

Even when I go to ride, if I turn my head suddenly and surprise it—there is that smell!

Such a peculiar odor, too! I have spent hours in trying to analyze it, to find what it smelled like.

It is not bad—at first, and very gentle, but quite the subtlest, most enduring odor I ever met.

In this damp weather it is awful, I wake up in the night and find it hanging over me.

It used to disturb me at first. I thought seriously of burning the house—to reach the smell.

But now I am used to it. The only thing I can think of that it is like is the *color* of the paper! A yellow smell.

There is a very funny mark on this wall, low down, near the mopboard. A streak that runs round the room. It goes behind every piece of furniture, except the bed, a long, straight, even *smooch*, as if it had been rubbed over and over.

I wonder how it was done and who did it, and what they did it for. Round and round and round—round and round and round—it makes me dizzy!

* * * * *

I really have discovered something at last.

Through watching so much at night, when it changes so, I have finally found out.

The front pattern *does* move—and no wonder! The woman behind shakes it!

Sometimes I think there are a great many women behind, and sometimes only one, and she crawls around fast, and her crawling shakes it all over.

Then in the very bright spots she keeps still, and in the very shady spots she just takes hold of the bars and shakes them hard.

And she is all the time trying to climb through. But nobody could climb through that pattern—it strangles so; I think that is why it has so many heads.

They get through, and then the pattern strangles them off and turns them upside down, and makes their eyes white!

If those heads were covered or taken off it would not be half so bad.

* * * * *

I think that woman gets out in the daytime!

And I'll tell you why—privately—I've seen her!

I can see her out of every one of my windows!

It is the same woman, I know, for she is always creeping, and most women do not creep by daylight.

I see her in that long shaded lane, creeping up and down. I see her in those dark grape arbors, creeping all around the garden.

I see her on that long road under the trees, creeping along, and when a carriage comes she hides under the blackberry vines.

I don't blame her a bit. It must be very humiliating to be caught creeping by daylight!

I always lock the door when I creep by daylight. I can't do it at night, for I know John would suspect something at once.

And John is so queer now, that I don't want to irritate him. I wish he would take another room! Besides, I don't want anybody to get that woman out at night but myself.

I often wonder if I could see her out of all the windows at once.

But, turn as fast as I can, I can only see out of one at one time.

And though I always see her, she *may* be able to creep faster than I can turn!

I have watched her sometimes away off in the open country, creeping as fast as a cloud shadow in a high wind.

* * * * *

If only that top pattern could be gotten off from the under one! I mean to try it, little by little.

I have found out another funny thing, but I shan't tell it this time! It does not do to trust people too much.

There are only two more days to get this paper off, and I believe John is beginning to notice. I don't like the look in his eyes.

And I heard him ask Jennie a lot of professional questions about me. She had a very good report to give.

She said I slept a good deal in the daytime.

John knows I don't sleep very well at night, for all I'm so quiet!

He asked me all sorts of questions, too, and pretended to be very loving and kind.

As if I couldn't see through him!

Still, I don't wonder he acts so, sleeping under this paper for three months.

It only interests me, but I feel sure John and Jennie are secretly affected by it.

* * * * *

Hurrah! This is the last day, but it is enough. John to stay in town over night, and won't be out until this evening.

Jennie wanted to sleep with me—the sly thing! but I told her I should undoubtedly rest better for a night all alone.

That was clever, for really I wasn't alone a bit! As soon as it was moonlight and that poor thing began to crawl and shake the pattern, I got up and ran to help her.

I pulled and she shook, I shook and she pulled, and before morning we had peeled off yards of that paper.

A strip about as high as my head and half around the room.

And then when the sun came and that awful pattern began to laugh at me, I declared I would finish it to-day!

We go away to-morrow, and they are moving all my furniture down again to leave things as they were before.

Jennie looked at the wall in amazement, but I told her merrily that I did it out of pure spite at the vicious thing.

She laughed and said she wouldn't mind doing it herself, but
I must not get tired.

How she betrayed herself that time!

But I am here, and no person touches this paper but me,—
not *alive*!

She tried to get me out of the room—it was too patent! But I
said it was so quiet and empty and clean now that I believed I
would lie down again and sleep all I could; and not to wake
me even for dinner—I would call when I woke.

So now she is gone, and the servants are gone, and the things
are gone, and there is nothing left but that great bedstead
nailed down, with the canvas mattress we found on it.

We shall sleep downstairs to-night, and take the boat home
to-morrow.

I quite enjoy the room, now it is bare again.

How those children did tear about here!

This bedstead is fairly gnawed!

But I must get to work.

I have locked the door and thrown the key down into the
front path.

I don't want to go out, and I don't want to have anybody
come in, till John comes.

I want to astonish him.

I've got a rope up here that even Jennie did not find. If that
woman does get out, and tries to get away, I can tie her!

But I forgot I could not reach far without anything to
stand on!

This bed will *not* move!

I tried to lift and push it until I was lame, and then I got
so angry I bit off a little piece at one corner—but it hurt my
teeth.

Then I peeled off all the paper I could reach standing on the
floor. It sticks horribly and the pattern just enjoys it! All those
strangled heads and bulbous eyes and waddling fungus
growths just shriek with derision!

I am getting angry enough to do something desperate. To

jump out of the window would be admirable exercise, but the bars are too strong even to try.

Besides I wouldn't do it. Of course not. I know well enough that a step like that is improper and might be misconstrued.

I don't like to *look* out of the windows even—there are so many of those creeping women, and they creep so fast.

I wonder if they all come out of that wall-paper as I did?

But I am securely fastened now by my well-hidden rope—you don't get *me* out in the road there!

I suppose I shall have to get back behind the pattern when it comes night, and that is hard!

It is so pleasant to be out in this great room and creep around as I please!

I don't want to go outside. I won't, even if Jennie asks me to.

For outside you have to creep on the ground, and everything is green instead of yellow.

But here I can creep smoothly on the floor, and my shoulder just fits in that long smooch around the wall, so I cannot lose my way.

Why there's John at the door!

It is no use, young man, you can't open it!

How he does call and pound!

Now he's crying for an axe.

It would be a shame to break down that beautiful door!

"John dear!" said I in the gentlest voice, "the key is down by the front steps, under a plantain leaf!"

That silenced him for a few moments.

Then he said—very quietly indeed, "Open the door, my darling!"

"I can't," said I. "The key is down by the front door under a plantain leaf!"

And then I said it again, several times, very gently and slowly, and said it so often that he had to go and see, and he got it of course, and came in. He stopped short by the door.

"What is the matter?" he cried. "For God's sake, what are you doing!"

I kept on creeping just the same, but I looked at him over my shoulder.

"I've got out at last," said I, "in spite of you and Jane! And I've pulled off most of the paper, so you can't put me back!"

Now why should that man have fainted? But he did, and right across my path by the wall, so that I had to creep over him every time!

THE ROCKING-CHAIR

A waving spot of sunshine, a signal light that caught the eye at once in a waste of commonplace houses, and all the dreary dimness of a narrow city street.

Across some low roof that made a gap in the wall of masonry, shot a level, brilliant beam of the just-setting sun, touching the golden head of a girl in an open window.

She sat in a high-backed rocking-chair with brass mountings that glittered as it swung, rocking slowly back and forth, never lifting her head, but fairly lighting up the street with the glory of her sunlit hair.

We two stopped and stared, and, so staring, caught sight of a small sign in a lower window—"Furnished Lodgings." With a common impulse we crossed the street and knocked at the dingy front door.

Slow, even footsteps approached from within, and a soft girlish laugh ceased suddenly as the door opened, showing us an old woman, with a dull, expressionless face and faded eyes.

Yes, she had rooms to let. Yes, we could see them. No, there was no service. No, there were no meals. So murmuring monotonously, she led the way up-stairs. It was an ordinary house enough, on a poor sort of street, a house in no way remarkable or unlike its fellows.

She showed us two rooms, connected, neither better nor worse than most of their class, rooms without a striking feature about them, unless it was the great brass-bound chair we found still rocking gently by the window.

But the gold-haired girl was nowhere to be seen.

I fancied I heard the light rustle of girlish robes in the inner chamber—a breath of that low laugh—but the door leading to this apartment was locked, and when I asked the woman if we could see the other rooms she said she had no other rooms to let.

A few words aside with Hal, and we decided to take these two, and move in at once. There was no reason we should not. We were looking for lodgings when that swinging sunbeam caught our eyes, and the accommodations were fully as good as we could pay for. So we closed our bargain on the spot, returned to our deserted boarding-house for a few belongings, and were settled anew that night.

Hal and I were young newspaper men, "penny-a-liners," part of that struggling crowd of aspirants who are to literature what squires and pages were to knighthood in olden days. We were winning our spurs. So far it was slow work, unpleasant and ill-paid—so was squireship and pagehood, I am sure; menial service and laborious polishing of armor; long running afoot while the master rode. But the squire could at least honor his lord and leader, while we, alas! had small honor for those above us in our profession, with but too good reason. We, of course, should do far nobler things when these same spurs were won!

Now it may have been mere literary instinct—the grasping at "material" of the pot-boiling writers of the day, and it may have been another kind of instinct—the unacknowledged attraction of the fair unknown; but, whatever the reason, the place had drawn us both, and here we were.

Unbroken friendship begun in babyhood held us two together, all the more closely because Hal was a merry, prosaic, clear-headed fellow, and I sensitive and romantic.

The fearless frankness of family life we shared, but held the right to unapproachable reserves, and so kept love unstrained.

We examined our new quarters with interest. The front room, Hal's, was rather big and bare. The back room, mine, rather small and bare.

He preferred that room, I am convinced, because of the window and the chair. I preferred the other, because of the locked door. We neither of us mentioned these prejudices.

"Are you sure you would not rather have this room?" asked Hal, conscious, perhaps, of an ulterior motive in his choice.

"No, indeed," said I, with a similar reservation; "you only have the street and I have a real 'view' from my window. The only thing I begrudge you is the chair!"

"You may come and rock therein at any hour of the day or night," said he magnanimously. "It is tremendously comfortable, for all its black looks."

It was a comfortable chair, a very comfortable chair, and we both used it a great deal. A very high-backed chair, curving a little forward at the top, with heavy square corners. These corners, the ends of the rockers, the great sharp knobs that tipped the arms, and every other point and angle were mounted in brass.

"Might be used for a battering-ram!" said Hal.

He sat smoking in it, rocking slowly and complacently by the window, while I lounged on the foot of the bed, and watched a pale young moon sink slowly over the western housetops.

It went out of sight at last, and the room grew darker and darker till I could only see Hal's handsome head and the curving chair-back move slowly to and fro against the dim sky.

"What brought us here so suddenly, Maurice?" he asked, out of the dark.

"Three reasons," I answered. "Our need of lodgings, the suitability of these, and a beautiful head."

"Correct," said he. "Anything else?"

"Nothing you would admit the existence of, my sternly logical friend. But I am conscious of a certain compulsion, or at least attraction, in the case, which does not seem wholly accounted for, even by golden hair."

"For once I will agree with you," said Hal. "I feel the same way myself, and I am not impressionable."

We were silent for a little. I may have closed my eyes,—it may have been longer than I thought, but it did not seem another moment when something brushed softly against my arm, and Hal in his great chair was rocking beside me.

"Excuse me," said he, seeing me start. "This chair evidently 'walks,' I've seen 'em before."

So had I, on carpets, but there was no carpet here, and I thought I was awake.

He pulled the heavy thing back to the window again, and we went to bed.

Our door was open, and we could talk back and forth, but presently I dropped off and slept heavily until morning. But I must have dreamed most vividly, for he accused me of rocking in his chair half the night; said he could see my outline clearly against the starlight.

"No," said I, "you dreamed it. You've got rocking-chair on the brain."

"Dream it is, then," he answered cheerily. "Better a nightmare than a contradiction; a vampire than a quarrel! Come on, let's go to breakfast!"

We wondered greatly as the days went by that we saw nothing of our golden-haired charmer. But we wondered in silence, and neither mentioned it to the other.

Sometimes I heard her light movements in the room next mine, or the soft laugh somewhere in the house; but the mother's slow, even steps were more frequent, and even she was not often visible.

All either of us saw of the girl, to my knowledge, was from the street, for she still availed herself of our chair by the window. This we disapproved of, on principle, the more so as we left the doors locked, and her presence proved the possession of another key. No; there was the door in my room! But I did not mention the idea. Under the circumstances, however, we made no complaint, and used to rush stealthily and swiftly up-stairs, hoping to surprise her. But we never succeeded. Only the chair was often found still rocking, and sometimes I fancied a faint sweet odor lingering about, an odor strangely saddening and suggestive. But one day when I thought Hal was there I rushed in unceremoniously and caught her. It was but a glimpse—a swift, light, noiseless sweep—she vanished into my own room. Following her with apologies for such a sudden entrance, I was too late. The envious door was locked again.

Our landlady's fair daughter was evidently shy enough when brought to bay, but strangely willing to take liberties in our absence.

Still, I had seen her, and for that sight would have forgiven much. Hers was a strange beauty, infinitely attractive yet infinitely perplexing. I marveled in secret, and longed with painful eagerness for another meeting; but I said nothing to Hal of my surprising her—it did not seem fair to the girl! She might have some good reason for going there; perhaps I could meet her again.

So I took to coming home early, on one excuse or another, and inventing all manner of errands to get to the room when Hal was not in.

But it was not until after numberless surprises on that point, finding him there when I supposed him downtown, and noticing something a little forced in his needless explanations, that I began to wonder if he might not be on the same quest.

Soon I was sure of it. I reached the corner of the street one evening just at sunset, and—yes, there was the rhythmic swing of that bright head in the dark frame of the open window. There also was Hal in the street below. She looked out, she smiled. He let himself in and went up-stairs.

I quickened my pace. I was in time to see the movement stop, the fair head turn, and Hal standing beyond her in the shadow.

I passed the door, passed the street, walked an hour—two hours—got a late supper somewhere, and came back about bedtime with a sharp and bitter feeling in my heart that I strove in vain to reason down. Why he had not as good a right to meet her as I it were hard to say, and yet I was strangely angry with him.

When I returned the lamplight shone behind the white curtain, and the shadow of the great chair stood motionless against it. Another shadow crossed—Hal—smoking. I went up.

He greeted me effusively and asked why I was so late. Where I got supper. Was unnaturally cheerful. There was a sudden dreadful sense of concealment between us. But he told nothing and I asked nothing, and we went silently to bed.

I blamed him for saying no word about our fair mystery, and yet I had said none concerning my own meeting. I racked my brain with questions as to how much he had really seen of her; if she had talked to him; what she had told him; how long she had stayed.

I tossed all night and Hal was sleepless too, for I heard him rocking for hours, by the window, by the bed, close to my door. I never knew a rocking-chair to "walk" as that one did.

Towards morning the steady creak and swing was too much for my nerves or temper.

"For goodness' sake, Hal, do stop that and go to bed!"

"What?" came a sleepy voice.

"Don't fool!" said I, "I haven't slept a wink to-night for your everlasting rocking. Now do leave off and go to bed."

"Go to bed! I've been in bed all night and I wish you had! Can't you use the chair without blaming me for it?"

And all the time I *heard* him rock, rock, rock, over by the hall door!

I rose stealthily and entered the room, meaning to surprise the ill-timed joker and convict him in the act.

Both rooms were full of the dim phosphorescence of reflected moonlight; I knew them even in the dark; and yet I stumbled just inside the door, and fell heavily.

Hal was out of bed in a moment and had struck a light.

"Are you hurt, my dear boy?"

I was hurt, and solely by his fault, for the chair was not where I supposed, but close to my bedroom door, where he must have left it to leap into bed when he heard me coming. So it was in no amiable humor that I refused his offers of assistance and limped back to my own sleepless pillow. I had struck my ankle on one of those brass-tipped rockers, and it pained me severely. I never saw a chair so made to hurt as that one. It was so large and heavy and ill-balanced, and every joint and corner so shod with brass. Hal and I had punished ourselves enough on it before, especially in the dark when we forgot where the thing was standing, but never so severely as this. It was not like Hal to play such tricks, and both heart and ankle ached as I crept into bed again to toss and doze and dream and fitfully start till morning.

Hal was kindness itself, but he would insist that he had been asleep and I rocking all night, till I grew actually angry with him.

"That's carrying a joke too far," I said at last. "I don't mind a joke, even when it hurts, but there are limits."

"Yes, there are!" said he, significantly, and we dropped the subject.

Several days passed. Hal had repeated meetings with the gold-haired damsel; this I saw from the street; but save for these bitter glimpses I waited vainly.

It was hard to bear, harder almost than the growing estrangement between Hal and me, and that cut deeply. I think that at last either one of us would have been glad to go away by himself, but neither was willing to leave the other to the room, the chair, the beautiful unknown.

Coming home one morning unexpectedly, I found the dull-faced landlady arranging the rooms, and quite laid myself out to make an impression upon her, to no purpose.

"That is a fine old chair you have there," said I, as she stood mechanically polishing the brass corners with her apron.

She looked at the darkly glittering thing with almost a flash of pride.

"Yes," said she, "a fine chair!"

"Is it old?" I pursued.

"Very old," she answered briefly.

"But I thought rocking-chairs were a modern American invention?" said I.

She looked at me apathetically.

"It is Spanish," she said, "Spanish oak, Spanish leather, Spanish brass, Spanish————." I did not catch the last word, and she left the room without another.

It was a strange ill-balanced thing, that chair, though so easy and comfortable to sit in. The rockers were long and sharp behind, always lying in wait for the unwary, but cut short in front: and the back was so high and so heavy on top, that what with its weight and the shortness of the front rockers, it tipped forward with an ease and a violence equally astonishing.

This I knew from experience, as it had plunged over upon me during some of our frequent encounters. Hal also was a sufferer, but in spite of our manifold bruises, neither of us would have had the chair removed, for did not she sit in it, evening after evening, and rock there in the golden light of the setting sun.

So, evening after evening, we two fled from our work as early as possible, and hurried home alone, by separate ways, to the dingy street and the glorified window.

I could not endure forever. When Hal came home first, I, lingering in the street below, could see through our window that lovely head and his in close proximity. When I came first, it was to catch perhaps a quick glance from above—a bewildering smile—no more. She was always gone when I reached the room, and the inner door of my chamber irrevocably locked.

At times I even caught the click of the latch, heard the flutter of loose robes on the other side; and sometimes this daily disappointment, this constant agony of hope deferred, would bring me to my knees by that door begging her to open to me, crying to her in every term of passionate endearment and persuasion that tortured heart of man could think to use.

Hal had neither word nor look for me now, save those of studied politeness and cold indifference, and how could I behave otherwise to him, so proven to my face a liar?

I saw him from the street one night, in the broad level sunlight, sitting in that chair, with the beautiful head on his shoulder. It was more than I could bear. If he had won, and won so utterly, I would ask but to speak to her once, and say farewell to both forever. So I heavily climbed the stairs, knocked loudly, and entered at Hal's "Come in!" only to find him sitting there alone, smoking—yes, smoking in the chair which but a moment since had held her too!

He had but just lit the cigar, a paltry device to blind my eyes.

"Look here, Hal," said I, "I can't stand this any longer. May I ask you one thing? Let me see her once, just once, that I may say good-bye, and then neither of you need see me again!"

Hal rose to his feet and looked me straight in the eye. Then he threw that whole cigar out of the window, and walked to within two feet of me.

"Are you crazy," he said. "*I* ask her! *I!* I have never had speech of her in my life! And *you*—" He stopped and turned away.

"And I what?" I would have it out now whatever came.

"And you have seen her day after day—talked with her—I need not repeat all that my eyes have seen!"

"You need not, indeed," said I. "It would tax even your invention. I have never seen her in this room but once, and then but for a fleeting glimpse—no word. From the street I have seen her often—with you!"

He turned very white and walked from me to the window, then turned again.

"I have never seen her in this room for even such a moment as you own to. From the street I have seen her often—*with you!*"

We looked at each other.

"Do you mean to say," I inquired slowly, "that I did not see you just now sitting in that chair, by that window, with her in your arms?"

"Stop!" he cried, throwing out his hand with a fierce gesture. It struck sharply on the corner of the chair-back. He wiped the blood mechanically from the three-cornered cut, looking fixedly at me.

"I saw you," said I.

"You did not!" said he.

I turned slowly on my heel and went into my room. I could not bear to tell that man, my more than brother, that he lied.

I sat down on my bed with my head on my hands, and presently I heard Hal's door open and shut, his step on the stair, the front door slam behind him. He had gone, I knew not where, and if he went to his death and a word of mine would have stopped him, I would not have said it. I do not know how long I sat there, in the company of hopeless love and jealousy and hate.

Suddenly, out of the silence of the empty room, came the steady swing and creak of the great chair. Perhaps—it must be! I sprang to my feet and noiselessly opened the door. There she sat by the window, looking out, and—yes—she threw a kiss to some one below. Ah, how beautiful she was! How beautiful! I made a step toward her. I held out my hands, I uttered I know not what—when all at once came Hal's quick step upon the stairs.

She heard it, too, and, giving me one look, one subtle, mysterious, triumphant look, slipped past me and into my room just as Hal burst in. He saw her go. He came straight to me and I thought he would have struck me down where I stood.

"Out of my way," he cried. "I will speak to her. Is it not enough to see?"—he motioned toward the window with his wounded hand—"Let me pass!"

"She is not there," I answered. "She has gone through into the other room."

A light laugh sounded close by us, a faint, soft, silver laugh, almost at my elbow.

He flung me from his path, threw open the door, and entered. The room was empty.

"Where have you hidden her?" he demanded. I coldly pointed to the other door.

"So her room opens into yours, does it?" he muttered with a bitter smile. "No wonder you preferred the 'view!' Perhaps I can open it too?" And he laid his hand upon the latch.

I smiled then, for bitter experience had taught me that it was always locked, locked to all my prayers and entreaties. Let him kneel there as I had! But it opened under his hand! I sprang to his side, and we looked into—a closet, two by four, as bare and shallow as an empty coffin!

He turned to me, as white with rage as I was with terror. I was not thinking of him.

"What have you done with her?" he cried. And then contemptuously—"That I should stop to question a liar!"

I paid no heed to him, but walked back into the other room, where the great chair rocked by the window.

He followed me, furious with disappointment, and laid his hand upon the swaying back, his strong fingers closing on it till the nails were white.

"Will you leave this place?" said he.

"No," said I.

"I will live no longer with a liar and a traitor," said he.

"Then you will have to kill yourself," said I.

With a muttered oath he sprang upon me, but caught his foot in the long rocker, and fell heavily.

So wild a wave of hate rose in my heart that I could have trampled upon him where he lay—killed him like a dog—but with a mighty effort I turned from him and left the room.

When I returned it was broad day. Early and still, not sunrise yet, but full of hard, clear light on roof and wall and roadway. I stopped on the lower floor to find the landlady and announce my immediate departure. Door after door I knocked at, tried and opened; room after room I entered and searched thoroughly; in all that house, from cellar to garret, was no furnished room but ours, no sign of human occupancy. Dust, dust, and cobwebs everywhere. Nothing else.

With a strange sinking of the heart I came back to our own door.

Surely I heard the landlady's slow, even step inside, and that soft, low laugh. I rushed in.

The room was empty of all life; both rooms utterly empty.

Yes, of all life; for, with the love of a lifetime surging in my heart, I sprang to where Hal lay beneath the window, and found him dead.

Dead, and most horribly dead. Three heavy marks—blows—three deep, three cornered gashes—I started to my feet—even the chair had gone!

Again the whispered laugh. Out of that house of terror I fled desperately.

From the street I cast one shuddering glance at the fateful window.

The risen sun was gilding all the housetops, and its level rays, striking the high panes on the building opposite, shone back in a calm glory on the great chair by the window, the sweet face, down-dropped eyes, and swaying golden head.

THROUGH THIS

The dawn colors creep up my bedroom wall, softly, slowly.

Darkness, dim gray, dull blue, soft lavender, clear pink, pale yellow, warm gold—sunlight.

A new day.

With the great sunrise great thoughts come.

I rise with the world. I live, I can help. Here close at hand lie the sweet home duties through which my life shall touch the others! Through this man made happier and stronger by my living; through these rosy babies sleeping here in the growing light; through this small, sweet, well-ordered home, whose restful influence shall touch all comers; through me too, perhaps—there's the baker, I must get up, or this bright purpose fades.

How well the fire burns! Its swift kindling and gathering roar speak of accomplishment. The rich odor of coffee steals through the house.

John likes morning-glories on the breakfast table—scented flowers are better with lighter meals. All is ready—healthful, dainty, delicious.

The clean-aproned little ones smile milky-mouthed over their bowls of mush. John kisses me good-bye so happily.

Through this dear work, well done, I shall reach, I shall help—but I must get the dishes done and not dream.

"Good morning! Soap, please, the same kind. Coffee, rice, two boxes of gelatine. That's all, I think. Oh—crackers! Good morning."

There, I forgot the eggs! I can make these go, I guess. Now to soak the tapioca. Now the beets on, they take so long. I'll bake the potatoes—they don't go in yet. Now babykins must have her bath and nap.

A clean hour and a half before dinner. I can get those little nightgowns cut and basted. How bright the sun is! Amaranth lies on the grass under the rosebush, stretching her paws among the warm, green blades. The kittens tumble over her. She's brought them three mice this week. Baby and Jack are on the warm grass too—happy, safe, well. Careful, dear! Don't go away from little sister!

By and by when they are grown, I can—O there! the bell!

Ah, well!—yes—I'd like to have joined. I believe in it, but I can't now. Home duties forbid. This is my work. Through this, in time—there's the bell again, and it waked the baby!

As if I could buy a sewing machine every week! I'll put out a bulletin, stating my needs for the benefit of agents. I don't believe in buying at the door anyway, yet I suppose they must live. Yes, dear! Mamma's coming!

I wonder if torchon would look better, or Hamburg? It's softer but it looks older. Oh, here's that knit edging grandma sent me. Bless her dear heart!

There! I meant to have swept the bed-room this morning so as to have more time to-morrow. Perhaps I can before dinner. It does look dreadfully. I'll just put the potatoes in. Baked potatoes are so good! I love to see Jack dig into them with his little spoon.

John says I cook steak better than anyone he ever saw.

Yes, dear?

Is that so? Why, I should think they'd *know* better. Can't the people do anything about it?

Why no—not *personally*—but I should think *you* might. What are men for if they can't keep the city in order.

Cream on the pudding, dear?

That was a good dinner. I like to cook. I think housework is noble if you do it in a right spirit.

That pipe must be seen to before long. I'll speak to John about it. Coal's pretty low, too.

Guess I'll put on my best boots, I want to run down town for a few moments—in case mother comes and can stay with baby. I wonder if mother wouldn't like to join that—she has time enough. But she doesn't seem to be a bit interested in outside things. I ought to take baby out in her carriage, but it's so heavy with Jack, and yet Jack can't walk a great way. Besides, if mother comes I needn't. Maybe we'll all go in the car—but that's such an undertaking! Three o'clock!

Jack! Jack! Don't do that—here—wait a moment.

I ought to answer Jennie's letter. She writes such splendid things, but I don't go with her in half she says. A woman cannot do that way and keep a family going. I'll write to her this evening.

Of course, if one *could*, I'd like as well as anyone to be in those great live currents of thought and action. Jennie and I were full of it in school. How long ago that seems. But I never thought then of being so happy. Jennie isn't happy, I know—she can't be, poor thing, till she's a wife and mother.

O, there comes mother! Jack, deary, open the gate for Grandma! So glad you could come, mother dear! Can you stay awhile and let me go down town on a few errands?

Mother looks real tired. I wish she would go out more and have some outside interests. Mary and the children are too much for her, I think. Harry ought not to have brought them home. Mother needs rest. She's brought up one family.

There, I've forgotten my list, I hurried so. Thread, elastic, buttons; what was that other thing? Maybe I'll think of it.

How awfully cheap! How can they make them at that price! Three, please. I guess with these I can make the others last through the year. They're so pretty, too. How much are these? Jack's got to have a new coat before long—not to-day.

O dear! I've missed that car, and mother can't stay after five! I'll cut across and hurry.

Why the milk hasn't come, and John's got to go out early to-night. I wish the election was over.

I'm sorry, dear, but the milk was so late I couldn't make it. Yes, I'll speak to him. O, no, I guess not; he's a very reliable man, usually, and the milk's good. Hush, hush, baby! Papa's talking!

Good night, dear, don't be too late.

Sleep, baby, sleep!
The large stars are the sheep,
The little stars are the lambs, I guess,
And the fair moon is the shepherdess.
Sleep, baby, sleep!

How pretty they look! Thank God, they keep so well.

It's no use, I can't write a letter to-night—especially to Jennie. I'm too tired. I'll go to bed early. John hates to have me wait up for him late. I'll go now, if it is before dark—then get up early tomorrow and get the sweeping done. How loud the crickets are! The evening shades creep down my bedroom wall—softly—slowly.

Warm gold—pale yellow—clear pink—soft lavender—dull blue—dim gray—darkness.

THE BOYS AND
THE BUTTER

Young Holdfast and J. Edwards Fernald sat grimly at their father's table, being seen and not heard, and eating what was set before them, asking no questions for conscience' sake, as they had been duly reared. But in their hearts were most unchristian feelings toward a venerable aunt, by name Miss Jane McCoy.

They knew, with the keen observation of childhood, that it was only a sense of hospitality, and duty to a relative, which made their father and mother polite to her—polite, but not cordial.

Mr. Fernald, a professed Christian, did his best to love his wife's aunt, who came as near being an "enemy" as anyone he knew. But Mahala, his wife, was of a less saintly nature, and made no pretense of more than decent courtesy.

"I don't like her and I won't pretend to; it's not honest!" she protested to her husband, when he remonstrated with her upon her want of natural affection. "I can't help her being my aunt—we are not commanded to honor our aunts and uncles, Jonathan E."

Mrs. Fernald's honesty was of an iron hardness and heroic mould. She would have died rather than have told a lie, and classed as lies any forms of evasion, deceit, concealment or even artistic exaggeration.

Her two sons, thus starkly reared, found their only imaginative license in secret converse between themselves, sacredly guarded by a pact of mutual faith, which was stronger than any outward compulsion. They kicked each other under the table, while enduring this visitation; exchanged dark glances concerning the object of their common dislike, and discussed her personal peculiarities with caustic comment later, when they should have been asleep.

Miss McCoy was not an endearing old lady. She was heavily built, and gobbled her food, carefully selecting the best. Her clothing was elaborate, but not beautiful, and on close approach aroused a suspicion of deferred laundry bills.

Among many causes for dislike for her aunt, Mrs. Fernald cherished this point especially. On one of these unwelcome visits she had been at some pains to carry up hot water for the Saturday evening bath, which was all the New England conscience of those days exacted, and the old lady had neglected it not only once but twice.

"Goodness sake, Aunt Jane! aren't you ever going to take a bath?"

"Nonsense!" replied her visitor. "I don't believe in all this wetting and slopping. The Scripture says, 'Whoso washeth his feet, his whole body shall be made clean.'"

Miss McCoy had numberless theories for other people's conduct, usually backed by well-chosen texts, and urged them with no regard for anybody's feelings. Even the authority of parents had no terrors for her.

Sipping her tea from the saucer with deep swattering inhalations, she fixed her prominent eyes upon the two boys as they ploughed their way through their bread and butter. Nothing must be left on the plates in the table ethics of that time. The meal was simple in the extreme. A New Hampshire farm furnished few luxuries, and the dish of quince preserves had already been depleted by her.

"Mahala," she said with solemn determination, "those boys eat too much butter."

Mrs. Fernald flushed up to the edging of her cap. "I think I must be the judge of what my children eat at my table, Aunt Jane," she answered, not too gently.

Here Mr. Fernald interposed with a "soft answer." (He had never lost faith in the efficacy of these wrath turners, even on long repeated failure. As a matter of fact, to his wife's temper, a soft answer, especially an intentionally soft answer, was a fresh aggravation.) "The missionary, now, he praised our butter; said he never got any butter in China, or wherever 'tis he lives."

"He is a man of God," announced Miss McCoy. "If there is anybody on this poor earth deserving reverence, it is a missionary. What they endure for the Gospel is a lesson for us all. When I am taken I intend to leave all I have to the Missionary Society. You know that."

They knew it and said nothing. Their patience with her was in no way mercenary.

"But what I am speaking of is children," she continued, not to be diverted from her fell purpose. "Children ought not to eat butter."

"They seem to thrive on it," Mrs. Fernald replied tartly. And in truth both the boys were sturdy little specimens of humanity, in spite of their luxurious food.

"It's bad for them. Makes them break out. Bad for the blood. And self-denial is good for children. 'It is better to bear the yoke in thy youth.'"

The youth in question spread its butter more thickly, and ate it with satisfaction, saying nothing.

"Look here, boys!" she suddenly assailed them. "If you will go without butter for a year—a whole year, till I come round again—I'll give each of you fifty dollars!"

This was an overwhelming proposition.

Butter was butter—almost the only alleviation of a dry and monotonous bill of fare, consisting largely of bread. Bread without butter! Brown bread without butter! No butter on potatoes! No butter on anything! The young imagination recoiled. And this measureless deprivation was to cover a whole year. A ninth or an eleventh of a lifetime to them respectively. About a fifth of all they could really remember. Countless days, each having three meals; weeks, months, the long dry butterless vista stretched before them like Siberian exile to a Russian prisoner.

But, on the other hand, there was the fifty dollars. Fifty dollars would buy a horse, a gun, tools, knives—a farm, maybe. It could be put in the bank and drawn on for life, doubtless. Fifty dollars at that time was like five hundred to-day, and to a child it was a fortune.

Even their mother wavered in her resentment as she considered the fifty dollars, and the father did not waver at all, but thought it a Godsend.

"Let 'em choose," said Miss McCoy.

Stern is the stock of the Granite State. Self-denial is the essense of their religion; and economy, to give it a favorable name, is for them Nature's first law.

The struggle was brief. Holdfast laid down his thick-spread slice. J. Edwards laid down his. "Yes, ma'am," said one after the other. Thank you, ma'am. We'll do it."

* * * * *

It was a long year. Milk did not take the place of it. Gravy and drippings, freely given by their mother, did not take the place of it, nor did the infrequent portions of preserves. Nothing met the same want. And if their health was improved by the abstinence it was in no way visible to the naked eye. They were well, but they were well before.

As to the moral effect—it was complex. An extorted sacrifice has not the same odor of sanctity as a voluntary one. Even when made willingly, if the willingness is purchased, the effect seems somewhat confused. Butter was not renounced, only postponed, and as the year wore on the young ascetics, in their secret conferences, indulged in wild visions of oleaginous excess so soon as the period of dearth should be over.

But most they refreshed their souls with plans for the spending and the saving of the hard-earned wealth that was coming to them. Holdfast was for saving his, and being a rich man—richer than Captain Briggs or Deacon Holbrook. But at times he wavered, spurred by the imagination of J. Edwards, and invested that magic sum in joys unnumbered.

The habit of self-denial was perhaps being established, but so was the habit of discounting the future, of indulging in wild plans of self-gratification when the ship came in.

* * * * *

Even for butterless boys, time passes, and the endless year at last drew to a close. They counted the months, they counted the weeks, they counted the days. Thanksgiving itself shone pale by contrast with this coming festival of joy and triumph. As it drew nearer and nearer their excitement increased, and they could not forget it even in the passing visit of a real missionary, a live one, who had been to those dark lands where the heathen go naked, worship idols and throw their children to the crocodiles.

They were taken to hear him, of course, and not only so, but he came to supper at their house and won their young hearts by the stories he told them. Gray of hair and beard was the preacher and sternly devout, but he had a twinkling eye none the less, and told tales of wonder and amazement that were sometimes almost funny and always interesting.

"Do not imagine, my young friends," he said, after filling them with delicious horror at the unspeakable wickedness of those "godless lands," "that the the heathen are wholly without morality. The Chinese, among whom I have labored for many years, are more honest than some Christians. Their business honor is a lesson to us all. But works alone cannot save." And he questioned them as to their religious state, receiving satisfactory answers.

The town turned out to hear him; and, when he went on his circuit, preaching, exhorting, describing the hardships and dangers of missionary life, the joys of soul-saving, and urging his hearers to contribute to this great duty of preaching the Gospel to all creatures, they had a sort of revival season; and arranged for a great missionary church meeting with a special collection when he should return.

The town talked missionary and thought missionary; dreamed missionary, it might well be; and garrets were ransacked to make up missionary boxes to send to the heathen. But Holdfast and J. Edwards mingled their interest in those unfortunate savages with a passionate desire for butter, and a longing for money such as they had never known before.

Then Miss McCoy returned.

They knew the day, the hour. They watched their father drive down to meet the stage, and tormented their mother with questions as to whether she would give it to them before supper or after.

"I'm sure I don't know!" she snapped at last. "I'll be thankful when it's over and done with, I'm sure! A mighty foolish business, I think!"

Then they saw the old chaise turn the corner. What? Only one in it! The boys rushed to the gate—the mother, too.

"What is it, Jonathan? Didn't she come?"

"Oh, father!"

"Where is she, father?"

"She's not coming," said Mr. Fernald. "Says she's going to stay with Cousin Sarah, so's to be in town and go to all the missionary doin's. But she's sent it."

Then he was besieged, as soon as the horse was put up, by three pairs of busy hands; they came to the supper table, whereon was a full two pounds of delicious butter, and sat down with tingling impatience.

The blessing was asked in all due form—a blessing ten miles long, it seemed to the youngsters, and then the long, fat envelope came out of Mr. Fernald's pocket.

"She must have written a lot," he said, taking out two folded papers, and then a letter.

"My dear great-nephews," ran this epistle, "as your parents have assured me that you have kept your promise, and denied yourselves butter for the space of a year, here is the fifty dollars I promised to each of you—wisely invested."

Mr. Fernald opened the papers. To Holdfast Fernald and to J. Edwards Fernald, duly made out, receipted, signed and sealed were two $50 life memberships in the Missionary Society!

Poor children! The younger one burst into wild weeping. The older seized the butter dish and cast it to the floor, for which he had to be punished, of course, but the punishment added nothing to his grief and rage.

When they were alone at last, and able to speak for sobbing, those gentle youths exchanged their sentiments; and these were of the nature of blasphemy and rebellion against God. They had learned at one fell blow the hideous lesson of human depravity. People lied—grown people—religious people—they lied! You couldn't trust them! They had been deceived, betrayed, robbed! They had lost the actual joy renounced, and the potential joy promised and withheld. The money they might someday earn, but not heaven itself could give back that year of butter. And all this in the name of religion—and of missionaries! Wild, seething outrage filled their hearts at first; slower results would follow.

* * * * *

The pious enthusiasm of the little town was at its height. The religious imagination, rather starved on the bald alternatives of Calvinism, found rich food in these glowing tales of danger, devotion, sometimes martyrdom; while the spirit of rigid economy, used to daylong saving from the cradle to the grave, took passionate delight in the success of these noble evangelists who went so far afield to save lost souls.

Out of their narrow means they had scraped still further; denied themselves necessaries where no pleasures remained; and when the crowning meeting was announced, the big collection meeting, with the wonderful brother from the Church in Asia to address them again, the meeting house was packed in floor and gallery.

Hearts were warm and open, souls were full of enthusiasm for the great work, wave on wave of intense feeling streamed through the crowded house.

Only in the Fernalds pew was a spirit out of tune.

Mr. Fernald, good man though he was, had not yet forgiven. His wife had not tried.

"Don't talk to me!" she had cried passionately, when he had urged a reconciliation. "Forgive your enemies! Yes, but she hasn't done any harm to *me!* It's my boys she's hurt! It don't say one word about forgiving other people's enemies!"

Yet Mrs. Fernald, for all her anger, seemed to have some inner source of consolation, denied her husband, over which she nodded to herself from time to time, drawing in her thin lips, and wagging her head decisively.

Vengeful bitterness and impotent rage possessed the hearts of Holdfast and J. Edwards.

This state of mind in young and old was not improved when,

on arriving at the meeting a little late, they had found the head of the pew was occupied by Miss McCoy.

It was neither the time nor the place for a demonstration. No other seats were vacant, and Mrs. Fernald marched in and sat next to her, looking straight at the pulpit. Next came the boys, and murder was in their hearts. Last, Mr. Fernald, inwardly praying for a more Christian spirit, but not getting it.

Holdfast and young J. Edwards dared not speak in church or make any protest; but they smelled the cardamum seeds in the champing jaws beyond their mother, and they cast black looks at each other and very secretly showed clenched fists, held low.

In fierce inward rebellion they sat through the earlier speeches, and when the time came for the address of the occasion, even the deep voice of the brother from Asia failed to stir them. Was he not a missionary, and were not missionaries and all their works proved false?

But what was this?

The address was over; the collection, in cash, was in the piled plates at the foot of the pulpit. The collection in goods was enumerated and described with full names given.

Then the hero of the hour was seen to confer with the other reverend brothers, and to rise and come forward, raising his hand for silence.

"Dearly beloved brethren and sisters," he said, "in this time of thanksgiving for gifts spiritual and temporal I wish to ask your patience for a moment more, that we may do justice. There has come to my ears a tale concerning one of our recent gifts which I wish you to hear, that judgment may be done in Israel.

"One among us has brought to the House of the Lord a tainted offering—an offering stained with cruelty and falsehood. Two young children of our flock were bribed a year ago to renounce one of the scant pleasures of their lives, for a year's time—a whole long year of a child's life. They were bribed with a promise—a promise of untold wealth to a child, of fifty dollars each."

The congregation drew a long breath.

Those who knew of the Fernald boys' endeavor (and who in that friendly radius did not?) looked at them eagerly. Those who recognized Miss McCoy looked at her, too, and they were many. She sat, fanning herself, with a small, straight-handled palmleaf fan, striving to appear unconscious.

"When the time was up," the clear voice went on remorsefully, "the year of struggle and privation, and the eager hearts of childhood expected the reward; instead of keeping the given word, each child was given a paid life membership in our society!"

Again the house drew in its breath. Did not the end justify the means?

He went on:

"I have conferred with my fellow members, and we are united in our repudiation of this gift. The money is not ours. It was obtained by trick which the heathen themselves would scorn."

There was a shocked pause. Miss McCoy was purple in the face, and only kept her place for fear of drawing more attention if she strove to escape.

"I name no names," the speaker continued, "and I regret the burden laid upon me to thus expose this possibly well-meant transaction, but what we have at stake to-night is not this handful of silver, not the feelings of one sinner, but two children's souls. Are we to have their sense of justice outraged in impressionable youth? Are they to believe with the Psalmist that all men are liars? Are they to feel anger and blame for the great work to which our lives are given because in its name they were deceived and robbed? No, my brothers, we clear our skirts of ignominy. In the name of the society, I shall return this money to its rightful owners. 'Whoso offendeth one of these little ones, it were better that a millstone be hanged about his neck and he cast into the depths of the sea.'"

MRS. BEAZLEY'S DEEDS

Mrs. William Beazley was crouching on the floor of her living-room over the store in a most peculiar attitude. It was what a doctor would call the "knee-chest position"; and the woman's pale, dragged out appearance quite justified the idea.

She was as one scrubbing a floor and then laying her cheek to it, a rather undignified little pile of bones, albeit discreetly covered with stringy calico.

A hard voice from below suddenly called "Maria!" and when she jumped nervously, and hurried downstairs in answer, the cause of the position became apparent—she had been listening at a stovepipe hole.

In the store sat Mr. Beazley, quite comfortable in his back-tilted chair, enjoying a leisurely pipe and as leisurely a conversation with another smoking, back-tilting man, beside the empty stove.

"This lady wants some cotton elastic," said he; "you know where those dew-dabs are better'n I do."

A customer, also in stringy calico, stood at the counter. Mrs. Beazley waited on her with the swift precision of long practice, and much friendliness besides, going with her to the wagon afterwards, and standing there to chat, her thin little hand on the wheel as if to delay it.

"Maria!" called Mr. Beazley.

"Oh, good land!" said Mrs. Janeway, gathering up the reins.

"Well—good-by, Mrs. Janeway—do come around when you can; I can't seem to get down to Rockwell."

"Maria!" She hurried in. "Ain't supper ready yet?" inquired Mr. Beazley.

"It'll be ready at six, same as it always is," she replied wearily, turning again to the door. But her friend had driven off and she went slowly up-stairs.

Luella was there. Luella was only fourteen, but a big, courageous-looking girl, and prematurely wise from many maternal confidences. "Now you sit down and rest," she said. "I'll set the table and call Willie and everything. Baby's asleep all right."

Willie, shrilly summoned from the window, left his water wheel reluctantly and came in dripping and muddy.

"Never mind, mother," said Luella. "I'll fix him up in no time; supper's all ready."

"I can't eat a thing," said Mrs. Beazley, "I'm so worried!" She vibrated nervously in the wooden rocker by the small front window. Her thin hands gripped the arms; her mouth quivered—a soft little mouth that seemed to miss the smiles naturally belonging to it.

"It's another of them deeds!" she was saying over and over in her mind. "He'll do it. He's no right to do it, but he will; he always does. He don't care what I want—nor the children."

When the supper was over, Willie went to bed, and Luella minding the store and the baby, Mr. Beazley tipped back his chair and took to his toothpick. "I've got another deed for you to sign, Mrs. Beazley," said he. "Justice Fielden said he'd be along to-night some time, and we can fix it before him—save takin' it to town."

"What's it about?" she demanded. "I've signed away enough already. What you sellin' now."

Mr. Beazley eyed her contemptuously. The protest that had no power of resistance won scant consideration from a man like him.

"It's a confounded foolish law," said he, meditatively. "What do women know about business, anyway! You just tell him you're perfectly willin' and under no compulsion, and sign the paper—that's all you have to do!"

"You might as well tell me what you're doin'—I have to read the deed anyhow."

"Much you'll make out of readin' the deed," said he, with

some dry amusement, "and Justice Fielden lookin' on and waitin' for you!"

"You're going to sell the Rockford lot—I know it!" said she. "How can you do it, William! The very last piece of what father left me!—and it's mine—you can't sell it—I don't sign!"

Mr. Beazley minded her outcry no more than he minded the squawking of a to-be beheaded hen.

"Seems to me you know a lot," he observed, eyeing her with shrewd scrutiny. Then without a word he rose to his lank height, went out to the woodshed and hunted about, returning with an old piece of tin. This he took up-stairs with him, and a sound of hammering told Mrs. Beazley that one source of information was closed to her completely.

"You'd better not take that up, Mrs. Beazley," said he, returning. "It makes it drafty round your feet up there. I always wondered at them intuitions of yours—guess they wasn't so remarkable after all."

"Now before Mr. Fielden comes, seein' as you are so far on to this business, we may as well talk it out. I suppose you'll admit that you're a woman—and that you don't know anything about business, and that it's a man's place to take care of his family to the best of his ability."

"You just go ahead and say what you want to—you needn't wait for any admits from me! What I know is my father left me a lot o' land—left it to me—to take care of me and the children, and you've sold it all—in spite of me—but this one lot."

"We've sold it, Mrs. Beazley; you've signed the deeds."

"Yes, I know I have—you made me."

"Now, Mrs. Beazley! Haven't you always told Justice Fielden that you were under no compulsion?"

"O yes—I told him so—what's the use of fightin' over everything! But that house in Rockford is mine—where I was brought up—and I want to keep it for the children. If you'd only live there, William, I'd take boarders and be glad to—to keep the old home! and you could sell that water power—or lease it—"

Mr. Beazley's face darkened. "You're talking nonsense, Mrs. Beazley—and too much of it. 'Women are words and

men are deeds' is a good sayin'. But what's more to the purpose is Bible sayin'—this fool law is a mere formality—you
know the real law—'Wives submit yourselves to your husbands!'"

He lit his pipe and rose to go outside, adding, "Oh, by the
way, here 'tis Friday night, and I clean forgot to tell you—
there's a boarder comin' to-morrow."

"A boarder—for who?"

"For you, I guess—you'll see more of her than I shall, seein'
as it's a woman."

"William Beazley! Have you gone and taken a boarder without even askin' me?" The little woman's hands shook with excitement. Her voice rose in a plaintive crescendo, with a
helpless break at the end.

"Saves a lot of trouble, you see; now you'll have no time to
worry over it; and yet you've got a day to put her room in
order."

"Her room! What room? We've got no room for ourselves
over this store. William—I won't have it! I can't—I haven't the
strength!"

"Oh, nonsense, Mrs. Beazley! You've got nothin' to do but
keep house for a small family—and tend the store now and
then when I'm busy. As to room, give her Luella's, of course.
She can sleep on the couch, and Willie can sleep in the attic.
Why, Morris Whiting's wife has six boarders—down at Ord-
ways' there'e eight."

"Yes—and they are near dead, both of them women! It's
little they get from their boarders! Just trouble and work and
the insultin' manners of those city people—and their husbands
pocketing all the money. And now you expect me—in four
rooms—to turn my children out of doors to take one—and a
woman at that; more trouble'n three men! I won't, I tell you!"

Luella came in at this point and put a sympathetic arm
around her. "Bert Fielden was in just now," she told her father.
"He says his father had to go to the city and won't be back for
some time—left word for you about it."

"Oh, well," said Mr. Beazley philosophically, "a few days
more or less won't make much difference, I guess. That bein'

the case you better help your mother wash up and then go to bed, both of you," and he took himself off to lounge on the steps of the store, smoking serenely.

Next day at supper time the boarder came. Mr. Beazley met her at the station and brought her and her modest trunk back with him. He took occasion on the journey to inform the lady that one reason for his making the arrangement was that he thought his wife needed company—intelligent company of her own sex.

"She's nervous and notional and kinder dreads it, now it's all arranged," he said; "but I know she'll like you first rate."

He himself was most favorably impressed, for the woman was fairly young, undeniably good looking, and had a sensible, prompt friendliness that was most attractive.

The drive was quite a long one and slower than mere length accounted for, owing to the nature of rural roads in mountain districts; and Mr. Beazley found himself talking more freely than was his habit with strangers, and pointing out the attractive features of the place with fluency.

Miss Lawrence was observant, interested, appreciative.

"There ought to be good water power in that river," she suggested; "what a fine place for a mill. Why, there was a mill, wasn't there?"

"Yes," said he. "That place belonged to my wife's father. Her father had a mill there in the old times when we had tanneries and saw mills all along in this country. They've cut out most of the hemlock now."

"That's a pleasant looking house on it, too. Do you live there?"

"No—we live quite a piece beyond—up at Shade City. This is Rockwell we're going through. It's a growin' place—if the railroad ever gets in here as they talk about."

Mr. Beazley looked wise. He knew a good deal more about that railroad than was worth mentioning to a woman. Meanwhile he speculated inwardly on his companion's probable standing and profession.

"She's Miss, all right, and no chicken," he said to himself, "but looks young enough, too. Can't have much money or she'd not be boardin' with us, up here. Schoolma'am, I guess."

"Find school-teachin' pretty wearin'?" he hazarded.

"School teaching? Oh, there are harder professions than that," she replied lightly. "Do I look so tired?

"I have a friend in the girl's high school who gets very much exhausted by summer time," she pursued. "When I am tired I prefer the sea; but this year I wanted a perfectly quiet place—and I believe I've found one. Oh, how pretty, it is!" she cried as they rounded a steep hill shoulder and skirted the river to their destination. Shade City was well named, in part at least, for it stood in a crack of the mountains and saw neither sunrise nor sunset.

The southern sun warmed it at midday, and the north wind cooled it well; there was hardly room for the river and the road; and the "City" consisted of five or six houses, a blacksmith shop and "the store," strung along the narrow banks.

But the little pass had its strategic value for a country trader, lying between wide mountain valleys and concentrating all their local traffic.

"Maria!" called Mr. Beazley. "Here's Miss Lawrence, I'll take her trunk up right now. Luella! Show Miss Lawrence where her room is! You can't miss it, Miss Lawrence—we haven't got so many."

Mrs. Beazley's welcome left much to be desired; Luella wore an air of subdued hostility, and Willie, caught by his father in unobserved derision, was cuffed and warned to behave or he'd be sorry.

But Miss Lawrence took no notice. She came down to supper simply dressed, fresh and cheerful. She talked gaily, approved the food, soon won Luella's interest, and captured Willie by a small mechanical puzzle she brought out of her pocket. Her hostess remained cold, however, and stood out for some days against the constant friendliness of her undesired guest.

"I'll take care of my own room," said Miss Lawrence. "I like to, and then I've so little to do here—and you have so much. What would I prefer to eat? Whatever you have—it's a change I'm after, you know—not just what I get at home."

After a little while, Mrs. Beazley owned to a friend and

customer that her boarder was "no more trouble than a man, and a sight more agreeable."

"What does she do all the time?" asked the visitor. "You've got no piazza."

"She ain't the piazza kind," answered Mrs. Beazley. "She's doing what they call nature study. She tramps off with an opera glass and a book—Willie likes to go with her, and she's tellin' him a lot about birds and plants and stones and things. She gets mushrooms, too—and cooks them herself—and eats them. Says they are better than meat and cheaper. I don't like to touch them myself, but it does save money."

In about a week Mrs. Beazley hauled down her flag and capitulated. In two she grew friendly—in three, confidential, and when she heard through Luella and Bert Fielden that his father would soon be back now—her burden of trouble overflowed—the overhanging loss of her last bit of property.

"It's not only because it's our old place and I love it," she said; "and it's not only because it would be so much better for the children—though that's enough—but it would be better business to live there—and I can't make him see it!"

"He thinks he sees way beyond it, doesn't he?"

"Of course—but you know how men are! Oh, no, you don't; you're not married. He's all for buyin' and sellin' and makin' money, and I think half the time he loses and won't let me know."

"The store seems to be popular, doesn't it?"

"Not so much as it would be if he'd attend to it. But he won't stock up as he ought to—and he takes everything he can scrape and puts it into land—and then sells that and gets more. And he swaps horses, and buys up stuff at 'andoos' and sells it again—he's always speculatin'. And he won't let me send Luella to school—nor Willie half the time—and now—but I've no business talkin' to you like this, Miss Lawrence!"

"If it's any relief to your mind, Mrs. Beazley, I wish you would. It is barely possible that I may be of some use. My father is in the real estate business and knows a good deal about these mountain lands."

"Well, it's no great story—I'm not complainin' of Mr. Beazley, understand—only about this property. It does seem as if it was mine—and I do have to sign deeds—but he will sell it off!"

"Why do you let him, if you feel sure he is wrong!"

"Let him!—Oh, well you ain't married! Let him! Miss, Lawrence, you don't know men!"

"But still, Mrs. Beazley, if you want to keep your property—"

"O, Miss Lawrence, you don't understand—here am I and here's the children, and none of us can get away, and if I don't do as he says I must, he takes it out of us—that's all. You can't do nothin' with a man like that—and him with the Bible on his side!"

Miss Lawrence meditated for some moments.

"Have you ever thought of leaving him?" she ventured.

"Oh, yes, I've thought of it; my sister's always wantin' me to. But I don't believe in divorce—and if I did, this is New York state and I couldn't get it."

"It's pretty hard on the children, isn't it?"

"That's what I can't get reconciled to. I've had five children, Miss Lawrence. My oldest boy went off when he was only twelve, he couldn't stand his father—he used to punish him so—seems as if he did it to make me give in. So he never had proper schoolin' and can't earn much—he's fifteen now—I don't hear from him very often, and he never was very strong." Mrs. Beazley's eyes filled. "He hates the city, too, and he'd come back to me any day—if it wasn't for his father."

"You had five, you say?"

"Yes, there was a baby between Willie and this one—but it died. We're so far up from a doctor, and he wouldn't hitch up—said it was all my nonsense till it was too late! And this baby's delicate—just the way he was!" The tears ran down now, but the faded little woman wiped them off resignedly and went on.

"It's worst now for Luella. Luella's at an age when she oughtn't to be tendin' store the whole time—she ought to be at a good school. There's too many young fellows hangin' around here already. Luella's large for her age, and pretty. I was good lookin' when I was Luella's age, Miss Lawrence, and I got married not much later—girls don't know nothin!"

Miss Lawrence studied her unhappy little face with attention.

"How old should you think I was, Mrs. Beazley?"

Mrs. Beazley, struggling between politeness and keen observation, guessed twenty-seven.

"Ten years short," she answered cheerfully. "I was thirty-seven this very month."

"What!" cried the worn woman in calico. "You're older'n I am! I'm only thirty-two!"

"Yes, I'm a lot older, you see, and I'm going to presume on my age now, and on some business experience, and commit the unpardonable sin of interfering between man and wife—in the interest of the children. It seems to me, Mrs. Beazley, that you owe it them to make a stand.

"Think now—before it is too late. If you kept possession of this property in Rockwell, and had control of your share of what has been sold heretofore—could you live on it?"

"Why, I guess so. There's the house, my sister's in it now—she takes boarders and pays us rent—she thinks I get the money. We could make something that way."

"How much land is there?"

"There's six acres in all. There's the home lot right there in town, and the strip next to it down to the falls—we own the falls—both sides."

"Isn't that rather valuable? You could lease the water power, I should think."

"There was some talk of a 'lectric company takin' it—but it fell through. He wouldn't sell to them—said he'd sell nothin' to Sam Hunt—just because he was an old friend of mine. Sam keeps a good store down to Rockwell, and he was in that company—got it up, I think. Mr. Beazley was always jealous of Sam—and 'twan't me at all he wanted—'twas my sister."

"But, Mrs. Beazley, think. If you and your sister could keep house together you could make a home for the children, and your boy would come back to you. If you leased or sold the falls you could afford to send Luella away to school. Willie could go to school in town—the baby would do better down there where there is more sunlight, I'm sure—why do you not make a stand for the children's sake?"

Mrs. Beazley looked at her with a faint glimmer of hope. "If I only could," she said.

"Has Mr. Beazley any property of his own?" pursued Miss Lawrence.

"Property! He's got debts. Old ones and new ones. He was in debt when I married him—and he's made more."

"But the proceeds of these sales you tell me of?"

"Oh, he has some trick about that. He banks it in my name or something—so his creditors can't get it. He always gets ahead of everybody."

"M-m-m," said Miss Lawrence.

* * * * *

Mr. Beazley had a long ride before him the next day; he was to drive to Princeville for supplies.

An early breakfast was prepared and consumed, with much fault finding on his part—and he started off by six o'clock in a bad temper, unrestrained by the presence of Miss Lawrence, who had not come down.

"Whoa! Hold up!" he cried, stopping the horses with a spiteful yank as they had just settled into the collar.

"Maria!"

"Well—what you forgotten?"

"Forgot nothin'! I've remembered something; see that you're on hand tonight—don't go gallivantin' down to Rockwell or anywhere just because I'm off. Justice Fielden's comin' up and we've got to settle that business I told you about. See't you're here! Gid ap!"

The big wagon lumbered off across the bridge, around the corner, into the hidden wood road.

When Mr. Beazley returned the late dusk had fallen thickly in the narrow pass. He was angry at being late, for he had counted much on having this legal formality in his own house—where he could keep a sterner hand on his wife.

He was tired, too, and in a cruel temper, as the sweating horses showed.

"Willie!" he shouted. "Here you, Willie! Come and take the horses!" No hurrying, frightened child appeared.

"Maria!" he yelled. "Maria! Where's that young one! Lu-ella! Maria!"

He clambered down, swearing under his breath; and rushed to the closed front door. It was locked.

"What in Halifax!" he muttered, shaking and banging vainly. Then he tried the side door—the back door—the woodshed—all were locked and the windows shut tight with sticks over them. His face darkened with anger.

"They've gone off—the whole of them—and I told her she'd got to be here to-night. Gone to Rockwell, of course, leavin' the store, too. We'll have a nice time when she comes back! That young one needs a lickin'."

He attended to the horses after a while, leaving the loaded wagon in the barn, and then broke a pane of glass in a kitchen window and let himself in.

A damp, clean, soapy smell greeted him. He struck matches and looked for a lamp. There was none. The room was absolutely empty. So were the closet, pantry and cellar. So were the four rooms up-stairs and the attic. So was the store.

"Halifax!" said Mr. Beazley. He was thoroughly mystified now, and his rage died in bewilderment.

A knocking at the door called him.

It was not Justice Fielden, however, but Sam Hunt.

"I heard you brought up a load of goods, today," said he easily; "and I thought you might like to sell 'em. I bought out the rest of the stuff this morning, and the store, and the good-will o' the business—and this lot isn't much by itself."

Mr. Beazley looked at him with a blackening countenance.

"You bought out this store, did you? I'd like to know who you bought it of!"

"Why, the owner, of course! Mrs. Beazley; paid cash on the nail, too. I've bought it, lock, stock and barrel—cows, horses, hens and cats. You don't own the wagon, even. As to your clothes—they're in that trunk yonder. However, keep your stuff—you'll need some capital," with this generous parting shot Mr. Hunt drove off.

Mr. Beazley retired to the barn. He had no wish to consult his neighbors for further knowledge.

Mrs. Beazley had gone to her sister's, no doubt.

And she had dared to take this advantage of him—of the fact that the property stood in her name—Sam Hunt had put her up to it. He'd have the law on them—it was a conspiracy.

Then he went to sleep on the hay, muttering vengeance for the morrow.

The strange atmosphere awoke him early, and he breakfasted on some crackers from his wagon.

Then he grimly set forth on foot for the village, refusing offered lifts from the loads of grinning men who passed him. He presented himself at the door of his wife's house in the village at an early hour. Her sister opened it.

"Well," she said, holding the door-knob in her hand, "What do you want at this time in the morning?"

"I want my family," said he. "I'll have you know a man has some rights in his family at any rate."

"There's no family of yours in this house, William Beazley," said she grimly. "No, I'm not a liar—never had that reputation. You can come in and search the house if you please—after the boarders are up."

"Where is my wife?" he demanded.

"I don't know, thank goodness, and I don't think you'll find her very soon either," she added to herself, as he turned and marched off without further words.

In the course of the morning he presented himself at Justice Fielden's office.

"Gone off, has she?" inquired the Judge genially. "O just gone visiting, I guess. Forgot to leave word."

"It's not only that, I want to know my rights in this case, Judge. I've been to the bank—and she's drawn every cent. Every cent of my property."

"Wasn't it her property, Mr. Beazley?"

"Some of it was, and some of it wasn't. All I've made since we was married was in there, too. I've speculated quite a bit, you know, buying and selling—there was considerable money."

"How on earth could she get your money out of the bank?" asked Mr. Fielden.

"Why, it was in her name, of course; matter of business, you understand."

"Why, yes; I understand, I guess. Well, I don't see exactly what you can do about it, Mr. Beazley. You technically gave her the property, you see, and she's taken it—that's all there is to it."

"She's sold out the store!" broke in Mr. Beazley, "all the stock, the fixtures—she couldn't do that, could she?"

"Appears as if she had, don't it? It was rather overbearin' I do think, and you can bring suit for compensation for your services—you tended the store, of course?"

"If I knew where she was—" said Mr. Beazley slowly, with a grinding motion of this fingers. "But she's clean gone—and the children, too."

"If she remains away that constitutes desertion, of course," said the Judge briskly, "and your remedy is clear. You can get a separation—in due time. If you cared to live in another state long enough you could get a divorce—not in New York, though. Being in New York, and not knowing where your wife is, I don't just see what you can do about it. Do you care to employ detectives?"

"No," said Mr. Beazley, "not yet."

Suddenly he started up.

"There's Miss Lawrence," said he. "She'll know something," and he darted out after her.

She came into the little office, calm, smiling, daintily arrayed.

"Do you know where my wife is, Miss Lawrence?" he demanded.

"Yes," she replied pleasantly.

"Well—where is she?"

"That I am not at liberty to tell you, Mr. Beazley. But any communication you may wish to make to her you can make through me. And I can attend to any immediate business. She has given me power of attorney."

Justice Fielden's small eyes were twinkling.

"You never knew you had a counsel learned in the law at your place, did you? Miss Lawrence is the best woman lawyer in New York, Mr. Beazley—just going kinder incog[nito] for a vacation."

"Are you at the bottom of all this deviltry?" said the angry man, turning upon her fiercely.

"If you mean that Mrs. Beazley is acting under my advice, yes. I found that she had larger business interests than she supposed, and that they were not being well managed. I happened to be informed as to real estate values in this locality, and was able to help her. We needed a good deal of ready money to take advantage of our opportunity, and Mr. Hunt was willing to help us out on the stock."

He set his teeth and looked at her with growing fury, to which she paid no attention whatever.

"I advised Mrs. Beazley to take the children and go away for a complete change and rest, and to leave me to settle this matter. I was of the opinion that you and I could make business arrangements more amicably perhaps."

"What do you mean by business arrangements?" he asked.

"We are prepared to make you this offer: If you will sign the deed of separation I have here, agreeing to waive all rights in the children and live out of the state, we will give you five thousand dollars. In case you reappear in the state you will be liable for debts, and for—you remember that little matter of the wood lot deal?"

"That's a fair offer, I think," said Justice Fielden. "I always told you that wood lot matter would get you into trouble if your wife got on to it—and cared to push it. I think you'd better take up with this proposition."

"What's she going to do—a woman alone? What are the children going to do? A man can't give up his family this way."

"You need not be at all concerned about that," she answered. "Mrs. Beazley's plans are open and aboveboard. She is going to enlarge her house and keep boarders. Her sister is to marry Mr. Hunt, as you doubtless know. The children are to be properly educated. There is nothing you need fear for your family."

"And how about me? I—if I could just talk to her?"

"That is exactly what I advised my client to avoid. She has gone to a quiet, pleasant place for this summer. She needs a long rest, and you and I can settle this little matter without any feeling, you see."

"What with summers in quiet places, and enlarging the

house, you seem to have found a good deal more in that property than I did," said he with a sneer.

"That is not improbable," she replied sweetly. "Here is the agreement; take the offer or leave it."

"And if I don't take it? Then what'll you do?"

"Nothing. You may continue to live here if you insist—and pay your debts by your own exertions. You can get employment, no doubt, of your friends and neighbors."

Mr. Beazley looked out of the window. Quite a number of his friends and neighbors were gathered together around Hunt's store, and as each new arrival was told the story, they slapped their thighs and roared with laughter.

Judge Fielden smiling dryly, threw up the sash.

"Clean as a whistle!" he heard Sturgis Black's strident voice. "Not so much as a cat to kick! Nobody to holler at! No young ones to lick! Nothin' whatsomever to eat! You should a heard him bangin' on the door!"

"And him a luggin' in that boarder just to spite her," crowed old Sam Wiley—"that was the last straw I guess."

"Well, he was always an enterprisin' man," said Horace Johnson. "Better at specilatin' with his wife's property than workin' with his hands. Guess he'll have to hunt a job now, though."

"He ain't likely to git one in a hurry—not in this county—unless Sam Hunt'll take him in." Wiley yelled again at this.

"Have you got that deed drawn up?" said Mr. Beazley harshly—"I'll sign."

TURNED

In her soft-carpeted, thick-curtained, richly furnished chamber, Mrs. Marroner lay sobbing on the wide, soft bed.

She sobbed bitterly, chokingly, despairingly; her shoulders heaved and shook convulsively; her hands were tight-clenched. She had forgotten her elaborate dress, the more elaborate bedcover; forgotten her dignity, her self-control, her pride. In her mind was an overwhelming, unbelievable horror, an immeasurable loss, a turbulent, struggling mass of emotion.

In her reserved, superior, Boston-bred life, she had never dreamed that it would be possible for her to feel so many things at once, and with such trampling intensity.

She tried to cool her feelings into thoughts; to stiffen them into words; to control herself—and could not. It brought vaguely to her mind an awful moment in the breakers at York Beach, one summer in girlhood when she had been swimming under water and could not find the top.

In her uncarpeted, thin-curtained, poorly furnished chamber on the top floor, Gerta Petersen lay sobbing on the narrow, hard bed.

She was of larger frame than her mistress, grandly built and strong; but all her proud young womanhood was prostrate now, convulsed with agony, dissolved in tears. She did not try to control herself. She wept for two.

If Mrs. Marroner suffered more from the wreck and ruin of a longer love—perhaps a deeper one; if her tastes were finer, her ideals loftier; if she bore the pangs of bitter jealousy and outraged pride, Gerta had personal shame to meet, a hopeless future, and a looming present which filled her with unreasoning terror.

She had come like a meek young goddess into that perfectly ordered house, strong, beautiful, full of goodwill and eager obedience, but ignorant and childish—a girl of eighteen.

Mr. Marroner had frankly admired her, and so had his wife. They discussed her visible perfections and as visible limitations with that perfect confidence which they had so long enjoyed. Mrs. Marroner was not a jealous woman. She had never been jealous in her life—till now.

Gerta had stayed and learned their ways. They had both been fond of her. Even the cook was fond of her. She was what is called "willing," was unusually teachable and plastic; and Mrs. Marroner, with her early habits of giving instruction, tried to educate her somewhat.

"I never saw anyone so docile," Mrs. Marroner had often commented. "It is perfection in a servant, but almost a defect in character. She is so helpless and confiding."

She was precisely that: a tall, rosy-cheeked baby; rich womanhood without, helpless infancy within. Her braided wealth of dead-gold hair, her grave blue eyes, her mighty shoulders, and long, firmly moulded limbs seemed those of a primal earth spirit; but she was only an ignorant child, with a child's weakness.

When Mr. Marroner had to go abroad for his firm, unwillingly, hating to leave his wife, he had told her he felt quite safe to leave her in Gerta's hands—she would take care of her.

"Be good to your mistress, Gerta," he told the girl that last morning at breakfast. "I leave her to you to take care of. I shall be back in a month at latest."

Then he turned, smiling, to his wife. "And you must take care of Gerta, too," he said. "I expect you'll have her ready for college when I get back."

This was seven months ago. Business had delayed him from week to week, from month to month. He wrote to his wife, long, loving, frequent letters, deeply regretting the delay, explaining how necessary, how profitable it was, congratulating her on the wide resources she had; her well-filled, well-balanced mind, her many interests.

"If I should be eliminated from your scheme of things, by any of those 'acts of God' mentioned on the tickets, I do not feel that you would be an utter wreck," he said. "That is very comforting to me. Your life is so rich and wide that no one loss, even a great one, would wholly cripple you. But nothing of the sort is likely to happen, and I shall be home again in three weeks—if this thing gets settled. And you will be looking so lovely, with that eager light in your eyes and the changing flush I know so well—and love so well! My dear wife! We shall have to have a new honeymoon—other moons come every month, why shouldn't the mellifluous kind?"

He often asked after "little Gerta," sometimes enclosed a picture postcard to her, joked his wife about her laborious efforts to educate "the child," was so loving and merry and wise—

All this was racing through Mrs. Marroner's mind as she lay there with the broad, hemstitched border of fine linen sheeting crushed and twisted in one hand, and the other holding a sodden handkerchief.

She had tried to teach Gerta, and had grown to love the patient, sweet-natured child, in spite of her dullness. At work with her hands, she was clever, if not quick, and could keep small accounts from week to week. But to the woman who held a Ph.D., who had been on the faculty of a college, it was like baby-tending.

Perhaps having no babies of her own made her love the big child the more, though the years between them were but fifteen.

To the girl she seemed quite old, of course; and her young heart was full of grateful affection for the patient care which made her feel so much at home in this new land.

And then she had noticed a shadow on the girl's bright face. She looked nervous, anxious, worried. When the bell rang, she seemed startled, and would rush hurriedly to the door. Her peals of frank laughter no longer rose from the area gate as she stood talking with the always admiring tradesmen.

Mrs. Marroner had labored long to teach her more reserve with men, and flattered herself that her words were at last effective. She suspected the girl of homesickness, which was denied. She suspected her of illness, which was denied also. At last she suspected her of something which could not be denied.

For a long time she refused to believe it, waiting. Then she had to believe it, but schooled herself to patience and understanding. "The poor child," she said. "She is here without a mother—she is so foolish and yielding—I must not be too stern with her." And she tried to win the girl's confidence with wise, kind words.

But Gerta had literally thrown herself at her feet and begged her with streaming tears not to turn her away. She would admit nothing, explain nothing, but frantically promised to work for Mrs. Marroner as long as she lived—if only she would keep her.

Revolving the problem carefully in her mind, Mrs. Marroner thought she would keep her, at least for the present. She tried to repress her sense of ingratitude in one she had so sincerely tried to help, and the cold, contemptuous anger she had always felt for such weakness.

"The thing to do now," she said to herself, "is to see her through this safely. The child's life should not be hurt any more than is unavoidable. I will ask Dr. Bleet about it—what a comfort a woman doctor is! I'll stand by the poor, foolish thing till it's over, and then get her back to Sweden somehow with her baby. How they do come where they are not wanted—and don't come where they are wanted!" And Mrs. Marroner, sitting alone in the quiet, spacious beauty of the house, almost envied Gerta.

Then came the deluge.

She had sent the girl out for needed air toward dark. The late mail came; she took it in herself. One letter for her—her husband's letter. She knew the postmark, the stamp, the kind of typewriting. She impulsively kissed it in the dim hall. No one would suspect Mrs. Marroner of kissing her husband's letters—but she did, often.

She looked over the others. One was for Gerta, and not

from Sweden. It looked precisely like her own. This struck her as a little odd, but Mr. Marroner had several times sent messages and cards to the girl. She laid the letter on the hall table and took hers to her room.

"My poor child," it began. What letter of hers had been sad enough to warrant that?

"I am deeply concerned at the news you send." What news to so concern him had she written? "You must bear it bravely, little girl. I shall be home soon, and will take care of you, of course. I hope there is not immediate anxiety—you do not say. Here is money, in case you need it. I expect to get home in a month at latest. If you have to go, be sure to leave your address at my office. Cheer up—be brave—I will take care of you."

The letter was typewritten, which was not unusual. It was unsigned, which was unusual. It enclosed an American bill—fifty dollars. It did not seem in the least like any letter she had ever had from her husband, or any letter she could imagine him writing. But a strange, cold feeling was creeping over her, like a flood rising around a house.

She utterly refused to admit the ideas which began to bob and push about outside her mind, and to force themselves in. Yet under the pressure of these repudiated thoughts she went downstairs and brought up the other letter—the letter to Gerta. She laid them side by side on a smooth dark space on the table; marched to the piano and played, with stern precision, refusing to think, till the girl came back. When she came in, Mrs. Marroner rose quietly and came to the table. "Here is a letter for you," she said.

The girl stepped forward eagerly, saw the two lying together there, hesitated, and looked at her mistress.

"Take yours, Gerta. Open it, please."

The girl turned frightened eyes upon her.

"I want you to read it, here," said Mrs. Marroner.

"Oh, ma'am—No! Please don't make me!"

"Why not?"

There seemed to be no reason at hand, and Gerta flushed more deeply and opened her letter. It was long; it was evidently puzzling to her; it began "My dear wife." She read it slowly.

"Are you sure it is your letter?" asked Mrs. Marroner. "Is not this one yours? Is not that one—mine?"

She held out the other letter to her.

"It is a mistake," Mrs. Marroner went on, with a hard quietness. She had lost her social bearings somehow, lost her usual keen sense of the proper thing to do. This was not life; this was a nightmare.

"Do you not see? Your letter was put in my envelope and my letter was put in your envelope. Now we understand it."

But poor Gerta had no antechamber to her mind, no trained forces to preserve order while agony entered. The thing swept over her, resistless, overwhelming. She cowered before the outraged wrath she expected; and from some hidden cavern that wrath arose and swept over her in pale flame.

"Go and pack your trunk," said Mrs. Marroner. "You will leave my house tonight. Here is your money."

She laid down the fifty-dollar bill. She put with it a month's wages. She had no shadow of pity for those anguished eyes, those tears which she heard drop on the floor.

"Go to your room and pack," said Mrs. Marroner. And Gerta, always obedient, went.

Then Mrs. Marroner went to hers, and spent a time she never counted, lying on her face on the bed.

But the training of the twenty-eight years which had elapsed before her marriage; the life at college, both as student and teacher; the independent growth which she had made, formed a very different background for grief from that in Gerta's mind.

After a while Mrs. Marroner arose. She administered to herself a hot bath, a cold shower, a vigorous rubbing. "Now I can think," she said.

First she regretted the sentence of instant banishment. She went upstairs to see if it had been carried out. Poor Gerta! The tempest of her agony had worked itself out at last as in a child, and left her sleeping, the pillow wet, the lips still grieving, a big sob shuddering itself off now and then.

Mrs. Marroner stood and watched her, and as she watched she considered the helpless sweetness of the face; the

defenseless, unformed character; the docility and habit of obedience which made her so attractive—and so easily a victim.
Also she thought of the mighty force which had swept over
her; of the great process now working itself out through her;
of how pitiful and futile seemed any resistance she might have
made.

She softly returned to her own room, made up a little fire,
and sat by it, ignoring her feelings now, as she had before ignored her thoughts.

Here were two women and a man. One woman was a wife:
loving, trusting, affectionate. One was a servant: loving, trusting, affectionate—a young girl, an exile, a dependent; grateful
for any kindness; untrained, uneducated, childish. She ought,
of course, to have resisted temptation; but Mrs. Marroner was
wise enough to know how difficult temptation is to recognize
when it comes in the guise of friendship and from a source one
does not suspect.

Gerta might have done better in resisting the grocer's clerk;
had, indeed, with Mrs. Marroner's advice, resisted several.
But where respect was due, how could she criticize? Where
obedience was due, how could she refuse—with ignorance to
hold her blinded—until too late?

As the older, wiser woman forced herself to understand and
extenuate the girl's misdeed and foresee her ruined future, a
new feeling rose in her heart, strong, clear, and overmastering:
a sense of measureless condemnation for the man who had
done this thing. He knew. He understood. He could fully foresee and measure the consequences of his act. He appreciated to
the full the innocence, the ignorance, the grateful affection,
the habitual docility, of which he deliberately took advantage.

Mrs. Marroner rose to icy peaks of intellectual apprehen-
sion, from which her hours of frantic pain seemed far indeed
removed. He had done this thing under the same roof with
her—his wife. He had not frankly loved the younger woman,
broken with his wife, made a new marriage. That would have
been heart-break pure and simple. This was something else.

That letter, that wretched, cold, carefully guarded, unsigned
letter, that bill—far safer than a check—these did not speak of

affection. Some men can love two women at one time. This was not love.

Mrs. Marroner's sense of pity and outrage for herself, the wife, now spread suddenly into a perception of pity and outrage for the girl. All that splendid, clean young beauty, the hope of a happy life, with marriage and motherhood, honorable independence, even—these were nothing to that man. For his own pleasure he had chosen to rob her of her life's best joys.

He would "take care of her," said the letter. How? In what capacity?

And then, sweeping over both her feelings for herself, the wife, and Gerta, his victim, came a new flood, which literally lifted her to her feet. She rose and walked, her head held high. "This is the sin of man against woman," she said. "The offense is against womanhood. Against motherhood. Against—the child."

She stopped.

The child. His child. That, too, he sacrificed and injured—doomed to degradation.

Mrs. Marroner came of stern New England stock. She was not a Calvinist, hardly even a Unitarian, but the iron of Calvinism was in her soul: of that grim faith which held that most people had to be damned "for the glory of God."

Generations of ancestors who both preached and practiced stood behind her; people whose lives had been sternly moulded to their highest moments of religious conviction. In sweeping bursts of feeling, they achieved "conviction," and afterward they lived and died according to that conviction.

When Mr. Marroner reached home a few weeks later, following his letters too soon to expect an answer to either, he saw no wife upon the pier, though he had cabled, and found the house closed darkly. He let himself in with his latch-key, and stole softly upstairs, to surprise his wife.

No wife was there.

He rang the bell. No servant answered it.

He turned up light after light, searched the house from top to bottom; it was utterly empty. The kitchen wore a clean, bald, unsympathetic aspect. He left it and slowly mounted the stairs, completely dazed. The whole house was clean, in perfect order, wholly vacant.

One thing he felt perfectly sure of—she knew.

Yet was he sure? He must not assume too much. She might have been ill. She might have died. He started to his feet. No, they would have cabled him. He sat down again.

For any such change, if she had wanted him to know, she would have written. Perhaps she had, and he, returning so suddenly, had missed the letter. The thought was some comfort. It must be so. He turned to the telephone and again hesitated. If she had found out—if she had gone—utterly gone, without a word—should he announce it himself to friends and family?

He walked the floor; he searched everywhere for some letter, some word of explanation. Again and again he went to the telephone—and always stopped. He could not bear to ask: "Do you know where my wife is?"

The harmonious, beautiful rooms reminded him in a dumb, helpless way of her—like the remote smile on the face of the dead. He put out the lights, could not bear the darkness, turned them all on again.

It was a long night—

In the morning he went early to the office. In the accumulated mail was no letter from her. No one seemed to know of anything unusual. A friend asked after his wife—"Pretty glad to see you, I guess?" He answered evasively.

About eleven a man came to see him: John Hill, her lawyer. Her cousin, too. Mr. Marroner had never liked him. He liked him less now, for Mr. Hill merely handed him a letter, remarked, "I was requested to deliver this to you personally," and departed, looking like a person who is called on to kill something offensive.

"I have gone. I will care for Gerta. Good-bye. Marion."

That was all. There was no date, no address, no postmark, nothing but that.

In his anxiety and distress, he had fairly forgotten Gerta and all that. Her name aroused in him a sense of rage. She had come between him and his wife. She had taken his wife from him. That was the way he felt.

At first he said nothing, did nothing, lived on alone in his house, taking meals where he chose. When people asked him about his wife, he said she was traveling—for her health. He would not have it in the newspapers. Then, as time passed, as no enlightenment came to him, he resolved not to bear it any longer, and employed detectives. They blamed him for not having put them on the track earlier, but set to work, urged to the utmost secrecy.

What to him had been so blank a wall of mystery seemed not to embarrass them in the least. They made careful inquiries as to her "past," found where she had studied, where taught, and on what lines; that she had some little money of her own, that her doctor was Josephine L. Bleet, M.D., and many other bits of information.

As a result of careful and prolonged work, they finally told him that she had resumed teaching under one of her old professors, lived quietly, and apparently kept boarders, giving him town, street, and number, as if it were a matter of no difficulty whatever.

He had returned in early spring. It was autumn before he found her.

A quiet college town in the hills, a broad, shady street, a pleasant house standing in its own lawn, with trees and flowers about it. He had the address in his hand, and the number showed clear on the white gate. He walked up the straight gravel path and rang the bell. An elderly servant opened the door.

"Does Mrs. Marroner live here?"

"No, sir."

"This is number twenty-eight?"

"Yes, sir."

"Who does live here?"

"Miss Wheeling, sir."

Ah! Her maiden name. They had told him, but he had forgotten.

He stepped inside. "I would like to see her," he said.

He was ushered into a still parlor, cool and sweet with the scent of flowers, the flowers she had always loved best. It almost brought tears to his eyes. All their years of happiness rose in his mind again—the exquisite beginnings; the days of eager longing before she was really his; the deep, still beauty of her love.

Surely she would forgive him—she must forgive him. He would humble himself; he would tell her of his honest remorse—his absolute determination to be a different man.

Through the wide doorway there came in to him two women. One like a tall Madonna, bearing a baby in her arms.

Marion, calm, steady, definitely impersonal; nothing but a clear pallor to hint of inner stress.

Gerta, holding the child as a bulwark, with a new intelligence in her face, and her blue, adoring eyes fixed on her friend—not upon him.

He looked from one to the other dumbly.

And the woman who had been his wife asked quietly:

"What have you to say to us?"

OLD WATER

The lake lay glassy in level golden light. Where the long shadows of the wooded bank spread across it was dark, fathomless. Where the little cliff rose on the eastern shore its bright reflection went down endlessly.

Slowly across the open gold came a still canoe, sent swiftly and smoothly on by well-accustomed arms.

"How strong! How splendid! Ah! she is like a Valkyr!" said the poet; and Mrs. Osgood looked up at the dark bulk with appreciative eyes.

"You don't know how it delights me to have you speak like that!" she said softly. "I feel those things myself, but have not the gift of words. And Ellen is so practical."

"She could not be your daughter and not have a poetic soul," he answered, smiling gravely.

"I'm sure I hope so. But I have never felt sure! When she was little I read to her from the poets, always; but she did not care for them—unless it was what she called 'story poetry.' And as soon as she had any choice of her own she took to science."

"The poetry is there," he said, his eyes on the smooth brown arms, now more near. "That poise! That motion! It is the very soul of poetry—and the body! Her body is a poem!"

Mrs. Osgood watched the accurate landing, the strong pull that brought the canoe over the roller and up into the little boathouse. "Ellen is so practical!" she murmured. "She will not even admit her own beauty."

"She is unawakened," breathed the poet—"Unawakened!" And his big eyes glimmered as with a stir of hope.

"It's very brave of her, too," the mother went on. "She does not really love the water, and just makes herself go out on it. I think in her heart she's afraid—but will not admit it. O Ellen! Come here dear. This is Mr. Pendexter—the Poet."

Ellen gave her cool brown hand; a little wet even, as she had casually washed them at the water's edge; but he pressed it warmly, and uttered his admiration of her skill with the canoe.

"O that's nothing," said the girl. "Canoeing's dead easy."

"Will you teach it to me?" he asked. "I will be a most docile pupil."

She looked up and down his large frame with a somewhat questioning eye. It was big enough surely, and those great limbs must mean strength; but he lacked something of the balance and assured quickness which speaks of training.

"Can't you paddle?" she said.

"Forgive my ignorance—but I have never been in one of those graceful slim crafts. I shall be so glad to try."

"Mr. Pendexter has been more in Europe than America," her mother put in hastily, "and you must not imagine, my dear, that all men care for these things. I'm sure that if you are interested, my daughter will be very glad to teach you, Mr. Pendexter."

"Certainly," said Ellen. "I'll teach him in two tries. Want to start tomorrow morning? I'm usually out pretty early."

"I shall be delighted," he said. "We will greet Aurora together."

"The Dawn, dear," suggested her mother with an apologetic smile.

"O yes," the girl agreed. "I recognize Aurora, mama. Is dinner ready?"

"It will be when you are dressed," said her mother. "Put on your blue frock, dear—the light one."

"All right," said Ellen, and ran lightly up the path.

"Beautiful! Beautiful!" he murmured, his eyes following her flying figure. "Ah, madam! What it must be to you to have such a daughter! To see your own youth—but a moment passed—repeated before your eyes!" And he bent an admiring glance on the outlines of his hostess.

Mrs. Osgood appeared at dinner in a somewhat classic

gown, her fine hair banded with barbaric gold; and looked with satisfaction at her daughter, who shone like a juvenile Juno in her misty blue. Ellen had her mother's beauty and her father's strength. Her frame was large, her muscles had power under their flowing grace of line. She carried herself like a queen, but wore the cheerful unconscious air of a healthy schoolgirl, which she was.

Her appetite was so hearty that her mother almost feared it would pain the poet, but she soon observed that he too showed full appreciation of her chef's creations. Ellen too observed him, noting with frank disapproval that he ate freely of sweets and creams, and seemed to enjoy the coffee and liqueurs exceedingly.

"Ellen never takes coffee," Mrs. Osgood explained, as they sat in the luxurious drawing room, "she has some notion about training I believe."

"Mother! I am training!" the girl protested. "Not officially— there's no race on; but I like to keep in good condition. I'm stroke at college, Mr. Pindexter."

"*Pen*dexter, dear," her mother whispered.

The big man took his second demitasse, and sat near the girl.

"I can't tell you how much I admire it," he said, leaning forward. "You are like Nausicaa—like Atalanta—like the women of my dreams!"

She was not displeased with his open admiration—even athletic girls are not above enjoying praise—but she took it awkwardly.

"I don't believe in dreams," she said.

"No," he agreed, "No—one must not. And yet—have you never had a dream that haunts you—a dream that comes again?"

"I've had bad dreams," she admitted, "horrid ones; but not the same dream twice."

"What do you dream of when your dreams are terrible?"

"Beasts," she answered promptly. "Big beasts that jump at me! And I run and run—ugh!"

Mrs. Osgood sipped her coffee and watched them. There

was no young poet more promising than this. He represented all that her own girlhood had longed for—all that the highly prosperous mill-owner she married had utterly failed to give. If her daughter could have what she had missed!

"They say those dreams come from our remote past," she suggested. "Do you believe that, Mr. Pendexter?"

"Yes," he agreed, "from our racial infancy. From those long buried years of fear and pain."

"And when we have that queer feeling of *having been there before*—isn't that the same thing?"

"We do not know," said he. "Some say it is from a moment's delay in action of one-half of the brain. I cannot tell. To me it is more mysterious, more interesting, to think that when one has that wonderful sudden sense of previous acquaintance it means vague memories of a former life." And he looked at Ellen as if she had figured largely in his previous existence. "Have you ever had that feeling, Miss Osgood?"

The girl laughed rather shamefacedly. "I've had it about one thing," she said. "That's why I'm afraid of water."

"Afraid of water! You! A water goddess!"

"O, I don't encourage it, of course. But it's the only thing I ever was nervous about. I've had it from childhood—that horrid feeling!"

She shivered a little, and asked if he wouldn't like some music.

"Ah! You make music too?"

She laughed gaily. "Only with the pianola—or the other machine. Shall I start it?"

"A moment," he said. "In a moment. But tell me, will you not, of this dream of something terrible? I am so deeply interested."

"Why, it isn't much," she said. "I don't dream it, really—it comes when I'm awake. Only two or three times—once when I was about ten or eleven, and twice since. It's water—black, still, smooth water—way down below me. And I can't get away from it. I want to—and then something grabs me—ugh!"

She got up decidedly and went to the music stand. "If that's a relic of my past I must have been prematurely cut off by an enraged ape! Anyhow, I don't like water—unless it's wild ocean. What shall I play?"

He meant to rise next morning with the daylight, but failed to awaken; and when he did look out he saw the canoe shooting lightly home in time for breakfast.

She laughed at him for his laziness, but promised a lesson later, and was pleased to find that he could play tennis. He looked well in his white flannels, in fact his appearance was more admirable than his playing, and the girl beat him till he grew almost angry.

Mrs. Osgood watched delightedly on occasions where watching was agreeable, and on other occasions she took herself off with various excuses, and left them much together.

He expressed to her privately a question as to whether he was not too heavy for the canoe, but she reassured him.

"O, no, indeed, Mr. Pendexter; it's a specially wide canoe, and has air chambers in it—it can't sink." Her father had made it for her. "He's a heavy man himself, and loves canoeing."

So the stalwart poet was directed to step softly into the middle, and given the bow paddle.

It grieved him much that he could not see his fair instructress, and he proposed that they change places.

"No, indeed!" she said. "Trust you with the other paddle?— Not yet!"

Could he not at least face her, he suggested. At which she laughed wickedly, and told him he'd better learn to paddle forward before he tried to do it backward.

"If you want to look at me you might get another canoe and try to follow," she added, smiling; whereat he declared he would obey orders absolutely.

He sat all across the little rattan bow seat, and rolled up his sleeves as she did. She gave him the paddle, showed him how to hold it, and grinned silently as his mighty strokes swung them to right or left, for all her vigorous steering.

"Not so hard!" she said. "You are stronger than I, and your stroke is so far out you swing me around."

With a little patience he mastered the art sufficiently to wield a fairly serviceable bow paddle, but she would not trust him with the stern; and not all the beauties of the quiet lake consoled him for losing sight of her. Still, he reflected, she could see him. Perhaps that was why she kept him there in front!—and he sat straighter at the thought.

She did rather enjoy the well proportioned bulk of him, but she had small respect for his lack of dexterity, and felt a real dislike for the heavy fell of black hair on his arms and hands.

He tired of canoeing. One cannot direct speaking glances over one's shoulder, nor tender words; not with good effect, that is. At tennis he found her so steadily victor that he tired of that too. Golf she did not care for; horses he was unfamiliar with; and when she ran the car her hands and eyes and whole attention were on the machine. So he begged for walking.

"You must having charming walks in these woods," he said. "I own inferiority in many ways—but I can walk!"

"All right," she cheerily agreed, and tramped about the country with him, brisk and tireless.

Her mother watched breathlessly. She wholly admired this ox-eyed man with the velvet voice, the mouth so red under his soft mustache. She thought his poetry noble and musical beyond measure. Ellen thought it was "no mortal use."

"What on earth does he want to make over those old legends for, anyway!" she said, when her mother tried to win her to some appreciation. "Isn't there enough to write about today without going back to people who never existed anyhow—nothing but characters out of other people's stories?"

"They are parts of the world's poetic material, my dear; folklore, race-myths. They are among our universal images."

"Well, I don't like poetry about universal images, that's all. It's like mummies—sort of warmed over and dressed up!"

"I am so sorry!" said her mother, with some irritation. "Here we are honored with a visit from one of our very greatest poets—perhaps the greatest; and my own child hasn't sense enough to appreciate his beautiful work. You are so like your father!"

"Well, I can't help it," said Ellen. "I don't like those foolish old stories about people who never did anything useful, and hadn't an idea in their heads except being in love and killing somebody! They had no sense, and no courage, and no decency!"

Her mother tried to win her to some admission of merit in his other work.

"It's no use, mama! You may have your poet, and get all the esthetic satisfaction you can out of it. And I'll be polite to him, of course. But I don't like his stuff."

"Not his 'Lyrics of the Day,' dear? And 'The Woods'?"

"No, mumsy, not even those. I don't believe he ever saw a sunrise—unless he got up on purpose and set himself before it like a camera! And woods! Why he don't know one tree from another!"

Her mother almost despaired of her; but the poet was not discouraged.

"Ah! Mrs. Osgood! Since you honor me with your confidence I can but thank you and try my fate. It is so beautiful, this budding soul—not opened yet! So close—so almost hard! But when its rosy petals do unfold—"

He did not, however, give his confidence to Mrs. Osgood beyond this gentle poetic outside view of a sort of floricultural intent. He told her nothing of the storm of passion which was growing within him; a passion of such seething intensity as would have alarmed that gentle soul exceedingly and make her doubt, perhaps, the wisdom of her selection.

She remained in a state of eager but restrained emotion; saying little to Ellen lest she alarm her, but hoping that the girl would find happiness with this great soul.

The great soul, meanwhile, pursued his way, using every art he knew—and his experience was not narrow—to reach the heart of the brown and ruddy nymph beside him.

She was ignorant and young. Too whole-souled in her indifference to really appreciate the stress he labored under; much less to sympathize. On the contrary she took a mischievous delight in teasing him, doing harm without knowing it, like a playful child. She teased him about his tennis playing, about his paddling, about his driving; allowed that perhaps he might play golf well, but she didn't care for golf herself—it was too slow; mocked even his walking expeditions.

"He don't want to walk!" she said gaily to her mother one night at dinner. "He just wants to go somewhere and arrange himself gracefully under a tree and read to me about Eloise, or Araminta or somebody; all slim and white and wavy and golden-haired; and how they killed themselves for love!"

She laughed frankly at him, and he laughed with her; but his heart was hot and dark within him. The longer he pursued and failed the fiercer was his desire for her. Already he had loved longer than was usual to him. Never before had his overwhelming advances been so lightly parried and set aside.

"Will you take a walk with me this evening after dinner?" he proposed. "There is a most heavenly moon—and I cannot see to read to you. It must be strangely lovely—the moonlight—on your lake, is it not, Mrs. Osgood?"

"It is indeed," she warmly agreed, looking disapprovingly on the girl, who was still giggling softly at the memory of golden-haired Araminta. "Take him on the cliff walk, Ellen, and do try to be more appreciative of beauty!"

"Yes, mama," said Ellen, "I'll be good."

She was so good upon the moonlit walk; so gentle and sympathetic, and so honestly tried to find some point of agreement, that his feelings were too much for his judgment, and he seized her hand and kissed it. She pushed him away, too astonished for words.

"Why, Mr. Pendexter! What are you thinking of!"

Then he poured out his heart to her. He told her how he loved her—madly, passionately, irresistably. He begged her to listen to him.

"Ah! You young Diana! You do not know how I suffer! You are so young, so cold! So heavenly beautiful! Do not be cruel! Listen to me! Say you will be my wife! Give me one kiss! Just one!"

She was young, and cold, and ignorantly cruel. She laughed at him, laughed mercilessly, and turned away.

He followed her, the blood pounding in his veins, his voice shaken with the intensity of his emotions. He caught her hand and drew her toward him again. She broke from him with a little cry, and ran. He followed, hotly, madly; rushed upon her, caught her, held her fast.

"You shall love me! You shall!" he cried. His hands were hot and trembling, but he held her close and turned her face to his.

"I will not!" she cried, struggling. "Let me go! I hate you, I tell you. I hate you! You are—disgusting!" She pushed as far from him as he could.

They had reached the top of the little cliff opposite the house. Huge dark pines hung over them, their wide boughs swaying softly.

The water lay below in the shadow, smooth and oil-black.

The girl looked down at it, and a sudden shudder shook her tense frame. She gave a low moan and hid her face in her hands.

"Ah!" he cried. "It is your fate! Our fate! We have lived through this before! We will die together if we cannot live together!"

He caught her to him, kissed her madly, passionately, and together they went down into the black water.

* * * * *

"It's pretty lucky I could swim," said Ellen, as she hurried home. "And he couldn't. The poor man! O, the poor man! He must have been crazy!"

MAKING A CHANGE

"WA-A-A-A-A! WAA-A-A-AAA!"

Frank Gordins set down his coffee cup so hard that it spilled over into the saucer.

"Is there no way to stop that child crying?" he demanded.

"I do not know of any," said his wife, so definitely and politely that the words seemed cut off by machinery.

"*I do*," said his mother with even more definiteness, but less politeness.

Young Mrs. Gordins looked at her mother-in-law from under her delicate level brows, and said nothing. But the weary lines about her eyes deepened; she had been kept awake nearly all night, and for many nights.

So had he. So, as a matter of fact, had his mother. She had not the care of the baby—but lay awake wishing she had.

"There's no need at all for that child's crying so, Frank. If Julia would only let me—"

"It's no use talking about it," said Julia. "If Frank is not satisfied with the child's mother, he must say so—perhaps we can make a change."

This was ominously gentle. Julia's nerves were at the breaking point. Upon her tired ears, her sensitive mother's heart, the grating wail from the next room fell like a lash—burnt in like fire. Her ears were hypersensitive, always. She had been an ardent musician before her marriage, and had taught quite successfully on both piano and violin. To any mother a child's cry is painful; to a musical mother it is torment.

But if her ears were sensitive, so was her conscience. If her nerves were weak, her pride was strong. The child was her child, it was her duty to take care of it, and take care of it she would. She spent her days in unremitting devotion to its needs and to the care of her neat flat; and her nights had long since ceased to refresh her.

Again the weary cry rose to a wail.

"It does seem to be time for a change of treatment," suggested the older woman acidly.

"Or a change of residence," offered the younger, in a deadly quiet voice.

"Well, by Jupiter! There'll be a change of some kind, and p. d. q.!" said the son and husband, rising to his feet.

His mother rose also, and left the room, holding her head high and refusing to show any effects of that last thrust.

Frank Gordins glared at his wife. His nerves were raw, too. It does not benefit anyone in health or character to be continuously deprived of sleep. Some enlightened persons use that deprivation as a form of torture.

She stirred her coffee with mechanical calm, her eyes sullenly bent on her plate.

"I will not stand having Mother spoken to like that," he stated with decision.

"I will not stand having her interfere with my methods of bringing up children."

"Your methods! Why, Julia, my mother knows more about taking care of babies than you'll ever learn! She has the real love of it—and the practical experience. Why can't you *let* her take care of the kid—and we'll all have some peace!"

She lifted her eyes and looked at him; deep inscrutable wells of angry light. He had not the faintest appreciation of her state of mind. When people say they are "nearly crazy" from weariness, they state a practical fact. The old phrase which describes reason as "tottering on her throne" is also a clear one.

Julia was more near the verge of complete disaster than the family dreamed. The conditions were so simple, so usual, so inevitable.

Here was Frank Gordins, well brought up, the only son of a very capable and idolatrously affectionate mother. He had fallen deeply and desperately in love with the exalted beauty and fine mind of the young music teacher, and his mother had approved. She too loved music and admired beauty.

Her tiny store in the savings bank did not allow of a separate home, and Julia had cordially welcomed her to share in their household.

Here was affection, propriety, and peace. Here was a noble devotion on the part of the young wife, who so worshipped her husband that she used to wish she had been the greatest musician on earth—that she might give it up for him! She had given up her music, perforce, for many months, and missed it more than she knew.

She bent her mind to the decoration and artistic management of their little apartment, finding her standards difficult to maintain by the ever-changing inefficiency of her help. The musical temperament does not always include patience, nor, necessarily, the power of management.

When the baby came, her heart overflowed with utter devotion and thankfulness; she was his wife—the mother of his child. Her happiness lifted and pushed within till she longed more than ever for her music, for the free-pouring current of expression, to give forth her love and pride and happiness. She had not the gift of words.

So now she looked at her husband, dumbly, while wild visions of separation, of secret flight—even of self-destruction—swung dizzily across her mental vision. All she said was, "All right, Frank. We'll make a change. And you shall have—some peace."

"Thank goodness for that, Jule! You do look tired, Girlie—let Mother see to His Nibs, and try to get a nap, can't you?"

"Yes," she said. "Yes . . . I think I will." Her voice had a peculiar note in it. If Frank had been an alienist, or even a general physician, he would have noticed it. But his work lay in electric coils, in dynamos and copper wiring—not in women's nerves—and he did not notice it.

He kissed her and went out, throwing back his shoulders and drawing a long breath of relief as he left the house behind him and entered his own world.

"This being married—and bringing up children—is not what

it's cracked up to be." That was the feeling in the back of his mind. But it did not find full admission, much less expression.

When a friend asked him, "All well at home?" he said, "Yes, thank you—pretty fair. Kid cries a good deal—but that's natural, I suppose."

He dismissed the whole matter from his mind and bent his faculties to a man's task—how he can earn enough to support a wife, a mother, and a son.

At home his mother sat in her small room, looking out of the window at the ground-glass one just across the "well," and thinking hard.

By the disorderly little breakfast table his wife remained motionless, her chin in her hands, her big eyes staring at nothing, trying to formulate in her weary mind some reliable reason why she should not do what she was thinking of doing. But her mind was too exhausted to serve her properly.

Sleep—Sleep—Sleep—that was the one thing she wanted. Then his mother could take care of the baby all she wanted to, and Frank could have some peace. . . . Oh, dear! It was time for the child's bath.

She gave it to him mechanically. On the stroke of the hour, she prepared the sterilized milk and arranged the little one comfortably with his bottle. He snuggled down, enjoying it, while she stood watching him.

She emptied the tub, put the bath apron to dry, picked up all the towels and sponges and varied appurtenances of the elaborate performance of bathing the first-born, and then sat staring straight before her, more weary than ever, but growing inwardly determined.

Greta had cleared the table, with heavy heels and hands, and was now rattling dishes in the kitchen. At every slam, the young mother winced, and when the girl's high voice began a sort of doleful chant over her work, young Mrs. Gordins rose to her feet with a shiver and made her decision.

She carefully picked up the child and his bottle, and carried him to his grandmother's room.

"Would you mind looking after Albert?" she asked in a flat, quiet voice. "I think I'll try to get some sleep."

"Oh, I shall be delighted," replied her mother-in-law. She said it in a tone of cold politeness, but Julia did not notice. She laid the child on the bed and stood looking at him in the same dull way for a little while, then went out without another word.

Mrs. Gordins, senior, sat watching the baby for some long moments. "He's a perfectly lovely child!" she said softly, gloating over his rosy beauty. "There's not a *thing* the matter with him! It's just her absurd ideas. She's so irregular with him! To think of letting that child cry for an hour! He is nervous because she is. And of course she couldn't feed him till after his bath—of course not!"

She continued in these sarcastic meditations for some time, taking the empty bottle away from the small wet mouth, that sucked on for a few moments aimlessly and then was quiet in sleep.

"I could take care of him so that he'd *never* cry!" she continued to herself, rocking slowly back and forth. "And I could take care of twenty like him—and enjoy it! I believe I'll go off somewhere and do it. Give Julia a rest. Change of residence, indeed!"

She rocked and planned, pleased to have her grandson with her, even while asleep.

Greta had gone out on some errand of her own. The rooms were very quiet. Suddenly the old lady held up her head and sniffed. She rose swiftly to her feet and sprang to the gas jet— no, it was shut off tightly. She went back to the dining-room— all right there.

"That foolish girl has left the range going and it's blown out!" she thought, and went to the kitchen. No, the little room was fresh and clean, every burner turned off.

"Funny! It must come in from the hall." She opened the door. No, the hall gave only its usual odor of diffused basement. Then the parlor—nothing there. The little alcove called by the renting agent "the music room," where Julia's closed piano and violin case stood dumb and dusty—nothing there.

"It's in her room—and she's asleep!" said Mrs. Gordins, senior; and she tried to open the door. It was locked. She knocked—there was no answer; knocked louder—shook it—rattled the knob. No answer.

Then Mrs. Gordins thought quickly. "It may be an accident, and nobody must know. Frank mustn't know. I'm glad Greta's out. I *must* get in somehow!" She looked at the transom, and the stout rod Frank had himself put up for the portieres Julia loved.

"I believe I can do it, at a pinch."

She was a remarkably active woman of her years, but no memory of earlier gymnastic feats could quite cover the exercise. She hastily brought the step-ladder. From its top she could see in, and what she saw made her determine recklessly.

Grabbing the pole with small strong hands, she thrust her light frame bravely through the opening, turning clumsily but successfully, and dropping breathlessly and somewhat bruised to the floor, she flew to open the windows and doors.

When Julia opened her eyes she found loving arms around her, and wise, tender words to soothe and reassure.

"Don't say a thing, dearie—I understand. I *understand*, I tell you! Oh, my dear girl—my precious daughter! We haven't been half good enough to you, Frank and I! But cheer up now—I've got the *loveliest* plan to tell you about! We *are* going to make a change! Listen now!"

And while the pale young mother lay quiet, petted and waited on to her heart's content, great plans were discussed and decided on.

Frank Gordins was pleased when the baby "outgrew his crying spells." He spoke of it to his wife.

"Yes," she said sweetly. "He has better care."

"I knew you'd learn," said he, proudly.

"I have!" she agreed. "I've learned—ever so much!"

He was pleased, too, vastly pleased, to have her health improve rapidly and steadily, the delicate pink come back to her cheeks, the soft light to her eyes; and when she made music for him in the evening, soft music, with shut doors—not to waken Albert—he felt as if his days of courtship had come again.

Greta the hammer-footed had gone, and an amazing French matron who came in by the day had taken her place. He asked no questions as to this person's peculiarities, and did not know that she did the purchasing and planned the meals, meals of such new delicacy and careful variance as gave him much delight. Neither did he know that her wages were greater than her predecessor's. He turned over the same sum weekly, and did not pursue details.

He was pleased also that his mother seemed to have taken a new lease of life. She was so cheerful and brisk, so full of little jokes and stories—as he had known her in his boyhood; and above all she was so free and affectionate with Julia, that he was more than pleased.

"I tell you what it is!" he said to a bachelor friend. "You fellows don't know what you're missing!" And he brought one of them home to dinner—just to show him.

"Do you do all that on thirty-five a week?" his friend demanded.

"That's about it," he answered proudly.

"Well, your wife's a wonderful manager—that's all I can say. And you've got the best cook I ever saw, or heard of, or ate of—I suppose I might say—for five dollars."

Mr. Gordins was pleased and proud. But he was neither pleased nor proud when someone said to him, with displeasing frankness, "I shouldn't think you'd want your wife to be giving music lessons, Frank!"

He did not show surprise nor anger to his friend, but saved it for his wife. So surprised and so angry was he that he did a most unusual thing—he left his business and went home early in the afternoon. He opened the door of his flat. There was no one in it. He went through every room. No wife; no child; no mother; no servant.

The elevator boy heard him banging about, opening and shutting doors, and grinned happily. When Mr. Gordins came out, Charles volunteered some information.

"Young Mrs. Gordins is out, sir; but old Mrs. Gordins and the baby—they're upstairs. On the roof, I think."

Mr. Gordins went to the roof. There he found his mother, a smiling, cheerful nursemaid, and fifteen happy babies.

Mrs. Gordins, senior, rose to the occasion promptly.

"Welcome to my baby-garden, Frank," she said cheerfully. "I'm so glad you could get off in time to see it."

She took his arm and led him about, proudly exhibiting her sunny roof-garden, her sand-pile and big, shallow, zinc-lined pool, her flowers and vines, her seesaws, swings, and floor mattresses.

"You see how happy they are," she said. "Celia can manage very well for a few moments." And then she exhibited to him the whole upper flat, turned into a convenient place for many little ones to take their naps or to play in if the weather was bad.

"Where's Julia?" he demanded first.

"Julia will be in presently," she told him; "by five o'clock anyway. And the mothers come for the babies by then, too. I have them from nine or ten to five."

He was silent, both angry and hurt.

"We didn't tell you at first, my dear boy, because we knew you wouldn't like it, and we wanted to make sure it would go well. I rent the upper flat, you see—it is forty dollars a month, same as ours—and pay Celia five dollars a week, and pay Dr. Holbrook downstairs the same for looking over my little ones every day. She helped me to get them, too. The mothers pay me three dollars a week each, and don't have to keep a nursemaid. And I pay ten dollars a week board to Julia, and still have about ten of my own."

"And she gives music lessons?"

"Yes, she gives music lessons, just as she used to. She loves it, you know. You must have noticed how happy and well she is now—haven't you? And so am I. And so is Albert. You can't feel very badly about a thing that makes us all happy, can you?"

Just then Julia came in, radiant from a brisk walk, fresh and cheery, a big bunch of violets at her breast.

"Oh, Mother," she cried, "I've got tickets and we'll all go to hear Melba—if we can get Celia to come in for the evening."

She saw her husband, and a guilty flush rose to her brow as she met his reproachful eyes.

"Oh, Frank!" she begged, her arms around his neck. "Please don't mind! Please get used to it! Please be proud of us! Just think, we're all so happy, and we earn about a hundred dollars a week—all of us together. You see, I have Mother's ten to add to the house money, and twenty or more of my own!"

They had a long talk together that evening, just the two of them. She told him, at last, what a danger had hung over them—how near it came.

"And Mother showed me the way out, Frank. The way to have my mind again—and not lose you! She is a different woman herself now that she has her heart and hands full of babies. Albert does enjoy it so! And *you've* enjoyed it—till you found it out!

"And dear—my own love—I don't mind it now at all! I love my home, I love my work, I love my mother, I love you. And as to children—I wish I had six!"

He looked at her flushed, eager, lovely face, and drew her close to him.

"If it makes all of you as happy as that," he said, "I guess I can stand it."

And in after years he was heard to remark, "This being married and bringing up children is as easy as can be—when you learn how!"

MRS. ELDER'S IDEA

Did you ever repeat a word or phrase so often that it lost all meaning to you?

Did you ever eat at the same table, of the same diet, till the food had no taste to you?

Did you ever feel a sudden overmastering wave of revolt against the ceaseless monotony of your surroundings till you longed to escape anywhere at any cost?

That was the way Mrs. Elder felt on this gray, muggy morning, toward the familiar objects around her dining room, the familiar dishes on the table, even, for the moment, at the familiar figure at the other end of it.

It was Mr. Elder's idea of a pleasant breakfast to set up his preferred newspaper against the water pitcher, and read it as long as he could continue eating and drinking. Other people were welcome to do the same, he argued; *he* had no objection. It is true that there was but one newspaper.

Mrs. Elder was a woman naturally chatty, but skilled in silence. One cannot long converse with an absorbed opposing countenance which meets one's choicest anecdote, some minutes after the event, with a testy "What's that?"

She sat still, stirring her cool coffee, waiting to ring for it, hot, when he wanted more, and studying his familiar outlines with a dull fascination. She knew every line and tint, every curve and angle, every wrinkle in the loose-fitting coat, every moderate change in expression. They were only moderate, nowadays. Never any more did she see the looks she remembered so well, over twenty years ago; looks of admiration, of approval, of interest, of desire to please; looks with a deep kindling fire in them—

"I would thou wert either cold or hot," she was half consciously repeating to herself.

O yes, he was kind to her in most things; he was fond of her, even, she could admit that. He missed her, when she was not there, or would miss her—she seldom had a chance to test it. They had no quarrel, no complaint against each other; only a long, slow cooling, as of lava beds; the gradual evaporation of a fine fervor; that process of torpid, tepid, mutual accommodation which is complacently referred to by the worldly wise as "settling down."

"Had she no children?" will demand those whose psychological medicine closets hold but a few labels.

"For a Woman: A Husband, Home and Children. Good for whatever ails her."

"For a Man: Success, Money, A Good Wife."

"For a Child: Proper Care, Education, A Good Bringing Up."

There are no other persons to be doctored, and no other remedies.

Now Mrs. Elder had had children, four, fulfilling the formula announced by Mr. Grant Allen, some years since, that each couple must have four children, merely to preserve the balance of the population; two to replace their parents, and two to die. Two of hers had accordingly, died; and two, living, were now ready to replace their parents; that is they were grown up.

Theodore was of age, and had gone into business already, at a distance. Alice was of age, too; the lesser age allowed the weaker vessel, and also away from home. She was staying with an aunt in Boston, a wealthy aunt who insisted on maintaining her in luxury; but the girl insisted equally upon studying at the Institute of Technology, and threatened an early departure into the proud freedom of self support.

Mrs. Elder was fond of children, but these young persons were not children any more. She would have been glad to continue her ministrations; but however motherhood may seek to prolong its period of usefulness, childhood is evanescent; and youth, modern youth, serenely rebellious. The cycle which is supposed to so perfectly round out a woman's life, was closed for the present.

Mr. Elder projected a cup, without looking at it, or her; and Mrs. Elder rang, poured his coffee, modified it to his liking, and handed it back to him. She even took a fresh cup for herself, but found she did not want it.

There was a heavier shadow than usual between them this morning. As a general thing there was not a real cloud, only the bluish mist of distance in thick air; but now they had had a "difference," a decided difference.

Mr. Elder's concerns in life had never been similar to his wife's. She had tried, as is held to be the duty of wives, to interest herself in his, but with only a measurable success. Her own preferences had never amounted to more than topics of conversation, to him, and distasteful topics, at that. What was the use of continually talking about things, if you could not have them and ought not to want to?

She loved the city, thick and bustling, the glitter and surge of the big shops with their kaleidoscope exhibition of color and style, that changed even as you looked.

Her fondness for shopping was almost a passion; to her an unending delight; to him, a silly vice.

This attitude was reversed in the matter of tobacco; to him, an unending delight; to her a silly vice.

They had had arguments upon these lines, but that was years ago.

One of the reasons for Mrs. Elder's hard-bitten silence was Mr. Elder's extreme dislike of argument. Why argue, when you could not help yourself? that was his position; and not to be able to help herself was hers. How could she shop, to any advantage, when they lived an hour from town, and she had to ask for money to go with, or at least for money to shop with.

Just for once in her life had Mrs. Elder had an orgy of shopping. A widowed aunt of Mr. Elder, who had just paid them a not too agreeable visit, surprised her beyond words with a Christmas present of a hundred dollars. "It is conditional," she said grimly, holding the amazing yellow-backed treasure in her bony and somewhat purple hand. "You're not to tell

Herbert a word about it till it's spent. You're to go in town, early in January, some day when the sales are on, and spend it all. And half of it you're to spend on yourself. Promise, now."

Mrs. Elder had promised, but the last condition was a little stretched. She swore she had wanted the movable electric drop light and the little music machine, but Herbert and the children seemed to use them more than she did. Anyhow she had a day's shopping, which was the solace of barren years.

She liked the theatre, too, but that had been so wholly out of the question for so long that it did not trouble her, much.

As for Mr. Elder, he had to work in the city to maintain his family, but what he liked above everything else was the country; the real, wild, open country, where you could count your visible neighbors on your fingers, and leave them, visible, but not audible. They had compromised for twenty-two years, by living in Highvale, which was enough like a city to annoy him, and enough like the country to annoy her. She hated the country, it "got on her nerves."

Which brings us to the present difference between them.

Theodore being grown up and earning his living; Alice being well on the way to it, and a small expense at present; Mr. Elder had concluded that his financial resources would allow of the realization of his fondest hope—retirement. A real retirement, not only officially, from business, and its hated environment; but physically, into the remote and lonely situation which his soul loved. So he had sold his business and bought a farm.

They had talked about it all last evening; at least she had. Mr. Elder, as has been stated, was not much of a talker. He had seemed rather more preoccupied than usual during dinner; possibly he did realize in a dim way that the change would be extremely unwelcome to his wife. Then as they settled down to their usual quiet evening, wherein he was supremely comfortable in house-coat, slippers, cigars of the right sort, the books he loved, and a good light at the left back corner of his leather-cushioned chair; and wherein she read as long as she could stand it, sewed as long as she could stand it, and talked as long as he could stand it.

This time, he had, after strengthening himself with a preliminary cigar, heaved a sigh, and faced the inevitable.

"Oh, Grace," he said, laying down his book, as if this was a minor incident which had just occurred to him, "I've sold the business."

She dropped her work, and looked at him, startled. He went on, wishing to make all clear at once—he did hate discussion.

"Given up for good. It don't cost us much to live, now the children are practically off our hands. You know I've always hated office work; it's a great relief to be done with it, I assure you. . . . And I've bought that farm on Warren Hill. . . . We'll move out by October. I'd have left it till Spring—but I had a splendid chance to sell—and then I didn't dare wait lest I lose the farm. . . . No use keeping up two places. . . . Our lease is out in October you know."

He had left little gaps of silence between these blows, not longer than those required to heave up the axe for its full swing; and when he finished Mrs. Elder felt as if her head verily rolled in the basket. She moistened her lips, and looked at him rather piteously, saying nothing at first. She could not say anything.

He arose from the easy depth of the chair, and came round the table, giving her a cursory kiss, and a reassuring pat on the shoulder.

"I know you won't like it at first, Grace, but it will do you good—good for your nerves—open air—rest—and a garden. You can have a lovely garden—and" (this was a carefully thought out boon, really involving some intent of sacrifice) "and company, in summer. Have your friends come out!"

He sat down again feeling that the subject had been fully, fairly, and finally discussed. She thought differently. There arose in her a slow, boiling flood of long-suppressed rebellion. He could speak like this—he could do a thing like that—and she was expected to say "Yes, Herbert" to what amounted to penal servitude for life—to her.

But the habit of a score of years is strong, to say nothing of the habit of several scores of centuries, and out of that surging sea of resistance came only fatuous protests, and inefficacious pleas.

Mr. Elder had been making up his mind to take this step for many years, and it was now a fact accomplished. He had decided that it would be good for his wife even if she did not like it; and that conviction gave him added strength.

Against this formidable front of fact and theory she had nothing to advance save a pathetic array of likes and dislikes; feeble neglected things, weak from disuse. But he had generously determined to "let her talk it out" for that one evening; so she had talked from hour to hour—till she had at last realized that all this talk reached nowhere—the thing was done.

A dull cloud oppressed her dreams; she woke with a sense of impending calamity, and as the remembrance grew, into awakening pain. There was constraint between them at the breakfast table; a cold response from her when he went, with a fine effect of being cheerful and affectionate; and then Mrs. Elder was left alone to consider her future.

She was a woman of forty-two, in excellent health, and would have been extremely good-looking if she could have "dressed the part." Some women look best in evening dress, some in house gowns, some in street suits; the last was her kind.

She gave her orders for the day listlessly, noting with weary patience the inefficiency of the suburban maid, and then suddenly thinking of how much worse the servant question would become on Warren Hill.

"Perhaps he expects me to do the housework," she grimly remarked to herself. "And have company. Company!"

As a matter of fact, Mrs. Elder did not enjoy household visitors. They were to her a care, an added strain upon her housekeeping skill. Her idea of company was "seeing people"; the chance meeting in the street, the friendly face in a theatre crowd, the brisk easily-ended chatter of a "call" and now and then a real party—where one could dance. Should she ever dance again?

Mrs. Elder always considered it a special providence that brought Mrs. Gaylord, a neighbor, in to see her that day; and with her a visiting friend, Mrs. MacAvelly, rather a silent person, but sympathetic and suggestive. Mrs. Gaylord was profusely interested and even angry at Mr. Elder's heartlessness, as she called it; but Mrs. MacAvelly had merely assisted in the conversation, by gentle references to this and that story, book and play. Had she seen this? Had she read that? Did she think so and so was right to do what she did?

After they left, Mrs. Elder went down town, and bought a magazine or two which had been mentioned, and got a book from the little library.

She read, she was amazed, shocked, fascinated; she read more, and after a week of this inoculation, a strange light dawned upon her mind, quite suddenly and clearly.

"Why not?" she said to herself. And again, "Why not?" Even in the night she woke and lay smiling, while heavy breathing told of sleep beside her; saying inwardly, "Why not?"

It was only the end of August; there was a month yet.

She made plans, rapidly but quietly; consulting at length with several of her friends in Highvale, women with large establishments, large purses, and profoundly domestic tastes.

Mrs. Gaylord was rapturously interested, introducing her to other friends, and Mrs. MacAvelly wrote a little note from the city, mentioning several more; from more than one of these came large encouragement.

She wrote to her daughter also, and her son, whose business brought him to Boston that season. They had a talk in the soft-colored little parlor; Mrs. Elder smiling, flushed, eager and excited as a girl, as she announced her plans, under pledge of strictest secrecy.

"I don't care whether you agree or not!" she stoutly proclaimed. "But I'm going to do it. And you mustn't say one word. He never said a word till it was all done."

None the less she looked a little anxiously at Theodore. He soon reassured her. "Bully for you, Mama," he said. "You look about sixteen! Go ahead—I'll back you up."

Alice was profoundly pleased.

"How perfectly splendid, Mama! I'm so proud of you! What glorious times we'll have, won't we just?" And they discussed her plans with enthusiasm and glee.

Toward the middle of September Mr. Elder, immersed

though he was in frequent visits to that idol of his heart, the farm, began to notice the excitement in his wife's manner. "I hope you're not tiring yourself too much, packing," he said, and added, quite affectionately, "You won't hate it so much after a while, my dear."

"No, I won't," she admitted, with an ambiguous smile. "I think I might even like it, a little while, in Summer."

About the twentieth of the month she made up her mind to tell him, finding it harder than she had anticipated in the first proud moments of determination.

It was evening again and he had settled luxuriously into his big chair, surrounded by The Country Gentlemen, The Fruit-Grower, and The Breeder and Sportsman. She let him have one cigar, and then—"Herbert."

He was a moment or two in answering—coming up from the depths of his studies in "The Profits of Making Honey" with appropriate slowness. "Yes, Grace, what is it?"

"I am not going with you to the farm."

He smiled a little wearily. "Oh, yes you are, my dear; don't make a fuss about the inevitable."

She flushed at that and gathered courage. "I have made other arrangements," she said calmly. "I am going to board in Boston. I have rented a furnished floor. Theodore is going to hire one room, and Alice one. And we take our meals out. She is to have a position this year. They both approve—" She hesitated a moment, and added breathlessly, "I'm to be a professional shopper! I've got a lot of orders ahead. I can see my way half through the season already!"

She paused. So did he. He was not good at talking. "You seem to have it all arranged," he said drily.

"I have," she eagerly agreed. "It's all planned out."

"Where do I come in?" he asked, after a little.

She took him seriously. "There is plenty of room for you, dear, and you'll always be welcome. You might like it awhile—in Winter."

This time it was Mr. Elder who spent some hours in stating his likes and dislikes; but she explained how easily he could hire someone to pack and move for him—and how much happier he would be, when once well settled on the farm.

"You can get a nice housekeeper you see—for I shan't be costing you *anything* now!"

"I'm going to town next week," she added, "and we hope to see you by Christmas, at latest."

They did.

They had an unusually happy Christmas, and an unusually happy Summer following. From a sullen rage, Mr. Elder, in a serene rural solitude, simmered down to a grieved state of mind. When he did come to town, he found an eagerly delighted family; and a wife so roguishly young, so attractively dressed, so vivacious and happy and amusing, that the warmth of a sudden Indian Summer fell upon his heart.

Alice and Theodore chuckled in corners. "Just see Papa making love to Mama! Isn't it impressive?"

Mrs. Elder was certainly much impressed by it; and Mr. Elder found that two half homes and half a happy wife, were really more satisfying than one whole home, and a whole unhappy wife, withering in discontent.

In her new youth and gaiety of spirit, and her half-remorseful tenderness for him, she grew ever more desirable, and presently the Elder family maintained a city flat and a country home; and spent their happy years between them.

THE CHAIR OF ENGLISH

Dr. Irwin Manchester was calling on the wife of Dr. Richard Beale. Both of these gentlemen were Ph.D.s—not M.D.s or D.D.s or any other D.s as yet. The general public called them Professors, but in the little court of "The Faculty" of Everton University all were punctilious as to titles.

Dr. Manchester leaned rather forward in his chair, wearing a look as of one burdened with a painful duty. Mrs. Beale, a young-faced woman with a pleasant smile, sat quiet, watching him intently.

"I trust you feel assured that I speak most reluctantly," he said. "That only my sincere interest in you—in your welfare—your happiness—and that of your children—and of the college welfare, urges me to come to you." He spoke with a rather complicated hesitancy, picking his words with care. The direct look she gave him when he spoke of interest in her sent him wide afield at once, for further reasons; the children and the college combined seemed to steady him again.

"Pray, believe me," he concluded.

"Why should I not believe you?" she answered brightly. "You have always shown a friendly interest in us, and in the college. I may seem a little startled, naturally, but I assure you—" she gave him a swift, appreciative smile, "that I understand."

There was a moment's silence, and she added encouragingly, "I can see what an effort you are making, Dr. Manchester. It must be very hard indeed for you as a friend, as a gentleman, to come to me on an errand like this. Let me ask you to take this chair," she added, moving toward the other end of the long, low room, and motioning him to a big lounging chair that stretched comfortable arms against the background of a richly embroidered tall Japanese screen.

"This makes a little room by itself, you see," she added, seating herself in a low rocker near the window, "and we can be quite quiet."

The roses hung heavily on the latticed porch outside; the steady bees, with an occasional humming-bird, made a soft monotone beneath his words. She sat in silence, busying her fingers with a bit of needle-work, giving him close attention, asking now and then a question, while he laid before her his suspicions, his more than suspicions, concerning her husband and pretty Mrs. Rossiter, the new wife of the elderly president.

"I must hope it has not gone far—too far—as yet, Mrs. Beale. I cannot believe, knowing you, that any man could utterly forget you. But human nature is weak—we are all thrown together here in such a close way—Mrs. Rossiter is undeniably attractive—I think she had no intention of doing harm."

"Do you not think that our going away this Summer will break it all up—naturally?" she asked.

"Oh, unquestionably, unquestionably—at least for the time being. In other scenes and with you beside him it must come right. I feel sure that no further harm will come of it, Mrs. Beale—forewarned is forearmed, you know."

She meditated, tapping her thimbled finger softly on the window-sill, her eyes among the roses.

"Change will sometimes do wonders for a heart in temptation," she murmured.

"It is a joy to see you so brave, so rational," he said. "I knew you would be or I should not have dared to come. We have always discussed life very freely, very fully, and I felt sure you could face its emergencies with wisdom."

"I must be very *sure*, Dr. Manchester," she said suddenly. "There is always possibility of mistake—can you be a little more definite? I dislike to dwell on details, but I must really know my ground. Will you give me the exact grounds you have for belief?"

He drew a long breath. "You have the right to ask," he said. "It is only fair." Holding the Chair of English with some distinction, and sometimes putting forth in grave reviews scholarly articles of exquisite diction, Dr. Manchester was practiced expert in the use of words, and he used them now with delicate precision. Had the gentleman under discussion undertaken a similar errand he could never have done it so well—his was the Chair of Physics.

Mrs. Beale listened, her eyes on her work, her color changing a little now and then, while her visitor gave chapter and verse; a word here, a look there, an unavoidably overheard bit of conversation, the talk among the other members of the faculty, the growing comment, a surprised recognition of the two under circumstances which, to a less charitable mind, might have seemed too conclusive.

She faced him squarely at the end.

"I can hardly thank you, Dr. Manchester, for a blow like this, but I do wish you to rest assured that I appreciate your motives," and she smiled wanly.

He rose to go. "I can thank you, Mrs. Beale; I do thank you, for listening so quietly to what must have given pain; for your forbearance and understanding. I hope and believe that with prevision any serious danger may be averted."

Left alone Mona Beale watched the well-dressed, somewhat stiff figure well out of her garden gate and then turned to her telephone.

"Is Dr. Gates in? Oh, is that you, doctor? I'm so glad. Could you come and see me a moment, right now? Oh, no, nothing serious—I hope."

Dr. Gates was a "real doctor," a grizzled man, who had known Mona Beale when she was Mona Winsor—yes, and before the "Mona" was given her. He was the oldest established physician in the town, family doctor and family friend of successive generations of professors and professorins—the most popular individual on College Hill.

He came promptly with his long, heavy little bag in his hand.

"What's wrong, Mona? Baby got the croup? Richard caught the bubonic plague? Young Richard down with the measles? You're never sick!"

"No," said Mona. "I'm pretty strong, luckily. But I had to see you just the same. "Nobody's sick, but I think I'm—poisoned."

He gave her a quick look, drew her to the light, put his hands on her shoulders and turned her squarely toward him.

"Hm! Well, tell me about it."

She brought him to the same big chair by the golden storks and lilies and seated herself again in the rocker, not quiet now, but tense and earnest.

"Look here, Dr. Gates. You know everybody on this hill—you know what they talk about—what's going on? Now, I want to ask you something, and I want you to answer me square, as I know you will. It's a comfort to know a man who always speaks the truth—even if it's sometimes inconvenient.

"Doctor—there has been brought to me a story—about my husband and Mrs. Rossiter, a story with considerable evidence, and with the assertion that the—affair—is being talked about among the faculty. Is it true?"

"No," said Dr. Gates.

She gave a little gasping sigh, and leaned back in her chair for a moment. "I knew it," she said. "I *knew* it—I wasn't afraid, but I wanted evidence. Doctor—will you please tell me how you know?"

He gave a gruff little laugh. "Firstly, if there *was* such a thing going on it would be talked about all over the hill, these professors' wives have nothing else to discuss, apparently, but one another's affairs. And Mrs. Rossiter is so young and handsome, and your husband so popular, that they'd be 'on' if there was the shadow of a pin to hang anything to.

"Second, I've known Dick Beale ever since he was a kid; you two are part of my family, you know, and I happen to know that he's very much in love with his wife.

"Third, I've adopted this little Rossiter girl—she needs it, poor child. But I won't tell you how I know where her heart is—it's none of your business. Satisfied?"

Mona nodded, smiling happily, with wet eyes. "Now please tell me some more, Doctor. Dick has had a sort of offer from Harkness College—but he has not wanted to leave here. This is home, you know, we both love it. But if we went, do you happen to know who might be called to take his place?"

Dr. Gates meditated for a moment.

"I don't know as I can say, offhand. College politics are pretty thick and I don't pay much attention. But seems to me I did hear something at the Faculty Club—there's a smart young fellow from Princeton that they've had under discussion now and then for some time—brother-in-law or cousin or something of Dr. Manchester's, I believe. But you tell Dick to hang on—we can't spare him."

"Thank you, doctor! You do relieve my mind. I'm sorry to have troubled you, but I did want some scientific observation to back up my faith."

"All right, young lady. Next time don't listen to the serpent. These women have nothing to do but gossip—pay no attention to 'em!"

He went away, stopping to speak to cherry-cheeked little Doris in the garden. Mrs. Beale watched them affectionately, the child toddling eagerly forward, the big gray man stooping to her and gravely shaking the small fat hand.

"He's a *Dear!*" said Mrs. Beale, "A perfect *Dear!*"

* * * * *

She was unusually brilliant that night, unusually well-gowned, two golden roses in her soft hair. Richard Beale gazed at his wife with serene satisfaction.

"It's so lucky that you're not a high-flyer at fashion, Mona. Lucky for me, and lucky for all those men that you've saved the lives of!"

"Saved the lives of! What on earth do you mean, Dick?"

"Same as pins do, of course—by not eating them. But seriously, Mona—" he drew her down on his knee, and gazed admiringly at the soft silk, the delicate lace, the fair flushed face above, "seriously, it seems to me that you are far too handsome to be, as it were, wasted on one man!"

"You're not proposing polyandry, are you?" she answered. "Whom would you suggest as partners?"

"Our garden would become a graveyard if there were any,

and you know it, naughty girl! I'm sorry for all those other men in general, but in particular I should promptly exterminate them."

She nestled down till her head was on his shoulder, with a long sigh of content.

"Dick, dear—were you thinking at all of going to Harkness?"

"Why, no—not specially. It is pleasant to be wanted, but I'd rather stay here, I think. Unless—there's one thing that would send me to Harkness quick—that is if you wanted to go. Do you, Monalina?"

"I do not," she replied with decision.

* * * * *

Yet it was only the next day that Mrs. Richard Beale, attired with decorous richness and due care, entered the office of Horace Butts, of Butts & Henderson, Attorney-at-Law, and almost caused the hair of that respectable gentleman to rise upon his head. He would have been pleased if she had, by the way, as he had expended money, time and labor to produce that result—in vain. Presently he tipped back in his swivel chair, swung around to face her squarely, stared in unfeigned surprise:

"What do you mean, Mrs. Beale?"

"Exactly what I say, Mr. Butts. I have come to ask you to draw up the papers for an application for divorce."

"*You*—apply for divorce from Dick Beale! I've known you two long enough to know better than to believe you."

"I would far rather consult you than any other lawyer, Mr. Butts. But, of course—if you won't take the case—"

He pulled out a slide of the desk and took pen and paper.

"It's some kind of a joke—I can see that, but go ahead—I'll charge you for it! What grounds, please?"

"Statutory grounds, Mr. Butts."

He laid down his pen and stared at her again.

"Co-respondent known?"

"Trusting perfectly in your professional secrecy, Mr. Butts, yes—Mrs. President Rossiter."

"Any evidence?"

Here Mrs. Beale could no longer repress a twinkle in her eyes. "A witness," she said quietly. "A competent—and unbiased—witness, Dr. Irwin Manchester."

Mr. Butts leaned back again, and looked at her, his eyes narrowed. Mrs. Beale told him in succinct terms of Dr. Manchester's call and what he had said. She told him also of the opportunity her husband had of going to Harkness College, which would naturally put an end to this difficulty, and further told him of the gentleman from Princeton whose name had been mentioned repeatedly for a year or two past, as willing to come to Everton if an opening occurred.

"It seems to me," she continued soberly, "that the only self-respecting thing to do was to bring suit at once, here on the spot, where I have the advantage of such unimpeachable testimony."

She looked at Mr. Butts. Mr. Butts looked at her. Then the experienced lawyer rose from his chair and gravely shook hands with his visitor.

"Mrs. Beale," he said, "you have my sincerest sympathy. I will draw up the papers at once, and proceed to subpoena my witness. Perhaps it would be well to see the witness first?"

"That would be my idea," she gravely acquiesced.

* * * * *

A man may be extremely learned in the works of Beowulf and the Venerable Bede, yet unacquainted with the processes of the law. Mr. Butts looked severe as he sat in Mrs. Beale's parlor, facing Dr. Manchester (who had not in the least expected to meet him there), and drawing forth long folded papers which he laid upon his knee.

"I have come on an unpleasant errand, I fear, Dr. Manchester. Mrs. Richard Beale is bringing suit for absolute divorce, Mrs. Rossiter named as co-respondent, and I shall have to subpoena you as a witness."

The English professor seemed at a loss for words, but his expression was as of one whose house falls about his ears.

"I regret this painful publicity, Dr. Manchester," pursued the lawyer. "Mrs. Beale of course regrets it still more. But after what you have told her she feels that this is the proper course to take. It may be that you can help us to secure other witnesses, but in any case your testimony will be enough."

Dr. Manchester gazed fascinated at those terrifying "papers," while his nimble mind grasped with terrifying lucidity the consequences of his so testifying. He recovered his composure to some extent.

"My dear Mrs. Beale," he said, appealing to her. "I can quite sympathize with your feeling—quite—but surely you must know that there was nothing in what I said to you—as a friend—which could be construed into legal testimony. As you know I repeatedly assured you that I thought no real harm was done."

With growing assurance he revised his statements, trimmed and cut and modified, showing that his was only the attitude of a too-anxious friend, wishing to save all parties from distress.

The lady listened, the lawyer listened, the master of English used the language well. Then Mrs. Beale rose. "I fear that your natural agitation has affected your memory, Dr. Manchester—let me refresh it."

She rose and moved aside the gold-embroidered screen. Behind it, close to the big chair, was a dictagraph.

"Richard is always so interested in these inventions," she said. "We find this a great convenience, often."

She set the record turning, and Dr. Manchester had the pleasure of hearing in his own voice, his own words, of two days before. So had Mr. Butts.

Then was the majesty of the law, even without its real application, made manifest. Under the cold eyes of the lawyer, the hard, implacable gaze of the woman he had so villainously offended; seeing his reputation, his position, his salary and hope of other salaries departing, Dr. Manchester ate his own words, both those of to-day and those of the day previous.

Before the lawyer, the lady and the dictagraph, he abased himself, recanted, apologized, owned that his real purpose was to get Richard Beale out and his Princeton relative in. He pleaded with them piteously for concealment.

"I am not likely to mention it," said Mr. Butts.

"Nor I," said Mrs. Beale. "But I shall carefully keep the records. And I think, Dr. Manchester, if you were to take another position soon that it would be easier for you than after this matter gets out—if it ever should."

Next semester there was a new occupant of the Chair of English.

BEE WISE

"It's a queer name," said the man reporter.

"No queerer than the other," said the woman reporter. "There are two of them, you know—Beewise and Herways."

"It reminds me of something," he said, "some quotation—do you get it?"

"I think I do," she said. "But I won't tell. You have to consider for yourself." And she laughed quietly. But his education did not supply the phrase.

They were sent down, both of them, from different papers, to write up a pair of growing towns in California which had been built up so swiftly and yet so quietly that it was only now after they were well established and prosperous that the world had discovered something strange about them.

This seems improbable enough in the land of most unbridled and well-spurred reporters, but so it was.

One town was a little seaport, a tiny sheltered nook, rather cut off by the coast hills from previous adoption. The other lay up beyond those hills, in a delightful valley all its own with two most precious streams in it that used to tumble in roaring white during the rainy season down their steep little canyons to the sea, and trickled there, unseen, the rest of the year.

The man reporter wrote up the story in his best descriptive vein, adding embellishments where they seemed desirable, withholding such facts as appeared to contradict his treatment, and doing his best to cast over the whole a strong sex-interest and the glamor of vague suspicions.

The remarkable thing about the two towns was that their population consisted very largely of women and more largely of children, but there were men also, who seemed happy enough, and answered the questions of the reporters with good-will. They disclaimed, these men residents, anything peculiar or ultra-feminine in the settlements, and one hearty young Englishman assured them that the disproportion was no greater than in England. "Or in some of our New England towns," said another citizen, "where the men have all gone west or to the big cities, and there's a whole township of withering women-folks with a few ministers and hired men."

The woman reporter questioned more deeply perhaps, perhaps less offensively; at any rate she learned more than the other of the true nature of the sudden civic growth. After both of them had turned in their reports, after all the other papers had sent down representatives, and later magazine articles had been written with impressive pictures, after the accounts of permitted visitors and tourists had been given, there came to be a fuller knowledge than was possible at first, naturally, but no one got a clearer vision of it all than was given to the woman reporter that first day, when she discovered that the Mayor of Herways was an old college mate of hers.

The story was far better than the one she sent in, but she was a lady as well as a reporter, and respected confidence.

It appeared that the whole thing started in that college class, the year after the reporter had left it, being suddenly forced to drop education and take to earning a living. In the senior class was a group of girls of markedly different types, and yet so similar in their basic beliefs and ultimate purposes that they had grown through the four years of college life into a little "sorority" of their own. They called it "The Morning Club," which sounded innocent enough, and kept it secret among themselves. They were girls of strong character, all of them, each with a definite purpose as to her life work.

There was the one they all called "Mother," because her whole heart and brain were dominated by the love of children, the thought of children, the wish to care for children; and very close to her was the "Teacher," with a third, the "Nurse," forming a group within a group. These three had endless discussions among themselves, with big vague plans for future usefulness.

Then there was the "Minister," the "Doctor," and the far-seeing one they called the "Statesman." One sturdy, square-browed little girl was dubbed "Manager" for reasons frankly prominent, as with the "Artist" and the "Engineer." There were some dozen or twenty of them, all choosing various professions, but all alike in their determination to practice those professions, married or single, and in their vivid hope for better methods of living. "Advanced" in their ideas they were, even in an age of advancement, and held together in especial by the earnest words of the Minister, who was always urging upon them the power of solidarity.

Just before their graduation something happened. It happened to the Manager, and she called a special meeting to lay it before the club.

The Manager was a plain girl, strong and quiet. She was the one who always overflowed with plans and possessed the unusual faculty of carrying out the plans she made, a girl who had always looked forward to working hard for her own living of choice as well as necessity, and enjoyed the prospect.

"Girls!" said she, when they were all grouped and quiet. "I've news for you—splendid news! I wouldn't spring it on you like this, but we shall be all broken and scattered in a little while—it's just in time!" She looked around at their eager faces, enjoying the sensation created.

"Say—look here!" she suddenly interjected. "You aren't any of you engaged, are you?"

One hand was lifted, modestly.

"What does he *do?*" pursued the speaker. "I don't care who he is, and I know he's all right or you wouldn't look at him— but what does he *do?*"

"He isn't sure yet," meekly answered the Minister, "but he's to be a manufacturer, I think."

"No objection to your preaching, of course." This was hardly a question.

"He says he'll hear me every Sunday—if I'll let him off at home on week-days," the Minister replied with a little giggle.

They all smiled approval.

"He's all right," the Manager emphatically agreed. "Now

then girls—to put you out of your misery at once—what has happened to me is ten million dollars."

There was a pause, and then a joyous clapping of hands.

"Bully for you!"

"Hurrah for Margery!"

"You deserve it!"

"Say, you'll treat, won't you?"

They were as pleased as if the huge and sudden fortune were common property.

"Long lost uncle—or what, Marge?"

"Great uncle—my grandmother's brother. Went to California with the 'forty-niners'—got lost, for reasons of his own, I suspect. Found some prodigious gold mine—solid veins and nuggets, and spent quiet years in piling it up and investing it."

"When did he die?" asked the Nurse softly.

"He's not dead—but I'm afraid he soon will be," answered the Manager slowly. "It appears he's hired people to look up the family and see what they were like—said he didn't propose to ruin any feeble-minded people with all that money. He was pleased to like my record. Said—" she chuckled, "said I was a man after his own heart! And he's come on here to get acquainted and to make this over before he's gone. He says no dead man's bequest would be as safe as a live man's gift."

"And he's *given* you all that!"

"Solid and safe as can be. Says he's quite enough left to end his days in peace. He's pretty old. . . . Now then, girls—" She was all animation. "Here's my plan. Part of this property is land, land and water, in California. An upland valley, a little port on the coast—an economic base, you see—and capital to develop it. I propose that we form a combination, go out there, settle, build, manage—make a sample town—set a new example to the world—a place of woman's work and world-work too. . . . What do you say??"

They said nothing for the moment. This was a large proposition.

The Manager went on eagerly: "I'm not binding you to anything; this is a plain business offer. What I propose to do is to develop that little port, open a few industries and so on, build a reservoir up above and regulate the water supply—use it for power—have great gardens and vineyards. Oh, girls—it's California! We can make a little Eden! And as to Motherhood—" she looked around with a slow, tender smile, "there's no place better for babies!"

The Mother, the Nurse, and the Teacher all agreed to this.

"I've only got it roughly sketched out in my mind," pursued the speaker eagerly. "It will take time and care to work it all out right. But there's capital enough to tide us over first difficulties, and then it shall be just as solid and simple as any other place, a practical paying proposition, a perfectly natural little town, planned, built, and managed—" her voice grew solemn, "by women—for women—and *children!* A place that will be of real help to humanity.—Oh girls, it's such a chance!"

That was the beginning.

* * * * *

The woman reporter was profoundly interested. "I wish I could have stayed that year," she said soberly.

"I wish you had, Jean! But never mind—you can stay now. We need the right kind of work on our little local paper—not just reporting—you can do more than that, can't you?"

"I should hope so!" Jean answered heartily. "I spent six months on a little country paper—ran the whole thing nearly, except editorials and setting up. If there's room here for me I can tell you I'm coming—day before yesterday!" So the Woman Reporter came to Herways to work, and went up, o'nights, to Beewise to live, whereby she gradually learned in completeness what this bunch of women had done, and was able to prepare vivid little pamphlets of detailed explanations which paved the way for so many other regenerated towns.

And this is what they did:

The economic base was a large tract of land from the sea-coast hills back to the high rich valley beyond. Two spring-fed brooks ran from the opposite ends of the valley and fell steeply to the beach below through narrow cañons.

The first cash outlay of the Manager, after starting the cable line from beach to hill which made the whole growth possible, was to build a reservoir at either end, one of which furnished drinking water and irrigation in the long summer, the other a swimming pool and steady stream of power. The powerhouse in the cañon was supplemented by wind-mills on the heights and tide-mill on the beach, and among them they furnished light, heat, and power—clean, economical electric energy. Later they set up a solar engine which furnished additional force, to minimize labor and add to their producing capacity.

For supporting industries, to link them with the world, they had these: First a modest export of preserved fruits, exquisitely prepared, packed in the new fibre cartons which are more sanitary than tin and lighter than glass. In the hills they raised Angora goats, and from their wool supplied a little mill with high-grade down-soft yarn, and sent out fluffy blankets, flannels and knitted garments. Cotton too they raised, magnificent cotton, and silk of the best, and their own mill supplied their principal needs. Small mills, pretty and healthful, with bright-clad women singing at their looms for the short working hours. From these materials the designers and craftswomen, helped by the Artist, made garments, beautiful, comfortable, easy and lasting, and from year to year the demand for "Beewise" gowns and coats increased.

In a windy corner, far from their homes, they set up a tannery, and from the well-prepared hides of their goats they made various leather goods, gloves and shoes, "Beewise" shoes, that came to be known at last through the length and breadth of the land—a shoe that fitted the human foot, allowed for free action, and was pleasant to the eye. Many of the townspeople wore sandals and they were also made for merchandise.

Their wooded heights they treasured carefully. A forestry service was started, the whole area studied, and the best rate of planting and cutting established. Their gardens were rich and beautiful; they sold honey, and distilled perfumes.

"This place is to grow in value, not deteriorate," said the Manager, and she planted for the future.

At first they made a tent city, the tents dyed with rich colors, dry-floored and warm. Later, the Artist and the Architect and the Engineer to the fore, they built houses of stone and wood and heavy sheathing paper, making their concrete of the dead palm leaves and the loose bark of swift-growing eucalyptus, which was planted everywhere and rose over night almost, like the Beanstalk—houses beautiful, comfortable, sea-shell clean.

Steadily the Manager held forth to her associates on what she called "the business end" of their enterprise. "The whole thing must pay," she said, "else it cannot stand—it will not be imitated. We want to show what a bunch of women can do successfully. Men can help, but this time we will manage."

Among their first enterprises was a guest house, planned and arranged mainly for women and children. In connection with this was a pleasure garden for all manner of games, gymnastics and dancing, with wide courts and fields and roofed places for use in the rainy season.

There was a sanitarium, where the Doctor and the Nurse gathered helpers about them, attended to casual illness, to the needs of child-birth, and to such visitors who came to them as needed care.

Further there was a baby-garden that grew to a kindergarten, and that to a school, and in time the fame of their educational work spread far and wide, and there was a constantly increasing list of applicants, for "Beewise" was a Residence club; no one could live there without being admitted by the others.

The beach town, Herways, teemed with industry. At the little pier their small coast steamer landed, bringing such supplies as they did not make, leaving and taking passengers. Where the beach was level and safe they bathed and swam, having a water-pavilion for shelter and refreshment. From beach to hill-top ran a shuttle service of light cars; "Jacob's Ladder," they called it.

The broad plan of the Manager was this: with her initial capital to develop a working plant that would then run itself at a profit, and she was surprised to find how soon that profit appeared, and how considerable it was.

Then came in sufficient numbers, friends, relatives, curious strangers. These women had no objection to marrying on their own terms. And when a man is sufficiently in love he sees no serious objection to living in an earthly paradise and doing his share in building up a new community. But the men were carefully selected. They must prove clean health—for a high grade of motherhood was the continuing ideal of the group.

Visitors came, increasing in numbers as accommodations increased. But as the accommodations, even to land for tenting, must be applied for beforehand, there was no horde of gaping tourists to vulgarize the place.

As for working people—there were no other. Everyone in Herways and Beewise worked, especially the women—that was the prime condition of admission; every citizen must be clean physically and morally as far as could be ascertained, but no amount of negative virtues availed them if they were not valuable in social service. So they had eager applications from professional women as fast as the place was known, and some they made room for—in proportion. Of doctors they could maintain but a few; a dentist or two, a handful of nurses, more teachers, several artists of the more practical sort who made beauty for the use of their neighbors, and a few far-reaching world servants, who might live here, at least part of the time, and send their work broadcast, such as poets, writers and composers.

But most of the people were the more immediately necessary workers, the men who built and dug and ran the engines, the women who spun and wove and worked among the flowers, or vice versa if they chose, and those who attended to the daily wants of the community.

There were no servants in the old sense. The dainty houses had no kitchens, only the small electric outfit where those who would might prepare coffee and the like. Food was prepared in clean wide laboratories, attended by a few skilled experts, highly paid, who knew their business, and great progress was made in the study of nutrition, and in the keeping of all the people well. Nevertheless the food cost less than if prepared by many unskilled, ill-paid cooks in imperfect kitchens.

The great art of child-culture grew apace among them with

the best methods now known. Froebelian and Montessorian ideas and systems were honored and well used, and with the growing knowledge accumulated by years of observation and experience the right development of childhood at last became not merely an ideal, but a commonplace. Well-born children grew there like the roses they played among, raced and swam and swung, and knew only health, happiness and the joy of unconscious learning.

The two towns filled to their normal limits.

"Here we must stop," said the Manager in twenty years' time. "If we have more people here we shall develop the diseases of cities. But look at our financial standing—every cent laid out is now returned, the place is absolutely self-supporting and will grow richer as years pass. Now we'll swarm like the bees and start another—what do you say?"

And they did, beginning another rational paradise in another beautiful valley, safer and surer for the experience behind them.

But far wider than their own immediate increase was the spread of their ideas, of the proven truth of their idea, that a group of human beings could live together in such wise as to decrease the hours of labor, increase the value of the product, ensure health, peace and prosperity, and multiply human happiness beyond measure.

In every part of the world the thing was possible; wherever people could live at all they could live to better advantage. The economic base might vary widely, but wherever there were a few hundred women banded together their combined labor could produce wealth, and their combined motherhood ensure order, comfort, happiness, and the improvement of humanity.

"Go to the ant, thou sluggard, consider her ways and be wise."

HIS MOTHER

When a keen-witted, hard-headed, highly conscientious New England woman does let herself go, she goes, as she herself might describe it, "a good way."

Ellen Burrell was that kind of a woman, and she let herself go by marrying an Italian lover, a successful man enough, but hopelessly "a Dago" in the eyes of all Ellen's friends.

She was not sorry when his business took him west; not sorry when the cares and labors of carrying on life in strange scenes occupied her mind to the partial exclusion of new and painful thoughts; and, so greatly did these thoughts gain upon her in spite of all conscientious effort, not too overwhelmingly sorry when he died.

If a marriage proves personally unsympathetic the contracting parties are fortunate in possessing common interests; the more the better. When personally incompatible, it is added misfortune if they also disagree politically, religiously, or, as in this case, nationally.

There was bitter and growing misunderstanding, not in any way helped by Ellen's unflinching adherence to Duty, that special deity of the New Englander.

Mr. Martini being gone, she buried her hopes of romance with him, and turned her whole attention upon [her son] Jack— Giacomo his father had named him, but she preferred Jack.

Also being now her own mistress, she moved with her baby to another town, and left the "i" off the name she had acquired by marriage.

[There] followed the usual idyl of the only son of his mother, and she a widow; the years of hard work, of rigid economy, of careful instruction, such as many and many a widowed mother has spent in caring for her son.

But not even mother love could blind her wholly to his obvious faults and weaknesses worse than faults. He was a brilliantly beautiful child, a handsome boy, and as he grew to manhood this "fatal gift" seemed to work like a poison among his better qualities.

The teachers, with stroking hand upon those glossy curls, forgave him when his freckled and bristly-headed companions were promptly punished. When he sold papers, women bought from him because of his bright cheeks and brighter eyes. When he found summer employment as a grocer boy his back-door popularity quite turned his head.

His mother saved and planned for college, but he slipped quietly out of high school before graduation, his exit covered by a burst of precocious scandal in which most of the female gossips insisted that "she must have been to blame."

Mrs. Martin had no such illusions. In righteous horror she insisted on his going with her to the parents of the wretched girl, even more a child than he was, and promising to make amends as far as might be by marrying her when he was old enough.

"If they'll let you!" she said sternly. "If she'll have you—when she knows what a man ought to be!"

Jack was remorseful, self-extenuating, but the more he excused himself the less she could excuse him.

"Oh, pshaw, mother!" he protested. "You're makin' too much of it. It isn't such an awful thing. She'll get over it all right. Lots of the fellows are worse'n I am. I'm sorry of course that it came out that way—we were only havin' fun—"

"Fun!" she cried grimly. "Fun for you, perhaps—but how about her?"

She could not make him see the harm of what he had done, the cruel disproportion between his "fun" and that life-long injury and shame inflicted on a foolish, ignorant girl.

"She knew as much as I did!" he protested. "Why do you lay it all on me?"

"Because she's the one to suffer," she insisted, and steadily demanded that he make the offer of such protection as he could give the ruined child.

That night he went away.

He did not write for many months, then from a city more than a thousand miles away, and giving no address but General Delivery.

"I'm going to leave here soon," he said. "Have heard of a better job further south." He did not state what the job was, or where.

So for a few years she heard from him now and then, cheerful letters enough, sometimes sending her money, and boasting of success, sometimes speaking of great things in prospect, never of coming back.

Ellen Martin began to face the prospect of the rest of a lifetime alone. She was forty-five now. She was keener witted and harder headed than ever, but this mixture of sorrow and shame had softened her heart unrecognizably. Not to the lighthearted young rascal who had left such distress behind him, but to girls, to the yearly crop of fresh young creatures, blossoming out of childhood into girlhood, and paying such a terrible price for the follies incidental to youth plus ignorance plus temptation.

She began to study the subject seriously, and in one year's reading learned enough to bury her own grief deep out of sight under the piling griefs of others.

"I can't ever make up to that poor child for what my boy's done," she said, "nor to her parents. I don't wonder they won't take so much as a word from me." But secretly she mailed to the girl such casual sums as Jack sent her.

"He ought to have been taking care of her all this time," she thought. "I'll do what I can."

But the girl slipped out of sight altogether, left the town, and people judged by the silence of her family that they knew nothing of her, or knew no good.

Mrs. Martin sold what little she possessed, took what little she had saved, and went to the nearest large city.

"I don't suppose I can find her," she said solemnly to herself, looking blankly out of the black car window into the dim night spaces. "But there are others—hundreds of 'em— thousands of 'em—I can be some use, I guess—"

So she went into the business of girl saving.

This is new work. For long years we have had "Rescue Homes," "Magdalen Asylums," and the like, but each and all did their pitiful best after the wrong was done.

Modern society, stirring to new consciousness of its responsibility, is beginning to exert itself to secure the safety of young girls.

Mrs. Martin was eagerly interested, sternly practical, a woman of ability, and with no other ties. She proved a valuable assistant in more than one branch of the work, and studied eagerly.

Securing a room near one of the great Social Settlements, and visiting it often, she met others of the same spirit as herself; the earnest beginners, the wise old-timer, the blazing theorist, and that growing group of helpers who bring widely gathered facts and figures to help on the good work.

Her keen, deep feeling for the one poor little victim, lost and ruined through her own boy's fault, was now broadened into care for ignorant girlhood everywhere, and as it broadened, the bitterness of personal shame was lifted from her. She felt that she could now atone for Jack's misbehavior, and perhaps do more good, in the end, than he had done harm.

For a while she held the position of watchful matron in a railroad station; learning much of those other watchers, always looking for fresh material for their dreadful trade, and joyfully helping bewildered young visitors to escape such quick disaster.

She visited the night courts and learned how young girls are treated there; she read the reports of Vice Commissions, of various reformatory institutions, of the national and international societies now engaged in rescue or preventive work.

She learned the general character of these young victims, always young, averaging about seventeen. Many, very many, much younger; poor, of course; deficient in education, some having passed merely the lowest grades in schools, and a large proportion absolutely feeble witted—these were the kind of girls hired, lured, and often compelled to give themselves up to what the other half of the world calls "a social necessity."

"Surely," meditated Mrs. Martin, "they must mean a masculine necessity! Land alive! To imagine it's a necessity to those poor young ones—or to the rest of us women!"

Widening knowledge brings broader judgment also. Her fierce uncompromising New England conscience began to stretch enough to see that most young boys were as ignorant as the girls they ruined, and not only ignorant, but filled up from childhood with old sex-traditions, false and mischievous; teaching them that all this was not only necessary to their health, but rather commendable and fine.

This did not lift the hard-pressing pain from her own heart though. Jack knew—for she had taught him the simple facts in the case. He had deliberately chosen to accept the standards of boys who knew less; he had given way to his own worst weaknesses, without excuse.

"Unless it's his father that's in him!" she thought. "And that's my fault for giving him such a father! But I didn't know about those things then. Girls ought to. They ought to realize that it's not a question of losing their hearts, but of keeping their heads. What if they do fall in love! My heavens! Wouldn't I rather be a stark old maid a hundred times than go through what I've had to bear—and have to bear now—

"There's that poor young man, going from bad to worse, I don't doubt, and I can't stop him! Talk about a mother's prayer! Let the girls do some praying before it's too late."

She worked and studied and taught and helped; and filled her sore and empty heart with the grateful love of many a young girl whose life's happiness was owed to her.

In the process of her varied labors she became more and more skilled as a detective; not the miracle working literary figure with a magnifying glass, but a keen observer, whose accumulating knowledge of previous cases made each new one easier.

She became a probation officer, and learned much; a policewoman, and learned more. They offered her a good position as the head of a great reformatory for women, but she preferred to work "before the horse was stolen," she told them.

And in the course of time, as the special agent of a powerful society, with her police badge safe inside her coat, she undertook an important piece of work in one of our largest cities, a study of the recruiting among the working girls of great department stores for what we have learned to call "white slavery."

As she investigated the conditions of their work she wondered not that some were always dropping out of the ranks of "straight" living, but that so many remained in.

Take a young girl of ordinary stock and training, give her long, exhausting hours of work, pay so inefficient that she cannot even live comfortably, much less gratify her natural girlish desires for beauty and for "fun"; surround her with gleaming piles of all the lovely things she wants and cannot have—a torture of Tantalus, this; and also the walking embodiment of her foolish ambitions—the gaily clad shoppers who pass ever before her; then add, to make the pressure stronger, a continuous invitation from the men who need new material to meet their "necessities," and you have an environment which makes the continued virtue of so many of our young girls a miracle of noble womanhood.

Then one day she saw her son.

He was well dressed, too well dressed. His cigarette box was jewelled, his scarf pin a costly, glittering thing.

She started towards him, then checked herself, and studied his face hungrily. He was handsomer than ever, but not as she remembered him. That fresh, bright color, the soft, brilliant eyes, the winning smile—all were there but changed; harder, colder, more intentionally alluring. He had an air of practised charm, easy, indifferent, compelling, very effective with the little blue-eyed girl at the glove counter—why do they put such particularly pretty young girls at these counters? Merely a natural desire to promote business, of course. She nodded sternly and watched him a little, holding her heart in check. He was making graceful advances to the blue-eyed one which she received with an air of being quite used to the game and able to take care of herself; as a pert young mouse might fence awhile with an admiring cat.

Mrs. Martin was there apparently as a shopper, looking as interested in the bargain table of shirtwaists as any other middle-aged enthusiast. Now she came up swiftly, a love she could hardly believe surging up in her. "Jack, oh Jack!"

He greeted her with easy cordiality; took her to lunch forthwith; was full of questions about her work—and airily eluded any inquiry about his. He was with a commission house, he said, and only gave name and place when driven to it; then at a transcontinental distance.

And how was she doing? She looked well, handsomer than ever, he insisted.

That was a bad play. She had never been handsome. It showed the kind of compliments he was used to making, and how little he knew, or cared, about mothers.

He was delighted to get a glimpse of her—sorry he couldn't see more of her—he had to go back the next day—couldn't she go to the theatre with him that night?

No, she was sorry. She had an engagement. She, too, must return to her home city soon. She was doing well, had been working for a Social Settlement—no, he mustn't give her anything. He had a thick roll of bills.

Was he married, she suddenly asked.

He checked a smile, and answered with sudden fervor that he was going to be, as soon as he got a raise—that he'd bring her to see his mother when they could afford to come. He even took a photograph from his pocket and showed it proudly—her picture.

He watched his mother as she looked at it; and she, with the practised skill of long experience, by every look and tone and word and gesture, measured him.

She asked, as a mother must, about his life, where he had been all this time, why he had not written—

He owned his carelessness, gave a glib account of adventures and travels—too glib, too fluent, too impressive.

The practiced investigator felt him lie. A cold horror seized on her. This was not her boy. Her boy was dead. This was a man as hard and hollow as a brazen bell, a bell of base metal, ringing false at every stroke.

No love for her, no remorse for his idle youth and its wrong-going, no ambition for better things; he had thought it best to acknowledge her, and was throwing dust in her eyes. She was sure of it.

He went with her to her hotel; they said good-bye at the door—and as he turned away she spoke to the plainclothes man who was waiting there to help her in her work:

"Find where he lives, please; the man I was with."

Then she went to a telegraph office, not in the hotel, and wired to a friend in the city where he had told her he worked, asking about that commission house, and waited for an answer.

There was no such name and number there.

The man came back in the early evening. Said he'd had no end of trouble to follow him up, that the chap acted as if he knew he was being shadowed—but he'd managed to get considerable information—some of the police knew him. He had a bachelor apartment in a border-land district—fashionable and select in one direction, "anything but" in the other. Known to gamble a good bit. Known to have questionable friends. Known to be a gay one with the women. Suspected of worse than that by some.

"How does he live?" she asked. No one seemed to know.

Then Mrs. Martin began to do some detective work on her own account. It was a kind she was used to, and the more she learned the more familiar grew the trail. Presently she learned that this man, once her boy, was "Joe Mitchell," alias "Jerry Moore," one of the men who lived on the earnings of fallen women, women whose fall they first bring about, and then carefully prevent their ever rising.

She remembered the stories of three whom she had known personally, and more whom she had heard of, whose ruin was traced to this man; and, with all this evidence in hand, had close watch kept on the little blue-eyed glove-seller. Daily report told how he gradually won her confidence. The child wore a diamond ring, giggling and blushing showed it among her friends. There came a night when he took her to the theatre, then to a supper afterward, and then, drugged and half-conscious, to his own room.

He locked the door as he brought her in; he laid the helpless form down on his bed, standing a moment with a sneering smile.

Then, turning as he threw off his coat, he met the gray eyes of his mother.

"Just in time, I think, Jack," she said calmly. "This one can be saved anyhow. But I doubt if you can."

He tried every argument he knew, every cajolery, every plea. Was he not, after all, her son—her own boy? Surely she would not give him up—he would reform.

"If you were a leper, Jack—which would be less serious— they wouldn't consult me. I'd have to give you up. You are far more dangerous to society than that. I know your record now, for ten years back. I'm sorry, God knows how sorry—but that doesn't help those ruined lives you've left behind you.

"I'm thinking of the happy homes that might have been— the fine children and proud parents that might have been—but for you. It's got to stop right here. As for this child—she's my girl now. I'll take care of her—poor helpless little thing."

There were men present to take him away.

And having made the mistake of committing some of his worst offenses in a state where women help make laws to pro- tect themselves, he was "withdrawn from circulation" then and there.

His mother, with a black stone in her heart above the grave of her young love and pride, spent a long life in trying to do good enough to make up for her own share in his evil.

DR. CLAIR'S PLACE

"You must count your mercies," said her friendly adviser. "There's no cloud so dark but it has a silver lining, you know,—count your mercies."

She looked at her with dull eyes that had known no hope for many years. "Perhaps you will count them for me: Health, utterly broken and gone since I was twenty-four. Youth gone too—I am thirty-eight. Beauty—I never had it. Happiness—buried in shame and bitterness these fourteen years. Motherhood—had and lost. Usefulness—I am too weak even to support myself. I have no money. I have no friends. I have no home. I have no work. I have no hope in life." Then a dim glow of resolution flickered in those dull eyes. "And what is more I don't propose to bear it much longer."

It is astonishing what people will say to strangers on the cars. These two sat on the seat in front of me, and I had heard every syllable of their acquaintance, from the "Going far?" of the friendly adviser to this confidence of the proposed suicide. The offerer of cheerful commonplaces left before long, and I took her place, or rather the back-turned seat facing it, and studied the Despairing One.

Not a bad looking woman, but so sunk in internal misery that her expression was that of one who had been in prison for a lifetime. Her eyes had that burned out look, as hopeless as a cinder heap; her voice a dreary grating sound. The muscles of her face seemed to sag downward. She looked at the other passengers as if they were gray ghosts and she another. She looked at the rushing stretches we sped past as if the window were ground glass. She looked at me as if I were invisible.

"This," said I to myself, "is a case for Dr. Clair."

It was not difficult to make her acquaintance. There was no more protective tissues about her than about a skeleton. I think she would have showed the utter wreck of her life to any who asked to look, and not have realized their scrutiny. In fact it was not so much that she exhibited her misery, as that she was nothing but misery—whoever saw her, saw it.

I was a "graduate patient" of Dr. Clair, as it happened; and had the usual enthusiasms of this class. Also I had learned some rudiments of the method, as one must who has profited by it. By the merest touch of interest and considerate attention I had the "symptoms"—more than were needed; by a few indicated "cases I had known" I touched that spring of special pride in special misery which seems to be co-existent with life; and then I had an account which would have been more than enough for Dr. Clair to work on.

Then I appealed to that queer mingling of this pride and of the deep instinct of social service common to all humanity, which Dr. Clair had pointed out to me, and asked her—

"If you had an obscure and important physical disease, you'd be glad to leave your body to be of service to science, wouldn't you?" She would—anyone would, of course.

"You can't leave your mind for an autopsy very well, but there's one thing you can do—if you will; and that is, give this clear and prolonged self-study you have made, to a doctor I know who is profoundly interested in neurasthenia—melancholia—all that kind of thing. I really think you'd be a valuable—what shall I say—exhibit."

She gave a little muscular smile, a mere widening of the lips, the heavy gloom of her eyes unaltered.

"I have only money enough to go where I am going," she said. "I have just one thing to do there—that ought to be done before I—leave."

There was no air of tragedy about her. She was merely dead, or practically so.

"Dr. Clair's place is not far from there, as it happens, and I know her well enough to be sure she'd be glad to have you come. You won't mind if I give you the fare up there—purely as a scientific experiment? There are others who may profit by it, you see."

She took the money, looking at it as if she hardly knew what it was, saying dully: "All right—I'll go." And, after a pause, as if she had half forgotten it, "Thank you."

And some time later, she added: "My name is Octavia Welch."

Dr. Willy Clair—she was Southern, and really named Willy—was an eager successful young teacher, very young. Then she spent a year or two working with atypical children. Then, profoundly interested, she plunged into the study of medicine and became as eager and successful a doctor as she had been a teacher. She specialized in psychopathic work, developed methods of her own, and with the initial aid of some of her numerous "G. P.'s" established a sanatorium in Southern California. There are plenty of such for "lungers," but this was of quite another sort.

She married, in the course of her full and rich career, one of her patients, a young man who was brought to her by his mother—a despairing ruin. It took five years to make him over, but it was done and then they were married. He worshipped her; and she said he was the real mainstay of the business—and he was, as far as the business part of it went.

Dr. Clair was about forty when I sent Octavia Welch up there. She had been married some six years, and had, among her other assets, two splendid children. But other women have husbands and children, also splendid—no one else had a psycho-sanatorium. She didn't call it that; the name on the stationery was just "The Hills."

On the southern face of the Sierra Madres she had bought a high-lying bit of mesa-land and steep-sided arroyo, and gradually added to it both above and below, until it was now quite a large extent of land. Also she had her own water; had built a solid little reservoir in her deepest canyon; had sunk an artesian well far up in the hills behind, ran a windmill to keep the water up, and used the overflow for power as well as for irrigation. That had made the whole place such garden land as only Southern California knows. From year to year, the fame of the place increased, and its income also, she built and improved; and now it was the most wonderful combination of peaceful, silent wilderness and blossoming fertility.

The business end of it was very simply managed. On one of the steep flat-topped mesas, the one nearest the town that lay so pleasantly in the valley below, she had built a comfortable, solid little Center surrounded by small tent-houses. Here she took ordinary patients, and provided them not only with good medical advice but with good beds and good food, and further with both work and play.

"The trouble with Sanatoriums," said Dr. Clair to me—we were friends since the teaching period, and when I broke down at my teaching I came to her and was mended—"is that the sick folks have nothing to do but sit about and think of themselves and their 'cases.' Now I let the relatives come too; some well ones are a resource; and I have one or more regularly engaged persons whose business it is to keep them busy—and amused."

She did. She had for the weakest ones just chairs and hammocks; but these were moved from day to day so that the patient had new views. There was an excellent library, and all manner of magazines and papers. There were picture-puzzles too, with little rimmed trays to set them up in—they could be carried here and there, but not easily lost. Then there were all manner of easy things to learn to do; basket-work, spinning, weaving, knitting, embroidery; it cost very little to the patients and kept them occupied. For those who were able there was gardening and building—always some new little place going up, or a walk or something to make. Her people enjoyed life every day. All this was not compulsory, of course, but they mostly liked it.

In the evenings there was music, and dancing too, for those who were up to it; cards and so on, at the Center; while the others went off to their quiet little separate rooms. Everyone of them had a stove in it; they were as dry and warm as need be—which is more than you can say of most California places.

People wanted to come and board—well people, I mean— and from year to year she ran up more cheap comfortable little

shacks, each with its plumbing, electric lights and heating—
she had waterpower, you see, and a sort of cafeteria place
where they could eat together or buy food and take it to their
homes. I tell you it was popular. Mr. Wolsey (that's her husband, but she kept on as Dr. Clair) ran all this part of it, and
ran it well. He had been a hotel man.

All this was only a foundation for her real work with the
psychopathic cases. But it was a good foundation, and it paid
in more ways than one. She not only had the usual string of
Grateful Patients, but another group of friends among these
boarders. And there's one thing she did which is well worth
the notice of other people who are trying to help humanity—
or to make money—in the same way.

You know how a hotel will have a string of "rules and regu-
lations" strung up in every room? She had that—and more.
She had a "Plain Talk With Boarders" leaflet, which was freely
distributed—a most amusing and useful document. I haven't
one here to quote directly, but it ran like this:

> You come here of your own choice, for your own health and plea-
> sure, freely; and are free to go when dissatisfied. The comfort and
> happiness of such a place depends not only on the natural re-
> sources, on the quality of the accommodations, food, service and
> entertainment, but on the behavior of the guests.
>
> Each visitor is requested to put in a complaint at the office,
> not only of fault in the management, but of objectionable con-
> duct on the part of the patrons.
>
> Even without such complaint any visitor who is deemed
> detrimental in character of behavior will be requested to leave.

She did it too. She made the place so attractive, so *comfortable*, in every way so desirable, that there was usually a waiting
list; and if one of these fault-finding old women, or noisy, disagreeable young men, or desperately flirtatious persons got in,
Dr. Clair would have it out with them.

"I am sorry to announce that you have been black-balled by
seven of your fellow guests. I have investigated the complaints
and find them well founded. We herewith return your board

from date (that was always paid in advance) and shall require your room tomorrow."

People didn't like to own to a thing like that—not and tell the truth. They did tell all manner of lies about the place, of course; but she didn't mind—there were far more people to tell the truth. I can tell you a boarding-place that is as beautiful, as healthful, as exquisitely clean and comfortable, and as reasonable as hers in price, is pretty popular. Then, from year to year, she enlarged and developed her plan till she had, I believe, the only place in the world where a sick soul could go and be sure of help.

Here's what Octavia Welch wrote about it. She showed it to me years later:

I was dead—worse than dead—buried—decayed—gone to foul dirt. In my body I still walked heavily—but out of accumulated despair I had slowly gathered enough courage to drop that burden. Then I met the Friend on the train who sent me to Dr. Clair. . . .

I sent the post-card, and was met at the train, by a motor. We went up and up—even I could see how lovely the country was—up into the clear air, close to those shaggy, steep dry mountains.

We passed from ordinary streets with pretty homes through a region of pleasant groups of big and little houses which the driver said was the "boarding section," through a higher place where he said there were "lungers and such," on to "Dr. Clair's Place."

The Place was apparently just out of doors. I did not dream then of all the cunningly contrived walks and seats and shelters, the fruits and flowers just where they were wanted, the marvellous mixture of natural beauty and ingenious lovingkindness, which makes this place the wonder it is. All I saw was a big beautiful wide house, flower-hung, clean and quiet, and this nice woman, who received me in her office, just like any doctor, and said:

"I'm glad to see you, Mrs. Welch. I have the card announcing your coming, and you can be of very great service to me if you are willing. Please understand—I do not undertake to cure you; I do not criticize in the least your purpose to leave an unbearable world. That I think is the last human right—to cut short unbearable and useless pain. But if you are willing to let me study you awhile and experiment on you a little—it won't hurt, I assure you—"

Sitting limp and heavy, I looked at her, the old slow tears rolling down as usual. "You can do anything you want to," I said. "Even hurt—what's a little more pain?—if it's any use."

She made a thorough physical examination, blood-test and all. Then she let me tell her all I wanted to about myself, asking occasional questions, making notes, setting it all down on a sort of chart. "That's enough to show me the way for a start," she said. "Tell me—do you dread anaesthetics?"

"No," said I, "so that you give me enough."

"Enough to begin with," she said cheerfully. "May I show you your room?"

It was the prettiest room I had ever seen, as fair and shining as the inside of a shell.

"You are to have the bath treatment first," she said, "then a sleep—then food—I mean to keep you very busy for a while."

So I was put through an elaborate course of bathing, shampoo, and massage, and finally put to bed, in that quiet fragrant rosy room, so physically comfortable that even my corroding grief and shame were forgotten, and I slept.

It was late next day when I woke. Someone had been watching all the time, and at any sign of waking a gentle anaesthetic was given, quite unknown to me. My special attendant, a sweet-faced young giantess from Sweden, brought me a tray of breakfast and flowers, and asked if I liked music.

"It is here by your bed," she said. "Here is the card—you ask for what you like, and just regulate the sound as you please."

There was a light moveable telephone, with a little megaphone attached to the receiver, and a long list of records. I had only to order what I chose, and listen to it as close or as far off as I desired. Between certain hours there was a sort of "table d'hote" to which we could listen or not as we liked, and these other hours wherein we called for favorites. I found it very restful. There were books and magazines, if I chose, and a rose-draped balcony with a hammock where I could sit or lie, taking my music there if I preferred. I was bathed and oiled and rubbed and fed; I slept better than I knew at the time, for when the restless misery came up they promptly put me to sleep and kept me there.

Dr. Clair came in twice a day, with a notebook and pencil, asking me many careful questions; not as a physician to a patient, but as an inquiring scientific searcher for valuable truths. She told me about other cases, somewhat similar to my own, consulted me in a way, as to this or that bit of analysis she had made; and again and again as to certain points in my own case. Insensibly under her handling this grew more and more objective, more as if it were someone else who was suffering, and not myself.

"I want you to keep a record, if you will," she said, "when the worst paroxysms come, the overwhelming waves of despair, or that slow tidal ebb of misery—here's a little chart by your bed. When you feel the worst will you be so good as to try either of these three things, and note the result. The Music, as you have used it, noting the effect of the different airs. The Color—we have not introduced you to the color treatment yet—see here—"

She put in my hand a little card of buttons, as it were, with wire attachments. I pressed one; the room was darkened, save for the tiny glow by which I saw the color list. Then, playing on the others, I could fill the room with any lovely hue I chose, and see them driving, mingling, changing as I played.

"There," she said, "I would much like to have you make a study of these effects and note it for me. Then—don't laugh!— I want you to try tastes, also. Have you never noticed the close connection between a pleasant flavor and a state of mind?"

For this experiment I had a numbered set of little sweet-meats, each delicious and all beneficial, which I was to deliberately use when my misery was acute or wearing. Still further, she had a list of odors for similar use.

This bedroom and balcony treatment lasted a month, and at the end of that time I was so much stronger physically that Dr. Clair said, if I could stand it, she wanted to use certain physical tests on me. I almost hated to admit how much better I felt, but told her I would do anything she said. Then I was sent out with my attending maiden up the canyon to a certain halfway house. There I spent another month of physical enlargement. Part of it was slowly graduated mountain climbing; part was bathing and swimming in a long narrow pool. I grew gradually to feel the delight of mere ascent, so that every hilltop called me, and the joy of plain physical exhaustion and utter rest. To come down from a day on the mountain, to dip deep in that pure water and be rubbed by my ever careful masseuse; to eat heartily of the plain but delicious food, and sleep—out of doors now, on a pine needle bed—that was new life.

My misery and pain and shame seemed to fade into a remote past, as a wholesome rampart of bodily health grew up between me and it.

Then came the People.

This was her Secret. She had People there who were better than Music and Color and Fragrance and Sweetness,—People who lived up there with work and interests of their own, some teachers, some writers, some makers of various things, but all Associates in her wonderful cures.

It was the People who did it. First she made my body as strong as might be, and rebuilt my worn-out nerves with sleep—sleep—sleep. Then I had the right contact, Soul to Soul.

And now? Why now I am still under forty; I have a little cottage up here in these heavenly hills; I am a well woman; I earn my living by knitting and teaching it to others. And out of the waste and wreck of my life—which is of small consequence to me, I can myself serve to help new-comers. I am an Associate—even I! And I am Happy!

JOAN'S DEFENDER

Joan's mother was a poor defense. Her maternal instinct did not present that unbroken front of sterling courage, that measureless reserve of patience, that unfailing wisdom which we are taught to expect of it. Rather a broken reed was Mrs. Marsden, broken in spirit even before her health gave way, and her feeble nerves were unable to stand the strain of adjudicating the constant difficulties between Joan and Gerald.

"Mother! Mo-o-ther!" would rise a protesting wail from the little girl. "Gerald's pulling my hair!"

"Cry baby!" her brother would promptly retort. "Tell tale! Run to mother—do!"

Joan did—there was no one else to run to—but she got small comfort.

"One of you is as much to blame as the other," the invalid would proclaim. And if this did not seem to help much: "If he teases you, go into another room!"

Whether Mrs. Marsden supposed that her daughter was a movable body and her son a fixed star as it were, did not appear, but there was small comfort to be got from her.

"If you can't play nicely together you must be separated. If I hear anything more from you, I'll send you to your room—now be quiet!"

So Joan sulked, helplessly, submitted to much that was painful and more that was contumelious, and made little remonstrance. There was, of course, a last court of appeal, or rather a last threat—that of telling father.

"I'll tell father! I'll tell father! The you'll be sorry!" her tormentor would chant, jumping nimbly about just out of reach, if she had succeeded in any overt act of vengeance.

"I shall have to tell your father!" was the last resource of the mother on the sofa.

If father was told, no matter by whom, the result was always the same—he whipped them both. Not so violently, to be sure, and Joan secretly believed less violently in Gerald's case than in hers, but it was an ignominious and unsatisfying punishment which both avoided.

"Can't you manage to keep two children in order?" he would demand of his wife. "My mother managed eleven—and did the work of the house too."

"I wish I could, Bert, dear," she would meekly reply. "I do try—but they are so wearying. Gerald is too rough, I'm afraid. Joan is always complaining."

"I should think she was!" Mr. Marsden agreed irritably. "Trust a woman for that!"

And Joan, though but nine years old, felt that life was not worth living, being utterly unjust. She was a rather large-boned meager child, with a whiney voice, and a habit of crying, "Now stop!" whenever Gerald touched her. Her hair was long, fine and curly, a great trouble to her as well as to her mother. Both were generally on edge for the day, before those curls were all in order, and their principal use appeared to be as handles for Gerald, who was always pulling them. He was a year and a half older than Joan, but not much bigger, and of a somewhat puny build.

Their father, a burly, loud-voiced man, heavy of foot and of hand, looked at them both with ill-concealed disapproval, and did not hesitate to attribute the general deficiencies of his family wholly to their feeble mother and her "side of the house."

"I'm sure I was strong as a girl, Bert—you remember how I used to play tennis, and I could dance all night."

"Oh I remember," he would answer. "Blaming your poor health on me, I suppose—that seems to be the way nowadays. I don't notice that other women give out just because they're married and have two children—*two!*" he repeated scornfully, as if Mrs. Marsden's product were wholly negligible. "And one of them a girl!"

"Girls are no good!" Gerald quickly seconded. "Girls can't

fight or climb or do anything. And they're always hollering. Huh! I wouldn't be a girl—!" Words failed him.

Such was their case, as it says so often in the *Arabian Nights,* and then something pleasant happened. Uncle Arthur came for a little visit, and Joan liked him. He was mother's brother, not father's. He was big, like father, but gentle and pleasant, and he had such a nice voice, jolly but not loud.

Uncle Arthur was a western man, with a ranch, and a large family of his own. He had begun life as a physician, but weak lungs drove him into the open. No one would ever think of him now as ever having been an invalid.

He stayed for a week or so, having some business to settle which dragged on for more days than had been counted on, and gave careful attention to the whole family.

Joan was not old enough, nor Mrs. Marsden acute enough, to note the gradual disappearance of topic after topic from the conversation between Uncle Arthur and his host. But Mr. Marsden's idea of argument was volume of sound, speed in repetition, and a visible scorn for those who disagreed with him, and as Arthur Warren did not excel in these methods he sought for subjects of agreement. Not finding any, he contented himself with telling stories, or listening—for which there was large opportunity.

He bought sweetmeats for the children, and observed that Gerald got three-quarters, if not more; brought them presents, and found that if Gerald did not enjoy playing with Joan's toys, he did enjoy breaking them.

He sounded Gerald, as man to man, in regard to these habits, but that loyal son, who believed his father to be a type of all that was worthy, and who secretly had assumed the attitude of scorn adopted by that parent toward his visitor, although civil enough, was little moved by anything his uncle might say.

Dr. Warren was not at all severe with him. He believed in giving a child the benefit of every doubt, and especially the benefit of time.

"How can the youngster help being a pig?" he asked himself, sitting quite silent and watching Gerald play ball with a book just given to Joan, who cried "Now sto-op!" and tried to get it away from him.

"Madge Warren Marsden!" he began very seriously, when the children were quarreling mildly in the garden, and the house was quiet: "Do you think you're doing right by Joan—let alone Gerald? Is there no way that boy can be made to treat his sister decently?"

"Of course you take her part—I knew you would," she answered fretfully. "You always were partial to girls—having so many of your own, I suppose. But you've got no idea how irritating Joan is, and Gerald is extremely sensitive—she gets on his nerves. As for *my* nerves! I have none left! Of course those children ought to be separated. By and by when we can afford it, we mean to send Gerald to a good school; he's a very bright boy—you must have noticed that?"

"Oh yes, he's bright enough," her brother agreed. "And so is Joan, for that matter. But look here, Madge—this thing is pretty hard on you, isn't it—having these two irreconcilables to manage all the time?"

The ready tears rose and ran over. "Oh Arthur, it's awful! I do my best—but I never was good with children—with my nerves—*you* know, being a doctor."

He did know, rather more than she gave him credit for. She had responded to his interest with interminable details as to her symptoms and sensations, and while he sat patiently listening he had made a diagnosis which was fairly accurate. Nothing in particular was the matter with his sister except that fretful temper she was born with, idle habits, and the effects of an overbearing husband.

The temper he could not alter, the habits he could not change, nor the husband either, so he gave her up—she was out of his reach.

But Joan was a different proposition. Joan had his mother's eyes, his mother's smile—when she did smile; and though thin and nervous, she had no serious physical disability as yet.

"Joan worries you even more than Gerald, doesn't she?" he ventured. "It's often so with mothers."

"How well you understand, Arthur. Yes, indeed, I feel as if I knew just what to do with my boy, but Joan is a puzzle. She is so—unresponsive."

"Seems to me you would be much stronger if you were less worried over the children."

"Of course—but what can I do? It is my duty and I hope I can hold out."

"For the children's sake you ought to be stronger, Madge. See here, suppose you lend me Joan for a long visit. It would be no trouble at all to us—we have eight, you know, and all outdoors for them to romp in. I think it would do the child good."

The mother looked uncertain. "It's a long way to let her go—" she said.

"And it would do Gerald good, I verily believe," her brother continued. "I've often heard you say that she irritates him."

He could not bring himself to advance this opinion, but he could quote it.

"She does indeed, Arthur. I think Gerald would give almost no trouble if he was alone."

"And you are of some importance," he continued cheerfully. "How about that? Let me borrow Joan for a year—you'll be another woman when you get rested."

There was a good deal of discussion, and sturdy opposition from Mr. Marsden, who considered the feelings of a father quite outraged by the proposal; but as Dr. Warren did not push it, and as his wife suggested that in one way it would be an advantage—they could save toward Gerald's schooling—adding that her brother meant to pay all expenses, including tickets—he finally consented.

Joan was unaccountably reluctant. She clung to her mother, who said, "There! There!" and kissed her with much emotion. "It's only a visit, dearie—you'll be back to mother bye and bye!"

She kissed her father, who told her to be a good girl and mind her uncle and aunt. She would have kissed Gerald, but he said: "Oh shucks!" and drew away from her.

It was a silently snivelling little girl who sat by the window, with Uncle Arthur reading the paper beside her, a little girl who felt as if nobody loved her in the whole wide world. He put a big arm around her and drew her to him. She snuggled up with a long sigh of relief. He took her in his lap, held her close, and told her interesting things about the flying landscape. She nestled close to him, and then, starting up suddenly to look at something, her hair caught on his buttons and pulled sharply.

She cried, as was her habit, while he disentangled it.

"How'd you like to have it cut off?" he asked.

"*I'd* like it—but mother won't let me. She says it's my only beauty. And father won't let me either—says I want to be a tom-boy."

"Well, I'm in loco parentis now," said Uncle Arthur, "and I'll let you. Furthermore, I'll do it forthwith before it gets tangled up tonight."

He produced a pair of sharp little scissors, and a pocket-comb, and in a few minutes the small head looked like one of Sir Joshua Reynold's cherubs.

"You see I know how," he explained, as he snipped cautiously, "because I cut my own youngsters' on the ranch. I think you look prettier short than long," he told her, and she found the little mirror between the windows quite a comfort.

Before the end of that long journey the child was more quietly happy with her uncle than she had ever been with either her father or mother, and as for Gerald—the doctor's wise smile deepened.

"Irritated *him,* did she!" he murmured to himself. "The little skate! Why, I can just see her *heal* now she's escaped."

A big, high-lying California ranch, broad, restful sweeps of mesa and plain, purple hills rising behind. Flowers beyond dreams of heaven, fruit of every kind in gorgeous abundance. A cheerful Chinese cook and houseboy, who did their work well and seemed to enjoy it. The uncle she already loved, and an aunt who took her to her motherly heart at once.

Then the cousins—here was terror. And four of them boys—four! But which four? There they all were in a row, giggling happily, standing up to be counted, and to be introduced to their new cousin. All had short hair. All had bare feet. All had denim knickerbockers. And all had been racing and tumbling and turning somersaults on the cushiony Bermuda grass as Joan and her uncle drove up.

The biggest one was a girl, tall Hilda, and the baby was a girl, a darling dimpled thing, and two of the middle ones. But the four boys were quite as friendly as Hilda, and seeing that their visitor was strangely shy, Jack promptly proposed to show her his Belgian hares, and Harvey to exhibit his Angora goats, and the whole of them trooped off hilariously.

"What a forlorn child!" said Aunt Belle. "I'm glad you brought her, dear. Ours will do her good."

"I knew you'd mother her, Blessing," he said with a grateful kiss. "And if ever a poor kid needed mothering, it's that one. You see, my sister has married a noisy pig of a man—and doesn't seem to mind it much. But she's become an invalid—one of these sofa women; I don't know as she'll ever get over it. And the other child's rather a mean cuss, I'm afraid. They love him the best. So I thought we'd educate Joan a bit."

Joan's education was largely physical. A few weeks of free play, and then a few moments every day of the well-planned exercises Dr. Warren had invented for his children. There were two ponies to ride; there were hills to climb; there was work to do in the well-irrigated garden. There were games, and I am obliged to confess, fights. Every one of those children was taught what we used to grandiloquently call "the noble art of self-defense"; not only the skilled management of their hands, with swift "foot-work," but the subtler methods of jiu-jitsu.

"I took the course on purpose," the father explained to his friends, "and the kids take to it like ducks to water."

To her own great surprise, and her uncle's delight, Joan showed marked aptitude in her new studies. In the hours of definite instruction, from books or in nature study and laboratory work, she was happy and successful, but the rapture with which she learned to use her body was fine to see.

The lower reservoir made a good-sized swimming pool, and there she learned to float and dive. The big barn had a little simple apparatus for gymnastics in the rainy season, and the jolly companionship of all those bouncing cousins was an education in itself.

Dr. Warren gave her special care, watched her good, saw to it that she was early put to bed on the wide sleeping porch, and trained her as carefully as if she had some tremendous contest before her. He trained her mind as well as her body. Those children were taught to reason, as well as to remember; taught to think for themselves, and to see through fallacious arguments. In body and mind she grew strong.

At first she whimpered a good deal when things hurt her, but finding that the other children did not, and that, though patient with her, they evidently disliked her doing it, she learned to take her share of the casualties of vigorous childhood without complaint.

At the end of the year Dr. Warren wrote to his brother-in-law that it was not convenient for him to furnish the return ticket, or to take the trip himself, but if they could spare the child a while longer he would bring her back as agreed—that she was doing finely in all ways.

It was nearly two years when Joan Marsden, aged eleven, returned to her own home, a very different looking child from the one who left it so mournfully. She was much taller, larger, with a clear color, a light, firm step, a ready smile.

She greeted her father with no shadow of timidity, and rushed to her mother so eagerly as well-nigh to upset her.

"Why, child!" said the mother. "Where is your beautiful hair? Arthur—how could you?"

"It is much better for her health," he solemnly assured her. "You see how much stronger she looks. Better keep it short till she's fourteen or fifteen."

Gerald looked at his sister with mixed emotions. He had not grown as much. She was certainly as big as he was now. With her curls gone she was not so easy to hurt. However, there were other places. As an only child his disposition had not improved, and it was not long before that disposition led him to derisive remarks and then to personal annoyance, which increased as days passed.

She met him cheerfully. She met him patiently. She gave him fair warning. She sought to avoid his attacks, and withdrew herself to the far side of the garage, but he followed her.

"It is not fair, Gerald, and you know it," said Joan. "If you hurt me again, I shall have to do something to you."

"Oh you will, will you?" he jeered, much encouraged by her withdrawal, much amused by her threat. "Let's see you do it— smarty! 'Fraid cat!" and he struck her again, a blow neatly planted, where the deltoid meets the biceps and the bone is near the surface.

Joan did not say, "Now *stop!*" She did not whine, "*Please* don't!" She did not cry. She simply knocked him down.

And when he got up and rushed at her, furious, meaning to reduce this rebellious sister to her proper place, Joan set her teeth and gave him a clean thrashing.

"Will you give up?"

He did. He was glad to.

"Will you promise to behave? To let me alone?"

He promised.

She let him up, and even brushed off his dusty clothes.

"If you're mean to me any more, I'll do it again," she said calmly. "And if you want to tell mother—or father—or anybody—that I licked you, you may."

But Gerald did not want to.

THE VINTAGE

This is not a short story. It stretches out for generations. Its beginning was thousands of years ago, and its end is not yet in sight. Here we have only a glimpse, a cross section, touching sharply on a few lives.

There was a girl, in one our proudest Southern states, a girl of good family, and very proud of it. She wore a string of family names—Leslie Vauremont Barrington Montroy. There were more names, which they followed back for centuries, still with pride, but they could not put them all on one girl.

One other thing she was proud of, her blazing health. A big, vigorous girl, she was, smooth skinned, firm muscled, athletic, tireless, with the steady cheerfulness and courageous outlook which rest so largely on good health. Otherwise, not proud at all, a gentle, wholesome loving woman, loyal and tender.

She had lovers a plenty, among them two, who seemed to stand an even chance; one was Howard Faulkner, a young doctor, a friend, a neighbor, playmate from childhood; the other Rodger Moore, a college classmate and chum of the doctor, who had bought an estate next to the Montroys.

Moore was rich, but that did not weigh with Leslie. Faulkner had enough, and for that matter she would have married a gypsy, if she had loved him—and followed him to the world's end.

She chose Moore.

Faulkner suffered, but bore it well. He had known Leslie so long, he was so genuinely fond of her, that he cared enough for her happiness to wish for it even above his own. It was hard to listen to Moore, though, but he did not wish to tell him of his own hurt. And it was hard to watch them together, to see her round and well-tanned arms driving the canoe through the shaded reaches of the level winding river, with Moore treated as a mere student of the art of paddling—till she divined that he did not quite like that role, and let him do it, though he was not nearly so proficient.

At tennis, he beat her, he had had far more practice, and with sterner opponents, but her swiftness and strength of arm gave him an enjoyable game, none the less, and it was a joy to the eye to see her boyish delight in it.

She could outdance him easily and outride him, too, having been used to the saddle from childhood, and to the wild, wide country for many miles around. In the water she could distance him again, and seemed a triumphant glittering nymph as she swept smiling through the sunlit ripples.

Everywhere she carried the joy of her splendid vigor, the beauty of abounding health.

Howard Faulkner was glad for her, and glad for his friend.

Moore was tremendously in love. He had loved before, as he frankly admitted even though she did not ask him, but it was "as moonlight is to sunlight and as water is to wine" he told her. "Men are men—and women are women, you see. I was no different from other men. But you—you are different. You are like—it sounds cheap to say a goddess, but that's what I always think of, that victory thing—but all there—and so beautiful! I've never known a woman like you—within a thousand miles of you. You make me think of snow and wind and sunshine and pine trees; you're so *clean!* You are the kind of woman a man can worship."

She was, and he did. He was no poet, his praises were not novel, but he loved her with all his heart,—and body.

The day was set for the wedding.

Then a slight throat affection annoyed him. He took it to Dr. Faulkner and Faulkner's face went white. He asked a few necessary questions, but Moore saw the drift, and scouted the idea.

"Nonsense, Howard," he said. "That was years and years ago. I was entirely cured. Don't for heaven's sake, revive that bugaboo *now.*"

"Now is exactly when you must face it, Rodger," said his friend. "I'm sorry. I don't know anything more dreadful to tell a man, but you were not cured. You have syphilis in your system. You know the result—it is communicable—and inheritable. You cannot marry—not for years, nor till after the most thorough proof that it is gone."

Moore was as pale as the other, now, and as firm. "I don't doubt you're doing your duty, Howard, as you see it; but I tell you it's absurd. I've had the best treatment; I was thoroughly cured, I tell you."

"You can go through the tests again," Faulkner urged. "You can at least wait—the risk is too terrible for you to take—to let another take."

"It would be if there was any," said Moore doggedly. "You've got the thing on the brain, Howard. Talk about waiting!—with the invitations out and all of the county coming. What should I tell them, pray?"

"You can make some excuse, you can go to her father."

Moore laughed briefly. "Yes, and say good-bye. I will not have my life's happiness thwarted by one man's opinion, not while I have the verdict of certainly as good physicians on my side."

He was a determined man. This brief black incident in his past had long since been buried by that strong will, and he would not allow it to rise now like a skeleton at the feast.

Understand—he did not really in cold blood decide to offer such a risk to the women he loved. He refused to admit that there was a risk. And Faulkner? He was sure of his opinion but could not prove it without tests to which Moore would not submit; without time, which Moore would not allow.

He urged, he fairly begged, he used every argument and appeal he could think of to his friend, with the result that Moore would not come near him.

What else could he do? He was a physician with a high sense of professional honor. The physician must not betray his patient. . . .

So he held his tongue, and saw the woman he had loved so long, all white and radiant in her bridal glory, marry the man with the worst of communicable diseases.

The first baby was a boy. A boy who soon looked out on life with his mother's eyes, large, clear, truthful, brave, loving. A boy of marked intelligence, affectionate, devoted to both his adoring parents. A boy who was a hopeless cripple.

Leslie could not believe it.

She had borne strange ailments, unlooked-for distress, supposing it to be part of her condition; supporting herself always by her happiness with her husband, and with hope; murmuring to herself "and when the child came, lovely as a star"—

He came—not lovely to look at, but for all that a joy to her maternal heart.

The next one died at birth; and better so.

The next one never lived to be born.

Again and again she undertook the mother task, to mould and fashion with long love and patience another child; again and again illness and premature failure.

And the father, a man strong in his domestic feelings, worshipping his wife, idolizing the one frail little son who followed him about so lovingly, longing for other children who should grow to be strong men like himself, beautiful women like their mother—what did he feel? As the little blasted buds came and went, without even breathing, what did their father feel?

As a husband, too, as a lover, more of a lover rather than less, as years showed more clearly the sweet and noble character of his wife, what did he feel to watch the proud clean beauty of the woman he adored wither and disappear.

He had to watch it. He had to comfort her as he could, with every tenderness, every devotion, as her health weakened, her beauty fled from her, and the unmistakable ravages of the disease began to show.

She did not know what was the matter with her, or with her children. She never had known that there was such a danger before "a decent woman," though aware of some dark horror connected with "sin," impossible even to mention.

Her old family physician told her nothing—that was not his place.

Her minister told her that her affliction was "the will of God."

It is astonishing what a low opinion of God some people hold.

Leslie bore up bravely for her husband's sake, for her child's. That little crooked body, how she loved and tended it. That sweet young spirit, what a constant joy it was.

And her husband she idolized. His gentleness, his devotion, his endless patience, his continued tender admiration long after her relentless mirror told her that she was no longer pleasant to look at, even after she wore a veil when going out—these made her cling to him with adoring grateful love.

"You are so *good* to me, Rodger, dear!" she breathed, when the merciful darkness covered her face. "I never dreamed a man could be so good to a woman!"

A shudder shook him.

"I am not good, Leslie," he said with rigid quietness. "But I love you. God! How I love you!"

He did. He had from the beginning. The more she suffered, the more he loved her. The more he loved her, the more he suffered. It lasted for years.

When she was "taken away in the prime of her womanhood" by "the inscrutable Will Above," as the white-headed minister phrased it, Rodger was almost glad. He was glad, wholly glad, for her.

For a beautiful and vigorous young woman to see a slow repulsive disease gradually overwhelm her is a misery the end of which deserves gratitude.

Her absolute, exquisite love had been his, and he had done all that lay in his power to make her life bearable.

Her last words to him were: "You have made me happy, Rodger,—so happy! I—love—you. . . ."

Dr. Faulkner attended the funeral.

Father and son were inseparable. Rodger turned to that pathetic child, little Leslie (they had decided that, boy or girl, the child should bear that family name), with the grim determination that in so far as his life could serve, it should go to make up to the boy for his loss—his bitter loss and pain.

There was money enough.

There was the fine old place with all its freedom and beauty.

There was the subtlest, wisest education, bringing to the opening mind the wonders and beauties of life, developing all its power. There was travel, too, as soon as the boy was old enough to enjoy it; they went far and wide together, learning what the world was like.

There was music, too, unnumbered books, great pictures.

There was everything except companionship of his own age. He shrank from other boys, or perhaps they shrank from him. And he was so deeply content in his father's society that he seemed to miss nothing.

Together they went everywhere, together they stayed happily at home. As his father had been a playmate in the nursery and in the years of childhood, so he remained a playmate and schoolmate, studying with him, bringing all his long-trained patience and concentration to bear with the ceaseless purpose—"I will make up to him as far as I can. I will!"

Once, when the boy was about twelve years old, a small, weazened child, with the large beautiful head set low on the crooked shoulders, he sat in his father's arms one evening, in the big chair before the fire.

The large, rich room was very quiet; the red blaze held their eyes. They held each other close and were silent.

Then the child looked up into the man's eyes and asked soberly, "Father—why did God make me like this?" . . .

As he grew older, he grew stronger.

His face and head were of marked beauty, his eyes always the eyes of his mother.

He was a brilliant boy. With the help of tutors, he took a college course at home, his father always freshly interested.

"It's no use my going to college," said Leslie. "Colleges are for athletes, not students, as far as I can see. And I don't like the way the boys talk—from what I read of it."

So he lived with his father on the old place, in a companionship that grew with the years, and the boy was happy. His father watched him with ceaseless care, and so far as he could see, the boy was happy.

"If I can keep him so!" he murmured through set teeth. "No woman will love him—I must make up to him for everything."

For the boy's sake he kept himself young. He took unremitting care of his health.

"I must live," he said. "I shall live as long as he does, poor lad—perhaps. At any rate I must live as long as possible and be as strong as possible, for his sake."

So the man, who would gladly have died long since, set himself in all ways to preserve his health and remain with his son.

There came to the neighborhood for a summer's vacation a tall, sweet-faced girl, not at all like those Leslie had met, a woman, not a child. She had read as he had read. She had studied, was a college graduate, had traveled, too. More, she had worked as he had not. A little older than he, and of far wider experience, with a life of social enthusiasm and civic purpose.

She met the shy boy on a forest walk, and cheerfully made friends with him, taking the nettle firmly in both hands as it were.

"You feel badly because you are not like other folks," she said; "bless you, that's nothing to some of my friends, and they are jolly boys, too."

And she told him of this one and that one who bore worse physical disabilities by far, who had none of his compensating advantages, and who just went about their business like other people—"as far as they can, that is."

They became great friends. His father watched it with pleasure.

"He needs someone besides me," he thought, though there was a little jealous pain he would not admit. "She's a nice woman, a lady and all that, and her Settlement work and so on will interest him."

So they met often, and young Leslie grew more of a man,

visibly, from the fresh experience she brought to him, the new friends she introduced, the new lines of reading opened to his eager interest.

Through her he began to see the world, not as his father had always regarded it, as a place of other people and somewhere else, but as the place where he really lived, his own place, with duties, powers and responsibilities.

With her he somehow felt strong, straight, like other men. She did not seem to mind deformity. And then, in spite of himself, unexpectedly, irresistibly, he found that he loved her. . . .

This pain he took to his father, dumbly. "Take me away," he begged. "Let us go somewhere, anywhere. I love her, father! Such a thing as I have dared to love a woman! Let us go away, quickly."

His son must bear this, too; must love as men love; yet not even ask for happiness; he must suffer, and his father must see him bear it. This he had never looked for. The woman was a few years older, was not beautiful—but it had come. So they made preparations for a journey, a long one, far across the world.

But they met again in the forest paths, and had a clear talk. Leslie came to his father with shining eyes, walking as on air.

"She loves me, Father!" he said. "A woman loves me—loves *me!* She does not mind—she has made me feel that it does not matter. Oh—Father—she has lifted the load that has weighed on me since first I knew I was—different. It is gone, all gone, because it does not exist for her!

"Think, Father, think what it means. I can live in the world and work, do a real man's work. She says I can do more than many, that I am *needed.* Love, Father, for me, a home of my own. Even, perhaps," his face grew grave and reverent, his eyes bright with happy tears—"a little boy of my own, some day, to love as you have loved me."

And his father saw how all his days and nights of ceaseless devotion had in no way made up to the boy for losing the common things of life. He saw how this unhoped-for happiness had come like water to the desert and filled his barren life with flowers. He saw what it meant to his boy he so loved, to have the door so open to him.

And he his father, had to tell his son that he must never marry—and why. . . .

After a while the boy spoke, in a strange dead voice.

"All my little brothers and sisters? Was that—?"

"Yes" said the miserable man.

"And—my mother?" . . .

He nodded; he could not speak.

The boy stood still looking at the man, whose carefully fostered strength seemed all to have left him in an hour, and the resistless years to have swept down upon him like a flood of iron.

He came to him with a low cry—.

"Oh my poor father!"

THE UNNATURAL MOTHER

"Don't tell me!" said old Mis' Briggs, with a forbidding shake of the head. "No mother that was a mother would desert her own child for anything on earth!"

"And leaving it a care on the town, too!" put in Susannah Jacobs. "As if we hadn't enough to do to take care of our own!"

Miss Jacobs was a well-to-do old maid, owning a comfortable farm and homestead, and living alone with an impoverished cousin acting as general servant, companion, and protégée. Mis' Briggs, on the contrary, had had thirteen children, five of whom remained to bless her, so that what maternal feeling Miss Jacobs might lack, Mis' Briggs could certainly supply.

"I should think," piped little Martha Ann Simmons, the village dressmaker, "that she might a saved her young one first and then tried what she could do for the town."

Martha had been married, had lost her husband, and had one sickly boy to care for.

The youngest Briggs girl, still unmarried at thirty-six, and in her mother's eyes a most tender infant, now ventured to make a remark.

"You don't any of you seem to think what she did for all of us—if she hadn't left hers we should all have lost ours, sure."

"You ain't no call to judge, Maria 'Melia," her mother hastened to reply. "You've no children of your own, and you can't judge of a mother's duty. No mother ought to leave her child, whatever happens. The Lord gave it to her to take care of—he never gave her other people's. You needn't tell me!"

"She was an unnatural mother," repeated Miss Jacobs harshly, "as I said to begin with!"

"What is the story?" asked the City Boarder. The City Boarder was interested in stories from a business point of view, but they did not know that. "What did this woman do?" she asked.

There was no difficulty in eliciting particulars. The difficulty was rather in discriminating amidst their profusion and contradictoriness. But when the City Boarder got it clear in her mind, it was somewhat as follows:

The name of the much-condemned heroine was Esther Greenwood, and she lived and died here in Toddsville.

Toddsville was a mill village. The Todds lived on a beautiful eminence overlooking the little town, as the castles of robber barons on the Rhine used to overlook their little towns. The mills and the mill hands' houses were built close along the bed of the river. They had to be pretty close, because the valley was a narrow one, and the bordering hills were too steep for travel, but the water power was fine. Above the village was the reservoir, filling the entire valley save for a narrow road beside it, a fair blue smiling lake, edged with lilies and blue flag, rich in pickerel and perch. This lake gave them fish, it gave them ice, it gave the power that ran the mills that gave the town its bread. Blue Lake was both useful and ornamental.

In this pretty and industrious village Esther had grown up, the somewhat neglected child of a heart-broken widower. He had lost a young wife, and three fair babies before her—this one was left him, and he said he meant that she should have all the chance there was.

"That was what ailed her in the first place!" they all eagerly explained to the City Boarder. "She never knew what 'twas to have a mother, and she grew up a regular tomboy! Why, she used to roam the country for miles around, in all weather like an Injun! And her father wouldn't take no advice!"

This topic lent itself to eager discussion. The recreant father, it appeared, was a doctor, not their accepted standby, the resident physician of the neighborhood, but an alien doctor, possessed of "views."

"You never heard such things as he advocated," Miss Jacobs explained. "He wouldn't give no medicines, hardly; said 'nature' did the curing—he couldn't."

"And he couldn't either—that was clear," Mrs. Briggs agreed. "Look at his wife and children dying on his hands, as it were! 'Physician, heal thyself,' I say."

"But, Mother," Maria Amelia put in, "she was an invalid when he married her, they say; and those children died of polly—polly—what's that thing that nobody can help?"

"That may all be so," Miss Jacobs admitted, "but all the same, it's a doctor's business to give medicine. If 'nature' was all that was wanted, we needn't have any doctor at all!"

"I believe in medicine and plenty of it. I always gave my children a good clearance, spring and fall, whether anything ailed 'em or not, just to be on the safe side. And if there was anything the matter with 'em, they had plenty more. I never had anything to reproach myself with on that score," stated Mrs. Briggs, firmly. Then as a sort of concession to the family graveyard, she added piously, "The Lord giveth and the Lord taketh away."

"You should have seen the way he dressed that child!" pursued Miss Jacobs. "It was a reproach to the town. Why, you couldn't tell at a distance whether it was a boy or a girl. And barefoot! He let that child go barefoot till she was so big we was actually mortified to see her."

It appeared that a wild, healthy childhood had made Esther very different in her early womanhood from the meek, well-behaved damsels of the little place. She was well enough liked by those who knew her at all, and the children of the place adored her, but the worthy matrons shook their heads and prophesied no good of a girl who was "queer."

She was described with rich detail in reminiscence, how she wore her hair short till she was fifteen—"just shingled like a boy's—it did seem a shame that girl had no mother to look after her—and her clo'se was almost a scandal, even when she did put on shoes and stockings. Just gingham—brown gingham—and *short!*"

"I think she was a real nice girl," said Maria Amelia. "I can remember her just as well! She was so *nice* to us children. She was five or six years older than I was, and most girls that age won't have anything to do with little ones. But she was kind and pleasant. She'd take us berrying and on all sorts of walks, and teach us new games and tell us things. I don't remember anyone that ever did us the good she did!"

Maria Amelia's thin chest heaved with emotion, and there were tears in her eyes; but her mother took her up somewhat sharply.

"That sounds well I must say—right before your own mother that's toiled and slaved for you! It's all very well for a young thing that's got nothing on earth to do to make herself agreeable to young ones. That poor blinded father of hers never taught her to do the work a girl should—naturally he couldn't."

"At least he might have married again and given her another mother," said Susannah Jacobs, with decision, with so much decision, in fact, that the City Boarder studied her expression for a moment and concluded that if this recreant father had not married again it was not for lack of opportunity.

Mrs. Simmons cast an understanding glance upon Miss Jacobs, and nodded wisely.

"Yes, he ought to have done that, of course. A man's not fit to bring up children, anyhow. How can they? Mothers have the instinct—that is, all natural mothers have. But, dear me! There's some as don't seem to *be* mothers—even when they have a child!"

"You're quite right, Mis' Simmons," agreed the mother of thirteen. "It's a divine instinct, I say. I'm sorry for the child that lacks it. Now this Esther. We always knew she wan't like other girls—she never seemed to care for dress and company and things girls naturally do, but was always philandering over the hills with a parcel of young ones. There wan't a child in town but would run after her. She made more trouble 'n a little in families, the young ones quotin' what Aunt Esther said, and tellin' what Aunt Esther did to their own mothers, and she only a young girl. Why, she actually seemed to care more for them children than she did for beaux or anything—it wasn't natural!"

"But she did marry?" pursued the City Boarder.

"Marry! Yes, she married finally. We all thought she never

would, but she did. After the things her father taught her, it did seem as if he'd ruined *all* her chances. It's simply terrible the way that girl was trained."

"Him being a doctor," put in Mrs. Simmons, "made it different, I suppose."

"Doctor or no doctor," Miss Jacobs rigidly interposed, "it was a crying shame to have a young girl so instructed."

"Maria 'Melia," said her mother, "I want you should get me my smelling salts. They're up in the spare chamber, I believe. When your Aunt Marcia was here she had one of her spells—don't you remember?—and she asked for salts. Look in the top bureau drawer—they must be there."

Maria Amelia, thirty-six but unmarried, withdrew dutifully, and the other ladies drew closer to the City Boarder.

"It's the most shocking thing I ever heard of," murmured Mrs. Briggs. "Do you know he—a father—actually taught his daughter how babies come!"

There was a breathless hush.

"He did," eagerly chimed in the little dressmaker. "All the particulars. It was perfectly awful!"

"He said," continued Mrs. Briggs, "that he expected her to be a mother and that she ought to understand what was before her!"

"He was waited on by a committee of ladies from the church, married ladies, all older than he was," explained Miss Jacobs severely. "They told him it was creating a scandal in the town—and what do you think he said?"

There was another breathless silence.

Above, the steps of Maria Amelia were heard, approaching the stairs.

"It ain't there, Ma!"

"Well, you look in the highboy and in the top drawer; they're somewhere up there," her mother replied.

Then, in a sepulchral whisper:

"He told us—yes, ma'am, I was on that committee—he told us that until young women knew what was before them as mothers, they would not do their duty in choosing a father for their children! That was his expression—'choosing a father'!

A nice thing for a young girl to be thinking of—a father for her children!"

"Yes, and more than that," inserted Miss Jacobs, who, though not on the committee, seemed familiar with its workings. "He told them—" But Mrs. Briggs waved her aside and continued swiftly—

"He taught that innocent girl about—the Bad Disease! Actually!"

"He did!" said the dressmaker. "It got out, too, all over town. There wasn't a man here would have married her after that."

Miss Jacobs insisted on taking up the tale. "I understand that he said it was 'to protect her'! Protect her, indeed! Against matrimony! As if any man alive would want to marry a young girl who knew all the evil of life! I was brought up differently, I assure you!"

"Young girls should be kept innocent!" Mrs. Briggs solemnly proclaimed. "Why, when I was married I knew no more what was before me than a babe unborn, and my girls were all brought up so, too!"

Then, as Maria Amelia returned with the salts, she continued more loudly. "But she did marry after all. And a mighty queer husband she got, too. He was an artist or something, made pictures for the magazines and such as that, and they do say she met him first out in the hills. That's the first 'twas known of it here, anyhow—them two traipsing about all over; him with his painting things! They married and just settled down to live with her father, for she vowed she wouldn't leave him; and he said it didn't make no difference where he lived, he took his business with him."

"They seemed very happy together," said Maria Amelia.

"Happy! Well, they might have been, I suppose. It was a pretty queer family, I think." And her mother shook her head in retrospection. "They got on all right for a while; but the old man died, and those two—well, I don't call it housekeeping—the way they lived!"

"No," said Miss Jacobs. "They spent more time out-of-doors than they did in the house. She followed him around everywhere. And for open lovemaking—"

They all showed deep disapproval at this memory. All but the City Boarder and Maria Amelia.

"She had one child, a girl," continued Mrs. Briggs, "and it was just shocking to see how she neglected that child from the beginnin'. She never seemed to have no maternal feelin' at all!"

"But I thought you said she was very fond of children," remonstrated the City Boarder.

"Oh, *children*, yes. She'd take up with any dirty-faced brat in town, even them Canucks. I've seen her again and again with a whole swarm of the mill hands' young ones round her, goin' on some picnic or other—'open air school,' she used to call it—*such* notions as she had. But when it come to her own child! Why—" Here the speaker's voice sank to a horrified hush. "She never had no baby clo'se for it! Not a single-sock!"

The City Boarder was interested. "Why, what did she do with the little thing?"

"The Lord knows!" answered old Mis' Briggs. "She never would let us hardly see it when 'twas little. 'Shamed to, I don't doubt. But that's strange feelin's for a mother. Why, I was so proud of my babies! And I kept 'em lookin' so pretty! I'd 'a sat up all night and sewed and washed, but I'd 'a had my children look well!" And the poor old eyes filled with tears as she thought of the eight little graves in the churchyard, which she never failed to keep looking pretty, even now. "She just let that young one roll round in the grass like a puppy with hardly nothin' on! Why, a squaw does better. She does keep 'em done up for a spell! That child was treated worse 'n an Injun! We all done what we could, of course. We felt it no more 'n right. But she was real hateful about it, and we had to let her be."

"The child died?" asked the City Boarder.

"Died! Dear no! That's it you saw going by; a great strappin' girl she is, too, and promisin' to grow up well, thanks to Mrs. Stone's taking her. Mrs. Stone always thought a heap of Esther. It's a mercy to the child that she lost her mother, I do believe! How she ever survived that kind of treatment beats all! Why, that woman never seemed to have the first spark of maternal feeling to the end! She seemed just as fond of the other young ones after she had her own as she was before, and that's against nature. The way it happened was this. You see, they lived up the valley nearer to the lake than the village. He was away, and was coming home that night, it seems, driving from Drayton along the lake road. And she set out to meet him. She must 'a walked up to the dam to look for him; and we think maybe she saw the team clear across the lake. Maybe she thought he could get to the house and save little Esther in time—that's the only explanation we ever could put on it. But this is what she did; and you can judge for yourselves if any mother in her senses *could* 'a done such a thing! You see 'twas the time of that awful disaster, you've read of it, likely, that destroyed three villages. Well, she got to the dam and seen that 'twas givin' way—she was always great for knowin' all such things. And she just turned and ran. Jake Elder was up on the hill after a stray cow, and he seen her go. He was too far off to imagine what ailed her, but he said he never saw a woman run so in his life.

"And, if you'll believe it, she run right by her own house— never stopped—never looked at it. Just run for the village. Of course, she may have lost her head with the fright, but that wasn't like her. No, I think she had made up her mind to leave that innocent baby to die! She just ran down here and give warnin', and, of course, we sent word down valley on horseback, and there was no lives lost in all three villages. She started to run back as soon as we was 'roused, but 'twas too late then.

"Jake saw it all, though he was too far off to do a thing. He said he couldn't stir a foot, it was so awful. He seen the wagon drivin' along as nice as you please till it got close to the dam, and then Greenwood seemed to see the danger and shipped up like mad. He was the father, you know. But he wasn't quite in time—the dam give way and the water went over him like a tidal wave. She was almost to the gate when it struck the house and her—and we never found her body nor his for days and days. They was washed clear down river.

"Their house was strong, and it stood a little high and had some big trees between it and the lake, too. It was moved off the place and brought up against the side of the stone church down yonder, but 'twant wholly in pieces. And that child was found swimmin' round in its bed, most drowned, but not quite. The wonder is, it didn't die of a cold, but it's here yet—must have a strong constitution. Their folks never did nothing for it—so we had to keep it here."

"Well, now, Mother," said Maria Amelia Briggs. "It does seem to me that she did her duty. You know yourself that if she hadn't give warnin' all three of the villages would 'a been cleaned out—a matter of fifteen hundred people. And if she'd stopped to lug that child, she couldn't have got here in time. Don't you believe she was thinkin' of those mill-hands' children?"

"Maria 'Melia, I'm ashamed of you!" said old Mis' Briggs. "But you ain't married and ain't a mother. A mother's duty is to her own child! She neglected her own to look after other folks'—the Lord never gave her them other children to care for!"

"Yes," said Miss Jacobs, "and here's her child, a burden on the town! She was an unnatural mother!"

POETRY

One Girl of Many

1

One girl of many. Hungry from her birth.
Half-fed. Half-clothed. Untaught of woman's worth.
In joyless girlhood working for her bread.
At each small sorrow wishing she were dead,
5   Yet gay at little pleasures. Sunlight seems
Most bright & warm where it most seldom gleams.

2

One girl of many. Tawdry dress and old;
And not enough beneath to bar the cold.
The little that she had misspent because
10   She had no knowledge of our nature's laws.
Thinking in ignorance that it was best
To wear a stylish look, and—bear the rest.

3

One girl of many. With a human heart.
A woman's too; with nerves that feel the smart
15   Of each new pain as keenly as your own.
The old ones, through long use, have softer grown.
And yet in spite of use she holds the thought
Of might-be joys more than, perhaps, she ought.

4

One girl of many. But the fault is here;
20   Though she to all the others was so near;

One difference there was, which made a change.
No wrong thing, surely. Consequence most strange!
Alike in birth. Alike in life's rough way.
She, through no evil, was more fair than they.

5

25 So came the offer, "Leave this story cold
Where you may drudge and starve till you are old.
Come! I will give you rest. And food. And fire.
And fair apparel to your heart's desire;
Shelter. Protection. Kindness. Peace & Love.
30 Has your life anything you hold above?"

6

And she had *not*. In all her daily sight
There shone no vestige of the color *White*.
She had seen nothing in her narrow life
To make her venerate the title "Wife."
35 She knew no *reason* why the thing was wrong;
And instinct grows debased in ages long.

7

All things that she had ever yet desired
All dreams that her starved girlhood's heart had fired
All that life held of yet unknown delight
40 Shone, to her ignorance, in colors bright.
Shone near at hand and sure. If she had *known!*
But she was ignorant. She was alone.

8

And so she—sinned. I think we call it sin.
And found that every step she took therein
45 Made sinning easier and conscience weak.
And there was never one who cared to speak

A word to guide and warn her. If there were
I fear such help were thrown away on her.

9

Only one girl of many. Of the street.
In lowest depths. The story grows unmeet
For wellbred ears. Sorrow and sin and shame
Over and over till the blackened name
Sank out of sight without a hand to save.
Sin, shame, and sorrow. Sickness, & the grave.

10

Only one girl of many. Tis a need
Of man's existence to repeat the deed.
Social necessity. Men cannot live
Without what these disgraceful creatures give.
Black shame. Dishonor. Misery & Sin.
And men find needed health & life therein.

In Duty Bound

In duty bound, a life hemmed in
    Whichever way the spirit turns to look;
No chance of breaking out, except by sin;
      Not even room to shirk—
5   Simply to live, and work.

An obligation pre-imposed, unsought,
    Yet binding with the force of natural law;
The pressure of antagonistic thought;
      Aching within, each hour,
10   A sense of wasting power.

A house with roof so darkly low
    The heavy rafters shut the sunlight out;
One cannot stand erect without a blow;
      Until the soul inside
15   Cries for a grave—more wide.

A consciousness that if this thing endure,
    The common joys of life will dull the pain;
The high ideals of the grand and pure
      Die, as of course they must,
20   Of long disuse and rust.

That is the worst. It takes supernal strength
    To hold the attitude that brings the pain;
And they are few indeed but stoop at length
      To something less than best,
25   To find, in stooping, rest.

On the Pawtuxet

Broad and blue is the river, all bright in the sun;
The little waves sparkle, the little waves run;
The birds carol high, and the winds whisper low;
The boats beckon temptingly, row upon row;
5 Her hand is in mine as I help her step in.
Please Heaven, this day I shall lose or shall win—
      Broad and blue is the river.

Cool and gray is the river, the sun sinks apace,
And the rose-colored twilight glows soft in her face.
10 In the midst of the rose-color Venus doth shine,
And the blossoming wild grapes are sweeter than wine;
Tall trees rise above us, four bridges are past,
And my stroke's running slow as the current runs fast—
      Cool and gray is the river.

15 Smooth and black is the river, no sound as we float
Save the soft-lapping water in under the boat.
The white mists are rising, the moon's rising too,
And Venus, triumphant, rides high in the blue.
I hold the shawl round her, her hand is in mine,
20 And we drift under grape-blossoms sweeter than wine—
      Smooth and black is the river.

She Walketh Veiled and Sleeping

She walketh veiled and sleeping,
For she knoweth not her power;
She obeyeth but the pleading
Of her heart, and the high leading
5 Of her soul, unto this hour.
Slow advancing, halting, creeping,
Comes the Woman to the hour!—
She walketh veiled and sleeping,
For she knoweth not her power.

An Obstacle

I was climbing up a mountain-path
    With many things to do,
Important business of my own,
    And other people's too,
5 When I ran against a Prejudice
    That quite cut off the view.

My work was such as could not wait,
    My path quite clearly showed,
My strength and time were limited,
10   I carried quite a load;
And there that hulking Prejudice
    Sat all across the road.

So I spoke to him politely,
    For he was huge and high,
15 And begged that he would move a bit
    And let me travel by.
He smiled, but as for moving!—
    He didn't even try.

And then I reasoned quietly
20   With that colossal mule:
My time was short—no other path—
    The mountain winds were cool.
I argued like a Solomon;
    He sat there like a fool.

25 Then I flew into a passion,
    I danced and howled and swore.

I pelted and belabored him
　Till I was stiff and sore;
He got as mad as I did—
30　　But he sat there as before.

And then I begged him on my knees;
　I might be kneeling still
If so I hoped to move that mass
　Of obdurate ill-will—
35　As well invite the monument
　　To vacate Bunker Hill!

So I sat before him helpless,
　In an ecstasy of woe—
The mountain mists were rising fast,
40　　The sun was sinking slow—
When a sudden inspiration came,
　As sudden winds do blow.

I took my hat, I took my stick,
　My load I settled fair,
45　I approached that awful incubus
　With an absent-minded air—
And I walked directly through him,
　As if he wasn't there!

Similar Cases

There was once a little animal,
    No bigger than a fox,
And on five toes he scampered
    Over Tertiary rocks.
5   They called him Eohippus,
    And they called him very small,
And they thought him of no value—
    When they thought of him at all;
For the lumpish old Dinoceras
10   And Coryphodon so slow
Were the heavy aristocracy
    In days of long ago.

Said the little Eohippus,
    "I am going to be a horse!
15 And on my middle finger-nails
    To run my earthly course!
I'm going to have a flowing tail!
    I'm going to have a mane!
I'm going to stand fourteen hands high
20   On the psychozoic plain!"

The Coryphodon was horrified,
    The Dinoceras was shocked;
And they chased young Eohippus,
    But he skipped away and mocked.
25 Then they laughed enormous laughter,
    And they groaned enormous groans,
And they bade young Eohippus
    Go view his father's bones.

Said they, "You always were as small
30   And mean as now we see,
And that's conclusive evidence
    That you're always going to be.
What! Be a great, tall, handsome beast,
    With hoofs to gallop on?

35 *Why! You'd have to change your nature!"*
    Said the Loxolophodon.
They considered him disposed of,
    And retired with gait serene;
That was the way they argued
40   In "the early Eocene."

There was once an Anthropoidal Ape,
    Far smarter than the rest,
And everything that they could do
    He always did the best;
45 So they naturally disliked him,
    And they gave him shoulders cool,
And when they had to mention him
    They said he was a fool.

Cried this pretentious Ape one day,
50   "I'm going to be a Man!
And stand upright, and hunt, and fight,
    And conquer all I can!
I'm going to cut down forest trees,
    To make my houses higher!
55 I'm going to kill the Mastodon!
    I'm going to make a fire!"

Loud screamed the Anthropoidal Apes
    With laughter wild and gay;
They tried to catch that boastful one,
60   But he always got away.
So they yelled at him in chorus,
    Which he minded not a whit;

And they pelted him with cocoanuts,
    Which didn't seem to hit.
65 And then they gave him reasons
    Which they thought of much avail,
To prove how his preposterous
    Attempt was sure to fail.
Said the sages, "In the first place,
70   The thing cannot be done!
And, second, if it *could* be,
    It would not be any fun!
And, third, and most conclusive,
    And admitting no reply,
75 *You would have to change your nature!*
    We should like to see you try!"
They chuckled then triumphantly,
    These lean and hairy shapes,
For these things passed as arguments
80   With the Anthropoidal Apes.

There was once a Neolithic Man,
    An enterprising wight,
Who made his chopping implements
    Unusually bright.
85 Unusually clever he,
    Unusually brave,
And he drew delightful Mammoths
    On the borders of his cave.
To his Neolithic neighbors,
90   Who were startled and surprised,
Said he, "My friends, in course of time,
    We shall be civilized!
We are going to live in cities!
    We are going to fight in wars!
95 We are going to eat three times a day
    Without the natural cause!
We are going to turn life upside down
    About a thing called gold!
We are going to want the earth, and take

100 As much as we can hold!
  We are going to wear great piles of stuff
   Outside our proper skins!
  We are going to have Diseases!
   And Accomplishments!! And Sins!!!"

105 Then they all rose up in fury
   Against their boastful friend,
  For prehistoric patience
   Cometh quickly to an end.
  Said one, "This is chimerical!
110 Utopian! Absurd!"
  Said another, "What a stupid life!
   Too dull, upon my word!"
  Cried all, "Before such things can come,
   You idiotic child,
115 *You must alter Human Nature!"*
   And they all sat back and smiled.
  Thought they, "An answer to that last
   It will be hard to find!"
  It was a clinching argument
120 To the Neolithic Mind!

A Conservative

The garden beds I wandered by
   One bright and cheerful morn,
When I found a new-fledged butterfly
   A-sitting on a thorn,
5   A black and crimson butterfly,
   All doleful and forlorn.

I thought that life could have no sting
   To infant butterflies,
So I gazed on this unhappy thing
10   With wonder and surprise,
While sadly with his waving wing
   He wiped his weeping eyes.

Said I, "What can the matter be?
   Why weepest thou so sore?
15 With garden fair and sunlight free
   And flowers in goodly store—"
But he only turned away from me
   And burst into a roar.

Cried he, "My legs are thin and few
20   Where once I had a swarm!
Soft fuzzy fur—a joy to view—
   Once kept my body warm,
Before these flapping wing-things grew,
   To hamper and deform!"

25   At that outrageous bug I shot
   The fury of mine eye;

Said I, in scorn all burning hot,
   In rage and anger high,
"You ignominious idiot!
30   Those wings are made to fly!"

"I do not want to fly," said he,
   "I only want to squirm!"
And he drooped his wings dejectedly,
   But still his voice was firm;
35   "I do not want to be a fly!
   I want to be a worm!"

O yesterday of unknown lack!
   To-day of unknown bliss!
I left my fool in red and black,
40   The last I saw was this,—
The creature madly climbing back
   Into his chrysalis.

A Moonrise

The heavy mountains, lying huge and dim,
With uncouth outline breaking heaven's brim;
And while I watched and waited, o'er them soon,
Cloudy, enormous, spectral, rose the moon.

Too Much

There are who die without love, never seeing
The clear eyes shining, the bright wings fleeing.
Lonely they die, and ahungered, in bitterness knowing
They have not had their share of the good there was going.

5   There are who have and lose love, these most blessed,
In joy unstained which they have once possessed,
Lost while still dear, still sweet, still met by glad affection,—
An endless happiness in recollection.

And some have Love's full cup as he doth give it—
10   Have it, and drink of it, and, ah,—outlive it!
Full fed by Love's delights, o'erwearied, sated,
They die, not hungry—only suffocated.

To the Young Wife

Are you content, you pretty three-years' wife?
   Are you content and satisfied to live
   On what your loving husband loves to give,
      And give to him your life?

5 Are you content with work,—to toil alone,
   To clean things dirty and to soil things clean;
   To be a kitchen-maid, be called a queen,—
      Queen of a cook-stove throne?

Are you content to reign in that small space—
10   A wooden palace and a yard-fenced land—
   With other queens abundant on each hand,
      Each fastened in her place?

Are you content to rear your children so?
   Untaught yourself, untrained, perplexed, distressed,
15 Are you so sure your way is always best?
      That you can always know?

Have you forgotten how you used to long
   In days of ardent girlhood, to be great,
   To help the groaning world, to serve the state,
20   To be so wise—so strong?

And are you quite convinced this is the way,
   The only way a woman's duty lies—
   Knowing all women so have shut their eyes?
      Seeing the world to-day?

25   Have you no dream of life in fuller store?
        Of growing to be more than that you are?
        Doing the things you now do better far,
            Yet doing others—more?

       Losing no love, but finding as you grew
30   That as you entered upon nobler life
        You so became a richer, sweeter wife,
           A wiser mother too?

What holds you? Ah, my dear, it is your throne,
        Your paltry queenship in that narrow place,
35   Your antique labors, your restricted space,
          Your working all alone!

Be not deceived! 'Tis not your wifely bond
      That holds you, nor the mother's royal power,
      But selfish, slavish service hour by hour—
40   A life with no beyond!

Birth

Lord, I am born!
I have built me a body
Whose ways are all open,
Whose currents run free,
From the life that is thine
Flowing ever within me,
To the life that is mine
Flowing outward through me.

I am clothed, and my raiment
Fits smooth to the spirit,
The soul moves unhindered,
The body is free;
And the thought that my body
Falls short of expressing,
In texture and color
Unfoldeth on me.

I am housed, O my Father!
My body is sheltered,
My spirit has room
'Twixt the whole world and me,
I am guarded with beauty and strength,
And within it
Is room for still union,
And birth floweth free.

And the union and birth
Of the house, ever growing,
Have built me a city—

Have born me a state—
Where I live manifold,
30 Many-voiced, many-hearted,
Never dead, never weary,
And oh! never parted!
The life of The Human,
So subtle—so great!

35 Lord, I am born!
From inmost to outmost
The ways are all open,
The currents run free,
From thy voice in my soul
40 To my joy in the people—
I thank thee, O God,
For this body thou gavest,
Which enfoldeth the earth—
Is enfolded by thee!

Seeking

I went to look for Love among the roses, the roses,
The pretty winged boy with the arrow and the bow;
    In the fair and fragrant places,
    'Mid the Muses and the Graces,
5 At the feet of Aphrodite, with the roses all aglow.

Then I sought among the shrines where the rosy flames
      were leaping—
The rose and golden flames, never ceasing, never still—
    For the boy so fair and slender,
    The imperious, the tender,
10 With the whole world moving slowly to the music of his
will.

Sought, and found not for my seeking, till the sweet
      quest led me further,
And before me rose the temple, marble-based and gold
above,
    Where the long procession marches
    'Neath the incense-clouded arches
15 In the world-compelling worship of the mighty God of
Love.

Yea, I passed with bated breath to the holiest of holies,
And I lifted the great curtain from the Inmost,—the
      Most Fair,—
    Eager for the joy of finding,
    For the glory, beating, blinding,
20 Meeting but an empty darkness; darkness, silence—
nothing there.

Where is Love? I cried in anguish, while the temple
    reeled and faded;
Where is Love?—for I must find him, I must know and
    understand!
    Died the music and the laughter,
    Flames and roses dying after,
25 And the curtain I was holding fell to ashes in my hand.

Closed Doors

When it is night and the house is still,
    When it is day and guests are gone,
When the lights and colors and sounds that fill
    Leave the house empty and you alone:

5 Then you hear them stir—you hear them shift—
    You hear them through the walls and floors—
And the door-knobs turn and the latches lift
    On the closet doors.

Then you try to read and you try to think,
10   And you try to work—but the hour is late;
No play nor labor nor meat nor drink
    Will make them wait.

Well for you if the locks are good!
    Well for you if the bolts are strong,
15 And the panels heavy with oaken wood,
    And the chamber long.

Even so you can hear them plead—
    Hear them argue—hear them moan—
When the house is very still indeed,
20   And you are alone.

Blessed then is a step outside,
    Warm hands to hold you, eyes that smile,
The stir and noise of a world that's wide,
    To silence yours for a little while.

25 Fill your life with work and play!
   Fill your heart with joy and pain!
 Hold your friends while they will stay,
   Silent so shall these remain.

 But you can hear them when you hark—
30   Things you wish you had not known—
 When the house is very still and dark,
   And you are alone.

The Purpose

Serene she sat, full grown in human power,
Established in the service of the world,
Full-hearted, rich, strong with the age's life,
Wise with the womanhood of centuries,
5   With broad still brows and deep eyes lit beneath
With fire of inextinguishable love,
In beauty which the study of a life
Would fail to measure—beauty as of hills
Or the heart-stilling wonder of the sea.

10   Then came her lovers, awed and passionate,
With naught to offer she had not as much
Save only—manhood. Lovers made by God
To offer to her final power of choice
Their natural tribute of diverging gifts,
15   The man's inherent variance of growth,
That she, by choosing, build a better race.
Theirs the resistless longing to fulfill
Their nature's primal law at any cost,
The one great purpose of their parted life;
20   Love their first cause, love their determined end.

So she, from ardent, emulous appeal,
After the inner ruling of her heart
Chose him of all best mated to herself,
Best qualified to glorify The Child—
25   For this was she made woman—not for him.

Locked Inside

She beats upon her bolted door,
    With faint weak hands;
    Drearily walks the narrow floor;
Sullenly sits, blank walls before;
5   Despairing stands.

Life calls her, Duty, Pleasure, Gain—
    Her dreams respond;
But the blank daylights wax and wane,
Dull peace, sharp agony, slow pain—
10   No hope beyond.

Till she comes a thought! She lifts her head,
    The world grows wide!
A voice—as if clear words were said—
"Your door, o long imprisoned,
15   Is locked inside!"

The Artist

Here one of us is born, made as a lens,
Or else to lens-shape cruelly smooth-ground,
To gather light, the light that shines on all,
In concentrated flame it glows, pure fire,
5 With light a hundredfold, more light for all.

Come and receive, take with the eye or ear,
Take and be filled, illumined, overflowed;
Then go and shine again, your whole work lit,
Your whole heart warm and luminous and glad;
10 Go shine again—and spread the gladness wide;

Happy the lens! To gather skies of light
And focus it, making the splendor there!
Happy all we who are enriched therewith,
And redistribute ever, swift and far.

15 The artist is the intermediate lens
Of God, and so best gives Him to the world,
Intensified, interpreted, to us.

More Females of the Species

When the traveller in the pasture meets the he-bull in his
    pride,
He shouts to scare the monster, who will often turn
    aside;
But the milch cow, thus accosted, pins the traveller to the
    rail—
For the female of the species is deadlier than the male.

5   When Nag, the raging stallion, meets a careless man on
    foot,
He will sometimes not destroy him, even if the man
    don't shoot;
But the mare, if he should meet one, makes the bravest
    cowboy pale—
For the female of the species is more deadly than the male.

When our first colonial settlers met the Hurons and
    Choctaws
10 They were burned and scalped by the fury-breathing
    squaws;
'Twas the women, not the warriors, who in war-paint
    took the trail—
For the female of the species is more deadly than the
    male.

Man's timid heart is bursting with the thing he must not say
As to women, lest in speaking he should give himself
    away;
15 But when he meets a woman—see him tremble and turn
    pale—
For the female of the species is more deadly than the male.

Lay your money on the hen-fight! On the dog-fight
    fought by shes!
On the gory Ladies Prize-fight—there are none so fierce
    as these!
See small girls each other pounding, while their peaceful
    brothers wail—
20 For the female of the species is more deadly than the
    male.

So in history they tell us how all China shrieked and ran
Before the wholesale slaughter dealt by Mrs. Genghis
    Khan.
And Attila, the Scourge of God, who made all Europe
    quail,
Was a female of the species and more deadly than the
    male.

25 Red war with all its million dead is due to female rage,
The names of women murderers monopolize the page,
The ranks of a Napoleon are nothing to the tale
Of destruction wrought by females, far more deadly than
    the male.

In the baleful female infant this ferocity we spy,
30 It glares in bloodshot fury from the maiden's dewy eye,
But the really deadly female, when you see her at her
    best,
Has two babies at her petticoat and a suckling at her
    breast.

Yet hold! there is Another! A monster even worse!
The Terror of Humanity! Creation's direst curse!
35 Before whom men in thousands must tremble, shrink and
    fall—
A sanguinary Grandma—more deadly than the male!

Matriatism

Small is the thought of "Fatherland,"
With all its pride and worth;
With all its history of death;
Of fire and sword and wasted breath—
5   By the great new thought which quickeneth—
The thought of "Mother Earth."
Man fights for wealth and rule and pride,
For the "name" that is his alone;
Comes woman, wakening to her power,
10 Comes woman, opening the hour
That sees life as one growing flower,
All children as her own.

Fathers have fought for their Fatherland
With slaughter and death and dearth,
15 But mothers, in service and love's increase,
Will labor together for our release,
From a war-stained past to a world at peace,
Our fair, sweet Mother Earth.